LIMITLESS

A Born Assassin, Book 5

JACQUELINE PAWL

ALSO BY JACQUELINE PAWL

Defying Vesuvius

A BORN ASSASSIN SERIES

Helpless (prequel novella)

Nameless (prequel novella)

Merciless

Heartless

Ruthless

Fearless

Limitless

A Born Assassin Series Omnibus

THE LADY OF INNISLEE SERIES

Court of Vipers

Copyright © 2021 by Jacqueline Pawl

All rights reserved.

No part of this book may be reproduced in any form or by any electronic or mechanical means, including information storage and retrieval systems, without written permission from the author, except for the use of brief quotations in a book review.

To you, dear reader—
Prepare yourself!

(Muahahahahaha!)

I

PERCIVAL

"*ATTACK!*"

Chaos erupted as Nicholas's voice spilled out over the sea of tents and echoed off the city's exterior walls. Percival watched in horror and disbelief as the soldiers behind him unsheathed blades and turned on one another, steel ringing and blood spraying. Before his eyes, Tamriel's army fractured. Friends faced off against friends, brothers against sisters.

For a moment, Mercy looked stunned, then rage transformed her face. She dug her heels into Blackfoot's sides, positioning herself in front of Tamriel and his horse as the Qadar encircled them. Kaius snapped a command in Cirisian, and his elves drew their weapons, falling into a defensive formation.

Nicholas turned to a group of archers, whose arrows were nocked and aimed at Tamriel and the others. "LOOSE!"

"*NO!*" The cry wrenched free of Percival's lips as countless arrows flew through the air, soaring straight toward the king. His blood rushed in his ears. He couldn't watch Tamriel and the others die. Not after everything they'd just endured.

But none of the arrows struck flesh.

Two slate-gray forms—their bodies seemingly no more substantial than smoke—materialized before the king's entourage and thrust their hands out as if to catch the arrows. Percival only had time to register the furious expressions of Dayna and Adriel before a boom like a thunderclap rent the air. A blast of wind as solid as stone slammed into him, sending him and every cavalryman behind him tumbling off their horses. He landed shoulder-first on the ground, stunned and dazed. He brought his arms up over his head just as a wave of arrows—the very same arrows his uncle's treasonous soldiers had loosed—rained down on them.

Impossible.

He lifted his head in time to see Tamriel and Mercy exchange incredulous looks. Mercy's parents—the *ghosts* of her parents—stalked forward, murderous rage rippling off them with every step. Behind them, Cassia, Ino, Calum, and Matthias were all gaping, the weapons in their hands forgotten.

Again, the phantoms threw their hands outward. Another blast of solid air rammed into Percival, causing his ears to pop from the sudden shift in pressure. His head throbbed, and his shoulder ached where he'd landed on it. Out of the corner of his eye, he saw Nicholas stagger to his knees, teeth gritted.

"*Run!*" The voice was a woman's, but it wasn't one Percival recognized. It seemed to come from all around him. "*Tamriel, Bareea, run!*"

"What in the Creator's name—?" Nicholas cried as he snatched his sword and scrambled to his feet. He whirled around and narrowed his eyes at his dazed soldiers. "Get up! *Attack!*"

Before the words left his lips, Duomnodera and her warriors leap into motion, using the distraction to escort Tamriel and the others toward the city. Percival breathed a sigh of relief when he saw dozens upon dozens of city guards emerge from the open gate, ready to join the fight and defend their king—but it caught in his throat when they formed lines before the gate, every single crossbow aimed at Tamriel and the others. *Nicholas turned them against the king, too?* Percival thought with rising panic.

Duomnodera and the Qadar reacted immediately, pivoting and herding their small group along the city's exterior wall. The city guards fired on them even as they retreated, the crossbow bolts glancing harmlessly off the creatures' scales. Beyond Dayna and Adriel, Kaius and the Cirisians loosed arrow after arrow at the city guards, trying to buy the others time to escape. The traitors crumpled, white fletchings sticking out of their throats, their eyes, the gaps in their armor. Yet no matter how many the Cirisians struck down, more filled their places.

"Go, go, go!" Nicholas yelled, a vein pulsing in his forehead, as the soldiers shakily rose and reclaimed the weapons they had dropped. "Kill them! Don't let them escape!"

"Uncle, what the *hell* are you thinking?" Percival shouted, clutching his shoulder as he struggled to his feet. He glanced at Dayna and Adriel's flickering forms. Whatever power allowed them to appear seemed to be quickly running out. They'd given Tamriel and the others a chance to escape, but they wouldn't be able to hold off Nicholas's army much longer.

By the time he straightened, gripping his horse's saddle to keep himself from falling to another wall of solid air, the soldiers had resumed hacking and slashing at one another. In their identical silver plate mail, it was impossible to tell the treasonous soldiers from the faithful. Everything was blood and gore and death.

Percival winced at the agonized screams filling the air, the men and women dying around him. He couldn't see them, but he was certain that the five Daughters Tamriel had taken prisoner were fighting alongside Nicholas's men; his uncle would never have allowed such skilled fighters to remain in chains if he could use them for his own gain. Percival's only comfort was the knowledge that Arabelle and the other apprentices were not caught in the midst of the fighting. They'd been riding alongside Mercy and Faye. They were fleeing with Tamriel and the others, their small bodies shielded by the Qadar.

They're going to make it, Percival thought, his heart hammering against his ribcage. *They have to make it.*

He turned to his uncle, his blood boiling. *Liar! Traitor!* A flash of silver in his periphery caught his eye. A sword, lost by a fallen soldier.

Across the field, the ghosts lifted their hands again.

Percival dropped to the grass as another wave of solid air rolled over him, the impact rattling his bones. He gritted his teeth and reached out until his fingers closed around the sword's grip, then jumped to his feet. The weapon was impossibly heavy—heavier than it looked, heavy enough to make Percival's arm shake when he lifted it—but he did not falter. He would not watch his uncle kill his king, his friend.

While his uncle's back was to him, he lunged, angling the sword at Nicholas's heart.

Nicholas turned and lifted his own blade, looking almost bored as he knocked Percival's sword aside. Percival tried to regain his balance, but his uncle's fist connected with his cheek before he could strike again. The blow sent his spectacles flying, landing somewhere in the blood-soaked grass. The world went fuzzy as stars bloomed in his vision. He staggered backward and pressed his free hand to his throbbing face.

"I've told you time and time again that you're no swordsman," Nicholas growled. "Now get inside the city before you get yourself killed."

"I'm not taking orders from you." He lifted the sword again, trying to focus on his uncle's form. Before he could charge forward again, someone stepped between him and Nicholas. The stranger—a soldier—swiftly disarmed him, grabbed his free arm, and started tugging him toward the city gate. Percival snarled, "Let me go, damn you!"

He struggled against the man holding him, but the grip on his arm didn't waver. It didn't help that Percival could hardly see; he looked over his shoulder to find the fighting soldiers merely a mass of silver and red, blades flashing and blood splattering. Turning his head, he searched for a glimpse of Tamriel, some reassurance that his king, his old friend, had made his escape. As with the soldiers, however, he could not make out anything more than vague shapes in the distance. They were fleeing, but how many had they lost? How long would they be able to run before Nicholas's men caught up? The king could have been struck by a dozen arrows, could be bleeding out, and Percival would be none the wiser.

In the meantime, the ghosts of Mercy's parents were growing weaker, fainter; he didn't need his spectacles to know that. The gaps between their blows continued to lengthen. He only hoped Dayna and Adriel would be able to hold off the soldiers a little longer. Mercy and Tamriel had to survive.

"To your horses! Don't let the king get away!"

Armor clanked and clattered as soldiers ran to their horses and galloped after the king's company. Percival could hear the pounding of hooves and the twang of bows. He closed his eyes and sent a desperate prayer up to the Creator. *Please. Please, watch over them.*

He fought to free himself from the soldier's iron grip one last time, tugging at the hand clamped around his arm even though he knew it was a pointless endeavor. Even if he could get his hands on another sword, he was useless without his spectacles. By the Creator, he was useless *with* them.

"Quit fighting," the soldier grumbled as he dragged Percival through the city gate and dumped him unceremoniously on the cobblestone street. He looked down his nose at Percival and sneered, "Don't know why you're so upset about this. After he wins, he's going to make you king."

2
MERCY

"*Run! Tamriel, Bareea, run!*"

Liselle's shout echoed in Mercy's mind as Blackfoot raced across the grass, matching Tamriel's horse step for step. She looked over her shoulder at Cassia, knowing from her sister's pale face that she had recognized Liselle's voice. Somehow, Liselle, Dayna, and Adriel had manifested in the In-Between to save their lives. Mercy could still hear the booms thundering across the land, the panicked cries of the soldiers as they were flung to the ground by wave after wave of solid air. Whatever that strange power was, it had saved Mercy's life twice: first, when Faye and Lylia tried to kill her the night of the Assassins' attack, and now.

She turned to Tamriel, the wind snagging her hair and whipping it around her face. His dark eyes were fixed on a point on the horizon, burning with rage, and his knuckles were white around the reins. Kaius and the Cirisians were doing their best to hold off the city guards, but arrows and bolts still whizzed past. Some thudded against the Qadari warriors' scales, some sank harmlessly into the grass, and some managed to slip through the shield of bodies. Mercy's heart stuttered when one nearly hit Faye.

Catching her terrified expression, Faye called, "I'm fine. Don't worry about me. Arabelle, Indi, Zora, stay close!"

Mercy risked a glance back and found the Cirisians riding after them, bows in hand. When they could afford it, they twisted in their saddles and fired at the soldiers giving chase. Volley after volley sailed toward the soldiers riding after them. Five immediately went down, tumbling off their horses, but it wasn't nearly enough. In addition to Nicholas's traitorous army, guards continued streaming out of the city, joining the attack on their king.

Behind them, Percival pushed to his feet, a sword clenched in his fist.

"Tamriel, look!" she cried as Percival angled the sword at his uncle's heart.

From this distance, she couldn't make out the words they exchanged, but she *felt* the impact of Nicholas's fist against his nephew's cheek as surely as if she'd been the one struck. Percival stumbled backward in a daze, and a soldier began hauling him toward the city.

"*Damn it all,*" Tamriel snarled. "Blessed year, my ass."

Mercy turned forward, ignoring the pain shooting through her still-healing rib cage. Duomnodera and her warriors continued encircling Mercy, Tamriel, and their friends, ready to deflect any arrows that might fly their way.

"To your horses! Don't let the king get away!" Nicholas bellowed.

"Your parents—they're weakening," Faye gasped. "They won't be able to hold the soldiers much longer."

Ino let out a string of curses. "This isn't a battle we're going to win. We're outnumbered, as far as I can tell, and the city guard is going to skew the odds further in Nicholas's favor. Our only choice is to run and hope they don't catch up."

Mercy clutched Blackfoot's reins, her fingers itching for her daggers. After everything they'd been through, they deserved a peaceful, happy homecoming. How dare Nicholas take this victory away from them? How dare he turn on Tamriel? She had only known the general for a short time, but she'd come to respect him. When they were finalizing the plan for the attack on the Guild, he'd always had another strategy at hand, another move to make should one fall through. She should have guessed he had plotted something like this, too. Ghyslain had always warned them to be wary of the nobles.

How the hell did he figure out what Tamriel was planning? How did he know Tamriel hopes to free the slaves?

Tamriel's expression was dark, contorted in fury. He didn't look back as they raced along the city's exterior wall, arrows and bolts sailing past. They crossed the bridge spanning the Alynthi River and thundered toward the start of the king's highway. The city wall gradually curved away, leaving them exposed on all sides.

Nicholas's traitorous army chased them through the open fields and between the low, rolling hills of the Beltharan countryside. Eventually, Sandori faded from view, swallowed by the black, moonless night, and then the army faded away, too. Dayna and Adriel had bought them enough time to get a head start, but the Creator only knew how long it would take the traitors to catch up. Every second felt like a blessing.

They continued eastward with no destination in mind, their shock and adrenaline gradually giving way to exhaustion. When it grew so dark that they could barely see one another, let alone any pursuers on their heels, they relied on the Cirisians' enhanced night vision to guide them along the king's highway.

After what felt like an eternity, they stopped beside the bank of a river to let the horses rest and drink. Even the short break made Mercy anxious. They couldn't risk the horses dying of exhaustion, but if they slowed down for any longer than necessary, they would lose what little distance they had managed to put between themselves and Nicholas's troops. Mercy's only solace was the knowledge that their pursuers had to be equally cautious with their own mounts.

"What now?" Arabelle asked in a thin, wavering voice. Behind her, Indi and Zora were clutching each other tightly, trembling. "What do we do now? They're going to kill us!"

Faye wrapped an arm around the girl's shoulders. "Without the Cirisians to help them see, they'll have to stop and wait out the night. That means we can put miles between us and them by dawn. They're not going to catch up to us."

I hope you're right, Mercy thought. She tried to ignore the fatigue tugging at her, the drooping of her eyelids, the ache in her battered body. They would have to rest at some point, too. They could fight their exhaustion for as long as possible, but they were already weary and battered from the battle with the Guild.

Mercy absently ran her fingers through Blackfoot's thick mane as she watched Tamriel pace along the riverbank. She desperately wanted to go to him, to comfort him, but she could see that he needed some time to process this betrayal. It killed her to see him in so much pain.

"Our parents saved our lives," Matthias said in a raw voice, drawing her attention away from Tamriel. "How—How is that possible?"

"I don't know. Liselle protected me when I first arrived at the castle, but I always thought she was able to do it because Firesse summoned her from the Beyond. I have no clue how they were able to appear tonight."

"Considering everything that has happened, it's not really

important how they did it, though, is it?" Calum responded. "They saved our lives. Now we have to figure out a way to restore Tam's throne and kill that treasonous bastard."

Tamriel paused when he heard that. Mercy couldn't make out his expression, but she could feel the anger rippling off him as he growled, "When we do, we're going to make what Mercy did to Mother Illynor look *kind*."

3
PERCIVAL

Percival sat on the steps of the dais and glared at the soldiers surrounding him, guarding him like a governess would a misbehaving child. One of them had retrieved his spectacles from the battlefield, and he wiped at the lenses with the hem of his shirt. No matter how hard he scrubbed them, he couldn't get the flecks of dried blood from around the frames. His stomach churning, he jammed them on and let his head fall back to the step behind him, closing his eyes.

How long had Nicholas been plotting his coup? How many of Tamriel's soldiers had he managed to turn against their king?

And...what now?

Distantly, he heard the massive doors to the great hall swing open and countless people rush inside, speaking over one another. "Make way!" someone shouted. "Give him space, and for the Creator's sake, someone call for the healer!"

Percival followed his guards into the great hall and stopped dead when he saw his uncle standing in the midst of a group of soldiers, his hair matted with blood from a deep gash in his scalp. A young woman clad in blood-splattered armor ran off in search of Healer Tabris. Nicholas blinked dazedly, leaning against Rhiannon for support.

Thick, choking rage swept over Percival.

"What in the Creator's name were you thinking, betraying Tamriel? Have you lost your *mind?*" he exploded, his voice echoing throughout the room. He stormed toward the soldiers crowding around his uncle, but someone snagged his arm and yanked him back, nearly pulling his shoulder out of its socket. Percival glared at the man. "*Let me go.*"

"You can speak to him later."

"Like hell I can! He just turned against the king. I think I deserve some explanation. Now unhand me."

"I answer to your uncle, not you, whelp. You have two choices here: you can shut your mouth until a healer tends to him or I can lock you in your chambers until your uncle deigns to speak with you. What'll it be?"

Seeing that this would get him nowhere, Percival fell silent, setting his jaw. The soldier released his arm and shot him a smug look. "That's what I thought."

A moment later, a healer he didn't recognize swept into the room, his medicine bag swinging as he gestured for them to follow him into the throne room. Rhiannon slung one of Nicholas's arms across her shoulders to steady him as they followed the stranger. His uncle didn't even glance Percival's way as they passed.

Percival tried not to look at the portraits of past Myrellis kings as he trailed after the others. He couldn't imagine how furious Tamriel must be right now—if he was even still alive.

Guilt washed over him. He should have figured out his uncle was going to betray Tamriel. Nicholas had held meetings with several courtiers before they'd left the capital, and dozens more with officers and commanders during the march to the Keep; surely some of those meetings had been in preparation for this. By the Creator, why hadn't he seen it? Why hadn't he suspected it?

Because he's better at politics than you'll ever be, a small voice inside him whispered. *Because he has been playing this game for decades, while all you've ever done is read books and keep records.*

"Is the king dead, then?" Percival demanded. "Is the royal family—the one our family has been serving for *generations*—no more?"

"Make an effort to hide your admiration of them, Percival," Nicholas grunted as Rhiannon helped him slump onto the throne. The healer opened his medical bag and began to examine his wound. "I know Tamriel was your friend, but had he been allowed to continue his rule, he would have destroyed the country. Everything our family has fought and died for would be for nothing."

Was. Was your friend. Percival didn't hear anything after those words. "Is he dead?"

"As good as dead."

"What does that mean? And where is Healer Tabris?"

"It means my soldiers are hunting him, his friends, and his precious elven lover as we speak, and it's only a matter of time before they catch up. I hadn't planned for damned *ghosts* to show up." Nicholas winced as the healer began stitching the gash shut. "As for Healer Tabris, I don't know. He's likely off somewhere in the city, looking for work. He is loyal to your dear friend, so his services were no longer required. I don't trust him not to poison me."

"Rightly so, you bastard!" he seethed, storming toward the dais. "Tamriel was your king! He trusted you!"

One of the soldiers stepped in front of him and pulled his still-bloody sword from its sheath. "That's close enough."

"Let him pass. He's harmless. Actually, give us the room, please. I would like to speak with my nephew in private."

Percival's hands clenched into fists. He stood there,

silently fuming, until the last soldier cleared the room. The second the doors swung shut, he said, "Tell me why you did this."

Nicholas blinked at him, still slightly dazed. "I would have served Tamriel well had he not been on the verge of ruining our country. Even his father knew better than to free the slaves and give the Cirisor Islands to those savages. I fought too hard and lost too many good men to see that land slip through our grasp. I'm saving our kingdom."

Of course. The last Cirisian War had occurred around the time of Liselle's death; many of the soldiers and city guards had lost parents or grandparents to the fighting. Those men and women had died in service to their country. To their families, they were heroes—and in their eyes, Tamriel was going to throw all their sacrifices away. It was no wonder Nicholas had managed to turn them against their king.

Percival had been a baby when Nicholas nearly defeated the Feyndaran forces. He probably would have won the war once and for all if a wasting sickness hadn't claimed Percival's parents, leaving him to Nicholas's care. Although his uncle had never said it, Percival suspected Nicholas secretly blamed him for not dying alongside his parents.

"Do not think I have forgotten, nephew, your own participation in the freeing of several slaves. Do you know how much it cost me to reimburse the masters for the slaves you freed? How much it cost me to ensure their silence on the matter? Those slaves were precious investments."

"They are *people*."

"They're elves. They're an infestation in this world. There will always be more where they came from, but training them and teaching them to be proper servants takes time. Foolish boy."

Under his uncle's heavy gaze, Percival's anger waned, his shoulders slumping in defeat. "How did you figure all this out? How did you know I was working to free the slaves? Or that Tamriel was planning to give the Islands to the Cirisians?"

Did you hurt Hero and Ketojan? he wanted to ask, but he didn't dare. He had never met them; Cassia had been the link between them. Hero and Ketojan had found slaves desperate enough to risk fleeing the city, Cassia had told him when to expect them at the castle, and Percival and Ino had worked together to smuggle them out of the city. He would never forgive himself if something he did led to them being imprisoned—or worse, executed.

Nicholas shook his head. "I'm disappointed in you, Percival. Did you learn nothing from my lessons? There are always people willing to curry favor with powerful families. It doesn't take much to convince them to be your eyes and ears. How do you think I've managed to navigate the Beltharan and Rivosi courts for so long? I'm a warrior, not a courtier.

"I always hoped you would grow up to be like me. I prayed that you would put down your books and take up swordplay, but the joke was on me. When you did, you made a mockery of yourself and our family. For the Creator's sake, you can't hold a butter knife without straining your wrist." Percival ducked his head, a flush rising on his cheeks. Seeing his embarrassment, his uncle's voice softened. "Forgive me, nephew. All I meant to say was, some men are meant to wield power, and some are not. Some, like you, are simply meant to serve. It took me a long time to accept that, but I have."

Percival dropped onto the top step of the dais and buried his face in his hands, his emotions an ugly, tangled mess. Nicholas had planned everything perfectly. If not for the ghosts of Mercy's parents, Tamriel and all his allies would be dead. "What do you want from me, then?" he finally asked. "Are you really going to make me king?"

He couldn't imagine any idea more absurd, but Nicholas

nodded. "You will wear the crown, but you will be king in name only. I will make the decisions that will benefit our country and our family, and you will enact them."

A sour taste filled his mouth. *King.* He had never wanted to be king. He had never even wanted the prestige that accompanied his own family name. Even so... What choice did he have but to go along with his uncle's wishes, as he always had? If Tamriel truly would be dead in a matter of hours, as Nicholas had proclaimed, there would be no one of royal blood left to take the throne. The nobles would go to war, each claiming a right to the crown. Nicholas was more powerful than any of them; he had more men on his side, plus his years of military expertise. Percival accepting the throne might be the only way to keep the country from falling into civil war.

Maybe obeying his uncle wouldn't be so bad. If it would save his country and countless lives, he would do it—albeit begrudgingly. He would never forgive his uncle for killing his friend and king.

"Why me?" he managed to choke out. "Why not take the throne for yourself?"

"What good am I to anyone except as a strategist? I'm too old to raise heirs, and you're too softhearted to make the decisions a king needs to make for his subjects. With Riona Nevis as your queen, you'll strengthen the relationship between Beltharos and Rivosa and put an end to the border skirmishes. You'll sire lots of little princes and princesses and I'll ensure the kingdom runs smoothly. You may hate me for this now, but trust me when I say this is what is best for the future of our kingdom."

Percival's resolve crumbled, as it did every time they argued. A hollow ache filled his chest. His friends were likely dead. His kingdom's throne was empty. And it was all his uncle's fault.

Nicholas was the only family he had ever known. Instead of taking on the role of a father, however, he had become a puppet master, constantly maneuvering Percival into more strategic positions, better social circles. For eighteen years, Percival had been a piece in one big game of chess. Wherever his uncle bid him go, he went. What his uncle bid him do, he did. He could fight and shout and rage all he wanted, but they both knew he'd do as he was ordered. He had no other choice.

"...Fine. You win."

Nicholas nodded. Surprisingly, he did not look smug or triumphant. He was not a fool. He knew the cost of what he had done.

"Elias," he called, and a soldier strode into the room a moment later. "Send ravens to every major city in the kingdom. Tamriel Myrellis and his allies are now enemies of the crown, and they are to be arrested on sight—killed if they try to resist." He turned his good eye on Percival. "And alert them that King Percival Comyn's coronation will take place in three days."

4

TAMRIEL

The horses didn't even last until dawn.

The stars were faintly twinkling overhead, peeking out from between gaps in the fat gray clouds, when Tamriel's horse slowed to a walk. Even Blackfoot's pace was flagging; his tail swished back and forth with irritation. Mercy patted his neck and frowned. "We can't keep going. The horses can't take much more of this."

He nodded and gestured for their small group to stop. They'd been riding east for hours, following the king's highway through prairies and across countless bridges, but they were still well within reach of Nicholas's army. To make matters worse, the wide-open countryside and low, rolling hills offered little in the way of cover. If the horses were rested, they'd be able to reach Cyrna in two days, but every one of them was exhausted from the ride from the Forest of Flames. Now, it would take them twice that long—assuming Nicholas's army wouldn't catch up to them before then.

Rage filled Tamriel when he thought about his general's betrayal. He still hadn't fully recovered from the shock. If not for Dayna and Adriel, he and everyone he loved would be dead.

The memory of the heads staked to the city wall filled his mind. The bastard could have killed Tamriel anytime during their march from the Keep. He'd waited until they reached Sandori because he'd wanted Tamriel to see what he'd done. He had wanted Tamriel's murder to be a spectacle.

Be sure you do not make the mistake of trusting the wrong people, Nicholas had told him upon the general's arrival in Sandori. The irony of the statement was not lost on him now. *They always wait until your guard is down, until you are at your weakest, before they strike.*

That was before Nicholas had discovered he was planning to free the slaves. Tamriel still hadn't figured out how Nicholas learned about his sympathy for the elves. Had he overheard him speaking with Cassia or Percival? And now that Nicholas held the capital and the court in the palm of his hand, what would become of Percival? Tamriel doubted Nicholas would forgive his nephew's attack anytime soon.

He prayed his old friend would emerge from this mess unharmed.

Mercy laid a hand on his arm, startling him out of his reverie. "We will make Nicholas pay for this betrayal a thousand times over. But right now, we need to find somewhere to rest."

He sucked in a breath, swallowing his fury. Now was not the time to lose control, even if every fiber of his being screamed at him to turn around, find the traitor, and show him the true measure of his vengeance.

He scanned the land around them. Aside from a sparse patch of trees in the distance, there was no cover in sight. If they continued eastward, they could perhaps find a forest or valley in which to take shelter for a few hours. He dismounted, his entire body sore from so many hours of riding, and the others followed suit. "You're right. We'll go by foot until we can find somewhere to make camp."

"There's a farmhouse an hour's ride south of Knia Valley," Calum supplied. "Firesse used it for her troops before the attack on Sandori. It's secluded and the house is hidden by a windbreak."

"Do you think it's safe?"

He lifted a shoulder in a shrug. "It's the best of our limited options. We can't stray too close to the town—doubtless Nicholas has already sent out word that you're a wanted man—but we need somewhere to regroup and gather supplies. As long as we send scouts to watch the king's highway for Nicholas's troops, we should be fine for a few hours."

"Cassia and I can go into Knia Valley and buy anything we need," Faye suggested, glancing back at where Mercy's siblings were standing with Kaius and the rest of the Cirisians. "The guards won't be looking for us, and—"

"Absolutely not," Calum interrupted. "You're still healing. If you're wrong and it comes to a fight, you might not make it out alive."

She frowned at him. "Assuming you, Mercy, and His Majesty now have prices on your heads, you can't go. The Qadar and Cirisians will send the townspeople into a panic if they're spotted. We're the only ones who can slip in, buy what we need, and get out without attracting attention. If you're worried about our safety, Ino and Matthias can come along and protect us."

"But—"

"Good idea, Faye," Tamriel said to her, ignoring Calum's objection. "Just, please, be careful."

"We will. It'll be a good opportunity to see what the

people make of Nicholas's betrayal, too—if they rally behind their rightful king or the usurper."

Tamriel didn't respond. He knew with whom his subjects would side once they learned of his intentions to free the slaves and establish the Islands' independence.

But perhaps...perhaps there were more people like him—like Hero, Ketojan, and Percival—among his people. Perhaps he would find support from those who secretly desired to see the elves freed. He just needed to convince them to fight with him.

An hour later, they arrived at the farmhouse. Calum stared at his feet the entire walk up to the front porch, lost in memories of the last time he'd been here, when Drake still possessed him.

"Go ahead and rest," Kaius said as they neared the porch steps. "My people and I will take first watch. If we see anyone, we'll let you know."

"Are you sure?" Faye asked. "You all must be exhausted."

"No more than the rest of you." He offered her a weary smile. "Go on. We'll take inventory of our supplies while you sleep so you'll know what to buy in town."

Kaius wandered off to set patrols while Tamriel and the others unsaddled their horses. When he was finished, Tamriel slung his pack over his shoulder and followed Duomnodera and her warriors into the house. Ino and Matthias immediately headed to the bedrooms, the apprentices—half asleep already—stumbling after them. Cassia and Faye had already begun rifling through the kitchen, taking stock of how much food the Cirisians had left behind and how much they still needed to purchase. Tamriel tried not to think about how quickly what little coin they had would run out; beyond the contents of their coin purses and saddlebags, all they had were the clothes on their backs.

Calum was slumped in an armchair in the living room, and he straightened as Tamriel and the Qadar settled onto the worn settees. "We need to make a plan," he said immediately. "We need to figure out where we're going and how we're going to win back your throne."

"How about staking Nicholas's head to the city wall, along with those of every noble and soldier who supported him?" Tamriel responded darkly.

"Well, I figured that was a given. What are we going to do *leading up* to that?"

"I don't know. We have no known allies, no money, and barely any supplies. Nicholas has all that and more."

"Well, we need some kind of strategy. Nicholas's men are chasing us, and I really don't feel like dying anytime soon." Calum looked toward the front door as Mercy stepped through, tying her wild curls back with a strip of leather. Three strands immediately sprang out and fell into her face. She brushed them aside before perching on the arm of the settee and resting her hand on Tamriel's shoulder. Automatically, he reached up and laced his fingers through hers. Just that one touch tempered his anger by a fraction. After four weeks of not knowing whether she was alive or dead, he still marveled at the fact that she was here, free of the Guild.

"What advantages do we have?" she asked. "Aside from the Qadar and the Cirisians, I mean."

"Just the Cirisians," Duomnodera interjected before anyone could respond.

Tamriel sat up straighter. "I beg your pardon?"

"Just the Cirisians. My sisters are dead and their Guilds are destroyed, so we're returning to Gyr'malr. Our business here is finished. This is not our fight."

"You can't go! I am grateful for the aid you've given thus

far, but Nicholas Comyn has an army on his side. I need all the help I can get if I am to reclaim my throne."

Regret flashed through her eyes. "I swore that I would help you defeat Dwordraehulda—Illynor—and I upheld my vow without asking for anything in return. My people have fought and killed for yours, and now we would like to return to our homeland, away from this kingdom where loyalty belongs to the highest bidder. I'm sorry."

"You're a High Mother," Tamriel said desperately. "You can gather more warriors to fight. The burden wouldn't fall on the six of you. Please, speak to the other High Mothers and ask them if they'll fight for me. I can give you money, trade, weapons, whatever you desire. I need my throne if I am to free the slaves and help my people rebuild, and I'm woefully short on allies."

Duomnodera exchanged wary looks with her warriors. She spoke with them in Qadar for several long minutes before finally nodding. "Very well. My warriors and I will return to our land and speak with the leaders of the other factions. I expect, however, that they will not offer any aid."

He let out a relieved sigh. "A slim chance is better than none at all. Thank you."

"That helps, but we can't rely on the Qadar and the few dozen Cirisians we have here," Calum said, turning to Tamriel. "You need an army."

"I *had* an army."

Behind Calum, Cassia and Faye emerged from the kitchen, lingering in the doorway. At the sight of Cassia's headscarf, an idea struck Tamriel.

"We do have another advantage; one Nicholas will never be able to claim for himself..." he began, a smile slowly spreading across his lips. "The slaves."

For so long, he'd been terrified of what the nobles would do if he openly declared his support for the elves, if he made clear his intentions to free them. Now he was certain that no matter how much he worked to appease them, they would never support emancipating the slaves. They would have turned on him sooner or later.

He may not have his throne, but he was still the rightful king. His concern over whether the stuffy, self-absorbed nobles approved of his actions had ended the moment he saw the heads staked over the city gate. To hell with what the courtiers wanted. He was finished tiptoeing around them.

He was the king, and he was going to do what he should have done the moment he'd been crowned.

"I'm going to free the slaves."

Cassia smiled. "If you release them from their chains, they will fight for you, Your Majesty. I'm sure of it. They will take up arms and turn against their masters for a chance at freedom."

"They don't know the first thing about fighting," Calum objected.

"You'd be surprised at how well versed some of us have become at defending ourselves. We're far from helpless. With some training, it would not be hard for them to take up a sword or dagger." She lifted her chin and looked at Tamriel, conviction and excitement in her voice as she continued, "There are elves everywhere. If you offer them a place in your army, you might just be able to rally a force large enough to take on Nicholas's men."

"I think she's right," Mercy added. "Look how fiercely the Cirisians fought to free their brethren. Look at the lengths to which Kaius is willing to go to see slavery abolished. If you offer the elves the freedom they've been waiting for, they'll fight just as hard to get Nicholas off the throne."

A bud of hope bloomed within Tamriel. He slipped his free hand around Mercy's waist, tugging her close, and his heart swelled with gratitude as he looked to each person in turn. Even hurt, grieving, and exhausted, these people—*his people*—were willing to put their lives on the line to help him.

"I will never be able to repay you for this, but I swear to you," he said, beaming, "I will spend the rest of my life trying to validate your faith in me. Let's rest here for a few hours and get some sleep, then we'll start building our army."

5
FAYE

The house was dark and quiet when Faye woke up a few hours later, her body heavy and her mind groggy from too many days with far too little sleep. After Tamriel's proclamation, they'd all gone their separate ways—the Qadar to join the Cirisians in patrolling the surrounding land, and the rest of them to find bedrooms in the spacious farmhouse for some blessed rest. She and Mercy's siblings would ride out to Knia Valley shortly to gather supplies, then they'd all continue to Cyrna, hoping to stay ahead of the army.

She pressed a hand against her wounded side as she stood and moved to the window, wincing when her tender stitches pulled tight. With all the riding, her wound hadn't been healing well, but there was nothing she could do about that. She reached up and pushed the lace curtain aside. The sun was still high—it had to be early afternoon, at the latest—but the trees blocked most of the rays from reaching the house.

Kaius appeared in her view, twirling an arrow between his nimble fingers as he scanned the yard. The other Cirisians were nowhere in sight; they must still be sleeping or patrolling with the Qadar. The elves had surprised Faye with their willingness to serve as the guardians of the group. Even before Nicholas's betrayal, a Cirisian had trailed Mercy and Tamriel through the camp each night, watching over them alongside Tamriel's royal guard. They tended to keep to themselves, but they were fierce fighters, and she could tell that they respected Kaius. They cared about him, and he felt the same about them; it was obvious in everything he did. She had not forgotten that, after they freed Mercy from the Guild, he had made sure every one of his people made it out of the Keep before he fled.

As if sensing her thoughts, Kaius turned around, his tattooed lips spreading into a smile when he caught her watching him. He gestured for her to join him outside.

She nodded and let the curtain fall shut. A search of the closet rewarded her with a navy tunic and a pair of cotton pants close to her size. She had lost weight while bedridden by injury, and she had to roll the waistband a few times in order to make the pants fit. Still, clean clothes were better than nothing. She cinched her belt with her sheath of throwing knives, tucked a dagger into the leg of her boot, and slid her oyster-shucking knife into her sleeve before striding out of the room.

Kaius was waiting for her on the porch when she emerged, running her fingers through the tangles in her thick, waist-length hair. "Shouldn't you be resting right now?" she asked.

"I tried, but it's still strange to sleep indoors. It reminds me too much of when I lived in my master's manor. I had only just gone outside when I saw you. In fact, you were taking so long I was beginning to wonder if you'd gone back to sleep," he teased as he sat on the porch's top step. "I would have looked quite the fool standing around here waiting for you."

She sank down beside him and grinned. "I thought about it. We've been sleeping on the ground for so long I didn't want to leave my nice warm bed. I'm going to miss it when we leave." She studied him. "Do you miss the Islands? When this is all over, are you going to return there?"

"Cirisor has been my home for so long, I can't imagine living anywhere else. I don't know if I'd ever *want* to live anywhere else." He frowned thoughtfully as he stared out across the overgrown yard, watching the horses graze or doze in the shade. "When I was a slave, I dreamed of escaping and running to the Islands, but I was terrified that my master would find out what I was planning. The thought of what he would do to me if I were caught—or what he would do to the slaves I was leaving behind—kept me from running long after I should have fled."

"Did your master own many slaves?"

"Yes. He kept children around to tend to the household chores. It's not what you think," he said when Faye scowled, imagining what her former betrothed had no doubt planned to do to her after they were wed. "He didn't touch them or mistreat them. His children died young and he liked having kids around. It was just... I loved them, and I couldn't bear the thought of leaving them behind."

"You couldn't take them to Cirisor with you?"

"Not a chance. It was about ten years after Liselle's death, and it was far too dangerous with the humans hunting down runaway slaves. Besides, I was little more than a child myself. I wouldn't have been able to protect them if we were discovered." A wistful look passed across his face. His voice softened when he asked, "Do you want to know how I ended up leaving?"

She merely nodded, shocked by how much he was revealing. He had always seemed so closed-off whenever they'd spoken previously.

"One night, I returned to the slaves' quarters and found them all standing around my bed, waiting for me. One of the eldest boys, Liam, handed me a pouch of coin and told me that he and the others had been taking up odd jobs whenever they went into town. The younger ones begged for money or delivered orders for some of the shops while the older ones did mending or laundry. Together, they'd saved up enough money to fund my journey to the Islands. Every single one of them had contributed," he said, smiling. "They gave me the coin purse and a bag they'd already packed with food and clothes, then told me they'd meet me in the Islands one day. They'd seen me studying the map in my master's study when he wasn't around, and they knew that if I wasn't going to leave of my own volition, they'd have to help me claim my freedom."

Faye's heart swelled at the mental image of him surrounded by so many people who loved him. "And did they meet you in the Islands?"

"Over the years, some did. Others, I learned, were not lucky enough to make it all the way to Cirisor. I wouldn't be surprised if a few of the younger ones are still at the manor."

"When this is all over, you should go see them."

He picked at a piece of peeling paint on the railing. "I don't think they remember me."

She nudged his shoulder with hers. "Well, if you don't go, you'll never know. Judging by how fondly you talk about them and how much they seemed to love you, I think it would be pretty hard for them to forget you."

"Thank you, Faye," he murmured, at last meeting her gaze. His green eyes were bright against his bronze skin. "Maybe I will."

"What were the Islands like when you arrived?"

He raised a brow. "Why all the questions? A few weeks ago, you couldn't stand the sight of me."

"I didn't know if I could trust you. Now that I know I can, I'm curious." She didn't mention that listening to him helped keep her own memories at bay. Every time she closed her eyes, she saw the faces of the people she'd killed during Firesse's war. She had hoped the guilt would abate once she was free of the Guild, but she should have known better.

Besides, she liked listening to him talk. When she met him, she'd thought he spoke the common tongue without a hint of a Cirisian accent, but every so often, she caught the faint, rolling melody to his words. She had never heard anyone speak the way he did.

"So," she pressed. "The Islands."

"It took me two weeks to get there. Even though I had no idea what I would face when I arrived, I'll never forget the feeling of setting foot on the first Island and knowing I'd really made it—that I was finally free. Hunters from Firesse's clan found me within hours, and they brought me back to their camp and offered me a place among them.

"I did everything I could to show the others how grateful I was that they had given me a new family, a new life. In all honesty, I think some of them relegated the worst chores to me because they knew I would do them without fail." He chuckled softly. "They gave me a home when I had nothing. Firesse became like a little sister to me; I think I was drawn to her because she reminded me of some of the kids at my master's manor. The best day was when I went to my first *Ialathan* and got my tattoos. They marked me as a Cirisian and ensured that I could never be forced into slavery again.

"Now it's your turn," he announced before she could question him again. "You were just a child when you joined the Guild, correct?"

She looked away, cringing. "I was seven. I wish I could say I was as elated as you were in the Islands when I arrived at the Keep, but all I felt was an insatiable need for revenge.

Mother Illynor saw that and turned it against me. She turned me into *this*." She waved a hand down her body, gesturing with disgust to the knives strapped to her hip and the handle of the dagger sticking out of her boot. "The worst part is, the Keep became my home. I truly thought of the other girls as my sisters. They were horrible sometimes, but we all had an understanding. We were strays and runaways. We were the only family we had."

Kaius didn't respond for a few long moments. When she glanced at him, his eyes were full of sympathy. "Why did you leave home? Who hurt you?"

She considered telling him everything about Fredric, about her betrothed, about the fact that she had begged her parents to approve the match. She had only known her betrothed for a month, but in that short span of time he had altered her life in ways she never could have imagined. He had let her twin brother die, hired men to cripple her father, and after all that, the bastard had *still* claimed ownership of her. Because of him, she had decided to run away to the Guild. Because of him, she had nurtured the hatred within her heart for far too long.

Not anymore.

She was free of the Guild. The vengeful, bloodthirsty Assassin she had been died alongside Illynor. She would never forgive that monster for preying on her family, for deceiving them into thinking he could save her brother, but she would no longer allow that rage to consume her life.

Her brother died a long time ago. It was time her hunger for revenge died, as well.

She shook her head at the sympathy and anger mingling on Kaius's face, knowing what he had assumed when he asked the question. "My betrothed never laid a hand on me. He never did *anything*. He saw my family's world collapsing around us and let us believe he was our savior. After he sent men into our house to cripple my father, it just became too much. I couldn't marry him, and I couldn't watch my parents be harmed trying to protect me. So I left. I ran."

Faye ran a light finger along the throwing knives at her hip, a shiver of disgust rippling through her at the comfort the action brought. She'd run away because of her betrothed —she'd made the stupid, reckless decision to leave her family behind because of him—but the torture she had endured during her years in the Guild was the fault of no one but Illynor. For too long, the two had been interchangeable in her mind: her betrothed, who had preyed on a vulnerable, terrified family; and Illynor, who had taken a helpless little girl and rebuilt her into an unfeeling, ruthless assassin for her own gain.

They would not rule her life any longer.

✣ 6 ✣
MERCY

Mercy's eyes opened to pitch blackness. The cold, moist air of the Keep's dungeon surrounded her, its earthy scent filling her nose. *No. No, no, no, no! A tremor rolled through her. I can't be back here. I can't—I can't endure more of this.* She shifted, instantly becoming aware of the shackles clamped around her wrists and ankles, biting into her raw flesh. The slight movement caused the heavy chains to jangle, shattering the silence of the dungeon. She flinched at the sound.

She grabbed the shackle around her right wrist and tried to slip it over her hand. The metal cut into her skin, causing blood to well and trail down her arm. "Come on," she hissed, wincing at the needles of pain shooting through her. "Come on!"

The door on the opposite wall swung open, the wood scraping against the stone floor, and Mercy's heart stopped beating when Mother Illynor strode in.

"I told you you'd never be free of me," the Guildmother murmured in a voice as rough as stone. She stalked forward, fiendish delight pouring off her with every graceful step. Her black cloak tumbled from a clasp at her throat, the ruby set in the center seeming to glow under the light of the lantern in her hand. She stopped in the middle *of the room and set the lantern on the floor. Her eyes shone like chips of eudorite when she smiled at Mercy and crooned, "You're mine, Mercy. You will always be mine."*

"This isn't real," *she whispered. Again, she grasped the shackle and tried to pull it over her hand. Another wave of blood spilled out of her torn flesh, but the shackle didn't budge.*

"You're going to break your thumb if you continue that." Mother Illynor clicked her tongue as if she were scolding a petulant child. She stepped forward and placed a scaled fingertip below Mercy's chin, tipping her head back so she had no choice but to meet the Guildmother's hard gaze.

"You're dead," Mercy breathed, pretending her voice didn't waver, pretending she was not acutely aware that Illynor heard it. Every fiber of her being screamed at her to fight, but there was nothing she could do. She was weak, unarmed, and chained. "I killed you."

Mother Illynor reached into the folds of her cloak and pulled out a dagger. "Oh, Mercy, I thought you were smarter than that. Did you really think death would keep me from claiming you, my dear?"

She slashed Mercy's throat, carving her open from ear to ear.

"No—" Mercy choked out, a coppery tang filling her mouth, filling the air. With every frantic beat of her heart, more blood gushed out of her wound, soaking the front of her tattered tunic. Shadows crept in at the edges of her vision.

Mercy's head slumped forward, her eyelids falling shut. As the life drained out of her, Mother Illynor leaned so close her breath brushed Mercy's ear as she whispered, "Now you're going to join me in the Beyond."

A hand landed on Mercy's shoulder, startling her out of the nightmare. Her hand flew up to her throat, searching for the wound that wasn't there, before her eyes focused on Tamriel's concerned face. He was kneeling beside the bed, shirtless, his dark hair hanging in loose waves. He cupped her cheek, his palm cool against her flushed skin.

"You were crying in your sleep," he murmured, gently brushing away the tears with his thumb. "Nightmares?"

When she nodded, he leaned forward and pressed a soft kiss to her forehead. "I'm so sorry you have to endure this, my love. If I could bear this burden for you, I would do it in a heartbeat. Was it Illynor?"

She nodded again, not trusting her voice enough to speak. She had been having nightmares since she woke up in the Keep's dungeon, but they'd never been like this. She had never been so close to death in one before. *Did you think death would keep me from claiming you?* The echo of Illynor's voice sent a chill down her spine.

"Do you want to talk about it?"

"I don't even want to think about it." She kicked off the blankets tangled around her legs and sat up, trying to ignore the ache in her ribs. Most of the bruises had faded, but the bones would be sore for a long time to come. "They'll get easier as time goes on."

Tamriel's expression turned doubtful. He knew she was mostly saying it for his benefit, but he didn't try to argue. He kissed her again before crossing to the wardrobe against the far wall, hangers clacking as he searched for something to wear; he must have been in the middle of changing when she'd begun to thrash. She hugged her knees close to her chest and watched him move, admiring his muscles, toned from years of swordplay. After so many days under the hot sun, his skin had turned a dark bronze, almost the same shade as Kaius's. The crescent-shaped scar Calum had carved into his back stood out in sharp contrast, the tissue jagged and puckered.

Tamriel slipped a deep blue tunic over his head, then

turned to her. A grin spread across his lips when he caught her staring. "Have you just been sitting there ogling me?"

"Of course I was." She quickly braided her hair and tied it off with a piece of leather. "You're very pretty."

"I am not *pretty*."

"Just like a dashing prince out of a storybook."

His smile grew as he began strapping on his armor. "Does that make you my damsel in distress?"

"Please," she scoffed. "Here, let me help."

She slipped out of bed as he pulled on his breastplate. The brush of air against her bare legs sent goosebumps rippling across her skin, and she noticed Tamriel's gaze dip to the hem of her tunic as she approached. "Eyes up, Your Majesty."

"How can I help myself when you're so beautiful?"

She lifted onto her toes to kiss him before starting to work on the straps and clasps of his armor. Where the steel breastplate had once been smooth and shining, it now bore scratches and dents from countless weapons. "We haven't talked about Nicholas yet," she said softly. "How are you feeling about it? And I don't mean politically—we've had enough of that these past few months. I mean...are you okay?"

He looked down, toying with the edge of his gauntlet, and finally breathed, "I trusted him, Mercy. I made him my general, treated him as an honored guest, and he *betrayed* me." He shook his head, agony on his face. "He would have killed us all if your parents hadn't shown up. After we saw those... heads...on the wall, I just... Everything just fell apart."

Anger flooded Mercy—anger and fierce protectiveness. "That's exactly what the bastard intended. He wanted you to fall apart. He wanted to sow chaos among your troops. He knew you'd react so strongly because that's the kind of man you are— the kind of *king* you are. You care for your subjects more than anything." She finished with one strap and moved on to the next. "Nicholas is just like Illynor, and he'll die like her, too. I promise you that. We've been through even worse odds than this, and we've emerged victorious every time. We can do it again.

"I wish I could swear to you that we will all survive this, but I have no idea. What I *can* say for certain is that we will gather the slaves, we will build our army, and we will see Nicholas pay for his crimes." She reached up and cupped the side of his face, coaxing a smile from his lips. "I believe in you. Your friends believe in you. Nicholas will not win. Do you remember what you said when I told you we'd bring Firesse to justice?"

A spark of recognition lit his eyes. "I said justice abandoned us long ago."

"And what was my response?"

He glanced at the sword he had left leaning against the wardrobe. "*Then we'll just have to mete it out ourselves.*"

"That's right. And that's exactly what we're going to do." She tightened the last strap and stepped back. "There. Now you look like a proper king in your shining armor."

"I should hope so, as it's the only bit of regalia I have left." He secured the belt with his sheathed sword around his waist. "Do you think Percival is still alive? Or that Seren Pierce made it out of the city? His head wasn't on the wall."

"I think if Nicholas wanted to kill Percival, he would have done it when Percival attacked him. As for Pierce, I have no idea. I hope he and Nerida escaped or, at the very least, hid. We could use another ally."

"Tam? Mercy?" Calum called from down the hall, his voice muffled by the closed door. "Faye and the others are about to leave for town. Do you need any supplies?"

Tamriel kissed her temple and started toward the door. "Go ahead and get dressed, love. I'll speak to him."

Mercy watched him leave, shutting the door behind him,

before quickly changing. When she finished, she turned to the desk by the window. Her beautiful black and silver armor was spread out on its surface, glittering in the sliver of light that slipped in through the gap between the curtains. She donned the armor, and the weight of the chainmail tempered the nerves her nightmare had frayed. In it, she felt like she had before the Trial—invincible, unstoppable, *fearless*.

When she stepped into the living room, her Stryker-made daggers once again at her hips, she found Cassia sitting alone on the settee, a mug of tea in her hands. Little whorls of steam danced in the air in front of her face.

"Are Faye and the others outside?" Mercy asked as she sat down beside her sister.

"Yes. She's finishing saddling the horses."

Mercy studied Cassia. They were all exhausted, but Cassia looked even more so, like she might tip over with the slightest breeze. Her fair skin was almost transparent, underscored with blue veins and dark shadows. Her headscarf wasn't wrapped as neatly as it usually was; it hung loosely around her face, offering a glimpse of the disfigurement she was always so careful to keep hidden.

"Are you feeling alright, Cassia? Did you sleep?"

"I did, but not well. I keep thinking about our parents. What *happened*? How did they manage to appear like that? Why aren't we dead right now?"

In all the chaos, Mercy had not had a chance to properly explain how Dayna and Adriel had been able to appear in the In-Between. In all honesty, she didn't completely understand it herself.

"Tamriel told me about how Liselle protected you when you were on your contract, but I never expected to…to actually witness something like that." Cassia turned red-rimmed eyes on Mercy, her grip tightening on her mug. "How was it possible for them to come back from the Beyond? I thought the only reason Liselle was able to do it was because Firesse pulled her from the Beyond with her blood magic."

"I don't know," Mercy replied, hating that she didn't have the answers Cassia needed. "Liselle was summoned to torment the king, but she turned on Firesse when she recognized me in Sandori. Our parents appeared of their own volition to save us. I don't have any explanation for it. I wish I did."

"I need to see them again. I never even got to say goodbye." She sniffled, tears slipping through her lashes. "We knew there was a chance we wouldn't all make it out of the Keep alive, but I thought that after so many years apart, we would finally have a chance to be a real family for once." Cassia set the mug on the floor and dried her cheeks with her sleeve. "How do we contact them? How do we get them back?"

Mercy's heart broke for her sister. "I...don't think it works like that," she said softly, trying to ease the blow of the words. "When Liselle appeared to me in the Islands, she said she only had a little time to remain in the In-Between before she was pulled back to the Beyond. That's probably why she wasn't able to fully manifest last night. Considering how much power our parents used trying to fend off Nicholas's army, I don't know if they have enough strength left to contact us again."

"So they appear out of nowhere, save our lives, and disappear forever?"

"Cassia, consider how lucky we are. We should be dead right now, but they came back to protect us. Can you imagine any better way for them to show how much they love us?"

"I...suppose you're right." She stood on unsteady feet, her pale face made even starker by the deep violet of her scarf. She wrapped it tighter around her head, hiding her scars. "I just didn't expect to see them again. It—it rattled me."

"I understand. Are you sure you're fit to ride to Knia Valley?"

She nodded. "I need something to take my mind off everything. I'll see you in a few hours."

Cassia picked up her mug and walked into the kitchen. Mercy watched the door swing shut behind her, worry gnawing at her. Her siblings hadn't seen Dayna or Adriel in years. Ripping them away so suddenly—so soon after being reunited—was the cruelest joke the Creator could have played on them.

Mercy closed her eyes, picturing Dayna's delicate, feminine features and Adriel's piercing eyes, so like her own. "If you can hear me," she whispered, her voice thick with grief, "please tell me everything is going to be okay. Tell me we're going to make it through this."

She sat there for a few moments as Cassia moved around in the kitchen, her ears straining for an answer. When no response came, she swallowed the lump building in her throat and shoved her sorrow somewhere deep within her. Her parents had used up too much power, and Liselle had not even been strong enough to fully appear outside Sandori. Mercy didn't expect to ever see them again. She was fresh out of miracles.

❧ 7 ☙
TAMRIEL

The sun had already sunk below the windbreak when Faye, Cassia, Matthias, and Ino finally returned, followed by... Tamriel froze, stunned, when he recognized the man and woman riding on a snow-white mare between Mercy's brothers. A few paces back, a young elven woman rode behind Cassia. He slowly rose from the porch step he had been sharing with Calum as Seren Pierce and Nerida stopped their horse before him and dismounted.

"I bet your forgiveness, Your Majesty," Pierce said quickly, bowing low. His wife and Liri, their slave, did the same. "You entrusted the safety of the kingdom to Cassius and me, and we allowed this terrible mess. We had no idea the Astley and Burgess soldiers were going to attack. By the time we realized what was happening, they had already killed half of your supporters. I'm so sorry."

"I don't blame you for being taken by surprise, Pierce." Tamriel gestured for them to rise. "I never expected Nicholas to turn against me, either."

"I don't understand. The Comyns have supported the royal family for generations."

"Shocking, isn't it?" Calum asked dryly.

"I just—I can't believe it." Pierce seized his wife's hand, the blood draining from his face. "We hardly made it out of the capital alive. The Church bells started tolling, and chaos erupted throughout the city. The soldiers were running through the streets like madmen, blood dripping off their blades. Cassius and I were working in the castle. We made a run for it—to get to our wives—but they spotted us. I... I couldn't do anything but watch as one of the men ran him through with a sword. Some of Atlas's friends from the guard arrived then and fought them off so I could find Nerida and Liri and get out of the city."

"Your Majesty, do you know what happened to our son?" Nerida asked, tears welling in her eyes. "Is he alive?"

"I don't know, but I pray he is. I was separated from my royal guard when Nicholas turned the army against me."

She buried her face in her free hand. "Oh, Creator, let him be alive. Don't take both our children from us."

Faye jogged over to them while Ino, Matthias, and Cassia begin distributing supplies to the Cirisians. "Word of Nicholas's attack has already reached Knia Valley. Calum was right—he sent out ravens with news of his victory almost immediately. He is offering substantial rewards for the deaths of you, Calum, and Mercy, as well as anyone who travels with you or provides you aid. And he has announced that Percival will be coronated two days from now."

"Percival?" Tamriel repeated. He supposed it made sense; he had always suspected the nobles would stick a puppet in his place if they ever managed to overthrow him, and Percival was as good a puppet as any. Nicholas had been controlling him all his life. Of course he had leapt at the chance to do it on a grander scale.

At least now he knew his friend was alive.

"Do you have a plan to get your throne back, Your Majesty?"

He exchanged looks with Calum. "We're working on it. You have some thoughts on that?"

Pierce nodded. "Why don't we go inside and discuss it?"

"Sure. Calum, can you find Mercy, Kaius, and Duomnodera?"

Tamriel led them into the house while Calum ran off. Once they were all settled around the kitchen table, Tamriel explained his plan to recruit the slaves. To their credit, Seren Pierce and Nerida looked only *moderately* horrified at the thought of losing their property. Liri, sitting on the settee across the room, positively glowed.

"The slaves may agree to fight for you, Your Majesty," Pierce said when Tamriel finished, "but they're no match for a real army. You need soldiers of your own."

"We need to prepare for the worst," Nerida agreed. "Nicholas's family holds a lot of sway in the court, and his coffers are deep enough that he can buy any allies he can't persuade. If you're going to defeat him, you need a real army—a *foreign* army."

"I was afraid you'd come to that conclusion, as well," Tamriel groaned, sitting back in his chair. His grandfather, King Alaric, had been close with the Rivosi king, but Ghyslain had let the relationship between their kingdoms die after Liselle was killed. Considering his family's history, considering that Nicholas was certainly spreading word of Tamriel's sympathy for the elves, would they be willing to give him aid? Or would they capture him and his family and ship them off to Nicholas, eager to earn favor with the new monarch?

"We haven't always had good relations with the king of Rivosa," Pierce continued, "but Cassius Bacha used to belong to his court. The royal family won't take his murder lightly."

"They're all the way on the other side of the country,"

Calum objected. "Going to Rivosa means turning back and crossing paths with Nicholas's army in the process—not to mention the Assassins. I saw them fighting alongside Nicholas's men, which means they're now chasing us, too. Even if we were able to make it past them, Nicholas's land encompasses a large portion of the border. It's extremely unlike that we'd even be able to make it into Rivosa."

A name surfaced in Tamriel's mind from weeks before, when he'd overheard Percival and his uncle arguing. "Do you know a Rivosi noblewoman named Riona? She's Percival's betrothed, and Nicholas made it sound like she holds a lot of sway within the kingdom."

"The name sounds familiar."

"I thought so, too, but with everything else going on, I didn't have a chance to look into her."

"Riona..." Nerida mused. A second later, recognition flitted across her face. "She's the king's niece. Fourth or fifth in line for the throne, if I remember correctly, and a good bargaining chip for the king since his only daughter, Namira, is still a child."

"We're not going to find an ally in Rivosa, then," Mercy said, frowning. "The Rivosi king isn't going to pass up the opportunity to align himself with Beltharos's new king, regardless of whether or not he is legitimate. If we cross the border, he'll just hand us over to Nicholas."

"What does that leave?" Tamriel asked. "Cirisor and Gyr'malr?"

"Like I said, I'll try to gather as many warriors as I can, but I don't know how much aid the other High Mothers will pledge to your cause." Duomnodera looked to Kaius. "What of your people?"

"There are some elves who didn't fight with Firesse because they didn't support her hunger for vengeance. I bet they'll fight for His Majesty after they learn that he plans to free the slaves and pull his troops from the Islands."

"Nynev is there, too," Tamriel added. "She was going to try to take control of Firesse's clan. She's a gifted fighter and a talented archer. She'll fight."

"The Qadar and the Cirisians will help," Seren Pierce said, nodding, "but they're not going to be enough. You need Feyndara."

A stone sank in Tamriel's stomach. "I was afraid you were going to say that."

Queen Cerelia hated his family with a passion, claiming they stole the Cirisor Islands from her people. She'd cut off contact between their countries long before he'd been born and, to his knowledge, no one but the Strykers and a select few merchants were allowed on Feyndaran soil. Attempting to enter her country could be just as dangerous as turning back to face Nicholas's army.

"We don't have any other option, Your Majesty."

He groaned. "I know. That's the worst part."

Half an hour later, the horses were saddled and ready to leave. Half of Kaius's archers were already patrolling the king's highway, their quivers fully stocked thanks to Faye and the others, and the rest were waiting beside the opening in the windbreak. Tamriel shoved his small pack of food and clothes into his mare's saddlebag and climbed onto the saddle. Mercy, seated astride Blackfoot, immediately claimed the place to Tamriel's right as Duomnodera and her warriors closed ranks around their entire group.

"Your Majesty, if I may have a word?" Seren Pierce called, riding up to Tamriel's other side. "In light of everything, I need to apologize for our past...disagreements. I'm afraid I allowed the rift between your father and me to color my opinion of you. Once I learned the truth about my Elise's, uh, crimes," he said, stumbling a bit over the words, "I realized how unfairly I'd been treating you. I was one of your father's closest friends when we were younger, and I should have been his strongest supporter when he ascended the throne. I...I failed him. I will not do the same to you."

"I appreciate that, Seren. You are forgiven." He spurred his horse and started toward the opening in the windbreak, the rest of the horses falling into step behind him, Pierce, and Mercy. "I'll see you handsomely rewarded for your faithful service once my throne is restored."

"That is very gracious of you, but not necessary. You are my rightful king and are entitled to my fidelity and service. Most, if not all, of your supporters in the capital were killed the day I fled, but there must be more in the countryside. The Fitzroys, perhaps, and maybe the Clancys. I can write to them when we reach Cyrna. It's possible Nicholas has already swayed them to his side, but if he has not and they are willing to pledge troops to you, it would help your bid for the throne. It still won't be enough without Queen Cerelia's help, mind you, but every soldier helps."

"Be sure that you do not give away too many details. The last thing we need is them reporting our plan or our whereabouts to Nicholas."

"I'll be cautious, Your Majesty. Have you given any thought to how you're actually going to recruit the slaves to your army without the humans catching on?"

Tamriel merely nodded, refusing to offer any explanation. It wasn't that he didn't trust Pierce—the only people he was certain he could trust were the ones here with him—it was that he knew Nicholas would go to any length to learn how he was planning to reclaim his throne. He didn't want Pierce to have any more information than was absolutely necessary in case Nicholas got his hands on the seren or his family.

As Seren Pierce fell back to ride with Liri and the apprentices, Tamriel turned around to look at Ino, Matthias, and Cassia. While the others had been busy saddling the horses back at the farmhouse, Tamriel and Mercy had pulled them into one of the bedrooms to discuss that very same question: how were they going to get word of Tamriel's plans to the slaves without Nicholas or the city guards hearing of it? Ino had ventured a suggestion: using the safe houses scattered across the fishing sector to stage secret meetings with as many slaves as possible. It was risky, of course, but they had no other option.

❧ 8 ☙
PERCIVAL

"The council has assembled, my lord, and your uncle has requested your presence at the meeting," Percival's guard, whose name he had not bothered to learn, announced upon his arrival at the king's chambers. He stopped just beyond the threshold, the doors softly swinging shut behind him, and frowned at the tangled sheets strewn across one of the sitting room's lavish settees. "Did you sleep out here?"

"Yes. Are you going to run off and tell my uncle? I know he ordered you to report back to him anytime I so much as use the chamber pot." He bent down and picked up one of the throw pillows that had fallen onto the floor, tossing it aside. Last night, Percival had been deposited in the king's chambers and left under heavy guard. Even though he had been exhausted after the long journey, he had refused to sleep in the king's bed. The injustice of Nicholas's betrayal felt even more acute here. These rooms belonged to Tamriel and Mercy.

"Let me rephrase my earlier statement. Your uncle did not

request your presence at the council meeting. He demanded it. Let's go."

Percival scowled but followed him out of the room, three more guards immediately falling into step behind them. If Mercy and Tamriel were dead, then this was his new life: these guards, this guilt, this charade of playing at politics.

With a jolt of surprise, he realized that there was a bare spot of fabric on their tunics where the Myrellis family crest had once proudly shone. They had ripped the patches off their uniforms.

By the Creator, is no one in the castle loyal to Tamriel? he thought, outraged. How much had his uncle offered these guards—who had known Tamriel all his life—to betray him? *Am I the only one who sees how wrong this is?*

When they reached the council chamber, a guard pulled the doors open and stepped aside to let him enter. Nicholas was already seated at the head of the long table, various papers strewn across the dark wood. His good eye fixed on Percival as he shuffled inside and sank into the chair beside his uncle. The seating arrangement alone—Nicholas at the head, Percival at his side—left no doubt as to who truly held the power.

His throat tightened when Nicholas folded his hands and declared, "My nephew's coronation will take place two days from today. Nadra, have you spoken to the High Priestess about the ceremony?"

"I have, my lord. She has agreed to perform the ceremony."

"Excellent. I trust you have begun planning the banquet in our new king's honor."

As they discussed the coronation, Percival glanced around the table at the traitors surrounding him. Someone in this room could have killed Cassius Bacha. Someone in this room could have hurt Hero and Ketojan. Dunstan and Jocasta—the heads of the Astley household—were here, seated next to Corinne Burgess, the widow who had inherited her husband's massive estate and seemingly endless coffers. The three of them had provided the soldiers who killed Tamriel's supporters and joined the attack outside the city walls. They were the reason for the empty chairs around this table where Cassius and the others had once sat.

Leon Nadra caught Percival's eye. The boy was around his age, and he looked just as uncomfortable here as Percival felt. Perhaps the same thoughts were running through his mind.

Percival's gaze dropped to his hands, clasped loosely on the table before him. He would have given anything to be anywhere else at this moment. Even so, he sat straight-backed and tall, as his uncle had taught him; *Sit up, stay quiet, and make them think you're worthy of your family name.*

"I led countless men across the Cirisor Islands during the war, won battle after battle, and crafted unparalleled strategies for ridding that land of Feyndaran dogs. I prided myself on being adaptable, on anticipating every possible move my opponent could make," Nicholas was saying, his bitter tone drawing Percival's attention back to the conversation. "I didn't expect Creator-damned *ghosts* to show up and save Tamriel's life, and now we're scrambling to catch up to him and his allies."

Tamriel and Mercy are still alive, Percival realized with a rush of relief.

Nicholas leaned forward, frowning down at the map spread out before him. Little wooden figurines marked the position of his soldiers. "The Assassins are on his trail, as are my soldiers. His supporters are few and far between, but they exist, which makes him a threat to Percival's rule. As long as he is alive, he will not accept his defeat. I want him brought to me—dead or alive—before the wedding. Jocasta, have you—"

"Wedding?" Percival interrupted. "Whose wedding?"

"*Your* wedding. Before we left the Keep, I sent a raven to King Domhnall and arranged for your betrothed, the lovely Riona, to come and stay as a guest within the castle until you are married. If the weather has been kind, she and her entourage will arrive within a week, and the wedding will follow shortly afterward." He caught Percival's look of distaste and frowned. "You need a queen at your side, Percival. The sooner you secure an heir, the better."

Spare me your lectures, he wanted to retort, but he bit his tongue. The nobles surrounding him were some of the most powerful people in the kingdom. Talking back to his uncle like a petulant child wouldn't earn him anything but their scorn. He swallowed his objection and forced his voice to remain calm as he said, "Surely the wedding doesn't have to be so rushed, though? Tamriel will be dead and the threat to my rule will be eliminated. Can't Riona and I have some time to get to know one each other and see if this is a fitting match?"

"Young men are so picky," Landers chuckled before Nicholas could respond. "So caught up in dreams of true love. Your uncle would not have chosen Riona for you if he did not think she would be a capable queen. She's in line for the Rivosi throne and, I hear, is a well-respected member of her uncle's court. If it helps, it is rumored that she is stunningly beautiful."

"No, that doesn't help! Look at me!" He gestured to his spectacles—slightly crooked after being knocked off his face by Nicholas's punch—then to his unruly brown curls and long, lanky limbs. "Just...give us a little time to adjust," he implored Nicholas. "At least so I can learn more about her than just her name."

His uncle frowned. "It doesn't matter whether you know her. What matters is solidifying an alliance between the kingdom of Rivosa and us—and gaining access to the soldiers and substantial dowry Riona will bring with her. Whether you like her or not, you're to be married." His expression turned contemplative as his good eye swept over Percival—assessing, appraising. His lip curled in distaste. "Although, for my own sake, I hope you fall in love with her. It'll mean an end to your constant complaining and sulking. And my headaches."

Percival's hands clenched into fists as the courtiers chuckled. His ears burned.

"Besides," Nicholas said, smirking, "it's your crown that is going to be attractive to her, not you."

❦ 9 ❦
MERCY

They rode hard for the next two days, stopping only long enough to hunt, eat, and briefly rest before setting off again. Twice, they'd been roused from sleep by Kaius's scouts, warning of Nicholas's army. Both times, they had scrambled up from the cold, hard ground and hastily mounted their horses, adrenaline flooding their veins as they fled. According to the scouts, Nicholas's troops had split into groups of a hundred or so men to search the towns along the king's highway.

After the second sighting, Tamriel had insisted they abandon the highway altogether and continue through the plains and valleys, returning to the road only when they needed to cross one of the fishing sector's countless rivers. They were all stressed, anxious, hungry, and exhausted. Cassia had withdrawn even further into herself, and neither Ino's comforting words, Calum's concerned looks, nor Matthias's joking had been enough to draw her out of her grief. It pained Mercy to see her sister so distraught, but only time would help Cassia recover from the shock of seeing the ghosts.

"Finally," Mercy breathed when Cyrna appeared in the

distance before them, the buildings a dark cluster on the horizon.

"We're not safe yet," Tamriel muttered, looking like he would love nothing more than to collapse into bed. He slowed his horse to a walk and scanned the city and surrounding land. "I don't see Nicholas's men, but let's not forget he sent ravens ahead. The guards will be looking for us."

"That's where we come in." Ino gestured to himself, then to Faye and the others. Cassia blinked a few times and straightened, resting a hand on the hilt of the blade strapped to her thigh. The prospect of freeing more slaves seemed to liven her up a touch. "We'll let you know what we discover."

Without another word, he led his small group—Faye, Calum, Cassia, and Matthias—toward the city, leaving Mercy and everyone else to wait. When they reached the outskirts of the city, they would spread out and search for a safe house where Tamriel could address as many slaves as they could gather. The rest would be scattered on the streets nearby, acting as lookouts.

Blackfoot shifted beneath her, sensing her nerves. She patted his neck. "I hate having to sit here, completely useless."

"I do, too," Tamriel agreed, "but we don't have any other option. It's too dangerous for us to walk in there blind."

Mercy nodded, biting her lip as she watched their forms grow smaller with every passing minute.

He reached over and gently tugged the reins out of her left hand, interlacing their fingers. His grip tightened on hers almost imperceptibly, the only sign of his nerves.

"They're going to be okay," Kaius murmured. When Mercy glanced back, the archer's eyes were on Faye, his knuckles white around the grip of his bow. She wasn't entirely sure he had intended to speak aloud.

"I certainly hope so," she whispered.

"We found one," Faye announced an hour later, her hazel eyes bright with excitement. Beside her, Cassia was grinning, momentarily forgetting her grief. "We spoke to the owners—Mason and Lila—and they've agreed to host us for the night. We didn't mention the king will be joining us. That's a shock they'll have to endure when we arrive."

She tossed a handful of cloaks to Duomnodera, who began passing them around to the other Qadar. The Creator only knew what the people of the city would do if they realized a half-dozen of the most terrifying creatures in the world were in their midst. "Lila and I stopped at a shop and bought some cosmetics, as well." She handed a jar to Kaius, and another two to each of the elves beside him. "Use them to cover your tattoos."

Kaius nodded and turned back to translate her words to the Cirisians who did not speak the common tongue. As the Qadar shrugged on their cloaks, pulling up the hoods to hide their scaly, horned scalps, the Cirisians passed the jars of makeup around, helping each other smear the pigment across their faces and arms. It didn't cover the tattoos completely, but the sun would have already set by the time they reached the city, and Mercy doubted anyone would bother to question a group of skinny, ragged-looking elves. Without the ink marking them as Cirisians, they might as well be invisible.

"Here," Matthias said, his nose wrinkling with distaste as he pulled sashes of white silk from his saddlebags—slave sashes. "Mason gave these to us. No one will look twice at a few slaves running late-night errands."

"Lila and her husband know several elves who have been planning to escape and run to Cirisor," Faye told Mercy and

Tamriel as the Cirisians begrudgingly accepted the slave sashes. "They have agreed to gather as many as they can in their safe house, and to spread the word to any slaves they believe will be willing to risk sneaking out tonight. I don't know how many will actually show up—just *speaking* of rebellion is enough to get them killed—but I think Cassia is right about them fighting for their freedom. Even if only a handful come tonight, the slaves will whisper about what you've said. I don't doubt that elves all across the city will learn of your proposal before the week's end."

"You're awfully confident that we won't be captured and handed over to the guards the second we set foot in the city," Tamriel responded, nervously eyeing the houses in the distance. "How much is Nicholas offering for our capture?"

"A hundred thousand aurums for your body. Two hundred thousand for you alive."

"And only twenty-five thousand each for Mercy and me, dead or alive," Calum interjected. "It seems he considers us more inconveniences than actual threats, which is a little insulting."

"Until we have an army, he's right." Mercy turned to Tamriel and offered him a smile she hoped was reassuring. He had hidden his fear well over the past few days, but now, faced with the very real possibility that they could all be killed within the next few hours, terror flashed through his eyes. He blinked it away quickly, letting that court-made mask slip over his features. It may fool the others, but not her. For the moment, he was not a deposed king fighting to reclaim his throne—he was just an eighteen-year-old boy facing impossible odds.

"Tonight, we start building that army," she said, forcing her voice to remain calm, unfaltering. Beside her, Faye ran her fingers over the hilts of the throwing knives at her hip the way she did when she was nervous. "They will join us,

Tamriel. You just need to give them something worth dying for."

He glanced at the city, steeling himself for what they might face when they reached Cyrna. "Do you have any extra cloaks?" he asked Faye.

"Take mine," Seren Pierce said, passing him a bundle of slate gray wool. It was so unlike the seren's usual pomp and flash that it took Mercy aback.

"Is that really yours? It doesn't have nearly enough gems or embroidery."

Seren Pierce did not deign to respond as Nerida handed her own cloak to Mercy. As she and Tamriel slipped the cloaks over their armor, drawing them closed, the Cirisians finished covering their tattoos and donning the slave sashes. Faye frowned at the sight.

"I hate those things," she muttered, nodding to Kaius's sash. "After you reclaim your throne, Your Majesty, I suggest we burn them."

"I second that." He turned and surveyed their small group. In addition to Faye, the apprentices, and Mercy's siblings, they had fewer than three dozen Cirisians and six Qadari warriors. Every single one of them stared at Tamriel, awaiting his order.

"When we arrive at the safe house," he said, raising his voice for all of them to hear, "Kaius will assign you your positions. If you see any sign that the guards know we're here, you must alert the others immediately, and return to the safe house. Our priority is to protect the slaves. Understood?"

He paused, waiting for everyone in their party to nod or murmur their assent. "Good," he said, smiling with that mask he'd crafted during his long years in the court. Ever the brave prince, ever the confident king—at least, that was what he wanted the others to think. "Now, let's go gather an army."

10
FAYE

Faye lingered by the window in the safe house's small sitting room, nerves twisting her stomach. The Qadar and Cirisians were in position on the surrounding streets, keeping an eye out for city guards, but she didn't like being so close to the king's enemies. There were too many chances for something to go wrong.

She'd left Arabelle and the other young apprentices with Duomnodera. It was safer for them to be far from the safe house, but it felt strange to be away from them. After fleeing the Keep, the girls had practically attached themselves to her hip. Arabelle had begged to stay with her. Faye had, of course, refused. The girls were good fighters—Mother Illynor and Trytain had ensured that—but she didn't want to risk their safety.

Lila—the owner of the house—crossed the room and bowed to Tamriel. When they arrived, she'd been shocked to discover the king of Beltharos standing at her door, but she'd recovered from her surprise about as well as one could expect. "Is there anything I can do for you, Your Majesty?"

"You have already done more than enough. I'm beyond

grateful for your aid. And please, call me Tamriel." He shot her a dashing smile, and Faye grinned when the young woman positively *melted*. Lila was only a few years older than Faye, her gold-blonde hair braided and pinned into a bun at the nape of her neck. Her pale blue eyes sparkled with adoration as she watched Tamriel and Mercy shed their cloaks, revealing their fine armor. Faye couldn't deny feeling a little bit envious herself. She still wore her plain leather armor from the Guild.

"I hope her husband doesn't see the way she's fawning over Tamriel," Calum whispered as he passed. Lila hurriedly took their cloaks and led Mercy and Tamriel through the house, showing them to their room for the night.

"As if Mercy would allow her to get within five feet of him," she responded. She turned to the window and peered out at the dark street, the dim glow of the streetlamp on the corner illuminating the empty, cracked cobblestone road. No sign of guards or soldiers...yet. Spreading news of the clandestine meeting to random slaves wasn't the wisest idea they'd ever had, but Faye hoped the elves' desire for freedom would override any thoughts of handing Tamriel over to the authorities.

"You can stop worrying," Ino said from behind her, causing her to jump. He was so quiet she sometimes forgot he was here. He leaned past her and looked out at the street. "We may be in enemy territory, but Kaius and the others will alert us the second we're in danger. If something happens, we'll have plenty of time to get Mercy and the king out."

"We're sitting ducks here. We're just daring the guards to come kill us." She bit her lip and stepped away from the window, sinking onto the couch beside Cassia and Matthias. "How many slaves do you think will actually show up?"

"A dozen, maybe? Two dozen?" Matthias suggested, surveying the small room. "I don't know how many will risk leaving their masters' houses past sundown. Nothing good happens to lone slaves at night."

"Nothing good happens to slaves, period," Ino muttered.

"True," he conceded. "Even if they learn of Tamriel's offer, it's possible they'll interpret it as a ploy by the guards to capture any slaves who are thinking about escaping. That very thing happened in Blackhills when we were slaves. Rumors spread that the owner of a safe house across the city had come into some money and was willing to donate it to slaves in need of transport to the Islands."

Ino clapped a hand on his brother's shoulder. "Matthias was the one who figured out it was a trap. Said he had a bad feeling about it, and insisted on going ahead to make sure it was safe. When some time had passed and he had not yet returned, Cassia and I went after him and found him fighting with some of the city guards to free a young woman and her son. He only knocked them out—thank the Creator for that, because if he'd killed them, he certainly would have been executed—and luckily they woke up the next morning unable to recall who had beaten them into unconsciousness."

Matthias flashed her a cocky grin. "I've always been the most sensible of the three of us. And the most heroic."

Ino smacked the back of his head. "And the most arrogant."

Faye chuckled, and a small smile spread across Cassia's lips—like a ray of sunlight breaking through thick clouds. Out of all Mercy's siblings, Matthias was her favorite. Even when they had been riding to the Keep, knowing death awaited them, he had always been able to smile or crack a joke.

"In all honesty, I don't know if I would have done the same," Ino admitted. "As much as I wanted to help slaves like us, trying to free that woman and her child would have put Cassia and Matthias at risk, and I *always* put their safety first." He looked to his brother, admiration clear on his face. "You didn't even hesitate."

"Oh, just admit it. You could never be as caring or fearless as I am. Or as breathtakingly handsome, for that matter."

As the siblings bickered good-naturedly, Faye locked eyes with Calum, who was standing by the wall, watching with a wistful expression on his face. She still could hardly believe that he was related to them, to Mercy. It was obvious now that they were all together: Calum had the same angular face as Ino, the same crooked grin as Matthias. He shifted, looking uncomfortable. He and Mercy seemed to have made peace, but it was obvious he still didn't know his place within their family.

Take a walk? she mouthed to him, and he nodded, relieved. Without a word, they stepped outside, leaving the siblings to tease and mock each other.

For a few minutes, they wandered down the street in silence. Faye stared up at the stone buildings surrounding them, the shutters hanging crookedly from the second-floor windows, complete with sun-faded, peeling paint. This city was so similar to where she'd grown up. Fallmond was nowhere near this size, but the houses looked the same—all tall and narrow, lined up next to one another like dominos. She pictured her mother standing in the doorway of a house they passed, her apron dusted with flour. They'd never had much money, but her parents had tried their best not to let Faye or Fredric know that; their clothes had been hand-me-downs from the village kids, but they'd been patched and altered to fit, and they'd always scraped together enough coin to spend on treats at the annual Bounty Fest one town over.

That was, until Fredric fell ill. After that, they spent all their money on healers and miracle cures.

For the first time in years, homesickness hit Faye like a physical blow. After she burned her wedding dress, she had refused to let herself think about her home. If she had allowed herself to remember her mother's heartbroken sobs after she found Fredric's body, her father's agonized screams as her betrothed's lackeys broke his legs, she would have turned back into the helpless little girl she'd been when she fled. She would have curled up in her bed and never risen again.

She wrapped her arms around herself as they walked across the bridge that spanned the Bluejet River. Faye paused at the center and stared down at the water gurgling gently below them. It was so clear she could see all the way down to the bottom, which was littered with keys, coins, toys, and lockets. Calum looked at her questioningly.

"It's custom in the fishing sector to throw something into the river when a loved one passes," she explained. She leaned against the railing, and he moved to her side, watching the stars reflect off the water's surface. "The rivers connect all the cities in the sector, all the way from Lake Myrella to the Abraxas Sea. It's meant to represent that no matter where we go, our loved ones will be with us. They still watch over us from the Beyond." She thought back to Dayna and Adriel. "Perhaps there is more truth to that than I once believed."

"What did you throw in when your brother died?"

"An eyepatch." When he lifted a brow, she continued, "Fredric dreamed of becoming a pirate, and I was going to be his first mate. We were going to sail the world together, he said, and grow rich beyond our wildest dreams." She chuckled softly, staring down at her hands. "It sounds foolish when I say it out loud."

"I don't think it's foolish. You loved him."

"I would have followed him anywhere," she whispered, her voice small and meek. Aside from Mercy, she had never told anyone about Fredric. She was not entirely sure why she had felt compelled to tell Calum about her brother the day she'd helped him escape the capital. Perhaps she had simply needed someone to talk to after the horrors they'd witnessed during the war, and he'd been the only person around. Or perhaps some part of her had known he would understand.

She cleared her throat, swallowing her sorrow. "I never thanked you for saving me at the Keep."

"I didn't think you remembered that," he said, looking at her with surprise. "You were nearly unconscious. Anyway, you should be thanking Kaius, not me. He's the one who took care of you in the infirmary."

"I would have bled to death on the battlefield if you hadn't carried me into the castle. So, thank you."

"You're welcome. For what it's worth, I'm glad you made it."

"'For what it's worth'?"

"I don't know where we stand after everything that has happened," he confessed, staring down at the river. "I tried to have Tamriel killed. I almost killed Mercy. I tried to barter her freedom for Tamriel's life. I slaughtered countless people for Firesse—"

"That last one wasn't you."

"It was my body, my hands. I watched Dr—Drake murder them, and I *felt* his delight when he did it." He shuddered, stumbling over his father's name, before he raked his hands through his hair. "I don't know what you and I are to each other, or what I am to Mercy and Tam and the others. Hell, I hardly know *who* I am anymore."

"Then you should be glad you're still alive. You get a chance to figure it out."

"I suppose." He was quiet for a few long moments, then he asked, "What are we, Faye? Are we friends? Or just allies out of necessity? Where do we go when this is all over?"

"I... I don't know," she admitted, and she was not quite sure which question she was answering. In a way, he was no better than the man who had tried to buy her hand in marriage; he had manipulated Mercy to try and get what he had thought he wanted—Tamriel dead, Ghyslain blamed for the contract, and himself placed on the throne.

But...she had seen the agony in his eyes when Drake was possessing him. She had witnessed the desperate cry for help behind Drake's cruel sneer. He was no longer the man she had met in the Keep so many months ago. At his own father's hands, he had endured a torture she could not begin to comprehend, and he still fought back. He had saved Dayna and Adriel knowing he likely would not survive.

And after everything, here he was, standing before her. Considering all she had done for Firesse and Illynor, who was she to hold a grudge?

"I don't know where we go after this," she said, turning to him, "but I would very much like to be your friend."

He beamed at her, his grin as bright as the moon hanging high overhead. "I would like that, too, Faye."

11
MERCY

Two hours later, Mercy stood beside the kitchen counter as Tamriel greeted the fifteen slaves Mason had been able to gather. There were more who wanted to escape their chains, Mason had told them upon his return, but they had been wary of risking discovery by their masters or the city guards. They were right to be cautious, Mercy knew, but it was more than a little frustrating. Fifteen slaves wouldn't win Tamriel's throne back. They needed thousands of elves to take up arms against Nicholas and the corrupt nobility.

Give them time, she reminded herself. *Let them see that he is sincere. Let word spread to the others.*

Unfortunately, patience had never been her strong suit.

"Thank you for agreeing to speak with me," Tamriel repeated over and over again, shaking hands with each awestruck elf. While it was obvious they didn't have much in the way of respect or love for the royal family, it was entertaining to see the surprise on their faces when Tamriel greeted them as equals. Her chest swelled with pride as she watched Tamriel smile and clasp their hands. This was the king he would be once his throne was restored—a king of the people.

"Please, take a seat," he told the elves, gesturing to the couch and chairs they'd crammed into the small room. The slaves obeyed, casting wary glances at the strangers surrounding them. Faye and Kaius were standing in opposite corners at the back of the room, positioned next to the front windows so they could spot any guards approaching. Cassia, Matthias, and Ino were seated among the slaves, and Calum was standing with Mason and Lila at the mouth of the hall. All were heavily armed.

"I'm sure you're all aware that my throne was stolen from me," Tamriel began, a flicker of pain flashing across his face. "I've come here to ask you to help me reclaim it."

One of the elves let out a bark of laughter. He clapped a hand over his mouth as the others began to whisper to one another, looking uncertain whether Tamriel was joking or not.

"How, um, how would we do that, Your Majesty?" a redheaded girl not much older than Mercy asked. She fingered her white slave sash nervously, her eyes darting up to meet Tamriel's, then back down to the floor.

"More importantly," said another, bolder slave, "*why* would we do that? You're a wanted man, Your Majesty. If we help you, we'll be risking our lives."

"It's no small thing to ask you to risk your lives. I am well aware that you have no great love for my family, but if you do not wish to fight for me, perhaps you would be willing to fight for your freedom." Tamriel grinned at the surprise that rippled across their faces. "Nicholas Comyn orchestrated a coup because he learned that I intend to free the slaves and pull my troops from the Cirisor Islands. I intend to petition the queen of Feyndara for troops, but I need your support to reclaim my throne. If you are able-bodied enough to hold a sword, we will teach you how to wield it.

"When I reclaim the throne, my first act will be to declare slavery illegal across Beltharos. I promise you that as long as a Myrellis rules over this kingdom, you and your people will be free. Nicholas, however, will not be so kind."

"It's true," Cassia cut in, and all the slaves turned to face her. "For the last two years, His Majesty has been helping slaves escape from the capital. How many were you, Hero, and Ketojan able to smuggle out of the city?"

"Twenty-two," Tamriel responded. There was pride in his voice, but Mercy heard an undercurrent of pain. She knew he wished it had been more.

"The king is not offering you an empty promise," Cassia continued. "You are as much his subjects as the humans are, and he will see to it that the injustices you have suffered are set right. I would not be here, supporting him, if I did not believe he is the king Beltharos needs."

The elves exchanged glances, and Mercy felt a flutter of excitement at the hope on their faces. A few of them leaned forward, nodding along with Cassia's words.

"You would have us fight with you," the redhead said, turning back to Tamriel. "You would have us fight against Creator only knows how many trained, armored Beltharan soldiers. It'll be a slaughter."

This time, Kaius stepped forward. "Many of you know how to defend yourselves already. What you don't know, my people and I will teach you. I have three dozen Cirisian hunters and archers at my disposal, and, should you agree to fight for His Majesty, we will see that you are trained and prepared to take on Nicholas Comyn's army."

"Cirisians?" one of the slaves echoed, looking a little awed at the mention of the fabled elves.

Kaius nodded. "We have been defending ourselves against

Beltharan and Feyndaran soldiers for generations, with nothing more than the armor and weapons we have pilfered from the invading forces. If we can face them and live to tell the tale, rest assured that we can teach you to do the same. One of my people will remain here and train you in secret. When His Majesty returns with his army, we will regroup and prepare to face Nicholas's troops in the field."

The slaves whispered to one another again, some of them with expressions of hope and determination, others of fear and wariness. Mercy watched nervously as they deliberated, weighing what Tamriel and the others had said.

"Some of us have families," one of the elves finally said. He was tall and broad-chested like Ino, his muscles toned from years of manual labor. *Swordsman*, Mercy decided. He stood and looked at Tamriel. "I have no desire to see my daughter live her whole life in chains. I will stand by your side, Your Majesty, and when you call on me, I will fight beside you."

Some of the tension in Tamriel's shoulders released. "I'm grateful for your aid."

Another elf stood. "I'll fight, too."

"And me."

"And me."

One by one, the elves rose and pledged themselves to Tamriel's army. Mercy's spirits lifted as she watched Tamriel acknowledge and thank each one. It would be a long time before they had enough soldiers to take on Nicholas's army, but every person helped. This was the start of the army that would restore Tamriel's throne.

❧ 12 ☙
PERCIVAL

Percival swallowed tightly as the carriage rolled up to the Church of the Creator, and peered through the gap in the curtains over the window. The early morning sun was bright, the sky cloudless and impossibly blue. He had to squint to make out the noblemen and women waiting on the steps for a glimpse of Nicholas and him—their future king. His stomach clenched at the thought. He didn't want to be king. He had never wanted *any* of this.

"Are you ready?" Nicholas asked, appraising him from beneath lowered brows. His uncle was seated on the bench opposite him, dressed in a fitted black jacket, trousers, and shining leather boots. His usual sword had been swapped out for one with a handle of gleaming gold, rubies and sapphires inlaid in the hilt to match the crown Percival would soon wear.

Percival shook his head.

"I know it's nerve-wracking," Nicholas said, leaning close. "Everyone's eyes are going to be on you for no longer than an hour. After that, all you have to do is smile and accept their congratulations. Your duty to the kingdom is in name only. I will handle everything else. You needn't worry."

I needn't worry about the friend you tried to slaughter? he thought, biting back the retort. *I needn't worry that you have people hunting Tamriel, Mercy, and their allies as we speak? I needn't worry that I am about to commit treason?* Although Nicholas was confident in his army's abilities, they had yet to receive word that Tamriel, Mercy, and the others were dead; Percival refused to believe it until he saw their bodies with his own eyes. His king was alive, mounting a force to reclaim his throne. He was certain of it. All he had to do was wait and pray that Nicholas's men didn't catch up.

"Once Tamriel and the others are dead, you're going to send your soldiers to the Islands, aren't you?" he asked. "You're going to try and claim the Islands for Beltharos, and you're going to kill all the elves who stand against you. Do you expect me to just look the other way?"

The carriage halted before the Church steps and bobbed as the driver climbed down from his bench at the front.

"I am finally going to take control of the lands I fought and bled for. I lost good men and women in those battles—people who were more my family than your father was—and I can't watch their sacrifices go unavenged. Understand that I do not intend genocide, Percival. This is war. Any elves who surrender will be spared. The Cirisians will live as they always have, but their Islands will belong to our kingdom."

The door to the carriage swung open before Percival could respond. Nicholas leaned back and gestured for him to climb out first. Gathering his courage, Percival stood as tall as he could without hitting his head on the low ceiling, straightened his doublet, and stepped out onto the cobblestone road. A cheer rose from the gathered nobles the instant they saw him.

"By the Creator," he breathed, scanning the sea of excited

and expectant faces, the rainbow of silks and satins and laces. The council members knew the truth of who really held the power of the kingdom, but to the nobles gathered here, this was a valid coronation and an occasion for celebration.

He was in way, way over his head.

Nicholas followed him out and turned a beaming grin on the crowd. "Smile," he muttered to Percival, and he obeyed. The gesture was forced, hollow, and he was certain everyone saw straight through it as they made their way up the steps.

Two priestesses were waiting beside the open doors of the Church. They bowed to him and his uncle and led them down the aisle, seating them in the pew reserved for the royal family. As soon as they had taken their places, several of the royal guards who had been stationed along the walls slid onto the bench on either side of them and into the pew behind them. Then the nobles flooded in, chattering to one another as they took their seats. Percival tried to tune out their lighthearted conversations. How could they be acting like nothing was wrong? How could they ignore the fact that several of the pews were empty because the families who once supported the Myrellis royals were now dead or in hiding?

He turned forward and fixed his stare on the bowl-shaped altar. Once everyone was settled, the High Priestess emerged from the hallway at the rear of the dais, a line of a dozen priestesses trailing after her. All save for the High Priestess were dressed in the robes of the Church, rendering them nearly indistinguishable from one another—except one. Percival's attention snagged on the Cirisian woman in their ranks. The young elf's eyes remained trained on the floor as she took her place against the back wall with the other priestesses.

The High Priestess stepped to the edge of the dais. The Creator's holy eye symbol, embroidered in gold thread across her gown's fitted bodice, caught the light as she gestured for Percival to approach.

He stood, wiped his sweaty palms on his trousers, and made his way to the steps. As he approached, the High Priestess's eyes slid to Nicholas, and a shadow passed across her face before she blinked it away.

She held out her hand. One of the priestesses rushed forward and placed a well-worn copy of the Book of the Creator into her hand. It had to be decades, if not centuries, old, but the gold imprint of the Creator's eye was still as bright as the thread on her gown.

"We gather on this, the seventh day of Havenfall in the Year of the Creator 1326, to witness the coronation of Lord Percival Comyn, soon to be the twenty-fifth monarch of Beltharos," she announced, her voice echoing through the vast room. The nobles grew so quiet Percival could almost trick himself into thinking they were alone.

How many are secretly still loyal to the Myrellises? he wondered. Certainly, some of these people would have been outraged at the overthrow of their sovereign, wouldn't they? Tamriel had ruled for barely a month before he left for the Keep. He certainly wasn't mad or unstable like his father, and the nobles had put up with Ghyslain for decades.

"Will you, the people of Beltharos, accept this man as your sovereign from this day unto his last?"

Percival frowned as a *Yes* rose up from the crowd, and he had no doubt that if he looked over his shoulder, his uncle would be doing the same. The High Priestess was not following the traditional script for a coronation. She had left any mention of the Creator out of her question. He doubted anyone else had noticed, but it struck him as odd that she of all people would forget such a detail.

"Kneel, my lord, that you may swear your oath to your country and your people."

He climbed the steps and knelt on the top one, directly below the priestess.

"Percival Comyn, do you swear to govern your subjects fairly in accordance with the laws of Beltharos?"

His skin prickled under the heavy stares of the nobles. All of a sudden, his doublet felt too tight, the collar thick and choking. When he opened his mouth and said, "I shall," the voice that came out did not sound like his own.

"Do you promise to protect, guide, and provide for the people of your kingdom, in times of prosperity and in times of adversity, to the best of your ability for as long as you are able?"

"I do."

"Will you to your power ensure justice and mercy be executed in all your judgments, and, as the Creator himself once did, strive to rid your country of those black of heart and foul of deed?"

He fought not to let the surprise show on his face. *That* addition was certainly new. Although the High Priestess's tone had remained even, neutral, he got the distinct impression that the words had been directed at his uncle.

"My lord?" she prompted.

"I-I will."

She set the Book on the altar and gestured for the priestess carrying the crown to move forward. When she lifted it off the velvet pillow, the gemstones encrusted in the gold sent flashes of colorful light dancing around the room.

"I crown this man King Percival Comyn, the twenty-fifth sovereign of the great country of Beltharos, and the first king of the Comyn line," she said as she set the heavy crown on his head. "May your reign be prosperous, your life long and joyful, and your heart full of courage."

The nobles cheered as Percival rose, the crown wobbling with every slight movement. When he turned back to the pews, he did not miss the anger on his uncle's face. Fear for the High Priestess shot through him. She had altered the sacred, traditional words of the coronation; she had turned them into daggers to wield against his uncle, and he knew Nicholas would not forget the slight anytime soon.

Percival descended the steps. The nobles immediately swarmed him and his uncle as the High Priestess and the other priestesses filed out of the room. He forced another fake smile as the courtiers offered congratulations and well-wishes for the future.

A heavy hand landed on his shoulder. "You did well," Nicholas murmured. Percival tried to ignore the tiny spark of pride that lit up within him at the praise. Before the betrayal, he would have done anything to gain his uncle's approval—his *affection*—but now the feeling left a bitter taste in his mouth.

All hail the puppet-king of Beltharos.

After several long minutes, he caught sight of the Cirisian priestess glaring at him from across the room, making no effort to hide it. She held his gaze for a moment, her jaw set and eyes narrowed, before sharply pivoting on her heel and disappearing into the hall. Percival frowned, a sense of familiarity nagging at him. He had seen her around the city before. He wondered if, judging by the accusatory look she had shot him, she was a friend of Mercy or Tamriel.

The celebration dragged on, and his thoughts turned from the Cirisian woman to his conversations with various nobles. The men bowed to him and offered congratulations, while the women curtsied prettily and expressed their excitement for Lady Riona's visit. Nicholas and the council members must have already begun spreading the news about the impending royal wedding, he realized. He scanned the room and found his uncle standing halfway down the aisle, conversing with several members of the court. As much as Nicholas claimed to detest life in the court, he certainly enjoyed deceiving those around him. The courtiers didn't even see it. They saw the war hero, the brilliant strategist, the unfathomably rich nobleman. They had no idea he was using them.

And you're so much better off? a small voice whispered in his mind. *You didn't see it, either. Because of your blindness, he nearly killed your king.*

He winced. "I, ah, excuse me," he stammered suddenly, interrupting Marlena Nadra mid-sentence. She blinked at him, surprised. "I need to... I need a moment. Excuse me."

Without waiting for a response, he started toward the hall through which the priestesses had disappeared as fast as his heavy crown would allow. His neck ached from the weight. More than that, though, he needed a moment away from everyone, a moment to process everything that had happened over the past few days. Since the attack outside the city walls, he felt as if he had been sleepwalking, like he might one day wake up and realize everything that had happened was nothing more than a bad dream. Tamriel would be king. Mercy would be his queen.

He glanced over his shoulder as he neared the hall and jumped when he saw two guards walking just a few paces behind him. He'd been so lost in his thoughts he had not heard them approach. "Contrary to what my uncle may believe, I don't need to be watched everywhere I go," he snapped.

"He has ordered that we remain by your side, Your Majesty."

"Doesn't my word now outrank his?"

They both shot him knowing looks. They were under no illusions as to who truly held the power of the kingdom.

"Fine," he muttered through gritted teeth. He lifted the crown off his head and thrusted it at one of the guards. "Then you get to carry this blasted thing around."

They followed him down the hall, passing bedroom after bedroom. Percival didn't have any destination in mind; he just needed to get away from the pomp and circumstance of the celebration. Several priestesses paused and bowed when they saw him, which only served to dampen his already low mood.

It was no surprise that he found himself striding into the Church's vast library, breathing in the scents of ink, old parchment, and worn leather. Back in Westwater, he had spent hours holed up beside one of the bay windows in his familial estate's library, books stacked precariously on the floor, on the table, lined up across the windowsill. Some days, he went searching for a specific book. Others, he simply chose a shelf at random and worked his way across. He would read anything. At first, it had started as a way to escape his uncle's watchful eye; to recover from the humiliation of failing the simplest moves in his swordplay lessons; to forget the subtle barbs his uncle worked into every comment and critique. Eventually, the library had become his sanctuary.

He moved to a shelf and ran his fingers over the cracked and peeling spines of the books, smiling to himself at the simple comfort.

"*He was just made king, and the first thing he does is read a book?*" one of the guards whispered to the other. Percival pretended not to hear. Better they thought him inept than cowardly.

He plucked a book from the shelf at random—a thick tome on the history of the mining cities—and claimed a table in the middle of the room. When the guards merely lingered at the entrance, staring at him in incredulity, he glanced up and raised a brow. "You may want to take a seat, gentlemen. I have a feeling my uncle is going to be a while."

One sank into a chair, setting the crown atop the nearest table, while the other leaned against the bookshelves, his arms crossed loosely over his chest. Percival flipped the pages of his book every couple minutes, but he didn't read a word. His thoughts were too jumbled to focus.

King. The false title weighed heavily on his shoulders. What would become of him in the coming weeks? What would become of the kingdom his family had always strived to protect? As loath as he was to accept it, Tamriel, Mercy, and all their allies were likely dead; his uncle had sent the Daughters and hundreds of soldiers after them. Tamriel would not be returning. There wouldn't be a massive battle for the throne like in all the storybooks. Percival was on his own in a city—in a *kingdom*—where his uncle could buy whatever allies his silver tongue did not sway. He had the strength of an army at his back, the court at his side, and the puppet-king under his thumb. What did Percival have?

Guilt, anger, and a penchant for reading.

I'm going to spend the rest of my life on this Creator-forsaken throne.

The approach of soft footsteps drew his attention, and he looked up just as the Cirisian priestess walked in. She glanced at him, her expression darkening, then hurried toward the stacks at the far end of the room.

That was when an idea struck him.

The priestess might have cared little for him, but she had been loyal to Tamriel. If Percival could convince her to help him, he'd have an ally. Maybe she could get a letter to Hero and Ketojan. He might never have his uncle's strategic mind or the power of the throne, but he could defy his uncle in small ways. He could help slaves flee the city, just as he had before they left for the Keep.

He just needed *help*.

He stood, grabbed a quill, ink pot, and piece of parchment from one of the nearby tables, then returned to his seat and quickly flipped through the book. For several long minutes, all he did was skim the pages, occasionally scribbling what looked like a note to himself on the parchment. All the while, he listened to the priestess shuffling through old papers and silently prayed that she'd agree.

He glanced up at the guards, who both looked monumentally bored. The one at the table stared down at the jewels in the crown, likely wondering how much they wee worth. The other one gazed longingly toward the hall. Even from here, they could hear the chatter and laughter of the nobles.

While they weren't looking, Percival flipped over the parchment, scrawled a short note, and folded it into a square small enough to fit into his palm. He flipped a few more pages, then closed the book and carried it over to where the Cirisian priestess was working. Her lips pressed into a thin line when he approached.

"Do you have anything else by this author?" he asked, holding up the book. He was painfully aware of his guards listening in. They were already reporting everything he did to his uncle; the last thing he needed was to make Nicholas suspicious.

When she reached out to take it from him, he grabbed her hand and pressed the note to her palm. She frowned, her brows furrowing. *Read it,* he mouthed, shooting her an imploring look. *Please.*

She unfolded the paper and scanned the few lines of scrawl. "I don't know offhand," she said slowly, warily. His heart pounded against his ribs, a spark of hope lighting up within him. "We may have more tucked away somewhere. Give me some time to search and I'll have a message sent to you if I find anything."

Yes. That meant yes—or that she'd think about it, at least. He offered her a small, relieved smile. "Thank you."

She nodded and turned back to her work.

His steps considerably lighter, he returned the book to its shelf, then turned to his guards, letting out a long sigh. "I suppose we had better join the celebration once more. My uncle will certainly be looking for me by now." Even if his disappearance earned him a thorough tongue-lashing—or worse—later, it would have been worth it. He had no power of his own, but perhaps with the priestess's help, he could undermine his uncle. "Help me put that damned crown on again, won't you?"

The guard at the table rose and set the heavy crown on his head. His neck immediately began to ache from the weight. "Well," he muttered, starting down the hall, "let's get this over with."

When they returned to the main room of the Church, his uncle fixed him with a hard look. Percival offered Nicholas a shrug and wandered over to the closest group of nobles, planting a smile on his face. When asked about his whereabouts, his guards would tell Nicholas the truth—Percival had wanted to escape the stifling court and enjoy a few minutes of peace and quiet in the library. It certainly was not out of character.

When his uncle returned to his conversation, Percival allowed his smile to turn into a small smirk. His uncle was a brilliant strategist, always planning two or three steps ahead, but he had raised Percival. Percival might not have learned everything his uncle had tried to teach him, but perhaps he had learned *enough*.

Let the battle begin.

13
FAYE

Faye leaned against the wall after the meeting, watching Tamriel and Mercy hold hands, unable to keep foolishly wide grins from their faces. The love between them was palpable, and it made her heart soar that Mercy was finally happy. After everything Mercy had endured at the Guildmother's hands, she deserved it.

Tamriel introduced her as his future queen, and Lila, Mason, and the slaves swarmed around them, offering their support. A few bowed their heads in respect to Mercy, and one even called her 'Your Majesty'. Tamriel released her hand to allow the elves to admire the ring he'd given her, the sapphire as dark as a starless sky.

An ache grew in Faye's chest. What she would not give to feel that joy again, to undo all the terrible mistakes she had made. While she no longer belonged to the Guild, she still felt Mother Illynor's hold on her. The blood of innocents stained her hands. Sometimes, she woke late in the night, seized by memories she wished were not her own, memories she wished were merely nightmares. She would never forget the terror in her victims' eyes as she slaughtered them.

Calum stood at the mouth of the hallway. His mouth was a tight line, and although no tears trailed down his cheeks, his eyes were red-rimmed. She wondered if he was thinking of the young noblewoman he had loved.

In a twisted, selfish way, she envied him. He blamed himself for the deaths of the people Drake had killed during the war, but he'd not had a choice in the matter. She had, and yet she had elected to go along with the Guildmother's machinations. She would bear that knowledge—that guilt—for the rest of her life.

Across the room, Kaius had joined the group surrounding Mercy and Tamriel. He was speaking to a few of the elves, showing them the Cirisian tattoos that coiled along his arms, up his neck, around his face. She studied him for a few moments, noting the way his eyes lit up at the mention of his homeland. When the battle for Tamriel's throne was over, they would all go their separate ways: Mercy and Tamriel to rule; Kaius and the Cirisians to aid the newly-freed elves; and Faye and Calum to try and outrun the demons lurking within them. The thought saddened her.

Perhaps she would take him up on his offer of giving her a place in his clan.

First, though, she needed to restore Tamriel's throne and find her family.

She pushed off the wall and started toward the front door. "I need some fresh air," she said when Matthias glanced back questioningly.

"It's not wise for you to go out on your own," he responded, frowning. "Especially injured. If the guards find out we're here..."

"I'll be careful. I have my daggers. I can take care of myself."

His expression said he did not entirely believe her, but he let the subject drop. She stepped outside and closed the door behind her. A cool wind immediately wrapped around her, scented with the fresh water of the river and the leaves just beginning to turn shades of yellow and red. Autumn was swiftly approaching, and it was not welcome. It had once been her favorite season. Now, though, it only served to remind her of the Forest of Flames.

She wandered down the street with no destination in mind, reaching under the hem of her tunic to run her fingers along the hilts of her throwing knives. Tonight, the gesture did not comfort her as it once had. She scanned the buildings surrounding her. Most were dark, the windows shuttered or curtained off. Somewhere nearby, the Cirisians lurked in the alleys and atop the roofs, watching her with their strange night vision.

She crossed the bridge where she and Calum had stood earlier and continued aimlessly toward the center of town. As she neared the market square, the streets grow busier, despite the late hour. A couple of drunk fishermen at a street corner leered at her, their eyes lingering on her chest. She ducked her head and hurried past them.

"Help," a weak voice called as she passed a narrow alleyway. "Coin?"

She paused and peered into the darkness. What she had thought was just a pile of ratty old blankets was actually a man. His hair hung in long, greasy tangles around his face, emphasizing the sunken hollows of his cheeks and the shadows under his eyes.

"Can you help me?" he rasped. A shaft of moonlight illuminated the side of his face when he leaned forward, reaching for her, and she recognized the bright red rash immediately. *Fieldings' Plague*. He was one of many whose sickness had not disappeared after Firesse's death.

She shook her head. "I have no coin to give you. I'm sorry." What little money she'd been carrying had gone to buying supplies in Knia Valley. It would be a miracle if they had enough to feed themselves during the long trek to the coast, let alone to buy passage to Feyndara.

He slumped against the wall. "Be careful out here, girl. I've heard whispers that there are soldiers on the road. Something's happened in the capital, and it's making everyone nervous. Just watch your back."

As if in response, a shriek shattered the nighttime quiet. Faye jumped, automatically pulling a throwing knife from her belt as she ran toward the source of the sound. It had come from only a few streets down.

"Where do ye think yer goin', knife-ear?" a goading voice called as she turned the corner. Three guards were standing at the mouth of an alley beside a tavern, surrounding two cowering elves. The light spilling from the tavern's windows illuminated them enough for Faye to see the terror on the women's faces. Her anger surged. One of the elves tried to run, but the tallest guard reached out and snagged her arm, shoving her against the wall. She let out a yelp of pain when she hit the stone. "I told ye to wait just one minute," the Rivosan snarled, his voice slurred with drink. "We'll let ye go, sure, but not until ye provide some entertainment for me and my friends here."

Another guard, this one with balding hair and a round gut, grabbed the raven-haired woman and pulled her close. "I like this one the best. She's awfully pretty...for a knife-eared bitch."

"Get away from me, you drunken lout!" she cried, struggling to free herself from his grip.

He grabbed her hair and brought it close to his nose, inhaling deeply. His lips parted into a crooked grin. "You smell good, elf. Almost like—"

His mouth dropped open, his eyes going wide as he let out a wet, bloody gurgle. The elf shrieked and slipped out of his slackened grasp as he stumbled backward, clawing at the throwing knife embedded in his neck. The other two guards unsheathed their swords as Faye rushed at them, her face contorted with fury. She ducked under the swing of a blade and buried her dagger in the back of the guard's thigh. He howled with pain as she pulled it out, but his cry was silenced when she ducked behind him and slashed the blade in her other hand across his throat. Blood spurted from the wound, splattering across the elves and the remaining guard.

"Bitch!" the Rivosan spat as Faye released the dead guard. His body crumpled at her feet, his face frozen in shock. "Ye'll pay for that."

"I don't think so."

He lunged, slashing clumsily with his sword. She knocked the blow aside easily. He'd had far too much to drink. He swung his sword again, and Faye sidestepped. He stumbled from the momentum and tripped over one of his friend's outstretched arms. When he fell flat on his face in the street, Faye wasted no time in plunging her dagger into his back.

"Th-Thank you, my lady," one of the elves stammered as she rose, blood dripping off her daggers. Some of the tavern patrons had stepped outside to investigate the commotion; a small handful of them stood gaping just beyond the doors. A few muttered prayers to the Creator and returned to the tavern.

"Are you hurt?" Faye asked, ignoring the crowd the fight had drawn. Her pulse pounded in her ears, adrenaline flooding her veins.

"Nothing more than bruised pride," the elf assured her, her arms still wrapped tightly around the other woman. "Thank you for your kindness."

Faye nodded, her throat pinching at the sight of the three dead bodies surrounding her. Their blood pooled around her feet, coating her worn leather boots. "You need to leave before someone calls the guards." By the Creator, she did, too. If she needed to stay away from the safe-house all night, so be it. She wouldn't lead them to Tamriel. "Do you have somewhere to go?"

The other woman's eyes filled with tears. Under the blood splattered across her face, her skin was pale as the moon. "Nowhere we won't be treated exactly the same."

Faye glanced at the people lingering by the tavern doors, then looked down the street the way she had come. A few blocks away, two pairs of glistening eyes gleamed in the darkness. *The Cirisians.* She turned to the elves and lowered her voice. "Go with them," she told them, nodding to the cat-like eyes. "They will help you."

The women didn't need any more encouragement. They raced toward the elves, murmuring thank-you's as they passed. Faye turned to the tavern patrons. "If you don't want to join them," she said, nodding to the dead guards, "I'd suggest you return to your drinks and forget what you've seen here."

They hurried into the tavern, shoving each other in their haste to get away. It wasn't going to be long before more guards arrived; someone had likely run off to call them while she hadn't been paying attention.

The adrenaline began to fade, leaving Faye cold and empty. When she saw the guard grab the woman, she had acted on instinct. She hadn't even had to think about what she was doing. Her throwing knife had slid into her palm, and the next moment it was spinning end over end through the air.

Faye bent down and pulled the knife from the guard's neck. His head lolled, and warm blood dribbled onto her fingers. The feel of it nearly made her gag. *Some Assassin you are*, she thought miserably as she retreated into the alley. *Can't even stand the sight of a dead body.*

She only made it a few more yards before she slumped

against the wall of the tavern and dropped her head into her hands, being careful not to get any blood on her skin or hair. Just the cold wetness of it on her fingers sent shivers of disgust down her spine. Her stomach roiled and she sucked in a sharp breath, desperate not to lose her dinner.

She heard soft footsteps approach, but she did not look up.

Someone took her hands and gently pulled them away from her face. She opened her eyes to see Kaius crouching before her, pulling a worn handkerchief from his pocket. In the darkness, all she could make out were the outline of his body and the faint glimmer of his eyes as he began to scrub at the blood coating her fingers. He cleaned each one in turn, paying extra attention to the blood caked around her cuticles and calluses. His gaze never wavered from his work.

Silence stretched out between them, broken only by her sharp, ragged gasps.

Finally, Kaius set her hands on her lap. "Are you hurt anywhere?"

She shook her head. "The guards—"

"Don't worry about them. Myrabella is taking care of the —of them," he said, carefully avoiding the words '*bodies*' and '*corpses*.' "Can you stand?"

She nodded and pushed to her feet, loathing the fact that he was seeing this weakness within her. He knew how guilty she felt about the deaths of the people she had killed during the war, but she had never wanted him to see how much her mistakes haunted her. She didn't want his pity. She was raised to be a *Daughter of the Guild*, for the Creator's sake.

He reached out to steady her, but she backed away, pressing her hand flat against the tavern wall until her legs felt strong enough to support her. "I'm sorry for dragging you away from Tamriel and the others. I shouldn't have let a little blood get to me. If I'm the reason the guards find out Tamriel is here—"

"They won't," he promised. "Myrabella is going to clean up the mess, and then she'll wait nearby to make sure any guards who were called don't get anywhere near the safe house. It will be alright, Faye."

He led her out of the alley and toward the safe house. As they walked along the empty streets, her breathing eased and her trembling began to lessen.

"How did you know where I was?" she asked as they crossed the bridge.

"Ciaran and Myrabella told me they saw you leaving, and we followed you. You're a good fighter, but after everything with the Guild and Nicholas, I didn't want to leave you on your own."

"Thank you. It won't happen again."

He glanced at her sidelong, his green eyes bright in the darkness. "Do not be ashamed of the way you reacted to the deaths of those guards, Faye. Taking a life is never easy, no matter how many times you do it. You're strong. You have a good heart. The Guildmother never stole that from you."

She shuddered. "I don't want to kill anyone else. Ever."

His expression turned sorrowful. "If I could, I would do anything to make that possible."

They lapsed into silence again. After several minutes, the safe house came into view at the end of the block. The windows were tightly shuttered, as they had been when she left, but light only shone through the cracks in two of the rooms. The rest were dark. The slaves must have already left. The others were likely asleep, exhausted from their long journey. Kaius couldn't be faring any better—he and his people had been taking all the nighttime watches—and she was touched that he had come to her aid.

They approached the front door, but before Faye could

reach for the handle, Kaius grasped her elbow, stilling her. "After Firesse died," he said quietly, his slight Cirisian accent lilting his words, "I felt the same way you did. I never wanted to pick up a sword again. Just the sight of blood—the *smell* of it—made me queasy. Every night when I went to sleep, I could not stop picturing the sight of my people lying dead in the throne room, their bodies broken and bleeding. I knew every one of them by name. Some I had danced with at *Ialathan*. Some I had trained to become hunters and archers. Some I had rescued from Beltharan or Feyndaran soldiers. Their blood was on my hands as much as Firesse's.

"After I escaped and found refuge for the few people who had survived the battle, I wanted nothing more than to forget what had happened. What I had done. I'd had so many chances to choose a different path, and yet I followed Firesse. I helped her learn about blood magic so she could kill all those thousands of humans with the plague.

"Every night, I stood on the roof and prayed to the Old Gods for an answer. I could not lead my people out of the city without being caught by the guards, and I could not escape the guards without killing again. When I asked the gods for guidance, they sent me Hero and Ketojan, who told me about Tamriel's sympathy for my people. They told me everything he has done to free slaves behind his father's back. He—a human royal—has done more for my people than I ever have. Firesse and I freed slaves only to lead them into a slaughter. We freed them because we were angry and because we wanted to get back at the humans. Tamriel did it out of kindness and compassion."

He let go of her arm and glanced up at one of the second-floor windows, where she assumed Mercy and Tamriel were sleeping. "Fighting for him won't bring back my people, nor will it make my crimes disappear. But perhaps having a purpose beyond vengeance will make living with what I *have* done bearable. Perhaps, if I fight for him and see my people freed under his rule, I can begin to forgive myself. I think you need that—something to get you through this battle. Something to remind you why you fought so hard to be free of Mother Illynor. You saved Mercy and returned her to Tamriel. What is it *you* want?"

"I want to be Faye Cotheron again," she whispered, surprised at how much it hurt to admit it. Even when she had been fully devoted to the Guild, a small part of her had wondered what it would be like to return to her childhood home, to reclaim the life she had forsaken. "I want to work in the fields with my father again. I want to help my mother bake the pies she always used to make on my birthday. I want to see my brother's grave." Her voice broke on the last word.

Kaius smiled at her and reached for the door. "And so you shall."

14
PERCIVAL

Over the next few days, remarkably little changed. Percival was confined to the castle, shadowed by two or three guards at all times, per Nicholas's orders. During the first and second days, Percival made a point of following his uncle through the castle and accompanying him to council meetings, deliberately looking sullen and put-out by the events of the past few days. It didn't require much acting. At the meetings, he raised a few questions and offered some solutions to problems the council members brought up, but he spent most of his time listening, taking careful mental notes. They still hadn't heard any news of Tamriel and Mercy, but it was entirely possible they were dead, and word had simply not reached Sandori yet. He prayed that was not the case. After all, they had the Cirisians' night vision to help them flee. Perhaps they had made it farther than Nicholas had expected.

Beginning on the third day, he brought a book to every council meeting, pretending to look bored by the nobles' discussion. He wanted his uncle to believe he had accepted his fate as the puppet-king. He sulked at meals in the grand dining hall, trying not to let his worries about the Cirisian priestess show on his face. Could she have decided not to help him? Worse, could Nicholas have somehow intercepted a note from her? Every time he crossed paths with his uncle, he tensed, expecting a fist or a sharp comment, but nothing came...*yet*.

Percival resigned himself to waiting and listening. He occupied his time by gathering as much information as he could about the army's pursuit of Tamriel and Mercy, which wasn't much. Nicholas wasn't stupid; he took private meetings in the study to discuss the more sensitive matters of the court—matters to which Percival was not privy.

One night, as he and his guards left the library, he heard raised voices drifting from the study. He slowed—not enough to draw his guards' suspicion, but enough to catch a snippet of the conversation.

"You didn't give him a proper coronation!" his uncle was saying, sounding absolutely livid. "Those words have been said since Colm Myrellis's son became king. You denied him the blessing of the Creator!"

"That's because King Tamriel is still the ruler of this land under the eyes of the Creator," retorted a voice Percival immediately recognized as the High Priestess's.

"Tamriel is *dead*."

Percival's blood ran cold. He forced his pace not to falter as he continued to the stairs. Had a raven arrived? Had he just not heard the news?

"Until I see his body and give him the final rites, he is not. Show me his body—prove to me the Myrellis line is no more—and I will give your nephew the blessing." There was a pause, during which Percival pictured the High Priestess rising from one of the high-backed leather chairs and glaring down her nose at Nicholas. As cold and calculating as Nicholas could be, he was also a devout believer in the

Creator. "I cannot fathom how you, who values honor and loyalty above all else, found it within yourself to turn on your king. You will face punishment for it in the Beyond. Of that, I am certain."

"I did it for the good of my kingdom and my people. I will face no punishment for that."

The rest of their conversation was lost as Percival climbed the steps to the next floor. Their words echoed in his mind, along with all the subtle barbs the High Priestess had shot at Nicholas during the coronation: *Will you to your power ensure justice and mercy be executed in all your judgments, and, as the Creator himself once did, strive to rid your country of those black of heart and foul of deed?*

When they arrived at the king's chambers, the guards took up their positions on either side of the doors. Percival entered the large, lavish sitting room only to find a young elven woman standing in the middle of the room, dusting a vase on one of the low tables.

"Who are you?" he asked, pausing just beyond the threshold. The doors swung shut behind him, closing with a soft *click*. He knew the faces of all the slaves who attended him, and he had never seen her before.

She straightened, her curtain of deep brown hair falling over her shoulder. It hung nearly to her waist. No, he was certain he had never seen her before. He would have remembered that hair. "I'm a friend of Lethandris."

"Who?"

"The priestess to whom you gave the note." She set the feather duster down on the table and approached him. "My name is Celeste, Your Majesty."

He grimaced. "Just Percival, please. How did you get in here? The door was locked." That had been his one demand from Nicholas: he would stop fighting his uncle's demands for him to play the puppet, but he needed one space in the castle solely to himself. Nicholas wouldn't hesitate to search his rooms if he suspected Percival of working against him, but for now, the king's chambers were his alone.

She grinned up at him. "Climbed."

"*Climbed?*"

She nodded toward the balcony, and he gaped at her. One wrong step—one missed handhold—could have sent her tumbling four stories onto the sharp boulders in the shallows of the lake. He shoved the mental image of her slender body dashed across the rocks, bloodied and broken, out of his mind.

"After that, it was a simple matter of sneaking into the treasurer's office and adding my name to the list of slaves in the crown's ownership." As she spoke, she began working on the small buttons lining the front of his doublet. He went completely still when her graceful fingers brushed the hollow at the base of his throat. "Your friends Hero and Ketojan are alive."

"Truly?"

She nodded, and he let out a sigh of relief. "They've been in hiding since your uncle's coup, Your—Percival. I passed your note along to them, and they have agreed to help you in any way you need. Lethandris has agreed to help as well. Whatever you need, we're here for you. Have you any plans?"

"Not beyond finding a way to sneak slaves out of the city. My uncle knows that I helped Hero and Ketojan free several runaways before we left for the Keep. He's watching me carefully. It's not going to be easy, but I'll do anything. I can't just sit back and let them continue to suffer."

"That's very admirable. We'll find a way to help them." She shucked off his doublet, revealing the lightweight tunic he was wearing beneath it, and draped the doublet over the back of the nearest armchair. She frowned at the pile of pillows and blankets lying on his makeshift bed. "Is that where you've been sleeping all this time?"

He nodded. "These rooms belong to Tamriel and Mercy."

Sympathy filled Celeste's eyes at the pain in his voice. "I'm sure they're fine. From what I've heard of them, they seem very resourceful. I would not worry if I were you."

"I have nothing *but* worries."

In addition to his concerns about Tamriel and Mercy and his newfound role as 'king', Riona would be arriving in a matter of days, and his wedding would follow shortly afterward. The mere thought made him squirm.

"Tamriel and Mercy will return. Your uncle will lose his head for his crimes and you will no longer have to endure this viper's nest they call a court. Until then, I am happy to carry messages between you, Hero, Ketojan, and Lethandris. Do you need me to tell them anything?"

"Not at the moment, but...do you think there is any way I can see them? I could do with a few friendly faces right about now. And maybe we could come up with a way to get more slaves out of the city. I don't want them caught in the fighting when Tamriel returns."

"I'm sure something can be arranged." She glanced at the windows. Outside, the sky was dark and dotted with stars. "It'll be easier to get to them unseen if I go now. I'll have their response to you as soon as I can."

"Please tell me you're using the door from now on."

She flashed him another grin. "Only when it suits me."

"Where did you learn to climb like that?"

"I have my skills." She started toward the door, picking up her feather duster as she went.

"I'll need a way past my guards."

"Already thought of it," she called over her shoulder. With that, she stepped into the hall and closed the door behind her, leaving him alone.

He stared after her, awestruck. Then he walked over to the balcony and peered down into the dark churning waves far below. White spray flew into the air every time a wave hit one of the massive, algae-covered boulders. He shuddered and swiftly stepped away from the railing.

He had a really, really bad feeling about how she was going to sneak him out of his room.

15
TAMRIEL

"Fifteen elves in Cyrna," Mercy said as she donned her armor, the chainmail jangling softly. "Plus the two Faye saved, and maybe more now that they've had time to spread word to the other slaves in the city."

Tamriel nodded, securing the last strap of his breastplate as he stared out the window. Sunset had begun to paint the sky a deep red and cast the peaks of the houses in golden light. After leaving Cyrna, they had ridden hard and fast for Xilor, being careful to stay ahead of the approaching soldiers. According to Kaius's scouts, Nicholas's army was only a half-day's ride away. More worrisome was the fact that they had not yet spotted the Daughters.

He turned his head and winced at the knots between his shoulder blades. "Sometimes even the smallest force can make a difference."

Gauntleted arms slipped around his waist, and he turned to find Mercy looking up at him, the fiery reds of the sunset reflected in her eyes. He cupped her cheeks and brought her lips to his. "We have fought for our lives almost since the day we met," he murmured as he reluctantly pulled back. "We have endured so much pain and so much loss, but we've made it past every obstacle our enemies have set in our path. Through it all, and through everything there is to come, there is no one I would rather have by my side."

She smiled up at him, the small, private smile that made his heart soar—the smile she only shared with him. "If I have to be running for my life, I suppose being with you makes it a little more bearable."

"Creator willing, we won't be running for long."

She followed him out of the room and down the hall. Cyra and Hana, the twins who owned the safe-house, were sitting around the kitchen table with Calum and the others, their eyes darting to the front door every few seconds. Tamriel caught the eye of one of the sisters and offered her what he hoped was a reassuring smile, but her tight expression didn't change. Considering all they were risking by aiding Tamriel and the others, he wasn't surprised. They had all heard the whispers of what was happening in the capital in his absence: *Nicholas Comyn's nephew now sits on the throne*, a traveling merchant had told them. *The High Priestess refused to grant him the Creator's blessing in his coronation vows.*

He looked into the cramped living room. It was a small house, one just on the outskirts of the city, and there was barely enough room for the two-dozen-or-so slaves they had summoned. Tamriel drew in a steadying breath. He had thought speaking to the slaves would become easier with time, but so far, nothing had changed. He still had to go in there and look into their eyes, to see the hatred and anger they harbored for his family, to face the knowledge that many of those who pledged their blades for him would not survive to see him reclaim his throne.

It never became easier, asking them to risk their lives for him. And it was never anything less than shocking when every single one pledged him or herself to his growing army.

Some only did it out of a desire to be free, he knew. They supported him because he was their greatest chance at ridding the kingdom of slavery. They might not have any great love for him, but he didn't need them to love him. He needed them to help him do what was right.

He would not let them down.

Footsteps sounded behind him, and he looked back to see Kaius approaching, his face grim. "News?" Tamriel asked, noting the bow and quiver slung over the archer's shoulder, the dagger sheathed at his hip.

"The Assassins have been spotted. They're traveling with a group of soldiers only a few hours away. We need to leave soon if we're to have any chance of eluding them."

Tamriel nodded. "What of the city guards? Are your people in position?"

"They're watching the street, Your Majesty, as are the Qadar and Mercy's siblings. Any guards approach, we'll see them long before they see us."

"Good." He turned to the table, where Mercy, Faye, Pierce, Nerida, and Liri were speaking in low voices. Pierce blinked blearily up at him, his thinning brown hair uncombed and unruly. He and his wife were the least suited for the long rides, but they had not once complained about the journey. They had even sold their fine clothes and many of their belongings to provide them more money for the road. "Ready to speak to them?"

Mercy rose, the light shimmering on the links of her chainmail, and grinned at him. "Let's go meet our newest recruits, Your Majesty."

"Will you pledge yourselves to my cause?" Tamriel asked once he had finished his speech. "Will you join me in fighting for your freedom?"

There was a moment of silence, of contemplation, before one of the elves stood. "I will."

"Me, too."

"My brothers and I will fight for you," another said.

Tamriel let out a sigh of relief as the others pledged their support. Beside him, Mercy grinned at the elves, but her smile faltered when the front door opened and Kaius rushed inside. He kept his head down and his face turned away from the slaves as he approached them, but there was no mistaking the tension in his body.

"What's wrong?" Mercy asked, keeping her voice low.

"Someone told the guards you're here. They've gathered a company of thirty men and are approaching as we speak. My people can hold them off, but we need to get you out of the city. There could be more on the way."

Tamriel's hand closed around the grip of the sword at his hip. "How far are they?"

"A couple blocks."

He muttered a curse, then turned to Mercy. "Get the slaves out of the city. I'll hold them off."

Mercy shook her head. "They'll kill you!"

"What's wrong?" Faye asked, approaching from where she had been standing at the opposite side of the room.

"You two, get the slaves to safety," he said, ignoring her. "Get to the stables and flee the city. Kaius, stay here with me. If any guards make it past the archers, we'll take them down to buy the others time to escape."

"Tamriel, no—" Mercy began, laying her hand over his. "They're here for you. You need to come with us."

He stepped out of her reach as pounding footsteps echoed down the street. The guards were still a fair distance away, but they were getting closer, *fast*. "There's no time to argue! The guards are hunting me, so if I go with you, I'll be putting everyone's lives in danger. You need to get the slaves to safety. Go now!"

"Oh, by the Creator, they've found us!" one of the slaves cried, staring out the window.

He pushed Mercy and Faye toward the kitchen. "Go out the back door. Get the horses and follow the king's highway until you see a place to take shelter. I'll meet you there with everyone else."

Mercy turned and kissed his cheek. "Be careful." Then, she pulled her twin daggers and called to the elves: "Follow us! Quickly! Hurry!"

Tamriel drew his sword as they ran out of the house, several of the elves letting out cries of fear. Pierce, Nerida, and Liri ran after them. Beside him, Kaius unsheathed his dagger and crept toward the front door. He opened it a crack and looked outside. "They're almost upon us. Are you sure it's wise to fight?"

"They want me, but they won't hesitate to kill any slaves plotting to rebel. I won't let them harm unarmed subjects," he said as he moved toward the door. He could hear the archers firing arrows and shouting to one another in Cirisian as the guards approached. "That sounds like a lot more than thirty guards. How did they get so close without your people seeing them?"

"I don't—I don't know! I must have left a gap in the perimeter."

Out of the corner of his eye, he saw the last slave rush out of the room. Mercy glanced at him with fear in her eyes, then hurried after Faye and the others, slamming the kitchen door behind her.

Tamriel looked outside to find several dozen men and women in heavy armor darting from alley to alley, ducking behind whatever cover was available and firing crossbow bolts up at the Cirisians stationed on the roofs. In the darkness, it was nearly impossible to make them out, but one thing was certain by their weapons and armor: they were not guards.

They were soldiers.

Nicholas's army had found them.

One of the windows shattered, shards of glass flying everywhere. Tamriel and Kaius ducked as the arrow flew through the room and hit the wall just above their heads. Kaius reached up and grabbed the note tied to the shaft. His eyes widened as he read. Then they narrowed in anger. "They demand your surrender. They have the house surrounded."

Another window exploded, showering them with glass. Tamriel winced as a shard cut a shallow gash in his cheek. "Surrender, Tamriel, and your allies will be spared!" someone shouted. "Step outside with your weapons lowered, and you'll be brought to the capital to face judgment. Your friends will be free to leave."

Tamriel snorted and shook the glass from his hair. "*Judgment.*"

"Do not comply, and we will kill them all," the soldier warned. "The deaths of all your allies will be on your hands."

He started to rise, infuriated, but Kaius caught his arm. "Are you *crazy?*"

"I'm not going to surrender. I don't have a death wish."

He moved to the window, being careful to stay out of sight. "I am your king!" he yelled. "If you support the traitor Nicholas Comyn, you are committing treason. Stand down!"

In answer, the head of an arrow punched through the wall two inches from Tamriel's arm.

Kaius ran over and grabbed his shoulder. "You should go with Mercy and the others. My people and I will hold them off."

He shook off Kaius's grip. "No. They'll only give chase."

The door flew open with a *crack!* and they whirled around to see Duomnodera, her five Qadari warriors, Calum, Ino, Matthias, and Cassia standing there, breathing hard. Their leather armor was splattered in blood. Duomnodera and the Qadar were, predictably, untouched.

Duomnodera lifted her mace, blood dripping from the spikes. "They want a battle," she said in her dry, rasping voice, "we'll give them a battle."

16
MERCY

"Where the hell did they come from?" Faye yelled as they ran down the street. An arrow whizzed over Mercy's shoulder and impaled itself in a shop sign. The slaves shrieked, covering their heads as they bolted into alleys for cover. Pierce grabbed Nerida and Liri and dragged them behind the steps leading up to a house. Mercy pressed her back against a door, the stone frame barely hiding her from their pursuers' view.

She leaned forward just enough to scan the street. Five soldiers were racing after them, their heavy armor clanking. One aimed an arrow at her, and she jerked back just before it flew past.

A few yards away, Faye was huddled at the mouth of an alley, out of sight of the soldiers. *How many?* she mouthed.

She held up five fingers.

Distract them for me. One, two, three.

They leapt from their hiding spots. Mercy unsheathed her daggers and hurled one at the archer. It was not as graceful as Faye's throwing knives, which sailed one after another past Mercy and into the startled soldiers, but it hit its mark. The archer crumpled. The four others fell into a pile in the middle of the road, Faye's knives buried in their eyes, their throats, the chinks in their armor.

Mercy rushed forward and grabbed the weapons as Faye ushered the others from their hiding spots. "Go, go, go!" she hissed as they sprinted down the empty street, away from the sounds of fighting drifting from the other side of the safe house.

"*Mercy!*" Faye snarled, her voice tight with fear. "Come on!"

She glanced toward the house. The Assassins had to be here. They must have come with the soldiers. They'd kill Tamriel if she didn't go back for him.

Just as she thought it, a dozen men and women rounded the side of the house, blades drawn and arrows at the ready. The archers fixed their sights on her and let the arrows fly. She dove, rolling out of their path, and jumped to her feet. She clutched her aching rib cage as she sprinted toward where Faye was waiting at the end of the block, frantically waving her onward. Twice, she turned and loosed a throwing knife. She didn't look back long enough to confirm they'd hit their marks. She knew she had struck true.

The soldiers gave chase as she careened around the corner, nearly bowling Faye over in the process, and raced after the others. There were too many soldiers to stand and fight, and they couldn't risk the slaves getting hurt. She'd have to get the others to safety, then go back for Tamriel and Kaius. It would be easier to evade the soldiers on her own.

"Here," she panted, handing the remaining throwing knives to Faye. "I owe you two."

As they ran, several people in the surrounding houses opened the shutters and peered out, curious about the commotion, only to shrink back in fear when they saw the arrows whiz past. When Mercy and Faye caught up with the others on the next street, Faye took the lead, a knife in each hand. She did not hesitate to throw them at every unlucky soldier who stepped into their path. She barely had time to retrieve them before another appeared further down the street or in the mouth of an alley. Mercy silently cursed Kaius's archers as they ran. Judging by how many soldiers they'd already taken down, there had to be more than a hundred in the city. How could the Cirisians have missed them?

To the slaves' credit, they never faltered, never cowered in fear. They just kept pace with Faye, dragging each other along when some began to fall behind. Even Pierce, Nerida, and Liri remained close, their faces pale and drawn in terror.

Mercy breathed a sigh of relief when the stables appeared before them—or she would have, if she had any breath to spare. She bent over, sucking in lungfuls of air, as Faye rushed inside, startling the stablehand dozing against the wall. He spat curses as Faye began pulling horses from the stalls and snapping commands to the slaves.

"You'll have to ride two to a horse, or there won't be any left for Tamriel and the others," Mercy told them once she was finally able to speak. She swiped at the perspiration beading on her brow as she and Faye helped them secure saddles and reins. Most of the elves stared up at the beasts with fear in their eyes—she doubted any of them had ever ridden a horse before—but they listened carefully to Mercy's instructions before swinging themselves onto the saddles. They had no choice but to ride if they wanted to evade the soldiers.

The whole time, the stablehand looked on helplessly. He was only fifteen years old at most, and was wise enough not to challenge the two heavily-armed women stealing countless horses and supplies.

"They went this way!" someone cried, his voice nearly

drowned out by the stomping of heavy boots. Mercy muttered a curse and helped the last two elves onto their horse. Just a heartbeat later, one of the townspeople appeared a few blocks away, a half-dozen soldiers on his heels. He pointed to Mercy and Faye. "They're escaping! They stole two of my slaves!"

By the Creator, how many soldiers are there? Mercy turned to Seren Pierce. "Help Faye get the elves out of the city. I'll take out the soldiers."

He nodded and swung onto his horse. Beside him, Nerida held the reins of her own mare, Liri's arms wrapped tightly around her waist.

Faye ran over to her, Nightstorm trotting along behind her, and thrust her throwing knives into Mercy's hands. "Use these, and be safe. I'll see you soon, my friend."

Mercy turned to the approaching soldiers as Faye mounted her mare and led the others toward the king's highway at a gallop. The stablehand merely watched, open-mouthed, as they thundered down the road and disappeared around the block.

"Stop!" one of the soldiers shouted, pointing his sword straight at Mercy. Thank the Creator, none of them were armed with bows or crossbows. "Stop, thief! Those slaves are personal property!"

"They are *people*!" She whirled around and offered the stablehand a tight smile. "You should probably go home. This is going to get messy."

He practically tripped over his own feet in his haste to leave.

As soon as he was out of sight, Mercy lifted a throwing knife. "Drop your weapons," she called to the soldiers. "Tuck your tails and run, and you'll survive the night."

"I should be saying that to you," one retorted.

With two flicks of her wrist, the soldiers to either side of him crumpled. The villager yelped and ducked behind a pillar as the leader gaped at his fallen comrades. "It's the Assassin!" he shouted to his men. "There's a bounty on her head. Get her!"

"Wrong choice."

Mercy traded the last throwing knife for her twin daggers, twisting the pommels so they formed one dual-bladed staff, as the soldiers barreled toward her.

The leader reached her first, swinging his sword straight at her neck. She blocked the blow, dropped low, and thrust upward with one end of her staff. The blade slipped under the bottom of his breastplate, piercing him straight through his stomach. He let out a cry of pain and stumbled backward, blood pouring out from under his armor.

She jumped to her feet as the three remaining men surrounded her.

"Surrender," one growled. Just behind him, the leader dropped his sword and fell face-first onto the cobblestone. He didn't move again.

"Never."

"We have orders to take the king alive if possible," another guard, one who couldn't be more than a few years older than she, said. "We've no such restrictions when it comes to you. Surrender and you will come to no further harm."

"You think you can kill me? I'm insulted."

She lunged, aiming her blade for his throat. He parried, leaping back, and slashed at her weapon-wielding arm. The blade grazed her chainmail as she turned, locking blades with the soldier on her left. A twist of her wrist sent his sword skittering across the street. He lunged for it, and the second he turned his back to her, she jammed the blade through his skull. Hot blood spilled over her hands. She planted a foot on his back and shoved him off the end of the double-sided dagger, then spun to face her two remaining opponents.

The young one was standing slightly farther back than the other. His eyes widened when he saw the blood dripping off her blade. The other soldier leapt forward, slashing at her with a snarl. She danced back, looking for an opening, but he swung his sword again and again.

"Attack, you coward!" he snapped at the younger soldier.

Both of them lunged for her. With the speed and strength of their attacks, it was all Mercy could do to hold them off. Her arms trembled, her ribs ached, and her still-healing fingers throbbed. She leapt back, just out of reach of their swords. She was wasting time. She needed to get to Tamriel.

Movement flashed in the corner of her eye. An archer had climbed onto one of the nearby rooftops.

The younger soldier aimed his sword straight at her heart. She smiled. There was too much power behind the blow. She sidestepped into the middle of the street, allowing herself to be fully visible to the archer, and hooked her foot around the soldier's ankle. He pitched forward, hitting the cobblestone with a moan and a clang of armor. She turned to the older soldier as the archer on the roof nocked an arrow and took aim. She didn't betray the fact that she had spotted him as she twisted the double-sided dagger apart.

The older soldier's blade flashed in the moonlight. She caught his sword with one dagger and their blades locked.

"Give up," the soldier hissed, leaning into their locked blades. Her arm shuddered with exhaustion. "You're weak and clearly injured. Give up."

She smiled. Then she slammed the dagger in her right hand into the chink in his armor between his breastplate and his shoulder, straight into the soft, vulnerable flesh of his underarm. He howled with pain. She let go of the dagger, grabbed his shoulder, and pulled him in front of her just as the archer loosed his arrow.

Thud.

Hot blood sprayed across her face when the arrow pierced the soldier's throat. His eyes widened, his mouth gaping, as he choked. Mercy released him and grabbed one of Faye's throwing knives as the archer scrambled for another arrow. His fingers closed around empty air when the knife buried itself in his neck. He dropped his bow, his hands scrabbling at the hilt sticking out of his flesh, and staggered dangerously close to the edge of the steeply-pitched roof.

Mercy turned back to the young soldier. He was on his feet now, and he flinched when the archer let out a choked scream, which was abruptly cut off by the crunch of bone against cobblestone. He dropped his sword. "P-Please," he choked out. "Please don't kill me."

She stalked forward, lifting her blood-coated blades. "Who is the rightful king?"

"T-Tamriel Myrellis," he stammered, shrinking away from her. "Please, I was just following my commander's orders. I didn't know what Nicholas Comyn was planning, and after it happened, there was nothing I could do. I'm sorry."

He sounded sincere, and she didn't sense anything behind his words other than genuine terror. Creator damn her, she actually *pitied* him. She lowered her daggers. "I'm going to find the king. Help me protect him, and if you manage to survive the fight, perhaps His Majesty will pardon you. Hurt him, and I'll make you wish you had died with the others. Got it?"

His head bobbed up and down.

"Grab your sword."

As he stooped to retrieve his weapon, Mercy ran to the archer, who, despite the throwing knife to the neck and the fall off the roof, was still alive—but just barely. He let out a low, agonized moan as Mercy buried her dagger in his eye socket, killing him swiftly. She returned her daggers to their sheaths, then tucked Faye's throwing knives into her belt. Three left. When the soldier jogged over to her, steadfastly avoiding looking at the dead bodies, she gestured for him to lead the way. When they passed the pillar behind which the townsman had hidden, they found him still huddled there, hugging his knees to his chest. Mercy ignored him and waved the soldier onward.

I'm coming, Tamriel, she thought, wishing he could hear her. *Creator, please don't let me be too late.*

17
MERCY

Everything had devolved into chaos by the time Mercy and the soldier—Ewan, she'd learned—arrived at the rear of the safe house. She crept forward and peered around to the front of the building. Cirisian archers were still crouching atop the surrounding roofs, firing down at the soldiers. The traitors faced off against Cirisian fighters and Qadari warriors, many of them moving too fast to track in the darkness. A lantern hanging over a neighboring house provided a little light by which to see, but other than that, they were fighting with only the moonlight and their night vision to aid them.

"This way!" Mercy hissed, waving Ewan toward the back door of the safe house. "Go inside first." He was terrified of her, but that didn't mean she trusted him enough to turn her back on him.

He opened the door, and immediately, the clashing of swords, the ringing of blades, and the crash of furniture breaking rushed over them. They ran through the kitchen and into the living room. Mercy searched the sea of faces until she spotted Tamriel and Kaius standing back-to-back on the opposite side of the room, slashing out at the four men surrounding them. Cassia, Calum, Ino, and Matthias were scattered throughout the room, their blades splattering blood across the ruined furniture and scratched walls. They appeared to be winning; the soldiers' numbers were dwindling, but it would only take one lucky strike to end Tamriel's life. Luckily, the Daughters were nowhere in sight. Perhaps Mercy had been wrong about them being nearby.

"There he is," Mercy told Ewan, pointing. She pulled her daggers from their sheaths. Together, they fought their way through the bodies crammed into the small room. The floor was cluttered with bodies, shards of glass, and pieces of broken furniture.

Tamriel spotted them when they were halfway across the room. His brows rose in surprise. He quickly turned back to the soldiers he had been fighting, striking with newfound ferocity.

Mercy dodged a swinging blade and rushed to his side. "Faye and the others are safe. Time for us to get out of here."

He nodded, lunging forward, feinting left, and striking at a soldier's side. When he darted back, Ewan took his place and forced his brother-at-arms back with a series of quick blows. Tamriel watched him with a questioning look.

"He's on our side," Mercy told him. "I think. I hope. Kaius, can you—"

"I heard you," the archer said, not looking away from the soldiers slashing at him. "Go on; we'll keep them occupied. As soon as you make it out the door, I'll give the order to retreat."

Mercy looked across the room to where her brothers and sister were fighting beside Calum. She caught Ino's eye and jerked her chin toward the kitchen. He nodded. *Right behind you.*

A soldier rushed toward her and she met him with her

twin daggers. Three quick slashes, and he fell at her feet, dead. "Tamriel, come on!" she called, her voice barely distinguishable over the sounds of the fighting.

He killed another soldier and moved to her side, panting hard. "After you...my love," he forced out with a pained, tired smile. His dark hair was slicked to his forehead with sweat, and he brushed it back with a swipe of one armored forearm, leaving a smear of blood across his face.

They began carving a path toward the kitchen door, blades scraping flesh and armor and bone. Once the traitors realized that they were trying to escape, the soldiers rushed forward, attempting to block their exit. One lunged at Tamriel, but before his sword could hit flesh, Ewan's blade flew out and severed the man's head from his body. He offered Tamriel a small bow before turning back to the fight.

"Right now would be a perfect time for your parents to show up," Tamriel shouted to Mercy.

"You can say that again!"

After what felt like an eternity, they reached the kitchen. Tamriel shoved the door open, then grabbed Mercy's hand and led her toward the back door. Just before the living room fell out of sight, Mercy glanced back to see Kaius fighting his way to the front of the house, Calum, Cassia, Matthias, and Ino on his heels.

They emerged onto the street, the cool nighttime air a shock after the stifling heat of the safe house. Tamriel released her hand and slumped against the wall, sucking in ragged breaths. Somewhere on the other side of the house, Kaius shouted a command in Cirisian to his archers and fighters.

"Let's... Let's go," Tamriel panted. They took off at a run down the street, the same way Mercy and Faye had led the slaves. Gradually, the sounds of the battle faded behind them.

Her stomach twisted into knots knowing Calum and her siblings were still there, still fighting for their lives. *We shouldn't have left them. We should go back for them. I should go back for them.*

Tamriel grabbed her arm and pulled her forward. "We can't help them," he said, sensing her thoughts. "The soldiers will pursue us once they realize we've gone. The farther I am from them, the safer they'll be."

She shook her head and jerked out of his grasp. "They're my family. I can't leave them behind." She turned and ran toward the safe house, Tamriel's curses trailing after her.

"Calum's my family, too!" he called. "Do you think it's easy for me to leave him?"

"No. That's why I have to go back." Before she made it more than a few yards, the rear door of the safe house burst open and several soldiers spilled out, swords raised. Mercy stumbled back, bumping into Tamriel as the soldiers surrounded them.

"This is why we *run*," he hissed as he lifted his sword.

She unsheathed her daggers, opening her mouth to retort, when she heard his breath hitch. She didn't even need to look to know what he'd spotted.

The Daughters had arrived.

"Mercy! Tamriel! Duck!"

Tamriel grabbed her shoulders and yanked her down, covering her body with his own, as more arrows and crossbow bolts than she could count whizzed over their heads. The soldiers surrounding them let out cries of pain as the sharp projectiles pierced their flesh. Some didn't make any sound at all before they dropped their weapons and slumped to the ground. Mercy lifted her head and met the dead-eyed stare of a woman only a couple years her senior.

Tamriel helped her to her feet, and they both turned

toward their saviors. Five Daughters were standing in the middle of the street, bows and crossbows in hand. Blood was splattered across their faces and armor.

"Are you hurt?" Tanni asked, slinging her bow over her shoulder as she approached. The other Assassins—Hanna, Wren, Nerine, and Theodora—lowered their weapons and followed.

Mercy pushed Tamriel behind her, ignoring his objection. "That's close enough."

"We're not going to harm you. We want to help."

"You're working for Nicholas," Tamriel called, wariness in his voice. He glanced at the circle of dead bodies surrounding them. "You just want the bounty for yourselves."

Tanni shook her head and stopped a few yards from them, lifting her hands in surrender. Mercy tightened her grip on her daggers. Whatever game the Assassins were playing, she wasn't going to fall for it. She couldn't take on five at a time, but she could at least buy Tamriel time to escape.

"We don't have time to explain," Tanni said. Mercy could still hear Kaius and Duomnodera yelling to their warriors over the sounds of the fighting. "But I swear to you, we are on your side. We would never turn against the people who freed us from Mother Illynor."

Mercy narrowed her eyes, her heart still pounding hard. Tanni was right: they didn't have much time left. But still... "You were all too happy to serve her before."

"When His Majesty sent the messenger demanding the Guild's surrender, we begged Mother Illynor to give in, but she refused. She forced us to fight. If we didn't, she promised to kill us herself, and take her time doing it. She said there was no place for cowards among her ranks." Tanni swallowed, her throat bobbing, and a flicker of respect passed through her eyes as she looked to Tamriel. "You had every reason to want us dead, Your Majesty, but you offered us mercy. We have not forgotten that."

The other Assassins nodded, their expressions solemn.

On the other side of the safe house, Kaius yelled, "*Retaj!*" *Retreat!*

"Fine," Tamriel said. "Help our friends get out of the city alive, and you'll have earned your place among us."

In unison, the Daughters bowed to him, then ran off in the direction of the fight, nocking arrows and unsheathing blades. The second they turned the corner, Mercy grabbed Tamriel's hand, and together they raced through the narrow, winding streets until they arrived at the stables. They worked in tense, anxious silence to prepare as many horses as possible for their escape. Creator only knew how many soldiers were still in the city, searching for them.

Mercy had just finished securing Blackfoot's saddle when she heard a shout down the street. She turned and grinned when she saw their friends and family racing toward them. They were all coated in so much blood Mercy couldn't tell what was from their wounds and what was from their enemies, but all that mattered was that they were *alive*. Even the apprentices were unharmed. The three girls looked absolutely terrified, but they didn't have a speck of blood on them. Whichever Cirisian had been tasked with keeping them out of the fighting had done his job well.

"Mercy! Oh, thank the Creator!" Cassia threw her arms around Mercy's neck. "There were so many soldiers. I don't know where they all came from."

"Are you all okay? Is anyone hurt?" She pulled back and scanned her sister for injuries, then turned to the others. Ewan was leaning heavily against Wren, and a few of them were sporting deep gashes that would need sewing, but they all looked like they'd be able to ride. "Grab a horse and let's go."

"We'll watch your backs," Nerine said. "Go now. We'll be right behind you."

"We'll help you," Duomnodera said, gesturing to her warriors.

"Two to a horse!" Ino called, and the Cirisians immediately doubled up, working quickly to finish saddling the horses Mercy and Tamriel had pulled out of the stalls. He helped Cassia mount his stallion, then climbed up behind her and nocked an arrow. "You guide the horse, I'll shoot any bastards who try to give chase."

As soon as they were ready, Tamriel led them out of the city at a gallop. Matthias, seated in front of Mercy on Blackfoot's saddle, gripped the reins so tightly his knuckles turned white. As they neared the city limits, Mercy glanced back to see the Qadar and the Daughters forming a line in the middle of the street, loosing arrows and bolts at every soldier unlucky enough to get within their sight.

Mercy's tight grip on her brother didn't ease until the city faded into the distance. Her adrenaline quickly faded, leaving her chilled and shaking within her chainmail. The blood coating her had soaked through the links and stained her clothes, making them stick to her skin and reek of iron. When they finally slowed to a trot, Mercy leaned forward and rested her cheek on Matthias's back, her exhaustion finally catching up to her.

"Rest now, Bareea," Matthias whispered.

She shook her head, even as her eyelids began to drift shut of their own accord. "I'll rest when we find Faye and the others."

"The soldiers can still catch up to us, and you won't be able to fight as fiercely if you're exhausted. If you're going to insist on taking turns—which I have no doubt you will—fine. Just close your eyes for a little while."

"Promise you'll be here when I wake up?" she mumbled, remembering the terror she had felt when she woke up in the Forest of Flames to find him missing.

"I promise. I'm never leaving you again, Bareea. None of us are." He gently grasped the arms she had wrapped around his midsection, securing her to him so she wouldn't fall off the saddle. "Sleep now. I'll be here when you wake."

"You're not hurt? You're not lying to me?"

"I am perfect, Mercy. As always." She heard the smile in his voice, and it eased her worries enough for her to lean against him and close her eyes once more. Even through the blood wetting his armor, she could feel the warmth of his body, and it lulled her to a deep, dreamless sleep.

It felt like no time at all passed before Matthias gently nudged her awake. She opened her eyes to see that they had stopped in the middle of a valley, just a short distance from the king's highway. At the front of the group, Tamriel and Kaius were standing beside a large boulder, huddled over a scrap of paper.

"How long was I asleep?" she asked, grimacing as she massaged a kink in her neck.

"About an hour. We should be meeting Faye and the others somewhere around here. I'm assuming it is she who left the note," he said, nodding to the piece of parchment they were reading.

At a prod from her, he took the reins and guided Blackfoot over to them. "Where are Faye and the others?"

Kaius handed the note to Mercy, who scanned it and frowned. Only two words had been scrawled across the paper: *porsulli* and *parenti*. "Is that...Cirisian? What does it mean?"

The archer nodded, looking somewhat impressed. "She must have picked up some of our tongue during the war. She wrote 'pursued' and 'parents', albeit with several spelling mistakes. It must not have been safe for them to stop here. She's taking them to her parents' house in Fallmond."

⚜ 18 ⚜
PERCIVAL

A knock sounded on the doors to the king's chamber, waking Percival from fitful, nightmare-plagued sleep. In his dream, he had watched his uncle turn on Tamriel and Mercy again. Dozens of razor-sharp arrowheads flew toward the king's heart, but that time, the strange gray phantoms had not appeared. More arrows than he could count had filled his king's flesh, and he'd let out an anguished, inhuman scream of rage as Tamriel tumbled from his horse. Mercy had slumped to the ground a heartbeat after.

Someone rapped on the door again, and Percival cracked an eye open just as Celeste walked in, a tray of tea and pastries in her hands. He squinted against the sunlight streaming in through the wall of windows behind him as she set the tray on the ottoman.

"Did you sleep well, Percival?" she asked with a pleasant smile, pouring him a steaming cup of tea. She placed it into his hands, then perched on the couch opposite the one on which he was sprawled, his blankets tangled around his legs.

"No, I didn't," he mumbled, still caught halfway between the nightmare and reality. He pushed himself upright, took a sip of the scalding liquid, burned his tongue, and cursed. He set his cup on the tray and shoved his spectacles on, frowning at her. "You didn't warn me it was that hot."

She raised a brow. "I assumed you were familiar with the concept of tea. At the very least, that you understood the consequences of drinking water that had just finished boiling." She looked to the double doors leading to the king's bedroom. "You know, there is a nice comfortable bed just a room away. I'm sure Tamriel wouldn't mind you borrowing it. You don't have to sleep on the couch like a vagrant."

"Vagrants don't have couches," he muttered, biting into a pastry. "Besides, it's not the couch that's the problem. It's nightmares."

Her eyes filled with pity. "Care to talk about them?"

"I'd rather talk about anything else, actually. The weather. Your favorite color. The impact the mining industry has had on Beltharan-Rivosi trade."

"Ah. Is that what you've been reading about lately?" she asked, a smile playing across her lips. She cocked her head. "Sounds dull. Perhaps you can use it to lull you back to sleep after your nightmares wake you."

"I'd rather read about anything else. The weather. Your favorite color." He took another bite of pastry, ignoring the throbbing of his burned tongue. "When can I meet with Hero and Ketojan?"

"Tonight, in the Church. Lethandris snuck them into the vault last night so Nicholas's men couldn't find them."

"Will you be accompanying me?"

"Of course. I'm His Majesty's handmaid."

He cringed. "Don't call me 'His Majesty.' And are you sure? It'll be dangerous if we're discovered. My uncle will keep me alive to sit on the throne, but I can't promise he'll be merciful if he finds out we're planning to free slaves. You'll be risking your life."

"Do you think this is my first time risking my life?"

"Who are you?" he asked, and she beamed at him.

"I'm Percival Comyn's handmaid."

"Can't you answer anything seriously?"

"Can't you *try* to have some semblance of a sense of humor?" she retorted, lifting her chin and affecting an exaggerated, formal tone. "Or has all your academic study worn it away?"

She rose, rifling through the wardrobe the servants had brought up from his former room, while he munched on another pastry. When he was finished, she turned away while he changed—huffing something about 'modesty' under her breath—then secured all the buttons lining the front of his doublet. He studied the violet-and-gold brocade, the gold buttons, and the matching gold trim along the collar and cuffs. It was a far more formal piece than he would have ever picked out for himself. He had a suspicion he would blind someone if he were to step into direct sunlight.

"I can dress myself, you know."

"Not today, you can't."

"What's that supposed to mean?" When she didn't respond, he prompted, "Celeste?"

"Your betrothed, Lady Riona Nevis of Innislee, is arriving today," she said, watching for his reaction. Judging by her apologetic tone, she had heard the servants gossiping about his and Nicholas's frequent arguments on the topic.

He looked away. "Oh."

"Your uncle wants you to make a good impression."

"Why? He's going to marry me off regardless."

"I don't know, Your—Percival. Maybe your dread is unfounded. I've heard she's quite lovely."

He slumped onto the couch. "Unfounded? How would you like to marry a complete stranger? Being forced to make...*heirs?*" He choked on the last word.

"You don't want children?"

"Not at eighteen, and certainly not on my uncle's command. I just... Is it too much to want love?"

She was quiet for a few moments, then she said, "For royals, yes, it usually is."

"*I'm not a royal,*" he snapped, then immediately felt terrible for it when she shrank away, surprised by the anger in his voice. She was just being honest. It was not her fault he was in this situation. In fact, she was the only truly kind person he had spoken to since his uncle's coup. "I'm sorry, Celeste. I'm angry at my uncle and I'm taking it out on you."

"Apology accepted. Think of it no more." She closed the doors to the wardrobe, then walked over and picked up the breakfast tray. "Would you like your tea now that it's not going to burn you?"

"No, thank you."

Someone rapped on the door, and he groaned. "Five aurums says it's a guard come to tell me my bride has arrived."

"I'm not going to take that bet."

He stood as she balanced the tray in one hand and pulled the door open with the other. Sure enough—

"Your uncle would like you to join him in the great hall. Your betrothed's carriage has arrived at the city gates, and he asks that you be there to welcome her to the castle."

Percival stifled another groan. Celeste watched him with a sympathetic frown as he crossed the room and stopped before her. "Thank you for the food. And the company."

"You're welcome."

When he turned to follow the guard, she added, "Green."

"What?"

"Green. My favorite color. That's one more thing we have to talk about now."

Despite everything, a grin tugged at his lips. "I look forward to our discussion on the topic."

Creator curse him, the advisors were right.

Riona was stunningly, unbelievably, *painfully* beautiful.

Percival's jaw dropped when she stepped out of the carriage, her ebony skin shining in the early morning sunlight. She was clad in a gown of lavender silk with a high slit on one side of the skirt. Every step she took offered a glimpse of her long, toned legs. The top of her dress was sleeveless, exposing her arms, which were covered in gold bracelets that clinked gently with every little movement. A wide band of gold and amethyst was clamped around the upper part of her left arm.

"Pick your jaw up off the floor, nephew," Nicholas whispered, a smile in his voice.

Percival closed his mouth so quickly his teeth *clack*ed. They stood at the top of the steps outside the castle, watching Riona and her company of guards approach. Two of the half-dozen royal guards behind Percival stifled snickers. Heat crept up Percival's neck. He'd be lucky if he could form a sentence in the presence of his bride-to-be.

When Riona turned her head to murmur something to the finely-dressed man walking just behind her—an advisor, Percival assumed—he caught a glimpse of her long braids. Little gold beads decorated the strands around her face.

By the Creator, she's gorgeous.

He couldn't tear his eyes away from her.

It doesn't change anything, he told himself. *She's still a stranger. You've only ever exchanged letters.*

"I told you I'd find you a worthy wife," Nicholas murmured.

"Worthy?" he echoed. "Have you seen me? Can you see *her?*"

The guards snickered again.

He snapped to attention when Riona and her entourage

reached the bottom of the steps. She took her skirt in one hand and climbed the steps, smiling when she caught Percival staring at her—or rather, the vast amount of skin the gesture exposed. For a second, he forgot to breathe.

Quit acting like a fool!

She dropped into a graceful curtsy before them. "Lord Nicholas, Your Majesty, thank you for welcoming me into your beautiful city. I am honored to be your guest." Her words were lilted with a soft, rolling accent—the accent of Rivosi nobility.

"We are honored to have you," Nicholas responded smoothly, offering her a small bow.

Percival swallowed tightly and tried to remember how language worked. "Ah, yes, um... Thank you for traveling all this way." He cursed his tongue for tripping over the words. *It's because it's burned,* he told himself, not believing the lie in the slightest. Nicholas expected him to marry her? He expected him to produce *heirs* with her? He could hardly look her in the eye!

Riona gestured to the man standing beside her. "This is His Majesty's most trusted advisor, Lord Winslow. He has come to help with preparations for the wedding and discuss any arrangements that must be made between our kingdoms before the ceremony."

Lord Winslow bowed deeply. "I am at your disposal, my lord, Your Majesty."

Nicholas led them through the great hall and into the throne room, where servants had set up a table and chairs in the middle of the vast room. As they settled into their seats, servants moved around them and poured wine in shining crystal goblets. Percival sat stiffly beside his uncle, unable to keep his eyes off the stranger who was to be his wife.

Riona looked around the room, seeming to absorb every

detail before finally turning her attention to him. He was surprised to see that her eyes were a deep, striking blue.

"I trust your journey here was pleasant?" he asked.

"Very much so. I do not travel often, so I greatly appreciated the chance to see the land over which we are to rule."

His throat tightened.

"Perhaps after the wedding, you and I could tour the country," she continued, oblivious of the way her comment had affected him. "It would be nice to get to know your people."

He offered her a shallow nod. "Yes, it would be, wouldn't it?"

Nicholas pressed the heel of his boot into the top of Percival's foot as a warning. *Don't screw this up for us,* it said. He leaned forward and smiled at Lord Winslow. "King Domhnall was very amiable during the negotiations for the betrothal. I am overjoyed that he agreed to honor my nephew with such a lovely young woman. I can already tell she will make a wonderful queen."

The queen-to-be seemed not to care that she was being discussed as if she were not present. She merely swirled the wine in her goblet and took a small sip.

"My nephew has requested some time to get to know his bride, and I am inclined to grant his wish, if you agree. I am certain you would both like some time to relax and adjust to life here in Sandori before the wedding."

"That would be preferable, yes," Winslow said. "Traveling halfway across a country does take its toll."

"No doubt. I would like to throw a banquet in honor of our king and soon-to-be queen. It will be a wonderful opportunity for Riona to try some of the traditional fare and get a taste for life in the court. Shall we say three days from today?"

"Three days," Winslow echoed, nodding. "I look forward to it."

The way they're kissing up to each other, one would think they're the ones set to be married, Percival thought, fighting a smirk.

"It will be a chance for Percival and Riona to dance together in front of all the nobility," Nicholas added. "That should drum up some excitement for the impending wedding. Think of the tales that will be spread once they see their beautiful future queen!"

Ah, so that's his angle. This entire marriage was an opportunity for him to shift the court's attention off his coup. Riona and Percival would be the picture of the perfect royal family for the people of Beltharos, while Nicholas pulled the political strings in the background. Tamriel and the downfall of the Myrellis family would be all but forgotten.

The wine turned sour in his stomach.

"By the end of the feast, the people will be clamoring for the wedding!" Nicholas beamed. "This marriage will unify our countries like no other. I, my friend, have high hopes for the future."

"As do I," Riona cut in before Lord Winslow could respond. Her face was impassive, emotionless, but the glimmer in her eyes revealed that she had been listening to every word—and that, perhaps, his manipulative nature had not gone unnoticed. She turned to Percival and added in her rolling, melodic accent, "I look forward to ruling this lovely country beside you, Your Majesty."

19
TAMRIEL

The soft, lilting sounds of the Cirisian language woke Tamriel early the next morning. He rubbed his eyes with the heels of his palms, his skin still coated with the blood of the soldiers he'd fought mere hours before, and sat up. His muscles ached. After finding Faye's note, they had eventually found a small clearing beside a shallow stream where they could make camp for a few hours. Tamriel had not even bothered to remove his armor; he had simply dropped from his saddle, led his horse to the stream to drink, then laid down beside Mercy as the Cirisians tended wounds and set patrols. The apprentices, who had curled up together a few feet from them, were still asleep.

Mercy was already awake, speaking quietly with her siblings as they scrubbed the blood from their weapons and armor. For once, Calum had joined them. He was sitting cross-legged on the grass beside Ino, listening to Matthias tell a story as he changed the makeshift bandage around his forearm. The sight made Tamriel smile. Perhaps his cousin was finally coming back to life.

A few yards away, Kaius and several of the Cirisians were

huddled around a low-burning fire, roasting fish over the flames. Tamriel's stomach rumbled, but he forced himself to look away. There wasn't much food to go around, and the Cirisians had certainly earned all of it. They were the ones who had been hunting, scouting, and watching over their group every night. Without them, they wouldn't have survived the night after Nicholas's betrayal.

Kaius glanced up as Tamriel approached. "The Qadar and Assassins are watching the king's highway," he said in lieu of a greeting.

"How many did we lose?"

"Four." Pain and guilt flashed across his face. "I don't know how Nicholas's troops were able to sneak up on us, and in such great numbers, too. My people have been patrolling the land for days. They were watching the streets around the safe house all night. We should have had more warning."

He frowned, troubled. Kaius's scouts were exceptionally skilled; their enhanced vision gave them an advantage against Nicholas's human soldiers at night. The treasonous soldiers should not have been able to slip through their defenses so easily.

Tamriel gestured for Kaius to follow him to where the horses were grazing, well out of the Cirisians' earshot. "Where did the soldiers enter the city?"

"The southern side, I believe."

"And who was responsible for watching that area?"

A crease formed between Kaius's brows. "Are you insinuating that one of my people shirked his duties, while knowing his own clan members would be caught in the fight? If you ask me, I think someone alerted the soldiers to our location. Perhaps someone who previously tried to have you killed," he retorted, a hard glint in his eyes.

"That's everyone in this camp, Mercy included. You'll have to be more specific."

"*Calum*. He could have traded information about your whereabouts to a city guard in the hope of claiming the bounty on your head. Think about it—if he aided the soldiers in capturing you and handing you over to Nicholas, he would gain favor with the new king. He could go back to life in the court. It wouldn't be the first time he has betrayed you."

"You're wrong." He looked over Kaius's shoulder at his cousin, still sitting beside the bank. Calum brushed back a strand of hair and shot Mercy a crooked grin—one Tamriel hadn't seen on him in far too long. Despite everything, he looked genuinely *happy*. He had a real family for the first time. Tamriel was certain he wouldn't have done anything to compromise that, even if it would buy him favor with Nicholas Comyn. "Someone let the soldiers into the city, and it wasn't him."

"Why would my people help the humans?" Kaius asked, his tone turning defensive. "And why now? We all want to see you on the throne so our brethren can be freed. Nicholas would never agree to that."

"I can answer that."

They both whirled to see Ewan—the young soldier who had helped them fight their way out of the safe house—sprawled on the grass a few feet away, staring up at the sky. He'd been so quiet Tamriel hadn't realized he was there, listening. He looked half dead, his gaze distant, his face pale and underscored with deep shadows. When he shifted to look at them, Tamriel noticed the puddle of blood seeping out from under him.

"By the Creator, why didn't you tell someone you'd been hurt?" Tamriel exclaimed, stepping forward to examine the wound, but Ewan waved him off.

"I don't want to waste your supplies. They won't be of any use." He grimaced and pushed himself upright, his legs stretched out before him. Just that little movement turned his face gray and sallow. He was right; he had lost far too much blood to last more than another hour or two at most. Even so, Tamriel couldn't imagine lying there in pain for so long, slowly dying.

"There were two Cirisians," he began, and Kaius made a sound of disbelief. "Celandine and Gelso. They came to my commanding officer two days ago and told him that the king and his allies were heading to Xilor. Last night, they left their posts and led us to the safe house."

"Impossible," Kaius snarled. "They would never hand us over to Nicholas's soldiers."

"It's true! How else would I know their names?"

"You— You—" He scrambled for an explanation. Finding none, he turned on his heel and stormed toward the Cirisians, still sitting in a circle around the fire. Tamriel called for someone to attend to Ewan before following Kaius. Mercy and the others joined them.

Kaius snapped a command in Cirisian, and two of the elves leapt up and dragged a man and woman to their feet, blades pressed against their throats.

"Did you betray the king?" Kaius demanded, his face contorted in fury. He looked from Celandine to Gelso. "*Did you?*"

"Of course not," Celandine responded, taken aback. "Whatever could make you think that?"

"One of Nicholas's soldiers told us what you did. You told them where we were going! You led them straight to us!"

Her expression hardened. "Are you going to take the word of a human over us? Why would we turn on our own clan members?"

"That's what I want you to tell me. We lost four people last night. Four! Their deaths are on your hands." Kaius trembled with anger as he stared them down. "Tell me the truth."

"We didn't do anything," Gelso said.

"They left their posts last night," one of the elves murmured in a voice tinged with shock. A girl Tamriel's age stood and turned to Celandine and Gelso, sudden realization dawning on her face. "I saw them heading away from the safe house. I thought they had received new orders, but they must have been leaving to meet up with the soldiers."

"*Liar!*" Gelso hissed.

Tears welled in the girl's eyes. "Hawke is dead because of you! My brother is dead because of you! *How could you?*"

All the elves jumped to their feet, hurling insults at Celandine and Gelso in lightning-fast Cirisian. Tamriel rested a hand on Kaius's shoulder as the voices reached a cacophony. The archer looked back at him, devastated.

"They're your clan members. It's up to you how you wish to punish them, but they know our plans and they cannot be trusted."

Kaius looked away and nodded. Tamriel stepped back as Kaius pulled a dagger from his belt, and the elves instantly fell silent. "Hold them still," he commanded the elves holding Celandine and Gelso.

"Why did you do it?" Mercy asked, speaking up for the first time.

Gelso remained silent, but Celandine turned her glare on Tamriel. Hatred burned in her eyes. "His family has mistreated our people for generations. They turned their backs on us and allowed our ancestors to live in chains while they grew fat and rich off our labors."

"So you just did it for revenge?" Kaius asked, his mouth hanging open in shock. "You would have thrown away the future of our people for vengeance? Didn't you see how it destroyed Firesse?"

"Firesse was our *leader*. We pledged ourselves to fight for her—not for you, who allied with our enemy. He will never grant our people freedom. He is lying to you. He just wants to use you to regain his throne, and once he is king, he will send his soldiers to conquer our lands and slaughter our people."

"You're wrong."

"You could have killed him so many times," Mercy said. "Why would you betray him now?"

Celandine merely glared at her.

After a few beats of silence, Gelso muttered, "Nicholas never would have given the bounty to Cirisians, even if we handed him the king ourselves. So the human commander agreed to collect the bounty and split it among the three of us if we helped him capture Tamriel."

"He's going to turn his army on the Islands as soon as Tamriel is dead," Kaius said, bewildered. "*Why* would you help a man who wishes to see our people exterminated? Tamriel will make our lands independent."

"It doesn't matter who sits on the throne," Gelso said, at least having the decency to appear ashamed. "Regardless of who is king, the Islands will never be left alone. Beltharos will never give up on the war. But with the bounty, we could have freed some slaves on the journey to the Islands. *Some* free elves are better than none at all."

Tamriel gaped at them, stung by their betrayal. They had risked everyone's lives—had let four of their clan members die—because they did not trust him. Because revenge mattered more to them than the future of their people. "I swore to you I would free the slaves. I swore I would aid the elves in making the Islands an independent country. You can hate my family all you like, but my word is my bond."

"Have you anything else to say?" Kaius asked them stiffly, his voice ragged with pain. His fingers tightened around the grip of his dagger.

Gelso looked down at his feet and shook his head.

"I pray you don't live to see him reclaim his throne,"

Celandine said softly, glaring at Tamriel all the while. "I pray you don't live to see him betray you."

Grief and regret flashed across Kaius's face as he stepped forward, lifting his dagger. They all watched in silence as Kaius dragged his blade across Gelso's throat, then Celandine's. Tamriel winced at the sound of the elves' wet, gasping breaths, the soft *whump* of their bodies hitting the grass.

Kaius wiped his dagger clean on the grass, then stood and slipped it into its sheath. Tears streamed down his face, but there was no emotion in his voice when he shouldered past Tamriel and muttered, "The sun will rise soon. We should continue to Fallmond."

As he and the elves began packing up their belongings, Calum led the apprentices, who had been awakened by the shouting, over to the fire to eat. He was careful to stand between them and the bodies.

When Tamriel returned to Ewan, he found the young man once again sprawled on his back, his sightless eyes fixed on the twinkling stars just beginning to fade. Tamriel knelt beside the soldier and gently closed his lids, sadness sweeping over him. Without the information he had given them, Celandine and Gelso would have tried to attack them again. Creator only knew how many people they would have lost in the next battle. Ewan might have just saved all their lives.

"Rest now, soldier," he murmured. "Go now to the Creator's side, and there find peace eternal."

20
FAYE

The sun's rays beat down on Faye as she led her small group toward Fallmond. She wiped her brow with the back of her hand and tried to ignore the nervous energy coursing through her veins. What if her parents were no longer there? What if they had left, or something had happened to them? After Fredric's death, she should have been there for them. She should have tried to ease their grief. Instead, she had run away only a few days after they laid her brother to rest.

She closed her eyes when the tall, narrow houses of her hometown appeared in the distance. What she did—leaving them like that—was unforgivable. Would they even want to see her again?

She looked back at the elves riding behind her. Some of them were slumped against their riding partners, sleeping fitfully, while others simply guided their horses along in solemn silence. After leaving Xilor, they had ridden as fast as Faye had dared with so many inexperienced riders. They had been pursued by a few soldiers Faye managed to take down with her bow, but not before they shot two of the slaves.

Even now, their deaths hung heavily over their group. Tamriel had trusted her to get them out of the city safely, and she had failed.

She would not fail the rest.

They had stopped long enough to leave a note for the others where Tamriel had told her to meet them. She sent a prayer up to the Creator that the others had made it out of Xilor and found her message. After she hid the scrap of parchment, she and the elves had ridden hard for a few more hours, paused briefly to rest, then set off again shortly before dawn. That time, though, she had let them continue at a walk. She had told herself it was because they needed a reprieve from the breakneck pace she had set the day before, but that was not entirely true. Part of it was because she dreaded the thought of going home.

She had no idea what she would find when they arrived.

In her mind, at least, her parents were happy and healthy; her father still worked the fields and traveled to the market twice a week, and her mother sat by the fire and crafted her beautiful embroidery. Their lives were peaceful. She wasn't sure if she was ready to see the illusion shattered.

"What do I do, Nightstorm?" she murmured, running a hand along her horse's neck. The mare merely chuffed and continued plodding along. Faye sighed. "You're remarkably unsympathetic to my plight here, friend."

When they arrived at the outskirts of Fallmond, Faye led the elves through the side streets toward the north side of town, swallowing the ache of homesickness that swept through her. Her home lay a short ride away from the village, nestled between the mouth of a valley and the bank of a wide river. A lump formed in her throat as the cramped village streets gave way to dirt roads. The tall houses grew farther apart, carefully-pruned gardens turning to neatly-tilled fields.

Finally, they arrived.

Faye bit back a sob when she saw the squat one-story house her great-grandparents had built with their own hands. The walls were the same deep brown as the houses in the village, but they still bore the bright splashes of paint around the windowsills from her mother's childhood. Smoke billowed from the tall stone chimney. The plants spilling across the small field danced in the gentle breeze, filling the air with the same scent of herbs and dirt that had always clung to her father's tunic. Ivy trailed up the side of the small shed on the far side of the field.

The shutters were open, and she could hear her mother singing.

Numb, dazed, disbelieving, Faye pulled back on Nightstorm's reins, stopping the mare on the edge of the property. When she slipped off the saddle, her horse wandered off toward the river, her sides slick with sweat. Faye was vaguely aware of Seren Pierce and the others dismounting and trailing her up the skinny dirt path that led to the front door. As she passed the kitchen window, she spotted a flash of her mother's long black hair. Her mother was folding linens at the table, half-singing, half-humming an old folk song Faye's grandmother had loved.

Her vision turned blurry as she lifted her hand to knock on the front door.

"Who... By the Creator's grace..."

She turned toward the voice, her tears spilling over. A man stood just outside the door to the shed, a hoe in one hand, a cane in the other. His weathered face transformed when he saw her. "Faye? ...Is that you?"

She nodded, her heart swelling. "I'm here, Papa."

He dropped the cane and hoe and took several staggering steps forward. Beneath the hem of his cropped, dirt-streaked pants, she could see his gnarled, scarred shins. Her betrothed's lackeys had broken the bones so thoroughly it was a miracle he was even able to stand.

Nevertheless, he ran to her.

Lurching, hobbling steps, but he ran.

She met him in the middle of the field and threw her arms around him. He crushed her to him, his fingers knotting in her long hair, and burst into tears. Huge, wracking sobs shuddered through him. She squeezed her eyes shut. "I'm here, Papa."

"My... My baby girl," he gasped, the words muffled by her tunic. His arms tightened around her. "My baby girl is alive... By the Creator, my baby girl is...is *home*."

"Arthur? What's wrong? What's—" Her mother sucked in a sharp breath and broke into a sprint. Within moments, she crashed into them, tackling them in a hug. "My darling girl. *You've come home.*"

Once all their tears had dried, her father looped his arm through hers and leaned against her as they made their way toward the house. Her mother ushered Pierce and the others inside, not even questioning their presence. As Faye and her father trailed them into the house, she ran her fingers along the right side of the doorway, brushing the notches where her mother had tracked her and her brother's growth. Fredric had always been one inch shorter, and she had never tired of teasing him over it.

Be nice to him now, their father had scolded her, a faint smile gracing his lips. *One day he'll be bigger than you.*

She helped him onto the wooden rocking chair beside the fire and sat cross-legged on the floor beside him, just as she had done so many times as a child. He laid a hand on her shoulder and squeezed, and she leaned into the touch. "I missed you, Papa," she whispered.

"I missed you, too, my little lamb. More than you know."

"Faye—" her mother choked out. She was standing in the middle of the room, gaping at her. Nerida gently took her elbow and guided her to the couch. Pierce, Liri, and the elves stepped into the study or kitchen to give them privacy.

"I'll make some tea," Nerida said as Faye's mother sank onto the couch.

"Thank you." Faye shot her a grateful smile and watched her retreat to the kitchen. Then she looked down at her hands, her skin marred with calluses and old scars. The bumps and ridges seemed even more pronounced in the light of the fire. Eleven years in the Guild. Eleven years of her parents not knowing where she was—if she was even alive.

"I'm sorry for running away," she murmured, forcing the words past the lump in her throat. "I'm so, *so* sorry. I was weak, and I was afraid, and I didn't know what to do. And I— I couldn't marry that man." She refused to speak his name. Not in this house. Not here, where she had begged her parents to agree to the match so Fredric would live. Where she had watched her betrothed's lackeys shatter her father's legs. Not here. Not *ever*. "I was stupid and cowardly, and I hurt you both *so badly*. What I did was unforgivable."

"Nothing you could ever do is unforgivable, little lamb. Where did you go? Where have you been all this time?"

She gathered her courage and... "I found a Daughter of the Guild and told her what he did to you. She killed him, and then I... I went to the Keep with her," she said, shame and guilt sweeping over her when her father flinched at the mention of the Guild. Her mother anxiously twined a strand of black hair—now streaked through with gray—between her fingers. "Mama, Papa, I became a Daughter. And I made so many mistakes. I thought I could rid the world of men like him. Instead, I *became* him." Tears welled in her eyes, but she blinked them away, refusing to let them fall. "I didn't realize what Illynor did to me until it was too late. I killed... By the Creator, I killed so many people."

Her father's hand tightened on her shoulder. She hung her head, letting her thick hair block out everything around her. She couldn't bear to see the disappointment on their faces.

"I don't know what I'm doing," she whispered, her voice breaking. "I don't know how to fix this."

Wood creaked, and Faye peered through her hair to see her mother kneel before her. "Apology accepted," she said softly, placing a finger under Faye's chin and tipping her head up. "You're our daughter. All we want is for you to be happy."

"Truly?"

Her mother's eyes sparkled. "Truly."

"The Creator has returned you to us," her father added, leaning forward to kiss the top of her head. "Every day, I prayed that you were alive, that you would return to us. I never gave up hope that you were out there, somewhere. And now he has led you home."

Nerida returned then, a platter with three chipped teacups in her hands. Whorls of steam rose from the tea. Faye held her cup close, letting the heat warm her trembling hands. With great reluctance, she said, "I can't stay for long. I've sworn to help Tamriel Myrellis reclaim his throne from the traitor who seeks to kill him, and I need your help."

Her parents exchanged a long look, and her chest seized with fear. They must have heard the news of Nicholas's betrayal. They had to know how dangerous it would be to aid him.

She braced herself for rejection.

Then her mother smiled, set her teacup down, and said, "Tell us everything."

21
PERCIVAL

Percival was standing on the balcony, watching the reflection of the moon ripple on the lake's surface, when Celeste arrived. He raised a brow at the silver tray in her hands. "More tea? I don't know if we have time to indulge before our little midnight stroll."

She set it on one of the tables, then joined him on the balcony. Her shoulder brushed his when she leaned against the railing, staring up at the starry night sky. The wind caught her long hair and sent it dancing behind her. "Look who has developed a sense of humor. Scared of falling?"

"Scared of *landing*."

"Just hold on tight."

"Hadn't thought of that, thanks. What's the tea for?"

"It's warm milk. I told the guards I was bringing some to help you sleep. I...may have hinted that I would be attending you in other, more *private* ways, as well. That should buy us an hour or two before they come looking for me."

He whipped his head around so fast he winced. "Tell me you're joking. Riona's here!"

A mischievous glint sparkled in her eyes. "Are you that

offended by the idea of taking me to your bed? It's hard not to take that personally. You wouldn't be the first noble to have an affair with his servant."

"*Celeste!*" he hissed, a flush rising on his cheeks.

"Of course I'm joking. I offered each of the guards a drink out of the goodness of my heart. One was laced with something that will... Well, let's just say the poor man won't be straying far from the chamber pot until dawn, at the earliest. And the other I drugged with Ienna oil—not enough to knock him out, but enough to make him groggy and careless. We have plenty of time to sneak out and back in."

He gaped at her, half horrified and half impressed. "Who *are* you? How are you so good at this?"

"I'm just a lowly handmaid," she said, spreading her hands. "There's nothing more to tell."

He shook his head, ignoring the mirth in her voice. "How do you propose we do this? I'm very much praying this doesn't end with my body being dashed across the rocks."

She turned on her heel, strode into the bedroom, and returned a few moments later with a coil of rope.

"How in the Creator's name did you get *that* in here?" He crossed his arms. "Let me guess: you told the guards I like being tied up?"

"No, but that's good information to have. Never know when it'll come in handy." She winked, and his blush returned tenfold. Thank the Creator it was dark enough she probably couldn't see it.

She'd better not be able to see it.

"Right, ah, so—anyway," he stammered, his mouth suddenly dry. *I take back everything I said to Tamriel in camp that night. I don't need love. Just books. Books never turn me into a bumbling, blushing idiot—no, it's always the fault of this terrible, infuriating, sarcastic girl.*

This smart, pretty, funny girl...

Creator, he was in over his head.

"So anyway," he said, ignoring the way she was grinning at him. "How did you get that in here? Or would I rather not know?"

She moved to the place where the balcony's railing met the castle's exterior wall and began tying off the rope. "I hid it among the sheets when I brought in fresh blankets the other day."

When she finished attaching the rope to the railing, she let the coil drop. He leaned over the railing and stared down at it, dangling in the empty air. At this height, the wind whipped around them, tugging at their hair and clothes. *I'm going to die. I am absolutely going to die.* She held out the rope, and he swallowed tightly. He wiped his sweaty palms on his trousers and accepted it.

"Brace your feet on the wall and ease your way down," she said, nodding encouragingly. "Whatever you do, don't look down."

He looked doubtfully at the rope. "Are you sure there isn't another way?"

"Not if you want to get out unseen. I hear your uncle is still meeting with Rhiannon, discussing the movement of the troops. I don't think you want him catching you sneaking out. Now go."

Before he could talk himself out of it, he gripped the rope with white knuckles and swung a leg over the railing. He eased himself over the side and placed his feet flat on the wall, exactly as she had told him. Already, the rope bit into the soft flesh of his hands. He had never built up calluses like the men and women of the guard.

"Loosen your grip," she hissed, holding her hair away from her face as she leaned over the railing. "Your fingers will go numb if you hold on that tightly."

"This isn't exactly easy," he muttered through gritted

teeth, but he followed her directions and began easing himself down the rope. His heart hammered in his chest so hard he could hear it pounding in his ears. It drowned out everything—her quiet encouragements, the strong wind, the crashing waves. As much as it called to him, he didn't allow himself to look down.

His arms began to ache. Sweat dampened his tunic and trailed down his forehead, plastering his hair to his head. His glasses quickly grew foggy, but there was nothing he could do about it, dangling in the air as he was. He slowly, *slowly*, made his way down the side of the castle blindly, his jaw clenched so tightly he feared he would break a tooth.

An eternity passed before his feet touched soft grass. He released the rope, falling backward onto the ground and letting out a relieved laugh. A few yards away, the manicured lawn gave way to the rocky shore of the lake. Spray from the tall waves flew into the air and hit him, cooling his warm body.

"Watch out," Celeste called. A moment later, he heard a soft *whump*.

He pulled off his glasses, wiped them off, and put them back on only to see the rope lying in a tangle beside him. His mouth dropped open as Celeste climbed over the railing and began scaling the wall with only her hands and feet. While he climbed, she had changed into a black tunic and fitted pants, traded her simple flats for sturdy ankle boots, and tied her hair into a long braid. He gaped at her as she descended as effortlessly as a spider. She dropped to the ground beside him and brushed back a strand of hair that had sprung free of her braid.

"Now you're just trying to impress me."

"Of course I am." She grabbed the rope, tossed it into a nearby bush, then extended a hand to him. "Finished resting?"

He took her hand and pushed to his feet, his limbs leaden and trembling slightly. He doubted he'd be able to walk tomorrow without wincing. "I have to ask once again, who *are* you?"

She gestured for him to follow her along the side of the castle. "I used to be a thief—a damn good one, too. Now come on."

When they reached the corner, she peeked at the front lawn, scanning for guards. "Seven," she murmured to him. "Follow me."

And then she was off.

He muttered a curse and scrambled to keep up as she darted toward the hedge maze. Two guards were walking the length of the gravel carriageway, while the rest wandered the grounds, their armor gleaming in the moonlight. Percival followed Celeste's lead and stayed low, his chest constricting with fear. If they were caught...

She dropped into a crouch behind the exterior wall of the maze and he stopped beside her, breathing hard. "You know you're insane, right?" he whispered.

"It's serving you well, is it not?" she responded before taking off again, creeping along the length of the hedge. When they reached the end, she nodded to the wall surrounding the castle grounds. "The moon is in the east, which means the light doesn't penetrate over there. See how the shadows are darkest at the base of the wall? You're going to use that to get out. Creep along the edge of the wall until you get to the gate, then slip out. I'll distract the guards. Meet me at the Church."

"Are you sure?"

"Have I not proven my skills yet?" She peered out over the top of the hedge, then pushed him toward the wall. "Go!"

He darted for the wall as she bolted from the cover of the maze, his heart hammering in his chest. He turned, pressing his back against the wall, just in time to see her make a run for the gate.

"Hey! Stop!"

The two guards walking the length of the carriageway unsheathed their swords and gave chase. Panic closed a fist around his throat. She was only a few yards away from the gate. She could make it.

Then she let out a cry and dropped to the grass, cradling her ankle.

No! She was going to be caught, and it was all his fault. She was going to be killed because of him.

He almost stepped out of the shadows, but her head jerked up and she looked straight at him, even though she shouldn't have been able to see him in the darkness. The moonlight caught the slight smile on her lips. He let out a breath. She was okay. She was only pretending to be injured.

The guards closed in on her. When they were almost upon her, she swept out a foot and knocked the legs out from under one of the men. He crashed onto his back as she sprang up, punched the other guard in the throat, and made a break for the far wall, leaving the gate unguarded and open for him.

"What the—"

The guards stumbled after her as the others, drawn by the commotion, rushed over. Percival crept toward the gate as she had instructed, watching in amazement as she began scaling the far wall.

Percival slipped through the gate and sprinted down the street. The voices of the guards faded as the distance between him and the castle grew. He turned a corner and darted into the first alley he saw, pressing his back to the wall and sucking in breath after breath. His tunic was soaked through with perspiration, and he felt as if he might simply keel over from how hard his heart was beating.

Letting out a quiet, incredulous laugh, he dropped his

head into his hands. Then he jerked back, hissing in pain when his sweat stung the tiny cuts the rope had carved into his hands.

Keep going, he told himself. *Keep going.* He crept down the alley, checked that the coast was clear, then started back in the direction of the Church. Every moan of the wind or creak of a house made him jump. He rubbed the goosebumps on his arms and hurried down the street.

"Creator, what have I done?" he muttered as he walked.

Despite his fatigue, despite the terror of what Nicholas would do to him if he was found, the answer filled him with pride. *I defied my uncle.*

"Good to see you again," Celeste said, slightly breathless, as she trailed Lethandris into the Church's archives and took her place beside Percival. They were below the main floor of the Church, surrounded by glass cases housing the Church's oldest and most valuable relics.

"How did you escape the guards?"

"Climbing the wall bought me enough time to outrun them. They couldn't follow in all their heavy armor."

He shook his head and turned to Hero and Ketojan, who were standing on the opposite side of the room, next to a case holding a manuscript that appeared to be centuries old. Ketojan's arms were crossed over his chest, his white hair cast in gold by the light of the lantern in Lethandris's hand.

"I don't know how you think you can help us," Ketojan said, drumming his fingers on his arms in agitation. "Your uncle has the capital on lockdown. His guards are manning the gates and checking every ship for runaways. It has been too dangerous for us to even leave the End since he returned. We're risking our necks just being here with you."

"There must be something we can do," he insisted, looking from Ketojan to Hero. "You worked with Tamriel, and it wasn't any safer to sneak slaves out when Ghyslain was king. There must be a way. It's a big city; people slip through the cracks."

"There are no cracks! Your uncle closed his fist around the city when he had all of Tamriel's supporters killed, and now we have no allies!" Ketojan looked away, pain flashing across his face. "You don't know what it was like watching his people take over the city," he said, his voice low. "The Astley and Burgess soldiers killed the nobles first—went from house to house and slaughtered them. If they tried to run, they struck them down in the street for everyone to see.

"Then they came to the End. They broke into people's houses searching for Cirisians or runaway slaves. Your uncle had figured out that someone in the End had been helping free the slaves on Tamriel's behalf. They were looking for *us*, and our people refused to give us up."

Hero nodded, tears welling in her eyes. "So many died," she breathed, her face pale. "Children, too."

Bile rose in Percival's throat. *Oh, Creator. Children?* "I'm so sorry. I had no idea. I'm going to find a way to make this right, I swear it."

Ketojan sighed. "I don't know how you can. Your uncle is a smart man. He knows how to wage war, and that's exactly what this is—war on a different battlefield. The five of us don't stand a chance against him."

"You're wrong," Percival snapped, surprised by the bite in his voice. He crossed the room and stopped right in front of the elf. "I need you to help me. Tamriel could be dead for all we know. Even if he's alive and he *does* find a way to challenge my uncle for his throne, he's going to need all the help he can get. We have to find little ways to undermine my uncle. I won't watch more elves suffer under the bonds of slavery."

Someone touched his arm, and he looked back to see Celeste standing behind him, her eyes full of sorrow. "Percival," she said quietly. "Go easy on them."

He glanced at them, and his anger faded when he recognized the look in their eyes: terror. For the first time since he had met them, they seemed lost, uncertain. They had just watched their friends—they had just watched *children*—die to keep their secret.

All the air left Percival's lungs, and he slumped against one of the glass cases. "I'm sorry. I know I'm asking a lot of you, but I can't do this on my own. I need help.

"My family has trading contracts across Beltharos and Rivosa. That means we need ships and bookkeepers to track expenses and profits. If I convince my uncle to allow me to oversee that, we can sneak slaves out of the city with the cargo. I'll get you the information about the shipments, and you can find slaves who are willing to risk running away. Celeste, could you help them sneak onto the ship?" he asked, and she nodded.

"I'll help, too," Lethandris said. "Sometimes slaves come to the Church and tell me some of the terrible things their masters have done to them. If they wish to escape, I can hide them here in the archives until you're able to get them out."

"Won't someone find them here?"

"The only one who is authorized to use this room is the High Priestess, and she's on your side. She believes Tamriel is still alive and will return to reclaim his kingdom. She'll take any opportunity to undermine Nicholas."

"I'm grateful for your aid." He offered Hero and Ketojan a pleading, hopeful look. "What do you say? You know the people of Beggars' End. They trust you. The slaves trust you."

Hero and Ketojan glanced at each other, an entire unspoken conversation seeming to pass between them in the span of a few seconds. "Fine," Ketojan said. "We'll help you."

"We owe Tamriel that much," Hero added.

He let out a sigh of relief, the weight on his shoulders lessening for the first time in days. "You won't regret it, I swear. I'll speak to my uncle in the morning about overseeing the shipping business, and I'll send a note through Celeste once I have news."

"We'll get to work procuring runaway slaves, but don't expect many to jump at the opportunity. They know your uncle's reputation well."

"It's getting late, Percival. We should return to the castle," Celeste said. She turned to the priestess and kissed her cheeks. "Thank you, Lethandris."

"Of course." She stepped back and smiled at Percival. "I am very glad you are not following in your uncle's footsteps. If you need any aid—anything at all—please let me know."

He dipped his head in respect. "I will. Thank you for trusting me."

She led them up the stairs and through the main room of the Church. This late, the prayer room was dark and empty. The light of Lethandris's lantern bobbed and flickered, casting long, dancing shadows as they made their way down the aisle.

"Be safe," she whispered as they left. "I'll pray for you."

The moment the doors swung shut behind them, Percival sank onto the top step and ran his hands through his hair. "I can't believe we just did that."

Celeste sat down beside him and nudged his shoulder with hers. "You're a lot braver than you give yourself credit for, Percival. Not many would have risked what you did tonight."

"I'm just trying to do what's right."

"And that's what makes you different from all the other nobles in this Creator-forsaken city. You did well tonight."

"Ha. Tell me that when we're actually able to *free* the

slaves. I still have to convince my uncle to let me help out with our business."

"I'm sure you'll find a way."

She started to stand up, but he caught her arm, stilling her. "I know we must return, but I have to ask. You were a thief?"

She looked away, biting her lip. "I did what I had to do to survive after I fled my master's home in Blackhills."

He remained quiet. This was the first time he had seen her confident swagger falter. The sadness in her voice made him ache, but he found himself hoping she'd keep talking. He wanted to know more about her; he'd listen to anything she was willing to share.

He suspected that she, like him, hadn't had many friends in her life.

When he didn't respond, she continued, "I went to Rivosa and fell in with a bunch of thieves and thugs. They're the ones who taught me all my skills. I'm not proud of that part of my life, but for a long time, I didn't see any other option. More than that, I was angry. I wanted the humans to hurt like I did when I was a slave. So I stole from them."

"What brought you here?"

She winced. "I tried to steal from the royal family and ended up getting one of my crew killed because of a stupid, stupid mistake. After that, I knew I couldn't continue down that road. It would have destroyed me. So I came to Sandori. I was praying in this Church, asking the Creator how I could turn my life around, when I met Lethandris. He knew she would be able to save me."

Before he could say a word, she rose and bounded down the steps. "That's enough of that. We should get back to the castle before your guards realize you're gone."

She started down the street and he fell into step behind her, his limbs aching. "Please tell me you're not going to make me climb up the side of the castle. I don't think I'll be able to make it even a foot off the ground."

"Don't worry your pretty little head, Your Majesty," she said over her shoulder, her usual grin once again tugging at her lips. "I always have a plan."

22
MERCY

Mercy sighed with relief when at last they arrived at Faye's childhood home. Tamriel dismounted at the edge of the field, and she and the others followed suit a moment later. Pain shot through her ribs when her feet hit the ground. Her broken bones had mended, but all the fighting and running in Xilor had left them sore. Tamriel shot her a concerned look when she moved to his side.

"I'm fine," she said, smiling wearily. "Just looking forward to finally resting."

He nodded, but the worry didn't leave his eyes. "At most, we have a day or two to recuperate and resupply. Now that the soldiers have found us, they won't be far behind; Duomnodera and the other Qadar can only hold them off for so long before word gets back to Nicholas that we're alive. The sooner we get to Feyndara, the better."

The front door opened and Faye ran out, a relieved laugh spilling from her lips. "I feared you'd never make it," she said as she pulled Mercy and Tamriel into a hug. "Any longer, and I'd have gone to hunt you down myself."

"You should have more faith in us."

Her friend stepped back, grinning. Then her eyes lifted to something over Mercy's shoulder and she went still. Her hand drifted to the throwing knives sheathed on her belt. "What are *they* doing here?"

Mercy didn't need to turn around to know that she had spotted the Daughters. "They're on our side. They helped us in Xilor. Believe me, I was as wary of trusting them as you are, but they haven't tried to kill us yet."

A shadow passed across her friend's face. Faye turned to Tamriel. "You approve of them traveling with us?"

"They saved our lives."

"Hm. Fine. But they don't go near the house, or my family—or the apprentices. They've caused enough damage as it is. I don't want them ruining this, too." When Tamriel nodded, she started toward the house. "Come inside. I want to introduce you to my parents."

That was when Mercy noticed the man and woman standing just beyond the front door. The woman—Faye's mother—was her spitting image, with the same high cheekbones, large hazel eyes, and long, elegant neck. Faye's father leaned heavily against his wife, a cane clutched in his hand. His lips spread into a wide grin as they approached.

"Mama, Papa, this is His Majesty King Tamriel Myrellis," Faye announced, beaming at them. "And this is my best friend, Mercy. She's going to be the queen of Beltharos."

Her parents dropped into low bows and welcomed them as Faye ran through introductions for the rest of their group, who were still lingering on the edge of the field, unsaddling their horses and unloading their packs. She must have told them what to expect; they didn't bat an eye at the heavily-armed Qadar and Cirisians. Mercy didn't miss the relief that passed across her friend's face when she saw Kaius alive and unharmed.

Once the introductions were finished, Faye took her father's arm and led him into the house, waving Mercy and Tamriel along. Her mother disappeared into the kitchen, murmuring something about preparing food. While Faye helped her father into his rocking chair, Mercy and the others settled onto the couch. She cast a furtive glance at Kaius. His eyes traveled slowly around the room, taking in the old books lined up across the fireplace's mantle, the dried bunch of roses hanging in the corner of the room, the drawing of a pirate ship tacked to the wall. His lips twitched into the ghost of a smile at the little stick-figure boy standing at the helm, a girl with long black hair at his side.

"What happened in Xilor?" Faye asked as she sank to the floor. The sight of her sitting there, the firelight reflecting in her large eyes, reminded Mercy of the scared young girl she had met in the Keep's infirmary eleven years earlier. Who would have guessed they'd one day end up back in her parents' home? "Did you figure out how the soldiers learned where we were?"

"We did," Tamriel answered quickly, saving Kaius from having to admit that two of his people had betrayed them. "Those responsible are no longer with us."

"Good. How many did we lose?"

"Four Cirisians, but it could have been much worse. The Qadar and Assassins kept the troops from pursuing us, but I doubt we have long before they regroup and track us down, which is why we should be leaving for Feyndara as soon as possible."

"Going there is a death sentence," her father said, shaking his head. "I don't know why you think the queen would help you. Even if she does agree, whatever she asks for in return will cost more than it's worth."

"No cost is too great for my kingdom. I'm not leaving my people in the hands of that traitor."

"I understand, but is there not another way? Is there no one else you could ask for aid? Rivosa?"

He shook his head. "Nicholas's nephew is betrothed to a member of the Rivosi king's family. He won't give up the chance for an alliance with a family as powerful and wealthy as the Comyns, especially knowing the odds stacked against us. Duomnodera has agreed to speak to the High Mothers in Gyr'malr, but there is no guarantee they will help. Same with the Cirisians. Feyndara is our best option."

"Then do what you must, but be wary. I would not put it past Queen Cerelia to take advantage of your desperation." His grip tightened on Faye's shoulder protectively. She lifted a hand and laid it over his. "Until you leave, our house is yours to use as you please. Give my wife a list of supplies you need, and she'll go to the market tomorrow morning and secure what she can for you. We don't have much coin to spare, but what we have is yours."

Tamriel dipped his head in respect. "I'm more grateful for your aid than I can express."

He dismissed Tamriel's words with a flick of his free hand. "My daughter told us all about the two of you. I can see that she would do anything for you, and you for her. It is an honor to have you in my house. My wife and I will gladly share what we have to help our king and future queen."

Calum stood and moved to the window, frowning, as if expecting Nicholas's troops to appear any second. Through the open shutters, Mercy could hear the apprentices laughing as her siblings chased them through the fields. The joyful sound lifted her spirits a fraction. "We're only a few days' ride from Cowayne, where we will hire a ship and crew to sail across the sea. I remember Hewlin mentioning a few he hires when he takes the Strykers to Feyndara. Hopefully they won't turn us over the second they realize who we are."

"When you leave for Cowayne, I'll lead my people and the

runaway slaves to the Islands," Kaius said, and Faye looked at him sharply. "They need to start training, and I need time to petition the other clans for fighters."

"You could come with us and then follow the coast north," Faye suggested, and Mercy heard the undercurrent of desperation under her friend's forced nonchalance. She didn't blame Faye for wanting to extend their time together. Even if Queen Cerelia ended up giving them the troops they needed to reclaim the throne, there was no guarantee any of them would survive this.

"Nicholas's men are looking for Tamriel. Like His Majesty said, they'll be searching even harder now that they know you're alive and close. The elves will be safer with me and my people, and it'll be easier for you to travel unnoticed without us. We'll meet up with you before the battle."

She nodded, looking dejected. "If that's what you think is best."

Tamriel rose and joined his cousin at the window, staring out at the small force they'd amassed. Their numbers weren't large, but Mercy knew beyond a shadow of a doubt that every one of them would give his or her life for their king. "It's settled then. Kaius, you and your people need a break from patrolling. Let the rest of us watch for Nicholas's troops while it's still light. We'll restock tomorrow and set out for Cowayne at dawn the day after."

Mercy stepped out of the house later that evening and scanned the field and surrounding land for Blackfoot. She grinned when she turned and found her stallion already loping toward her, his dark hide gleaming under the last strains of sunlight. "You knew I was coming, didn't you?" She offered him the apple Faye's mother had given her and he ate it eagerly, his breath warm on her palm. "Enjoy it while it lasts. After we get to Cowayne, we're not going to see each other for awhile. I can't take you to Feyndara with me."

He chuffed, munching on the apple. She ran her hand along his neck, gently working out the tangles in his long mane. "When we get back to Sandori, remind me to give you a bath, demon-horse." She grinned when his tail flicked in irritation. "You reek. But, to be fair, I don't smell much better after all this time on the road."

Behind her, the door swung open. She turned to find Faye standing there, fidgeting with the hem of her shirt. Faye had traded her leather armor and sheath of daggers for one of her mother's tunics, a white cotton top with pale blue flowers embroidered along the neckline and hem, and her hair hung in a damp sheet down her back. It was strange to see her in normal clothes—at the Keep, they'd had nothing but their armor and the worn hand-me-downs from the other Assassins—but that wasn't what gave Mercy pause. It was the mixture of sadness and fear on her friend's face.

She patted Blackfoot's neck once more before approaching Faye. "What's wrong?"

"M-My brother is buried by the river at the mouth of the glen." She nodded to the east, behind the house, where Mercy could see a range of low, rolling hills. "I haven't gone to see him yet, and I don't want to do it on my own. Will you go with me?"

"Of course I will."

Faye was quiet while they saddled their horses and followed the river toward the glen. For a long time, the only sounds were those of their horses and the soft gurgling of the water. Then Faye began to cry.

"Shh, it's alright," Mercy murmured, guiding Blackfoot closer to Faye's mare. She reached over and touched her friend's arm. "It's alright, Faye."

She looked down, her curtain of hair blocking Mercy's view of her face. "I just miss him so much. He was my first friend—my best friend. I haven't seen his grave since the day I ran away. Being here, seeing my family again... It was such a terrible mistake leaving them behind. I was a coward. A selfish, foolish coward."

The sun had already dipped below the horizon when they arrived at the mouth of the glen. Faye dismounted and led Mercy to a tall weeping willow beside the river, and they ducked through the fronds. A few paces away from the tree's massive trunk, a stone marker bearing Fredric's name and a quote from the Book of the Creator had been pressed into the dirt. Faye dropped to her knees in front of the gravestone and ran her fingers over the letters. Mercy knelt beside her and rested a hand on her friend's shoulder as her tears turned to sobs—great, shuddering sobs that wracked her whole body.

Mercy wrapped her arms around Faye and held her tightly, feeling her friend's trembling fingers dig into her back. A few tears slipped through her own lashes. Faye had had a life here, a family who loved her, and it had all been ripped away.

When the sobs eventually subsided, Faye pulled back and wiped her cheeks, her face flushed and puffy from crying. "Thank you for coming with me," she whispered, her voice raw and wavering.

Mercy offered her a small smile and tucked a strand of hair behind her ear. "Anything for you, sister."

Faye's face brightened at the word. She laughed shakily. "Some pair we are, huh? Do you think all this is ever going to get easier? Do you think we'll ever stop running?"

"From danger or our pasts?"

"Either."

"I don't know. It seems every time something finally goes right for us, the Creator decides to throw another obstacle in our path. Eventually, he has to get tired, doesn't he?" She looked through the swaying fronds toward the mouth of the glen, where Faye's home sat just beyond the hills. Then she studied her friend's red-rimmed eyes and shaky hands. As much as what she was about to say hurt, as much as Faye was going to hate her for saying it, she knew it was for the best. "Faye, your fight is over. You're free from the Guild. When we leave for Feyndara...you should stay here with your parents. You can have a family again. A life."

Faye stiffened. "B-But I can't leave you and Tamriel and the others. I promised I would help Tamriel reclaim his kingdom, and that is what I intend to do."

"It's your choice, but I know how killing affects you. I know that it makes you sick—Kaius told me what happened in Cyrna. He's worried about you, and so am I. You're not an Assassin anymore. You don't ever have to be an Assassin again. You can stay here and reclaim the life you left behind. You have endured enough."

Faye shook her head, but Mercy pushed on, laying her hand over her friend's. "Please, Faye, let me finish before you argue. I love you, and I'm ashamed that I haven't always been the best at showing it. You stood by me when no one else would. You turned against Illynor to free me, for the Creator's sake! Now let me do something for you. Let me help you find happiness. We're going to war, and I don't want to lose you."

For several long moments, Faye merely stared down at their joined hands. The weeping willow branches swayed around them, hiding them from the rest of the world. She could see Faye wrestling with how to respond. A small, selfish part of herself prayed that her friend would dismiss the idea outright. But Faye had risked so much to free her from the Guild; she deserved a break from all the death and destruction.

"I understand what you're doing," Faye finally said in a

quiet voice. "I know you want to protect me, but I can take care of myself. My place is by your side."

Mercy leaned forward. She didn't know if she could survive seeing Faye hurt in the coming battle. She'd do anything to keep from losing another person she loved. "Please," she whispered, even though it hurt to imagine leaving Faye behind, "think on what I've said. It's not just about protecting you. You may not get the chance to return. Promise me you'll consider it a little longer."

Faye looked at Fredric's grave marker and reluctantly nodded. "Fine. I'll consider it...but I can't promise my answer will change."

Mercy hugged her again and sent a silent prayer up to the Creator that she would come to her senses. They'd all seen enough war to last a lifetime.

She noticed something moving beyond the fronds, something too small to be one of their horses. The branches parted, and Kaius peered in, his concerned gaze going straight to Faye. *Is she okay?* he mouthed, and Mercy nodded.

"Someone's here to see you," she whispered to Faye as she pulled back. She stood and walked toward Blackfoot, leaving them to speak in private. Kaius whispered a quiet 'Thank you' when she passed.

She didn't look back, but she heard Kaius's soft footsteps on the grass as he went to Faye, and she smiled.

Creator, let them both survive the war.

23
FAYE

Faye looked up just as Kaius knelt before her. As his green eyes roved over her face, still puffy from crying, Mercy's words echoed in her mind: *He's worried about you.* She tried to ignore the pang the statement sent through her heart. They'd be marching to war in a matter of weeks; they had more important things to deal with than...whatever this was between them.

If she indulged this desire within her and he didn't survive...

"How did you know where I was?" she asked, being careful not to look at him. Here, below the canopy of the weeping willow, she could almost pretend it was just the two of them; there was no war, no bounty, no soldiers chasing them. It was a dangerous thought. They were friends. Nothing more.

There was a line between them they had yet to cross.

"I saw you leave the house and I...followed you," he admitted sheepishly. "I heard you crying." Kaius reached down and touched the grave marker, his expression tender. "Your brother?" he guessed, tracing the word COTHERON.

"My twin."

"I'm so sorry, Faye."

His fingers paused at the end of Fredric's name, and she felt the weight of his stare on her. Still, she refused to meet his eyes for fear of what she would see in them. She didn't want his pity, and she didn't want him to see how completely undone she had become over the past few weeks.

"Faye," he whispered, causing her heart to start pounding. "Why won't you look at me?"

She closed her eyes, and a tear rolled down her cheek.

After a moment's hesitation, Kaius reached up and cupped her face. Her breath hitched as his thumb grazed her skin, brushing the tear away. When she opened her eyes, Kaius smiled at her, his expression a mix of sympathy, sorrow, and...something she didn't want to name.

Her chest constricted at the tentative smile he gave her. "Please don't cry. I can't bear it."

"...Why do you always come for me? Why are you so nice?"

"Because you are kind, and strong, and wonderful, and it kills me to watch you blame yourself for everything that has happened to you. In the Islands, I saw countless soldiers suffer from night terrors after particularly bloody battles. Some could barely bring themselves to draw their weapons, even when facing an enemy. They couldn't stomach the thought of spilling more blood, of taking another life, even if it meant losing theirs. It's not shameful," he said, tilting her chin up when she tried to look away, "but it is wrong to try and hide it from everyone, to pretend you don't need help. Why won't you let me help you?"

She heard the real question hidden in his words: *Why won't you let me in?*

Suddenly, he was too close; his palm was too warm against her skin; her heart was beating too erratically. As much as she wanted to keep the truth hidden, buried somewhere deep inside, she knew she owed him an honest answer after everything he had done for her.

"Because I know what we're going to face when we return to Sandori. Because we're not all going to survive. Because everyone I love ends up being taken from me."

Because if I let myself, I will fall for you, and I won't be able to live with the pain of losing you.

Steeling her heart, she leaned back, out of his reach. His hand hovered in the air for a moment before he lowered it to his side and closed it into a fist. Pain flashed across his face. "I wish we had more time."

I do, too. More than you know.

She cast another glance at her brother's gravestone, her throat tightening. She would have loved to take Mercy up on her offer, to stay here with her family, but her duty was not yet done. For now, she was a soldier in Tamriel's army. "Maybe things will be different after the battle."

Kaius stood and offered her a hand up. *Ever the gentleman.* She accepted, and he squeezed her fingers once before letting go. "I certainly hope so."

He led her to their horses, and they rode in silence the entire way back to her parents' home. When the house appeared in the distance, the windows bright with flickering lantern light, he bade her goodnight and sweet dreams before guiding his horse to where several Cirisians were preparing to leave for patrols. She watched him, admiring the way the moonlight highlighted his bronze skin and strong, confident posture, until they disappeared down the dirt road that led to town.

I did the right thing, she told herself. *I made the right choice.*

"You're doing well, little lamb. Almost like you were never gone," her father said when she sat back on her heels and wiped at the perspiration beading across her brow. They'd been outside working in the field since dawn, and although the early autumn breeze was crisp and cool, it offered only a modicum of relief from the sun's relentless rays. For hours, they'd been working side by side, tending the neat rows of plants laden with ripe fruits and vegetables; watching the Cirisians attempt to teach the runaway slaves to wield sticks ike swords; and—most recently—listening to the apprentices' laughter as they raced Matthias and Ino from one side of the farm to the other. Faye smiled when Matthias pretended to trip, falling to his knees with exaggerated clumsiness.

"Go on without me!" he cried, his face contorted in pain. "I'll never make it!"

Indi, Zora, and Ino continued running, but Arabelle turned around and doubled over in laughter, completely forgetting about the race. She snorted when he struggled and failed to stand once, twice...then jumped up, threw her over his shoulder, and chased the others across the grass.

A wistful expression passed across her father's face as he watched them. "I never realized until now how much I missed that sound. That laughter. It was too quiet around here after you and Fredric...left."

"I never should have run away." She reached past him and plucked a fat, dark blackberry from the bush before him. She tossed that one to him, then pulled another for herself, savoring the sweet juice that burst across her tongue when she bit into it. "I'll be back once Tamriel and Mercy are on the throne. It won't be the same without Fredric, but I think —I think it'll be nice. We'll work outside every day, and we'll ride to the market together twice a week, to sell our produce and buy ingredients for Mama's blackberry pie. I think

Mama's cooking could rival those of the fancy chefs we'll meet in Queen Cerelia's court."

"I would love that, my dear, but is that truly what you wish to do?" Her father's hazel eyes—the exact same shade as her own—fixed on her face. He let out a long sigh and ran a hand through his thinning hair. "Don't think that I don't want you to stay here with us—by the Creator, I want that more than anything—but what a father desires for his daughter is not always what is best for her. When you were younger, I prayed every day that you and Fredric would grow up to leave this small village behind and make something of yourselves. Every time you spoke of sailing around the world, of finding riches and discovering uncharted lands, I prayed that was what the future held in store for you. The Creator had a different fate for your brother, but you... You have so much more to offer the kingdom, Faye. You weren't meant to live on this little farm and tend the same land your ancestors did. If that's what you decide, I won't stop you, but I don't want to see you tie yourself to this place—to a life you know won't make you happy—because you think you owe it to your mother and me. Do you understand me, Faye?"

"Who says I wouldn't be happy here?"

He shot her a knowing look. "I remember the wonder on your face every time you and your brother sat beside the fire and listened to me read stories of the Year of One Night. Fredric thought they were nice tales, but they never enchanted him the way they did you. Your favorites were the ones about the knights—the brave men and women who marched off to battle and conquered faraway cities in the name of the Creator's bride. I promised myself then that when you became old enough, I wouldn't stand in your way if you wanted to go off and see the world. No, more than that, I'd do anything to make it possible for you. I'd pray for your safety every day, and of course I would worry about you, but I could accept that you were never meant for a life of tending a farm."

Faye's heart swelled with affection. She threw her arms around her father. "I love you, Papa."

"I love you, too, my little lamb." He pulled back and kissed her cheek. "If you decide to continue your adventuring, I know you'll always come back. You never could resist your mother's baking. I doubt you'd be gone more than a month before you show up on our doorstep asking about dessert."

"You'll just fatten me up so much I won't be able to leave."

He shot her a mischievous grin, and the gesture transformed him into a younger man—the man she'd left behind eleven years ago "You'd do that yourself. Creator save anyone who gets in between you and your mother's blackberry pie."

Her mother stepped out of the house, Cassia trailing behind her, and climbed onto the bench of the wagon waiting on the little dirt road. Cassia checked the mules' reins once more before climbing up and waving Faye over. Then she turned and shouted for her brothers.

Faye rose and wiped the dirt from her trousers. "I've missed eleven years of birthdays. I have to make up for all those pies you got to eat without me. Want me to help you inside?"

"Am I some old man who can't hobble more than a few feet without keeling over?" he asked in mock offense. "Go on. I'll keep working. I've got the others to keep me company." He nodded to Tamriel, Mercy, Pierce, Nerida, and Liri, all of whom were scattered across the field, helping to tend the plants. A few rows over, Tamriel made a comment Faye couldn't hear, his lips curling in a teasing grin. Mercy threw a handful of blueberries at Tamriel's face and laughed when they bounced off his nose and scattered in the dirt. Earlier that morning, her father had frozen with shock when Tamriel had—unprompted—offered to help with the harvest, and then stuttered something about propriety and kings kneeling in the dirt.

"I don't think you'll have much produce left if they continue throwing it around like that."

"Psh. Let them have their fun. They've been through so much."

"Faye!" her mother called.

Ino and Matthias were already sprawled in the back of the wagon, panting from the races, when she approached. Both of them were grinning. Faye almost did a double take at Ino as she climbed up onto the bench and claimed the space Cassia had left beside her mother. She leaned back as her mother snapped the reins and the two mules lurched forward. Although the threat of Nicholas's troops still hung over them, it was as if they'd stumbled into a sanctuary when they arrived at the farm.

"Will you sing to me?" Faye asked, and her mother looked at her in surprise. "One of Grandma's favorites?"

"You've never liked my singing voice."

"Maybe you've gotten better over the last eleven years," she said teasingly, nudging her mother's side. Growing up, her mother had always sung—when she was cooking, when she was helping Faye's father in the field, when she was folding laundry, when she was fretting over Fredric. Her singing voice wasn't great, but it was home. "Please?"

"For you? Anything." She turned to Ino and Matthias. "You might want to cover your ears."

"What about me?" Cassia asked.

"You're sitting too close," Faye replied. "There's no saving you."

Her mother laughed, the sound spilling over Faye and warming her to the core. Then she burst into song. It was just as terrible, and wonderful, as Faye remembered.

24
MERCY

That night, for the first time in weeks, Mercy didn't have a single nightmare.

When she awoke, Mercy lay there, curled up beside Tamriel with his arm draped across her waist. It had taken weeks for her to be able to sleep through the night. The memory of dream-Illynor slashing her throat still haunted her, but she forced the image out of her mind as she rolled over, nuzzling Tamriel gently awake.

He groaned, blinking at her drowsily. "Remind me why I said we'd leave at dawn."

"I don't know why. That really was foolish," she teased. "Do you think we can take the mattress with us so we don't have to sleep on the ground anymore?"

"If the soldiers track us down, we can hide behind it and use it as a shield. That will definitely stop the arrows from hitting us," he agreed. Through the closed door, they could hear the others moving around, preparing food and packing their belongings for the long ride ahead of them. "When you're my queen, you're going to have to stop me from making these foolish decisions. I'd risk being caught by Nicholas's soldiers just for a full night's sleep."

She rolled over and straddled his hips, her curls tumbling around her face as she grinned down at him. *That* snapped him awake. "Just think how amazing it will feel when we're finally back in the castle with the nice downy mattresses."

"You're right. Forget about the kingdom and crown. I'll fight Nicholas to the death just for a chance to enjoy those downy mattresses and silk sheets again." Desire filled his eyes as he reached up and ran his finger lightly over her exposed thigh. A shiver trailed down her spine. "And the sight of you lying naked between them, my beautiful queen."

"Oh—By the Creator, I'm going to pretend I didn't hear that," Calum called through the door, eliciting a grumble of annoyance from Tamriel. Before Mercy could scramble off the bed, he continued, chuckling, "Don't worry, I'm not going to come in. I would really, *really* rather not. Faye's mother sent me to tell you to get dressed and come to breakfast. We'll be leaving within the hour, as long as you two are finished with your...um...sexy talk."

As his footsteps faded down the hall, Mercy leaned down, kissed Tamriel, and slipped out of bed. "You heard him. Time to get up, Your Majesty." She pulled the blankets off him, causing him to jolt upright and snatch them back.

"So very cruel. I miss privacy."

"All the more reason to get on the road so we can gather our army."

They dressed quickly, then joined the others at the kitchen table, where a surprisingly large array of plates and platters had been set out. They were all quiet as they finished breakfast and began cleaning the dishes, preparing the horses, and doing last-minute checks of their provisions. The past few days had been a welcome escape, but now reality was creeping back in. They'd be going their separate ways from here—the Cirisians to the Islands, the Qadar to Gyr'malr, and Tamriel and the others to Feyndara. The next time they met, they'd be marching to war.

The sun had just begun to rise when they heard hooves thundering down the dirt road. Mercy looked up from securing Blackfoot's saddle just as Duomnodera and her warriors appeared around the bend. Her mouth dropped open when she saw the four people riding behind them.

A few feet away, Tamriel froze in the middle of shoving something into one of his mare's saddlebags. He turned wide, shocked eyes upon Duomnodera as her small company came to a halt before him. Sitting behind the High Mother, clad in blood-splattered armor, were Atlas, Julien, Akiva, and Kova.

"How... How are you alive?" Tamriel stammered, looking as if he'd just seen the ghosts of Mercy's parents again. "I thought you all died outside Sandori."

"Have a little faith in us, Your Majesty," Atlas said as he dismounted, grinning widely. "We're resourceful."

"You're my royal guard. How did no one kill you on sight? They had to know you were loyal to me."

"The battle was so chaotic no one could tell who was on what side. It was a mess." Julien shook his head. "After we saw that you had made it out alive, we pretended that we had been fighting on Nicholas's side all along. We told the commanders Nicholas had been paying us to spy on you and report back, and they didn't even question it. The fools. Meanwhile, the traitor was so absorbed in securing his nephew's place on the throne that he didn't even think to look for us."

Behind them, the front door creaked as it swung open.

They all turned to look as Seren Pierce, Nerida, and Liri stepped outside and went still at the sight of the royal guards.

"Atlas?" Nerida said, her eyes filling with tears.

Atlas's jaw dropped. "Mother? Father?"

He ran to them and threw his arms around them, letting out a sound somewhere between a laugh and a sob. Nerida burst into tears, clutching her son close. Mercy glanced over her shoulder to see Julien watching them with a proud smile.

"All this time, he thought they were dead," Julien told her, his smile growing when Pierce backed out of the embrace and wiped his eyes with a sleeve. "I thought it was going to destroy him."

"How did you get here? How did Duomnodera find you?"

"After the battle, we joined one of the troops tasked with finding you. When we heard about that ambush in Xilor, we knew you had to be nearby. So, we snuck out of camp late at night, grabbed our horses, and ran, hoping we would find you before the rest of our company did. Unfortunately, a few of them heard us leaving and chased after us, but we took care of them," he said, gesturing to the dried blood splattered across his breastplate. "We were a few miles from Fallmond when your patrols found us."

Tamriel clasped his hand, then did the same with Akiva and Kova. "It's good to have you back."

"It's good to be back, Your Majesty," Akiva said, beaming.

"How far back are the other soldiers in your company?"

"Not close enough to be of any concern. By the time they manage to track us, we'll be long gone."

Seren Pierce, Nerida, Liri, and Atlas returned to their group. As they neared Julian, Seren Pierce stopped at looked up at the guard with an unreadable expression. "Do you love my son?"

Julien stiffened, fearing a trick or insult. After Leitha Cain discovered them being intimate in the castle, she'd had Julien shipped off to Blackhills and Atlas stationed in Beggars' End to hide the fact that there were so-called 'Unnaturals' in the guard.

After a moment's hesitation, he straightened and said, "Yes, sir. I love him more than anything."

Pierce nodded. "It may take some time for me to get used to...this," he said, gesturing between Atlas and Julien, "but I'll do my best. Thank you for protecting him."

"It was an honor, Seren."

Mercy smiled as they clasped hands. Behind his father, Atlas beamed.

The rest of their small force gradually wandered over: Kaius with the Cirisians and runaway slaves, Duomnodera and her warriors, Tanni and the Daughters, Mercy's siblings, the apprentices. Calum greeted the royal guards warmly, which surprised Mercy. She'd almost forgotten that he had worked alongside Master Oliver before he left to join the Strykers. She could tell by his expression that he saw the suspicion in their eyes—and he was trying not to be hurt by it. He'd once been friends with many members of the guard, and he had ruined it with one terrible mistake.

Lastly, Faye joined them, once again clad in her leather armor, blades strapped to her hips, wrists, and thighs. Her parents trailed behind her. Her father offered Mercy a grim smile, his eyes shining, while her mother surveyed their troops with trepidation. "Be careful," Faye's mother said, pulling Faye and her father into a hug.

Faye nodded, clutching her mother tight. She didn't try to convince her mother that there was no need to worry. They all knew better than that. They had no idea what they would face in Queen Cerelia's court, but they had no other option, no other potential allies.

When they reached the edge of the group, the Cirisians parted to allow them to pass. Faye caught Mercy's eye and mouthed, *I'm fighting with you.* Relief and sadness warred within Mercy. Part of her was glad to have her friend by her side, but she'd never forgive herself if Faye didn't survive the battle.

Sensing her thoughts, Faye set her hands on Mercy's shoulders. "Don't worry about me so much. Through thick and thin, I'll be right beside you, sister. Always."

She smiled. "Always."

Faye's parents bowed to Tamriel, who was standing at the edge of the group, watching their friends embrace and exchange goodbyes. "I wish you success on your journey, Your Majesty," her father said, still insisting on addressing Tamriel by his title.

"Thank you—both of you. You have no idea how grateful I am for your hospitality." He turned and took Faye's mother's hands. She blushed when he pressed a kiss to the back of each one. "Once I reclaim my throne, I hope you will allow me to repay you for your generosity."

"Just keep our daughter safe," she said, absolutely melting at his charm. "That will be repayment enough."

"I'll do everything in my power to see that she makes it home to you," he assured her. He returned to his horse and swung himself up onto the saddle. His gaze traveled over each of them in turn, finally coming to rest on Mercy. A burst of pride filled her at the sight of him sitting there, surveying his army, so different from the cynical, brooding prince she had met so many months ago.

"We will meet here three weeks from today," he announced. "Gather as many soldiers as you can, and be safe traveling across the fishing sector. Most of Nicholas's troops will be hunting me, but if they recognize you, they won't hesitate to attack."

He straightened and forced a smile Mercy was certain fooled everyone but her. He'd be brave for them, but she knew that if any of them came to harm, he'd bear the pain as surely as if he'd been the one struck by the blade. "Four weeks from today, we'll march to Sandori and fight for our kingdom, for the freedom of every elven man, woman, and child of this country, and for the Islands' independence."

A cheer rose up around Mercy, and hope filled her. Whatever they would face in Feyndara, they'd make it through.

We will secure aid from Queen Cerelia, and reclaim Tamriel's throne.

Tamriel beamed at her as she climbed onto Blackfoot's saddle. While the elves moved toward their horses and began to mount, Faye paused to exchange a few quiet words with Kaius. Mercy couldn't make them out, but she didn't miss the brush of their fingers as Kaius turned to follow his clan members. She bit her lip to keep from grinning. She didn't know if anything would come of whatever was between them, but she hoped so.

Faye hugged her parents. Before she had a chance to pull away, the apprentices darted forward and wrapped their arms around all three of them, making Faye laugh in surprise.

"I don't want you to go!" Arabelle cried. "I want to come with you!"

Faye turned and cupped the girl's cheek. "Hush now. It's safer for you here. I promise not to have too grand an adventure without you." Then she bent down and mock-whispered to the three apprentices, "While I'm gone, I'm going to need you to look after the old man for me. Can you do that?"

Three heads bobbed, while Faye's father scoffed and feigned offense.

"I'll see you before you know it," Faye told them, then mounted her horse and joined Mercy, Tamriel, and Mercy's siblings by the dirt road. Tamriel's royal guards spread out around them.

Seren Pierce, Nerida, and Liri joined Faye's parents and

the apprentices beside the house. They had decided the night before to remain in Fallmond with Faye's parents, both to help in the field and the market as well as to keep an ear out for news from the capital. If they learned anything important, Seren Pierce would send a raven to Rhys, the capital of Feyndara.

"We'll be back soon," Julien whispered to Atlas, who nodded sadly. Mercy could only imagine how hard it was for him to leave so soon after learning that his family was alive, but they didn't have a choice. "They'll be safe here. Right now, the king needs our protection."

Duomnodera and her warriors were the first to leave. They'd be riding to the northern coast at the edge of the Howling Mountains and returning to Gyr'malr to gather warriors for Tamriel's army. As much as Mercy disliked watching the formidable creatures go, leaving Tamriel vulnerable, they needed soldiers more than they needed protection.

Once they'd disappeared around the bend in the road, it was the elves' turn. Kaius dipped his head in respect to Tamriel as he passed, leading the Cirisians and runaway slaves behind him. Mercy pretended not to see the sadness on Faye's face as she watched him leave; she had a feeling anything she could say to comfort her friend would only embarrass her. She had never seen Faye so...*enamored*...of anyone before.

Finally, Tamriel let out a long breath and turned to her. "Ready?"

She reached across the distance between their horses and grabbed his hand. She was clad in her black and silver armor once again, the chainmail shining under the light of the rising sun, her twin daggers strapped to her hips.

She looked back at the others. Matthias, bright, funny, and sarcastic. Ino, quiet, selfless, and strong. Cassia, whose stubbornness and short temper—both qualities Mercy possessed—made her rash at times, but who had protected her time and time again. Faye, her best friend, her sister in every way but blood. Calum, her half-brother who had been here since the beginning, who had started her on this strange, twisted journey. Most of the time she wanted to throttle him, but when he wasn't mocking her or plotting to have Tamriel killed, she found herself truly enjoying his company. And the Daughters, who... Well, Mercy didn't have much affection for them, but the Assassins *had* saved all their lives in Xilor.

Soon, they'd be marching to war, and she could think of no one else she would rather have fighting beside her.

"Yes," she said to Tamriel, squeezing his hand. "I'm ready."

25
PERCIVAL

Music drifted through the corridors as Percival walked toward the great hall, tugging at the hem of his fine black velvet doublet. While most of the nobles and courtiers tended to favor embroidered tunics, Nicholas had insisted he dress in a style 'befitting his new position'—which Percival had interpreted to mean 'like a fraud.' The doublet had been pilfered from Tamriel's wardrobe and altered to fit Percival's thinner frame and longer arms. He doubted Tamriel had ever worn it—it showed no signs of wear, not even a frayed thread or loose button—but stealing it still felt wrong.

He walked into the great hall and paused, his eyes widening at the opulence of the celebration. He had known his uncle was preparing to make a spectacle of the banquet, of course, but this was a tacky display of his family's wealth. The braziers in the center of the room were lit, the flames illuminating the bright, silky fabrics draped across the high, arched ceiling. Portraits and paintings in gilded frames adorned each wall. Slaves in black dresses or tunics and fitted pants wove their way through the throngs of people, platters of food and drink held aloft. The humans ignored them completely, save to reach out and snag a gold goblet or silver plate.

When a slave passed him with a platter of wine-filled goblets, Percival grabbed one and drained it to the dregs. If he was to deal with his uncle, backstabbing nobles, and the prospect of a lifetime trapped in a loveless marriage, he was going to need it.

"I would prefer if you did not get drunk tonight."

He jumped when Riona appeared beside him, breathtaking in an emerald gown. *Celeste's favorite color.* The thought came to him unbidden, and he cringed inwardly. He shouldn't have been thinking of her. He shouldn't have thought of her half as often as he did. Riona frowned as he turned and handed the goblet to a passing slave. "I'm not getting drunk. It's just to help me through the night."

"Am I not pleasant enough company?" she asked, cocking her head. Every thought left his head when the firelight caught the gold pigment across her lids and full lips. In her fine silk gown—which, he did not fail to notice, clung to every curve of her body—and clinking gold bracelets, she looked ethereal.

He flushed and began to sputter an apology, but she merely laughed and slipped her arm into his. "I'm only joking. Although I would appreciate it if you stopped looking at me like you expect me to start speaking in tongues. I am to be your wife soon, you know."

"I'm sorry. I'm just nervous."

"Me too." She leaned in and lowered her voice conspiratorially. "I hate these mindless state functions. Such a waste of time and money."

"Really? I would have thought that you— Well, looking like that..." He bit his tongue, cursing himself for a fool, and wished she would stop looking at him with her piercing blue eyes. *How hard is it to hold a simple conversation?*

"You think because I'm pretty I enjoy these things? You think I like the way the nobles fawn over me? It's just like back home. I'm nothing more than a pretty doll to them, something to be paraded about when it suits them. I will admit, however, that I do enjoy the dresses." She ran a hand down the shiny silk, the movement drawing his attention to a pendant he hadn't noticed before. It was unlike any piece of jewelry he had ever seen: it looked like a chip of some kind of black stone or metal, hanging from a golden chain. The jagged edge of the pendant looked sharp enough to cut.

"That's an unusual necklace."

Her hand flew up to it. "It was my mother's. I never take it off."

He heard the note of sadness in her voice and politely let the subject drop.

Arm in arm, they made their way toward the throne room, but were stopped every few steps by some noble wishing them congratulations on their upcoming marriage. With each one, Percival felt his mood drop. More than anything, he would have loved to hide out in the library until the celebration was over.

His uncle, however, would not find that behavior fitting for a king.

Resigned to his role, he smiled at every passing face, accepted every well-wish with grace, and engaged in enough small talk to last him the rest of his life. For the most part, it was easy, if a little boring; at some point in the conversation, all attention turned to his beautiful bride-to-be, and all he had to do was look attentive while she charmed the court one noble at a time.

After what felt like an eternity, they arrived at the throne room. A line of tables laden with more dishes than he could possibly name ran up the center of the room. Another table —presumably for Nicholas, Percival, Riona, and Lord

Winslow—was set atop the dais before the throne, complete with gold plates, bowls, goblets, and utensils. Even the napkins had been crafted of cloth-of-gold.

"I think my uncle wants the court to match your jewelry," Percival said, nodding to the splashes of gold around the room.

"Apparently."

The musicians continued playing as Percival and Riona approached the head table, but he noticed the conversations around them hush whenever they passed one of the many tables scattered throughout the room. Every pair of eyes latched onto him and his wife-to-be. He forced himself to stand tall as, beside him, Riona smiled and waved at the young noblewomen enviously admiring her dress. Percival stiffened when he caught a group of men staring at Riona lecherously. Each of them was old enough to be her father.

"Relax," she murmured, just loud enough for him to hear over the music. Her smile never faltered. "It's all part of being a woman in the court."

"They shouldn't be looking at you like that."

"You looked at me like that when I arrived."

Heat crept up his neck. He prayed it did not show on his face. "I was surprised. I wasn't *lewd*."

"Whatever you were, don't worry about it. If they try anything, I'll put them in their places. I'm hardly helpless."

When they reached the table, Percival pulled her chair out for her. She sank into it gracefully, fanning her skirt out as he claimed his seat beside her.

"It's comforting to know my future husband is such a gentleman," Riona teased, and he offered her a tight smile before looking away. Any more marriage talk and he might need another glass of wine. Or two. Or ten.

After a few minutes, Nicholas and Lord Winslow joined them. Dozens of slaves flooded the room, each picking up a platter from the center table and presenting it to them. After Percival and the others had their pick of the dishes, the slaves circulated around the room and served the nobles. His plate was filled to overflowing in no time. He eyed the central table and bit back a groan. They hadn't even finished serving the first course. From the looks of it, they'd be here until dawn, and *still* have leftovers.

He focused on his plate as he ate, listening to the musicians play and the nobles chatter among themselves. As much as he wanted to down another glass of wine, he needed to keep his wits about him if he was to continue playing his uncle's game. More than that, he couldn't make a fool of himself. He would never do that to Riona. He may not want to marry her, but she was a foreigner in this kingdom. He was not so careless or cruel as to embarrass her in front of her future court.

Riona leaned over during the third course and whispered, "Do you really find me so repulsive you would rather stare at your plate than speak with me?" There was no venom in her words—only curiosity. It made him feel even worse for having ignored her.

"I'm sorry," he responded, clutching his fork and knife tightly. "I just...don't know what I'm doing. I wasn't meant for court life."

On his right, Nicholas made a sound of disapproval.

Percival closed his eyes, scowling. "I'm *trying*."

"Not hard enough."

"I think you're doing marvelously," Riona said with a pointed look at Nicholas. He merely sniffed and resumed eating.

The evening dragged on. Percival picked at his plate halfheartedly, politely engaging Riona and Lord Winslow in conversation until the slaves finished serving the seemingly endless courses. Several slaves stepped forward and cleared the plates from the three closest tables. Once they finished, a half-dozen guards dragged the tables to the sided of the room to provide space for dancing. As the music swelled, countless young couples approached the head table, bowed and offered their congratulations to Percival and Riona, then began dancing, the women's glittering skirts swishing in flashes of color and light.

When the last noble rose and strode away, Percival let his forced smile drop, his cheeks aching. "How are you so good at this?" he whispered to Riona, whose grin had been nothing short of radiant the entire night.

"Lots of practice," she responded. She looked at the musicians in the corner, who were playing a fast-paced, lighthearted tune, and a wistful expression came over her face.

Percival stood, his chair scraping against the stone, and held out a hand to Riona. "Would... Would you like to dance, my lady?"

Her eyes widened in surprise, then she smiled and stood, accepting his offered hand. "It would be my honor, Your Majesty."

He could feel Nicholas's stare on his back as he led Riona to the dance floor. Lord Winslow leaned over to murmur something to Nicholas as Riona turned to face him, her eyes sparkling with excitement. *See, Uncle? I can play your game. I can play the lovesick king.* Percival slipped a hand around her waist. They joined the dancing couples, quickly losing themselves in the quick, intricate steps.

Riona's smile grew as they swept across the floor, perfectly in sync with the dancers around them. Percival's tense, stiff posture soon relaxed, eased away by the song and the joy on his future bride's face. The nobles who weren't dancing had gathered around them and were clapping or stomping along to the beat. Several of them could not seem to take their eyes off Riona—but, unlike the creepy men from earlier, there was nothing lascivious or possessive about their gazes. They simply delighted in her beauty, her easy smile, her effortless grace. She was enchanting.

As they completed another circle around the dance floor, Percival caught his uncle's eye. The corner of Nicholas's mouth was lifted in an almost-smile, and he gave Percival a small, approving nod.

Riona leaned forward and said over the music, "You're an excellent dancer."

"As are you." It was true; every movement they made was perfectly executed, perfectly timed. Riona's shoulders were back, her chin high, her steps precise.

"If my position did not call me to court so often, I would have chosen to be a dancer. The Royal Theater of Innislee always hosts traveling plays, musicians, and dancers. When I was younger, I used to beg my father to take me there every week. I didn't care if I saw the same play a dozen times. I just enjoyed losing myself in the story—in the fantasy of it all."

He nodded. That was the same reason he had fallen in love with reading.

"Since I am bound to the court, however, I sponsor the training of the young girls who cannot afford dance lessons. Oh, you should see them perform at the spring's-end recital. It makes my heart swell just to see how happy they all are."

Again, sorrow flashed across her face for the briefest second, but she quickly hid it behind a smile. Sympathy flooded Percival. After the wedding, she would be living here, in the capital, with him. He had not even considered how much she was giving up to come to Beltharos. Her entire life was in Rivosa.

Percival spun her, and when she was again in his arms, he said, "Next spring, I would be honored to accompany you to their recital, if you will allow me."

She beamed at him, clearly surprised by his response. "It would be my pleasure, Your Majesty."

The next day, Percival glanced over his shoulder as he neared the shipping district, certain that his uncle had sent a guard to follow him and report back. Nicholas had finally given him permission to oversee their family's fabric trading business, even going so far as allowing him to leave the castle for the first time since the coronation. Apparently, he had been playing his role as the bored puppet-king well enough that Nicholas saw no harm in granting his request. Nicholas had even relaxed Percival's guard.

He was certain that was what his uncle wanted him to *think*, at least.

Percival scanned the busy street again. As far as he could see, no one was following him, but he knew his uncle better than that. There had to be royal guards lurking in the alleys, or mingling with the shoppers and pedestrians. No matter how useless he thought Percival was, Nicholas wouldn't let him wander the city alone.

Never underestimate your enemy. Never underestimate what he will do to win. Nicholas had said that over and over throughout Percival's childhood—most often when the friends he had made during the war came to visit their estate in Westwater. They had sat around the dining table for hours after dinner, drinking and reminiscing, and Nicholas had delighted in telling Percival stories of his victories. He could still picture the twinkle in Nicholas's good eye, could still hear the sounds of the men's laughter, could still remember stretching out before the fireplace and falling asleep to the rumble of his uncle's deep voice. He had never tired of his uncle's tales. They reminded him of the adventures of the valiant knights in his books, but his uncle was *real*. He was a real hero. And he had been *Percival's* hero.

When he arrived at the warehouse, he checked over his shoulder once more before stepping inside, cursing himself for his paranoia. Even if guards were following him, they wouldn't see him doing anything worthy of suspicion. As far as they knew, he was just doing this to fill his free time.

"Ah, Your Majesty, what an honor it is to see you again!" The supervisor of the warehouse, a portly, red-faced man named Levi, grinned widely as he made his way through the maze of boxes and shelves. He clasped Percival's hand and shook it vigorously. "It's been a long time since I last saw you, lad. Ten years, I think?"

"I believe so, yes. I'm sure my uncle told you I'll be overseeing this business on his behalf from now on."

"Oh, yes, Your Majesty. I'm delighted to be working with you. Although I'm not sure why you would choose to spend your time in this dingy place when you could be up in that nice castle. Running the country doesn't keep you busy enough?"

"Believe me, the castle gets old quickly. What's inventory like?" He started down the nearest row of boxes, eager to move the conversation away from his uncle and the kingdom.

"We're well-stocked. Just waiting on a shipment of Rivosi lace from Ravenglen. The workers ran into some trouble near the border, but they've assured me that none of the product was compromised. They should be arriving in a few days."

Levi continued yapping as Percival wandered the rows of boxes and shelves, inspecting the layout of the warehouse and asking questions about shipments and orders. Levi answered every one of his inquiries knowledgeably—as talkative and oblivious as the man was, Percival had to admit he knew the business well. When he finished exploring the first floor, they continued to the second, then the third. By the time they returned to the stairs, Levi's round cheeks had turned pink, and he was puffing from the quick pace Percival had set.

"I need a moment to catch my breath, Your Majesty. I'm sorry." He bent forward and braced his hands on his knees. "I'm not as young or thin as I used to be. More suited to sitting behind a desk these days, I'm afraid."

"Not a problem at all. Let's go to your office and you can tell me a little more about the business." Percival led the way down the stairs, being careful to keep his voice casual when he said, "I know many businesses around here stopped shipping to the fishing sector after the Cirisians' attacks. How many ships do we send east, on average?" If he and Celeste could get the runaway slaves out of the city, the ships would take them straight to the coast. From there, it would only be a short trek to the Islands—to freedom. The hardest part would be sneaking them past his uncle's guards.

"A week? One, maybe two. We lost a lot of business after Graystone and the other cities were destroyed, but we still have quite a few partners in Cyrna, Xilor, and Feyndara."

"And how well guarded are they?" *How hard will it be to sneak the slaves on board?*

"A half-dozen men for the really expensive shipments, not including the crew. Three for the rest."

Percival nodded, committing everything he had learned to memory. It wouldn't be easy hiding runaway slaves from a half-dozen guards, but after seeing Celeste trick the castle guards and scale the wall, he trusted in her ability to get them on board. Now he just needed to find out when the next shipment was going out.

Levi led him into the office, chattering on about some aspect of the textile industry or another. Percival pretended to listen as he took in the mess of papers scattered across the desktop. Parchment was everywhere: notes on inventory, shipment information, receipts and invoices, letters, calendars, workers' schedules. How Levi managed to find anything in the chaos was a mystery.

"Do you have a list of upcoming shipments?"

"Of course I do! Just, ah—Just a second." Levi frowned thoughtfully at the stacks of papers, then began shuffling through them. After several minutes, he pulled one out and presented it to Percival. "Told you I have it."

"Thank you." He scanned the list. There weren't many ships going east, but the first one went out that night. It would be tight—with a guard no doubt following him, he couldn't go anywhere near the End; he'd need to send Celeste to gather supplies and find the slaves Hero and Ketojan had procured.

"All right, I think I've seen everything I need. I'll let you know if I have any more questions." He shook Levi's hand again and smiled to himself as he stepped outside and started back toward the castle. This could turn out to be a foolish, dangerous plan, but if there was even a slight chance that he could help the slaves escape, he had to try.

He passed an alley, and movement in his periphery caught his attention. He stopped and turned around, but when he peered down the alley, it was empty. "Is someone there?"

No response came, and he felt a little foolish for talking to empty air. His paranoia was getting the better of him. Of course his uncle had sent a guard to watch him. He hadn't thought Nicholas would care whether he saw the guard, though.

Percival shook his head and hurried back to the castle, his pace a little quicker than before. He didn't see anyone out of the corner of his eye again, but he still had the distinct feeling of being watched the entire walk to the castle.

26

TAMRIEL

Relief flooded Tamriel when Cowayne appeared before them, tall masts and white sails peeking out over the roofs of the houses. Like Fishers' Cross, it had started as a small fishing town hundreds of years ago, but its position at the junction of the Abraxas Sea and the Bluejet River had made it a popular stop for sailors, merchants, and travelers alike. Before the Cirisian Wars, Feyndarans and Beltharans had come and gone from each other's shores, bringing coin and trade across the sea. Since Queen Cerelia closed her country to Beltharans, however, the village had lost a good portion of its population. Instead of sailing, many of the villagers had moved inland to farm along the rivers or work in larger cities.

Fortunately, a fair number of trading companies and fishermen still used the docks. While few Beltharan merchants were *officially* allowed into Feyndara, Tamriel knew there were plenty who smuggled goods in and out of the country. There was a lot of coin in trade, and a lot of people who were willing to risk being caught by the guards in order to earn some.

Hopefully, Tamriel and the others would find one willing to transport them across the sea.

He slowed his horse and looked at Calum as they neared the edge of town. "Do you remember the names of any of the men who take the Strykers to Feyndara?"

"I remember one. Korin. He's not a smuggler, though, so I don't know if he'll agree to take us to Feyndara considering the bounties on our heads. He's a greedy bastard."

Mercy touched the hilt of one of the daggers at her hips. "I'm sure he could be persuaded to help."

Tamriel rolled his eyes. "You can pressure him, but don't hurt him. The last thing we need is you drawing the attention of the guards."

"Fine." She glanced back and shot Faye a look that said she might not stick to that agreement—a look Tamriel chose to ignore.

They rode in silence through the streets. The guards, wearing lightweight cloaks to hide their armor, split from their group and continued down a parallel side street, being careful to keep Tamriel and the others within sight as much as possible. Tamriel hoped they would not stumble into any of Nicholas's men. They were still clad in their heavy armor— like the guards, they had donned loose, simple cloaks—but they no longer had the Cirisians or Qadar to cover them in a fight.

They passed a tavern, loud voices spilling out even in the middle of the day, and he deliberately avoided looking at the posters nailed to the front doors. He already knew what they contained: drawings of him, Calum, and Mercy, along with information about their bounties. He was grateful for the fact that, after so much time on the road, he looked nothing like the king in the drawing. His hair hung loose and unkempt, his clothing was worn and rumpled, scruff covered his jaw, and his skin was deeply tanned and underscored with shadows. The others didn't look any better.

Fortunately, no one they passed paid them any heed as they rode to the harbor. Merchants waved to them and shouted about their deals, and pedestrians were careful to move around their tall horses, but no one so much as glanced at them twice.

"He usually docks over there," Calum said, pointing down the shore. After a moment of searching, the tension on his face relaxed. "Thank the Creator, he's here."

They dismounted, and Tamriel gestured for the others to wait with the horses. He, Faye, and Mercy were careful to remain behind Calum as they approached Korin's ship. He wordlessly sent up a prayer that no one would recognize them, but as they neared the dock, he realized he needn't have worried. Most of the sailors around them were too busy loading or unloading their ships to notice a few bedraggled travelers.

"Korin!" Calum called as they walked toward the gangplank, his voice light and casual. He lifted a hand to his eyes to block the sun's glare and waved to a man standing on the deck of the ship. He was short, stocky, and barefoot, clad in a worn linen tunic and cropped pants. Curly blond hair poked out from below his floppy straw hat.

"Who are you?" He walked to the edge of the ship and jumped onto the dock. "Do I know you?"

"I'm a friend of Hewlin's. I need a favor."

The man studied Tamriel, Mercy, and Faye, his eyes narrowing. Tamriel stiffened, his heart pounding against his ribcage. The sight of the wanted posters flashed through his mind. *He knows. He recognizes us.* They could bribe him not to turn them over to the guards...if they had any money.

"Who're they?" Korin asked, peering up at Calum with a frown. Beside Tamriel, Mercy reached for one of the daggers hidden below her tunic. He lightly pressed his foot on top of hers in warning.

"They're the favor," Calum said, still smiling. "Look, why don't I buy you a pint at the tavern and we'll talk about it. Hm?"

Korin stared at them for a moment longer. Suddenly, realization transformed his face. "The king! He's—*Mmph!*"

He sputtered as Calum clapped a hand over his mouth. "Yes, he's the king," Calum whispered, never letting the smile drop. When he shifted, Tamriel saw the flash of silver in Calum's palm—a blade, pressed to Korin's stomach. *Sneaky bastard,* he thought, impressed. "He's also wanted by just about every guard in this city, which is why you need to keep your voice down. Can you do that for me?"

Korin nodded, and Calum stepped back, grinning. "Good. We need passage to Feyndara, and we're willing to pay handsomely for it."

"What business could you have in Feyndara?"

"That isn't your concern. Will you take us across the sea or not?"

"Beltharans aren't allowed on Feyndaran soil. Not most of us, anyway." It wasn't quite a refusal. Korin's eyes swept over Tamriel and the others, glittering hungrily. "How much are you willing to pay?"

"Double the bounty," Tamriel said.

"Let's see it."

"We don't have the money with us, you idiot," Calum cut in, his expression souring. "Every bandit on the king's highway would be all over us. You'll get your pay when he has his kingdom back. Now, do we have a deal or not?"

Korin hesitated, clearly torn between the prospect of coin now or double later. While the man deliberated, Calum glanced over his shoulder, and Tamriel's stomach dropped when fear flashed across his cousin's face. Tamriel followed his eyes to four soldiers in full metal armor walking toward them. They hadn't spotted them—that much was clear by their easy pace—but all it would take was a shout from Korin.

"Let's find another sailor to take us across the sea," Tamriel said, growing impatient and nervous. With their numbers, they could take out the guards easily, but word of the fight would get back to Nicholas. It wouldn't take him long to figure out why Tamriel had been spotted at the docks in Cowayne.

"No. The more people know you're here, the greater the chance of us being discovered. Korin will take us. He's just wondering how much more money he can squeeze out of you to keep your secret," Calum responded, eyeing the sailor with distaste.

Mercy shouldered past them. "If you enjoy having all your blood *inside* your body, I would accept the king's generous offer," she snarled at Korin. She didn't pull her blades; she didn't need to. Her tone said enough about her intentions.

Korin swallowed, his throat bobbing. Before he could answer, a deep voice behind them said, "Is there a problem here?"

Tamriel froze. Mercy reached into her cloak as Faye palmed one of her throwing knives. Calum shot them a warning look before turning to face the stranger. "No, of course no—" He paused in the middle of his sentence, a crooked grin splitting his face. "What are you *doing* here?"

Hearing the joy in his voice, they all turned to see Nerran, Hewlin, Amir, and Oren standing at the end of the dock. Nerran started to bow to Tamriel, but Amir grabbed his shoulder to stop him. Hewlin smacked the back of his head.

"Are you trying to get us all killed?" he hissed, before turning to Tamriel. "We left the capital after the massacre to continue our work in Rhys. We came here to speak to Korin about taking us to Feyndara, but it seems you beat us to it."

"Join us."

"Wait just a minute—" Korin began, stepping forward. Mercy unsheathed a dagger and he flinched, taking a step back. "Put the blade away, girl. I'm not going to do anything foolish. If I called out to the guards, you'd gut me. I'm not that stupid. But I also never said that I would take you to Feyndara. Nicholas Comyn has men looking for you all over. You can promise me all the money you want, but if you can't pay me first, I'm not taking you across the sea. There's no point in doing business with a dead man."

"How much did you offer him?" Hewlin asked.

"Double the bounty," Tamriel responded. He turned to Korin. "There must be some arrangement—"

There was a jangle of coins, then a coin purse went flying over his head. Korin reached up and caught it in one hand.

"There's your deposit," Hewlin said, his voice laced with a warning. "When we get to Feyndara, you'll get the rest, including a priceless Stryker-made sword. How's that?"

Korin pocketed the purse and straightened his hat. "That's a start. Climb aboard."

They followed him onto the ship. The entire time, Mercy muttered rude things about Korin under her breath. Faye and Nerran joined in as Korin led them below deck and showed them to their sleeping quarters—a large room with nothing but a few barrels and several hammocks strung up from posts.

"It's going to be tight," Korin said, gesturing to the room, "but I wasn't planning on having so many people on my ship. I still need places for my crew to sleep."

"No crew. We'll man it ourselves," Tamriel cut in. The others nodded—even Mercy and Faye, who, he was certain, had absolutely no idea how to sail. No matter. They'd learn quickly. It was better than trusting strangers not to give them away.

"Fine. I have a few more supplies to purchase, and then we'll be off."

"Amir and Oren will help you," Hewlin said immediately.

"So will my guards," Tamriel added.

Korin grumbled something about them not trusting him, but he didn't argue. He led Amir and Oren back up to the deck, leaving the rest of them to wait.

Calum immediately threw his arms around Hewlin and Nerran. "I can't believe you're here. For once, the Creator saw fit to give us *good* luck." He pulled back, looking ashamed. "The last time you saw me, I— My father—"

"You helped us get away from that crazy Cirisian girl," Nerran interrupted. "I still don't understand everything you said about your father controlling you or whatever, but I'm sorry we didn't see it sooner. I'm sorry we didn't help you."

"Forgiven. Completely forgiven." Calum smiled as he sank into one of the hammocks, seeming at ease for the first time in a long while. Until now, Tamriel had not realized how much the Strykers meant to his cousin, but it was obvious from Calum's relief that they were his family as much as Tamriel and Mercy. Perhaps more so. After all, he had never tried to kill *them*.

"You have to tell us everything that happened after we parted," Oren said, Amir nodding along.

Calum laughed. While they chatted, Tamriel turned to Mercy and Faye, both of whom were still gazing at the ladder Korin had just taken up to the deck with murderous looks on their faces. "I'm not going to be able to tolerate him long enough to reach Feyndara," Mercy muttered.

"Neither will I," Faye agreed.

"He wouldn't be my first choice as a captain, but he's willing to take us to Feyndara, and that's what's most important now," Tamriel said. "If the weather holds up, we'll reach

Feyndara in about a week. You only have to put up with him for that long."

"A week? I hate him after five minutes."

"Then it's a good thing we'll be on the open sea. Plenty of places to hide a body." Tamriel said it lightly, jokingly, but her expression turned contemplative. "Mercy, you can't kill him. Don't make me confiscate your daggers."

She laughed and crossed her arms over her chest. "I'd like to see you try."

27

MERCY

By some miracle, Mercy didn't gut Korin during their journey to Feyndara. Once they were on the sea and well away from Nicholas's soldiers, Korin kept mostly to himself, probably spending his free time counting the coins Hewlin had given him to pay for their passage.

From the moment they set sail, Mercy loved being on the open sea—the scent of the sea-salt air, the rush of the wind, the sparkle of sunlight on the water—but not everyone in their group fared as well as she. Calum and Atlas turned a sickly shade of green as soon as Beltharos faded behind them, and neither managed to keep down a meal longer than fifteen minutes. The Strykers comforted them when they felt like being kind and, when they didn't, teased them mercilessly. Even though their mocking could be harsh, it was clear Calum was glad to have them around. When they were not manning the ship, they reminisced about their year together, and Hewlin regaled them with stories of his travels during his youth.

The Daughters didn't speak to anyone, which didn't bother Mercy in the slightest. She was grateful to them for agreeing to fight for Tamriel, but that didn't mean she enjoyed having them around. The memories of their fists and feet striking her during her "second Trial" were still too raw.

Every day, Mercy, Faye, and Ino practiced sparring on the deck, daggers and swords flashing under the bright sunlight. The rocking of the ship provided a welcome challenge, especially on the third day of their journey, when the wind picked up and sent choppy waves slamming into the side of the ship. Ino might have been taller and stronger, but he was no match for the speed of the girls. More often than not, he was the first one to get knocked on his ass. Cassia sat on the side with Kova, Matthias, and Tamriel. The four of them offered feedback and laughed whenever someone snapped something snarky in response to their corrections.

For one blissful week, their lives were peaceful—happy even, considering the circumstances.

Then Korin spotted land.

Calum's feet hit the dock first, followed by Atlas's a second later.

"Thank the Creator," Atlas groaned, dropping to his knees. "I've never been so happy to see grass."

Julien clapped a hand on his shoulder. "Don't get too comfortable here. They still hate our guts."

One by one, they made their way onto the dock. A half-dozen Feyndaran guards in shining armor were already waiting for them at the end, their hands on the grips of their swords.

The eldest studied them with narrowed eyes, then turned to Korin. "As trusted traders and crafters, you and the Strykers are welcome on our queen's land, but who are these strangers? I've never seen them before."

"Do you remember the faces of everyone you see?" Calum asked skeptically, his face still tinged a faint green.

The guard leveled him a flat stare. "Yes."

"I am King Tamriel Myrellis," Tamriel said, pushing his way to the front of the group. "I've come to ask for an audience with Queen Cerelia about an urgent matter concerning my kingdom."

"Could the matter possibly be the fact that it is no longer *your* kingdom?"

"Show some respect," Ino snapped.

"I will not show respect to my queen's enemy."

"Hate me all you like, but I must speak to your queen," Tamriel said again, stepping between Ino and the guard. "Take us to her."

"Hmph. Very well."

The guards surrounded them. The eldest led them away from the docks, toward the heart of the city. Mercy couldn't help but gape as they made their way down the street. She'd known that Feyndara was densely forested, but she had never pictured it like *this*. Even inside the capital city, the trees lining the streets were tall—hundreds of feet tall—and thick-trunked, their canopies sending dappled light dancing over the cobblestones. Every building they passed was made of the same dark brown wood as the surrounding trees, and some of them—some of them were *in trees*.

The leader noticed her watching a child climbing down the ladder from one of the houses. "When one lives in a place as naturally beautiful as this, one wishes to keep it as close to nature as possible. By building in the trees, we're able to keep from cutting down too much of the forest."

"That's amazing," she responded, unable to hide the awe in her voice. Beside her, Tamriel tried to keep his expression impassive, unimpressed, but even his court-made mask was no match for the wonder of this city in the trees.

As they neared the heart of the city, it began to resemble Sandori. The buildings were wood instead of stone, but they were built in a similar style: tall and narrow, with sharply pitched roofs and shuttered windows. When they passed a market, Tamriel turned back to the Strykers and Korin, the latter of whom had been muttering about being paid since they left the docks. "Why don't you grab something to eat while we speak to the queen? We'll meet up with you later."

After they left, Tamriel and the others hired a few carriages from a stand by the market, and a few minutes later, they arrived before the castle. Mercy stepped out and tipped her head back to stare at the gleaming spires and tall turrets. Unlike the rest of the city, the castle was gray stone, with massive stained glass windows that spanned multiple floors. On foot, they passed through a gate and entered the lavish gardens surrounding the castle, rife with wildflowers, rose bushes, carefully-pruned hedges, and multiple ponds. A thin stream divided the grounds in two, and as they crossed the small, ornate bridge spanning the gap, Mercy peered down to see several colorful fish peeking out from the water, wide, unblinking eyes staring up at their party as they passed.

"Her Majesty's great-grandfather designed this garden for his eldest daughter, Acantha," one of the guards said with obvious pride. "She spent full days exploring the forests surrounding the city when she was a child and always told him about the beautiful things she found there. He had this designed, then dedicated to her on her sixteenth birthday."

"We may need to rethink the castle's landscaping when we return to Sandori," Tamriel whispered to her, and she nodded.

The guards escorted them through the ornate castle doors —the dark wood accented with swirling veins of gold and silver —and into the great hall. It was similar to the one in Myrellis Castle, with a soaring ceiling and stone supports lining either side of the room, but several of the walls were covered in murals of the forest, past Feyndaran rulers, and scenes from the Book of the Creator. The guard sent a servant to alert the queen of their request for an audience. While they awaited her response, Tamriel, Calum, and the royal guards turned to speak quietly with one another—likely to discuss how they were going to approach petitioning the queen for aid. Mercy and her siblings wandered around the room, admiring the murals.

"They're beautiful," Cassia murmured, staring up at a floor-to-ceiling painting of the past four Aasa queens. The portraits gazed down at them, their delicate, lovely faces betraying no emotion. Mercy recognized the women from her studies of Feyndaran history at the Keep:

Minerva, who ruled the country for only four years before passing away after the birth of her third child.

Acantha, who helped establish the Church of the Creator in Feyndara, and for whom the magnificent garden outside was dedicated.

Undine, who started the first Cirisian War.

Cerelia, who unknowingly held the fate of Tamriel's throne in her hands.

She studied the painting of Queen Cerelia, who looked to be about twenty-five. Her slate-gray eyes were striking coupled with her dark, wavy hair, pale skin, and deep violet gown. A crown of gold and rubies sat atop her carefully coiffed curls, the paint still bright and shiny even after decades.

"Her Majesty has agreed to grant you an audience," a servant called from the doorway. "She will see you now."

Mercy and her siblings followed the others into the throne room. Guards in full armor lined the room, a rose-and-thorn sigil—the Feyndaran royal crest—emblazoned on their breastplates and the pommels of their swords. Queen Cerelia was seated atop a wooden throne carved into a tangle of rose vines, her dark blue skirt fanned out around her legs. Several members of her family flanked her on either side. She watched in silence as Mercy and the others dropped into low bows before her.

Mercy studied the queen through her lashes. Although Cerelia was old—far older than any elf or human Mercy had ever met, since Daughters of the Guild did not often have the luxury of long lifespans—she had aged well. Her eyes were sharp and alert, the color of steel, and her gray hair hung in gentle waves all the way to the floor.

"Rise and tell me why you have come," Cerelia said, her voice echoing through the room.

Tamriel straightened. "Your Majesty, my kingdom has been stolen from me. I've come to ask for aid in reclaiming my throne."

"How did you allow this to happen?"

In her periphery, Mercy saw annoyance flash through Tamriel's eyes. "Your Majesty, if you're implying this was a result of my own shortcomings, I must inform you my only fault was in trusting my general and the oath of fealty he swore to my family. Several weeks ago, I led an army to Kismoro Keep to defeat the Assassins' Guild and free my country's future queen. I was unaware that my general had arranged to have my supporters murdered and my army turn on me. When we returned to the city, he and his traitorous soldiers attacked us," he said, gesturing to Mercy and the others. "We only narrowly escaped. While we have been on the run, he has taken over the kingdom and placed his nephew on the throne."

One of the men on the dais stepped forward and whispered something to the queen. She nodded and dismissed him with a wave before turning her attention to Tamriel. "Nicholas Comyn stole your throne. If I'm not mistaken, his family has been one of the greatest supporters of the Myrellis line. What changed?"

"He learned that I plan to free the slaves and help the Cirisor Islands establish itself as an independent country."

Several of the queen's family members exchanged surprised looks, but the queen's expression didn't change. "You do not have the power to give the Islands independence, for they do not belong to you. The land rightfully belongs to Feyndara."

"Some history books would say otherwise," Tamriel countered. "Both our countries have lost men to the wars. It is in our best interests to work together to establish the Islands as their own country, but we can only do that if I am on the throne. Nicholas Comyn will never relent. He will fight you for every inch of land, and you will lose countless soldiers. It won't be long before you lose the war, as well."

"He nearly defeated us before," one of the men said. "Perhaps it would be wise to—"

"If I wanted your counsel, General Cadriel, I would have asked for it," Cerelia interrupted, shooting her son a warning look. Cadriel nodded and stepped back to join the others as the queen again looked to Tamriel. "How many soldiers do you have?"

Here, Tamriel faltered. It was only for a second, but Mercy could tell by the narrowing of the queen's eyes that she had seen it. Her chest constricted in fear. *Don't turn us away. Help us. Help us reclaim Tamriel's kingdom,* she silently implored her.

"I am allied with a Cirisian leader and a High Mother of Gyr'malr. Both are currently gathering troops from their respective lands and will be joining us outside Sandori before the battle."

"So you have no soldiers of your own."

"I— Well, no," Tamriel admitted. Mercy moved closer,

wishing she could offer him help. "None except the people here with me. That is why I have come to ask you for aid. I would be greatly indebted to you if you help me reclaim my throne. Together, we could put all the years of animosity between our countries behind us."

Queen Cerelia drummed her fingernails on the arm of her throne. She was quiet for a few moments before she finally said, "I shall consider it. In the meantime, you will stay in the castle and dine with me and my family as my guests tonight. I would like to learn more about your proposal before I make a decision, but you look like you could use a meal and some rest. Lady Marieve will escort you to your rooms." She gestured to the young woman standing near the edge of the dais, clad in a beautiful gown of white lace. Marieve smiled and nodded gracefully. Mercy studied her face—the delicate features, the high cheekbones, the dark brown hair. Thank the Creator Marieve had never been to Beltharos, because Mercy never would have been able to impersonate her if she had attended the king's court. They looked nothing alike.

Tamriel bowed. "Thank you, Your Majesty."

The rest of them followed his lead, offering their gratitude. Marieve descended the steps of the dais and started toward the great hall. As they turned to leave, however, Queen Cerelia leaned forward and said, "You—the elven Assassin."

Mercy paused and turned around. "Yes, Your Majesty?"

Is she angry I impersonated her granddaughter? Does she even know about that?

"I've heard quite a lot about you—the Assassin who won the prince's heart. I would like to know more. Come to my chambers before dinner so we may speak in private."

It was not a question, but Mercy nodded and bowed anyway. "Yes, Your Majesty. It would be my honor."

28
PERCIVAL

Percival stared down at the door handle to the study and wavered, his stomach twisting into knots. The servant who had delivered the summons from Nicholas had not said anything more than *Your uncle wishes to speak to you,* but Percival had not missed the note of fear in the young man's voice.

He knows.

Percival swallowed tightly. He and Celeste had only been helping the slaves for a week now, but every time his uncle looked at him, he feared that Nicholas could see the truth on his face. Every time he heard a guard's footsteps outside his room, terror closed a cold fist around his heart. Every time, he became convinced the guards had come to drag him down to the dungeon.

You're just being paranoid, he reminded himself. He'd given his uncle no reason to doubt him. He had not returned to the warehouse since the day he spoke with Levi; he had simply given the information he'd found on the schedule to Celeste. Later that night, she had snuck the three slaves Hero and Ketojan had found onto the ship. None of the guards had spotted them. As far as he knew, the plot had gone off without a hitch.

There was no reason for his uncle to suspect him of anything.

He grabbed the handle and pushed the door open, being careful not to betray any hint of trepidation when he stuck his head in and said, "Uncle? You called for me?"

Nicholas looked up from the paper he was reading at the desk and motioned for him to enter. "Take a seat."

Percival obeyed, sinking into one of the high-backed leather chairs, and forced a pleasant smile. "What do you need?"

"I wanted to speak with you about your wedding."

Percival barely held back a sigh of relief.

Nicholas set the papers down and leaned forward. The skin around his good eye crinkled when he smiled. "I chose well when I picked Riona to be your wife, did I not? She's beautiful, intelligent, cultured, and she is already accustomed to life in a court. She will make a great queen for our people."

"Yes, she's...very interesting."

"I'm proud of you, nephew," he continued. "I know you were not eager to enter into an arranged marriage—we've quarreled about it far too often, and I'm sorry about that—but you have handled this entire situation with grace. I would be lying if I said I was not a little impressed."

Percival straightened, instantly suspicious. "Oh. Uh, thank you."

"Your display at the banquet last week—dancing with Riona—was inspired. The nobles are enamored with your foreign bride, which bodes well for your rule. She's the talk of the town. It's only a matter of time before they forget about Tamriel completely."

Percival's smile dropped. Bringing Riona here was only a ruse to distract the people from Nicholas's betrayal. "You didn't summon me here just to talk about Riona. What's the real reason?"

"I would like to schedule your wedding for two weeks from today. That should provide sufficient time for the council members to plan the ceremony and for talk of the banquet to subside. Can't give them too much all at once, can we now?"

Tamriel, Mercy, if you're going to attack, please let it be before the wedding.

"Two weeks is fine," he said dismissively, glancing toward the door. He was eager to return to his room and speak with Celeste about their next opportunity to free slaves. He'd grown accustomed to finding her waiting in the sitting room whenever he arrived, a sly smile on her lips as she teased him. It was nice to have one person with whom he could speak plainly—with whom he could be himself. He saw few friendly faces of late.

"Well...it would be fine," his uncle said slowly, sliding his chair back and pushing to his feet, "if there were not one small problem."

He rounded the desk and loomed over Percival, his expression hard. Percival's gaze dropped to the grip of the sword at Nicholas's hip. His heart began to pound.

"Three runaway slaves managed to sneak onto a ship headed for Cowayne early last week. The captain discovered them and turned them over to the guards in Cyrna, who then bestowed the punishment of twenty lashes to their backs and five lashes to the soles of their feet before returning them to their owners."

Nicholas's voice was cold, sharp as steel, and it took all of Percival's willpower to keep his face blank. If what Nicholas said was true, it was his fault the slaves had been captured. They'd be scarred for the rest of their lives because of him.

Nicholas bent down, forcing Percival to meet his eyes. "Do you know anything about this?"

"Of course not."

The back of Nicholas's hand cracked against Percival's cheek, sending his spectacles flying. He cradled the side of his face and glared up at his uncle. "I told you I don't know anything about it!"

Nicholas hit him again, and this time the force of the strike knocked him off the chair. He tumbled to the floor and landed on hands and knees, the taste of blood filling his mouth. Nicholas's ring had split his lip. "I had nothing to do with it, I swear!"

"You swear? Think twice before you give me your word, Percival. You've shown that it's not worth much."

"Says the man who turned on his king." Percival pushed to his feet and glared at his uncle. Standing before him, he was struck anew by how much larger his uncle was compared to him. They were both tall, but where he was wiry, his uncle was pure muscle. He could beat Percival to a pulp without breaking a sweat. "I. Did not. Help them," he growled.

Nicholas took a step forward, lifting a hand as if to hit him again, and Percival flinched. Creator curse him, he *flinched*. "Someone told them that the ship was going east. They knew exactly when the ship was being loaded, and when they would be able to sneak aboard. It's a terrible coincidence that they tried to escape on one of *our* ships the very day you went to the warehouse, isn't it?" He stepped forward again, and Percival shrank back, gingerly holding his swollen cheek. "I know you told them, Percival. You did it out of sympathy, out of the goodness of your heart, but you put me in a very unfortunate position. You are the king of Beltharos. It is your duty to uphold the laws of the land, or the people of this kingdom will turn against you. I turned against Tamriel because he was planning to free the slaves and make the

Islands independent. If the people of the court learn that you share his sympathy for the slaves, you will be next."

"So you're...what? Teaching me a lesson?" Percival spat, his fear morphing to fury. "You're trying to save my life? You don't care about me! All I've ever been to you is a pawn!"

"I gave up *everything* to raise you!" Nicholas roared, a vein pulsing in his forehead. "I gave up my victory in the Cirisian War for you!"

"And you've always blamed me for it!"

"Everything I have done was for the good of this family. I will not watch you throw it all away because of your ridiculous sympathies. You will forget about this foolish notion of helping the slaves, you will marry Riona, and you will play your part as the king of Beltharos. In the meantime, you will not leave this castle without my express permission. Have I made myself clear?"

Percival bent down, grabbed his spectacles, and shoved them on. By some small miracle, they had not broken when Nicholas knocked them off. "If I *had* helped those slaves, your warning would not be enough to deter me from trying again. I would spend every hour of every day working to free the slaves. You could beat me all you like, but you would never convince me that people deserve to be bought and sold—to be treated as less than *cattle*—because their ears are a different shape than ours. I would wear every bruise with honor, because I at least gave them a *chance* at freedom. *That* is what our family should stand for."

His uncle's fist flew out and connected with his gut. Percival doubled over, gasping for breath, as Nicholas leaned down and murmured, "Try it again. We'll see how noble you are when *you're* the one holding the whip."

"Step away from him."

Percival looked up to see Riona standing in the doorway. Her perfect, beautiful face looked as if it was hewn from granite, her blue eyes burning with fury. She looked ready to tear Nicholas apart with her bare hands.

"He is your king," she said, her voice trembling with anger. "Do not touch him again."

Nicholas straightened and bared his teeth in a cruel imitation of a grin. Percival slumped against the wall, his arms wrapped around his stomach as he tried not to lose his lunch. Nicholas snarled, "Return to your room, Riona. This is a private conversation."

"In a matter of weeks, he will be my king and my husband. I will not watch you treat him this way. Lay a hand on him again and I will call the guards."

He snorted. "Who do you think pays the guards?"

She lifted her chin and stepped further into the room. Five Rivosi guards filed in after her, their hands on the grips of their sheathed swords. "You do not pay my men, and they will not hesitate to throw you in the dungeon at a word from me. Do you think your precious guards will follow your commands when I am queen? You must have forgotten that Percival will not only have access to the Comyn family fortune, but also to the Beltharan and Rivosi royal coffers. We will be able to more than match whatever bribe you offer your guard in exchange for your freedom. Then we will see how you enjoy living in chains. Shall we leave, Percival?"

Her eyes never strayed from Nicholas as Percival staggered across the room and into the hall, letting out a sharp sigh of relief. He heard the saccharine smile in Riona's voice as she said, "See you at dinner, my lord," then left the room, her guards trailing behind her. The last one through the door closed it behind him.

Percival imagined his uncle standing in the middle of the study, gaping in disbelief, and a grim smile tugged at his lips. "What you did in there... That was incredible. Thank—"

Riona held up a hand. How much of their conversation

had she heard? Had she been listening the whole time? "If you wish to thank me, learn how to defend yourself so I don't have to do that again. You are the king. You must learn to act like it."

He blinked, taken aback by her bluntness. He didn't know her well, it was true, but her response was so unlike the polite, charming young woman with whom he had danced at the banquet.

Still, she had just saved him from his uncle, and he was grateful.

"Learn how to defend myself," he echoed. "You say that like it's simple, but you've never seen me try to wield a sword."

He had meant it as a joke, but she frowned. "You don't need a weapon. I believe I have proven words work just as well. How do you think I managed to last so long in my uncle's court? The council members think me too foolish for a seat at their table, the noblewomen resent me for my money and my looks, and the king sees me as nothing more than a prize to be sold to the highest bidder." She drew closer to him, her blue eyes fixated on his. He hardly dared to breathe as she continued in a low voice, quiet enough for only him to hear, "It has taken me years to eke out what little power I hold in my king's court. Now that I am here, I do not intend to waste a second obeying your uncle's whims after I become queen. I did enough of that in Rivosa. I will be queen of Beltharos, and I want a strong king beside me. Become that king."

Before Percival could respond, she turned on her heel and started down the hall, her guards following close behind. "I'll send a healer up to your room to tend to your face," she called over her shoulder. "Honorable or not, you can't show up to dinner with a bruise."

29
MERCY

"And finally, here are your chambers, Your Majesty," Marieve said as they approached a set of ornate double doors at the end of the guest wing. One by one, their companions had taken to their rooms to bathe and rest, leaving Mercy and Tamriel alone with the queen's granddaughter. Marieve's smile grew as she pushed the doors open and led them inside. Mercy took one step and stopped dead, her eyes growing wide as she took in the lavish, exquisite room.

A rug of gold and violet covered the stone floor. In the center of the sitting room sat a low wooden table whose legs had been carved to look like a tangle of roses and vines, similar to Queen Cerelia's throne. A velvet settee and several embroidered cushions surrounded it, the gold threads in the upholstery gleaming in the light streaming in through the wall of windows opposite them. Across the room, a massive four-poster bed carved into the same twining-vines style sat nestled among a matching desk and wardrobe. Panels of ivory silk hung from the sculpted canopy. Through a door to her left, Mercy glimpsed an enormous bath of white marble set into the floor, and a gold platter of soaps and oils waiting beside the faucets.

Marieve beamed at them. "Please make yourselves comfortable. I'll have a servant bring you some food shortly; I'm sure you're starving from your long journey. There are some spare clothes in the wardrobe, but I'll give you something from my own closet to wear to dinner tonight, my lady," she said, scanning Mercy from head to toe. "You look about my size. I'm sure I'll be able to find something that will suit you."

Mercy dipped her head in respect, ignoring the twitch of Tamriel's lips as he fought a grin. No doubt he was remembering all the weeks she had spent masquerading as Marieve. "Thank you, my lady."

Oblivious to the humor glittering in Tamriel's eyes, Marieve bowed and excused herself, quietly closing the door behind her. Mercy crossed the room, parted the curtains surrounding the bed, and flopped onto the mattress. She ran her hands over the fine sheets. "I know we're trying to gather forces to return to Sandori, but I could get used to this."

The bed dipped as Tamriel stretched out beside her, his tanned skin and dark hair stark against the ivory sheets. "No more bathing in rivers and hunting for our dinners."

"Are you sure you don't want to just stay here?"

"I don't think Queen Cerelia would care much for us moving into her home."

"We'll offer to cook dinner once a week. Maybe get her a nice floral arrangement to say thanks."

Tamriel chuckled. He rolled over and nuzzled her neck, his breath warm against her skin. "When you're my queen, you can redecorate our castle to your heart's content. We'll put this place to shame." He set a hand on her hip and tugged her close, leaving a trail of kisses up her neck and along her jaw. Then he rose onto one elbow and pressed a soft, tender kiss to her lips. "First, though," he breathed as he pulled back, "you need a bath."

She shoved him and he flopped onto the mattress beside her, laughing. "You're one to speak, *Your Majesty*." She teasingly tugged on a strand of his greasy, matted hair. They'd bathed at Faye's childhood home, but the days since—and the journey across the sea—had not been kind. "It's a wonder you weren't mistaken for a heathen and thrown in the dungeon. I'm sure those guards could smell you coming before we even docked."

"Remind me again why I bothered saving you from the Guild?"

She sat up, leaning over so she was staring straight down at him, a bare inch between their faces. "Because you love me."

"And who in the Creator's name authorized that? You've brought me nothing but trouble since I met you."

"Your life would be boring without me."

"That it would, my love." Without warning, he flipped her onto her back and shifted so he was straddling her hips, trapping her beneath him just as she had done to him in Fallmond. He laced his fingers through hers and pinned her arms to the mattress above her head. Heat rushed through her as he gazed down at her, love and desire in his eyes. "I've missed you."

"We've been together for the past month."

"We've been surrounded by soldiers and friends for the past month," he corrected. "I've missed *us*. I've missed talking to you. I've missed going to bed beside you and waking up with you in my arms. Collapsing from exhaustion and rising with the sun doesn't quite measure up." He dipped his head to kiss her, but before their lips could touch, he jerked back. "You really do need a bath, though."

Before she could come up with a snarky response, he

crawled off the bed and scooped her up in his arms. She let out a surprised yelp and wrapped her arms around his neck, laughing, as he started toward the bathing chamber. Sometimes she forgot how strong he was.

"Luckily for us," he said as he walked, "our hosts have given us *quite* an array of expensive soaps and oils. And you know what the best part is?"

"What?"

His lips curled into a seductive smile as he whispered, "The bath is big enough for two."

By the Creator, the bath was *divine*.

As was the bed.

After washing her hair, changing into a soft tunic, and curling up on the bed next to Tamriel for a short nap, Mercy was awakened by a light rap on the door. She carefully slipped out from under the arm Tamriel had slung around her and opened the door to find three pretty young servants standing before her. Two held trays of food—the scents from which made Mercy's mouth immediately start to water—and the third had a gown of violet silk draped across her arms. Mercy stepped aside to let the girls enter. The one holding the gown moved to the wardrobe to hang it, while the other girls set about arranging the food on the low table in the center of the room. Mercy watched them glance at the sleeping king sprawled out atop the blankets, partially visible through the curtains surrounding the bed, and grinned to herself. Despite everything they'd been through over the past few weeks— over the past few *months*, really—this moment was one of the most peaceful, one of the happiest, she'd ever had the privilege to experience.

The servants left without a word, and Mercy stretched

out on the mattress beside Tamriel. He stirred but didn't wake, shifting so he was pressed up against her, his face buried in the place where her neck met her shoulder. She brushed a strand of his soft, still-wet hair from his brow and closed her eyes.

Yes, in the midst of all this chaos, betrayal, war, and loss, this moment was a blessing.

An hour later, Tamriel had just finished tying off the laces at the back of Mercy's gown when a servant arrived to take Mercy to the queen. She turned to the polished metal mirror atop the desk and twisted her still-damp hair into a bun, tying it off with a strip of leather.

"Good luck," Tamriel whispered, leaning in to kiss her bare shoulder. "You look beautiful."

She smiled at his reflection. She *did* look beautiful. Marieve's gown was simple but stunning, a sheath of silk in a violet so dark it appeared almost black. The thin straps crossed between her shoulder blades and laced down the open back like a corset, all the way to the base of her spine. Months ago, she would have felt vulnerable and exposed in such a dress, but not anymore. Not when she looked into the mirror and saw a glimpse of the queen she would become.

"Are you ready, my lady?" the servant asked. When Mercy nodded, the servant led her down the hall and through the twisting corridors of the castle. Eventually, they arrived at a sitting room with a settee and several cushions, very much like the arrangement in the room she shared with Tamriel. A tray with a pot of tea and two teacups sat on the low table in the center. The servant guided her to one of the cushions. "Her Majesty will be with you shortly."

The servant slipped into the hall, leaving Mercy alone.

Oddly enough, there were no guards stationed outside the room. For whatever reason, the queen had not deemed her enough of a threat to have her watched while she was a guest in the castle. The thought should have put her at ease. Instead, the Assassin within her was a little insulted by the insinuation that she could not take down half the castle staff armed with only the tea service.

A few moments later, Queen Cerelia strode in, flanked by a half-dozen guards. She flicked her wrist, and they spread out across the room, their expressions blank as they watched Mercy rise and bow to the queen.

"Your Majesty," Mercy said, staring down at the floor as the queen took her seat on the settee.

"Please, be seated. There is no need for such formality. I simply wish to get to know you. There are a lot of rumors surrounding the Assassin who stole the prince's heart."

"I suspect only a fraction of them are true," she responded as she sank onto her cushion and began pouring the tea. She handed one cup to the queen and curled her hands around the other, letting the warmth soak into her fingers. "I'm sorry to disappoint you."

Cerelia cocked her head and stared at her. Seated, her long locks coiled on the floor, and the tips of her pointed ears peeked out through the fine strands. "Oh, I'm sure your story is far from disappointing. Tell me everything."

Mercy hesitated, dismayed at the command. But the queen's tone made it clear she would brook no argument, so Mercy did exactly as she was told: she explained everything, starting with her father trading her to the Guild and ending with Nicholas's betrayal. Through it all, the queen simply listened, her expression shifting from interest, to distaste, to mild surprise. By the time Mercy finished speaking, her untouched tea had gone cold. She set it on the table as she awaited the queen's response.

"Fascinating," Cerelia finally said, pursing her lips in thought. "Not only are you an Assassin, but you're an elf. Yet, despite his father's warnings and the dangers posed by the council, your prince stood by your side through it all. He marched a thousand men across the country to save you from that horrible Guildmother."

She straightened, her heart filling with pride and love. "Yes, he did. He saved my life."

"And this false king—this Nicholas Comyn—betrayed him because of his plans to free the slaves and establish the Islands as an independent country." She shook her head. "Treason is a terrible crime. It must not go unpunished."

"Does that mean you'll help us?"

"I have not made up my mind on the matter. I wished to speak with you first—to see what you had to say about your king—before I made my judgment. As capable a king as he appears to be, Tamriel Myrellis does not have an army. My soldiers would be fighting and dying for a royal family who has been our enemy for generations. How can I ask them to risk everything for a kingdom with whom we have been at war longer than most of them have been alive?"

Mercy leaned forward. "If you care about the fate of the elves and the Islands, you must help us. Aiding Tamriel in reclaiming his throne could be the action that begins to heal the rift between our countries. I know he has no intention of continuing this pointless, bloody war over Cirisor. Making the Islands an independent country would benefit both Beltharos and Feyndara."

Queen Cerelia gestured to the sapphire ring on Mercy's finger. "That's a beautiful piece of jewelry. Does it mean what I think it means? Does Tamriel intend to make you his queen?"

"He does."

Cerelia smiled then—a smile so wide and genuine it

caught Mercy off guard. "Then I offer you my sincerest congratulations. It is fortunate that you have found some happiness amidst all the pain and suffering you have endured. An elven queen. Perhaps it is time we reestablish our friendship with Beltharos. Your king does not seem as close-minded as those who came before him. Tell me, do you truly think the people will accept you as their queen? Will they be ruled by an elf?"

Mercy lifted her chin. "It may take some time for them to trust me, but I do not doubt that they will. Like you said, they are not all close-minded about elves. I have saved their king's life time and time again, I helped cure the plague, I defended the city from Firesse, and I took down the Guild. I am not their enemy."

"Then perhaps I judged you and your king too quickly. You both seem like very strong, confident leaders. I do not doubt that together, you would be a force with which to be reckoned." She glanced at the window and, seeing that the sun had begun to set, rose. Mercy followed suit. "It's almost time for dinner. One of my guards will see you to your chambers so you may fetch your king. Thank you for taking the time to speak with me. You have given me much to consider."

Mercy bowed and followed the guard out of the room, her steps light and her spirits high. The queen's piercing eyes and sharp tongue were intimidating, but she seemed intrigued by Tamriel's plans for his kingdom. She had been pleasantly surprised when Mercy mentioned his work to free the slaves.

We can do this, Tamriel, she thought, unable to fight back a hopeful grin. *We're going to reclaim our kingdom.*

30

TAMRIEL

Tamriel didn't miss the hope shining in Mercy's eyes when she returned to their room, and he felt his spirits lift. He moved closer to her as a Feyndaran guard led them to the dining hall. "I trust your meeting with the queen went well?"

"Very well." She beamed at him. "We may have found an ally in Feyndara after all."

"By the Creator, I hope so." He didn't know what he'd do if Queen Cerelia denied him aid. He trusted Kaius to train the runaway slaves, but even with his Cirisian fighters, the Daughters, and Duomnodera's Qadari warriors, he didn't have an army. Alone, they wouldn't stand a chance against Nicholas's men, especially if Tamriel was right about him allying with Rivosa.

They arrived at the grand dining hall to find Faye and the rest of their group already seated at the long table, surrounded by members of the queen's court. He bit back a grin at the bored expressions on the faces of his guards. They couldn't care less about court politics. Beside them, Calum was seated with the Strykers, smirking at something Nerran was saying. He caught Tamriel's eye and mouthed, *Good luck*.

The guard led them toward their seats at the opposite end of the table. The throne-like chair at the head was empty, but the queen's family had already taken their places around it: to the queen's right, her ancient-looking husband, Prince Dion; to her left, her eldest child and heir to the throne, Princess Nymh. The heir apparent was nearly identical to her mother, with a feminine, delicately-boned face and sharp gray eyes. She studied Tamriel and Mercy as they neared. Her two daughters, Jovi and Henna, ducked their heads to whisper to one another, ignoring the warning look their mother shot them.

"Here you are, Your Majesty, my lady," the guard said, pulling Mercy's chair out for her, then taking his place among the guards lining the walls of the room.

"I'm afraid we have not been formally introduced," the man across from Mercy said, dipping his head in respect. Tamriel recognized him from the throne room earlier that day. "I am General Cadriel, commander of Her Majesty's forces. I'll be fighting at your side if my mother decides to grant you the troops you've requested."

"It's an honor to meet you."

"The honor is all mine. I'm interested to learn more about your country, as I've never been there myself. Perhaps during this meal, you could enlighten me." He glanced toward the door, his entire countenance shifting when Lady Marieve walked in. "You've met my daughter already. I trust she made sure you have everything you need when she showed you to your chambers?"

"Of course I did, Father," she said as she sank into the seat next to him, then leaned over to kiss his cheek. "If Uncle Justus taught me anything, it was how to treat guests with the utmost hospitality. I even gave Lady Mercy one of my dresses. Doesn't she look marvelous?"

"It's a lovely gown," Mercy agreed, nodding. "Perhaps one day I'll be able to repay the favor."

"Yes! I would love to own a Beltharan gown. I'm sure your fashions must be very different from ours."

While Marieve chattered on, Cadriel leaned close to Tamriel and nodded to a man seated farther down the table, whose wavy black hair was markedly similar to that of the young man sitting beside him. "I'm sure you've not had the chance for proper introductions. That's my younger brother, Lord Justus, and his son, Alistair. I believe you've heard of him, no? Lord of Castle Rising? Guardian of the Islands?"

Tamriel vaguely remembered hearing the titles from one of his many childhood tutors, but he didn't know anything about Lord Justus beyond his name.

"Unfortunately, the demands of being general call me away from home far too often. He took my daughter under his wing after my wife passed, and has looked after her ever since, making sure she and Alistair have the best tutors in all of Feyndara. She's a bright young girl—the spitting image of her mother." He cast a sidelong glance at Tamriel. "She would make a wonderful queen for your people."

Oh.

Mercy shot the general an annoyed look, still nodding along to whatever Marieve was saying, but Cadriel didn't seem to notice. Marieve continued speaking, a smile plastered on her face as if she hadn't just heard her father's attempt to arrange a marriage between them. Even so, a slight flush rose on her cheeks.

"Well, actually—" Tamriel began, but the scraping of chairs against the stone floor interrupted him. Everyone at the table rose and bowed as the queen strode into the room, the large rubies set into her crown shining under the light of the crystal chandelier. Silence filled the dining hall as she made her way to her place at the head of the table. As soon as she was seated, everyone straightened and sat, resuming their conversations. Several servants filed into the room and began to serve wine.

As soon as the last goblet was distributed, the queen stood and raised her glass in a toast. "I would like to dedicate this meal to our guests, who have journeyed long and hard to be here with us tonight. They have faced hardships many of us can scarcely begin to imagine, and it is my honor to offer them a place at my table and in my home." Her gaze swept over Calum and the others, all seated far down the table, before finally coming to rest on Tamriel and Mercy. She smiled and lifted her glass higher. "To our guests, and to the start of a new friendship between our countries."

"Hear, hear!"

Course after course was brought in from the kitchens, so many Tamriel quickly lost count of how many dishes had been set before him. It seemed like every time he cleared his plate, another servant materialized just over his shoulder to whisk it away and replace it with a new one. And every time, Mercy insisted on taking the first bite to check for poison. At first, Tamriel had objected—killing him would get Cerelia no closer to winning the Cirisor Islands and, even if she had decided to poison him, he didn't want Mercy to be harmed in his stead—but she hadn't relented. He tensed every time she took a bite, fearing the worst, but her only reactions were those of contentment. Every dish was positively *divine*.

The gentle scraping of forks and knives filled the room, along with the chatter of conversation and occasional burst of laughter. At one point, Tamriel looked down the table to see

Julien grinning from ear-to-ear, Atlas hiding his smile behind the rim of his goblet, and Faye laughing so hard her face had turned red. A sudden pang of homesickness shot through him. What he wouldn't have given to be sitting in the castle at that moment, surrounded by these friends who had become his family. Before, he had never enjoyed his time in the court. He had taken for granted the few friends he'd had in the capital. Not anymore. Once he defeated Nicholas and reclaimed his throne, he and Mercy were going to build a court worth protecting—and every person who had accompanied him here would have a place in it, should they want it.

Mercy looked up from her dessert and whispered, "What are you thinking about?"

He reached over and grabbed her free hand, interlacing their fingers. "Our future."

Across the table, General Cadriel frowned at their joined hands. Since the meal began, he had thrice hinted not-at-all-subtly that Tamriel should take Marieve as his queen. The first time, Tamriel had politely refused, reminding him that he was betrothed to Mercy. The second and third, he had flat-out ignored. Judging by the stormy looks Mercy had been shooting the general, she would not forget his remarks anytime soon. Tamriel made a mental note to keep her well away from him on the battlefield. He didn't entirely trust her not to vent her anger against him in the midst of the chaos. Even with her sore ribs, he was certain that she would be the one to walk away from that fight.

After the final course was cleared away, the queen rose, and a hush settled over the room. Tamriel straightened when she focused on him. Had she made up her mind? Was she going to help him?

"You came to me asking for aid," she began, her voice carrying throughout the room. "You asked me to send my general and my soldiers into my enemy's land, to fight for *you*, whose family has been at war with mine for generations. When you first arrived, I was inclined to deny your request and have my guards place you on the first ship back to Beltharos. But then you spoke of your plans to free the slaves."

The queen's lips twitched into the ghost of a smile, and Mercy's fingers tightened around his.

"The kings who came before you would never have entertained the idea of granting the elves their freedom. Even your father gave in to the pressures from his court after they killed his love." She paused when Tamriel flinched at the mention of Ghyslain, sympathy passing across her face. While he and his father had never been close, the ache of Ghyslain's death lingered. "When you spoke of freeing the slaves and making the Islands an independent nation, you showed me that you are different from the other Myrellis kings. You are *better*, and your lady confirmed it when she spoke with me earlier," she said, nodding to Mercy. "You are the king who will bring justice for *all* the people of your kingdom. You are the king who will mend the rift between our countries. I will provide you the troops and supplies you need to defeat the traitor who stole your throne."

Tamriel let out a sharp, relieved breath. Dismissing court propriety, Mercy threw her arms around his neck and kissed his cheek. Down the table, Calum and the others let out a loud cheer.

The queen held up a hand. "I have not yet named my conditions. Several of my soldiers are going to die for you. That does not come without a price."

He stiffened, and Mercy's arms fell away. "What do you want?"

"In exchange for my troops, you will marry Lady Marieve—"

"Absolutely not," Mercy growled.

"—and the Cirisor Islands will become a vassal state, to be jointly ruled over by both Beltharos and Feyndara."

For a few moments, Tamriel simply gaped at her, unable to craft a response. He looked across the table to Marieve, who was staring down at her folded hands. He could tell by her guilty expression that she had known her grandmother was going to demand this of him.

Beside him, Mercy had not moved a muscle. He could feel the indignation, the rage, pouring off her. Betrayal was plain in her eyes as she glared at the queen. Everyone in the room had gone deathly quiet, watching in rapt attention as the tense silence stretched out between them.

The shock faded, anger sweeping in and taking its place. After everything they had endured, he would not give up Mercy. Not a chance.

"I will not marry her," Tamriel said. "I'm betrothed to Mercy. I *love* her."

"You're a royal, Your Majesty," Queen Cerelia responded, her voice soft and full of pity. "You do not have the luxury of marrying for love."

"I thought you approved of our marriage," Mercy cut in, her tone accusatory. Her knuckles were white around her fork and knife. Tamriel half expected her to hurl them at Cerelia. "You said we would be good leaders."

"If you had an army and were able to reclaim your throne on your own, I have no doubt that you would make an excellent queen. Alas, you do not. This is the cost of my help. Do not misunderstand me—I do not make this offer because I harbor any ill will toward either of you. My queendom has lost far too many soldiers to the Cirisian Wars. This is the only way I can ensure that their sacrifices are not for nothing. Believe me, this was not an easy decision to make."

Mercy snorted in disbelief.

"I will not marry Lady Marieve," Tamriel repeated,

pushing away from the table and staring down the queen. Mercy rose, as well. "I am betrothed to Mercy, and I intend to make her my queen. I am not going to cast her aside to regain my throne."

"If you do not accept my offer, you will be unable to defeat Nicholas Comyn on your own. Are you willing to leave your subjects under the rule of the man who stole your throne, who crowned a puppet in your place? Will you really prioritize your desires over what is best for your country?"

"Everything I do is for the good of my country," he snarled, eliciting gasps from the surrounding nobles. "I came here to gather an army so I could *protect* my subjects from a tyrant. Do not speak as if you know me."

"I know you will do anything to free the slaves, and I know you won't be able to live with the knowledge that you could have spared them from the suffering they will endure under the false king's rule. If you do not agree, you will be condemning them to a life in chains."

"No," Tamriel retorted, eyeing her coolly. "*You* will. If you ask this of me, the repercussions are on *you*."

He reached down and grabbed Mercy's hand. "Thank you for the meal, and for opening your home to us. I think it is time we retire for the night. I look forward to negotiating with you in the morning."

He felt the stares of the entire court on his back as he and Mercy walked toward the doors. Calum and the others rose and followed without a word. Matthias's expression was positively murderous—even more so than Ino's and Cassia's—but he knew better than to act on his anger. The guards they passed glared at them for their breach of etiquette, but Tamriel was too furious to care that he had just insulted the queen of Feyndara.

"Your Majesty," she called just as he reached the threshold.

Against his better judgment, he turned around.

"Consider what I've said. You cannot win your throne without my help."

"If getting your help means giving up the woman I love, I can damn well try." With that, he turned on his heel and walked out of the room.

31
FAYE

Faye scrambled to keep up with Mercy and Tamriel as they stormed into their room, bursting through the doors with such force that they cracked against the walls. Mercy dropped onto the settee while Tamriel paced, his face contorted in fury.

"The *gall!*" he seethed. "Holding my kingdom hostage unless I agree to marry her granddaughter? Now I know why my father was in no hurry to negotiate for peace between our countries. I would have given her *anything* in exchange for troops. *Anything* but this."

Cassia and Ino sank onto the settee beside Mercy, looking at their sister with concern in their eyes. Matthias moved behind her and rested a hand on her shoulder. Faye knew the expression on Mercy's face well—it was the same one she had often worn in the Guild; Mercy was fighting the urge to pick up her daggers and show the queen just what she thought of the proposal.

"We could kill her," Tanni suggested, lingering by the threshold with the rest of the Daughters.

"We're already fighting one army. We're not making it two," Tamriel snapped.

"The queen is bluffing," Calum said, stepping in front of the king. "She knows that by asking for something impossible, you'll be more inclined to give her what she really wants: Cirisor."

"I don't think so. You saw her face. She knows exactly what she's doing, and she's proud of it. She won't take no for an answer."

"Earlier, she kept asking me about the court," Mercy said, realization dawning. "She wanted to know if the court would accept having an elf as their queen. I thought she was just curious—that she was asking because she was afraid the court would turn on me—but she was asking to see if they would accept *any* elf as their queen. Marieve would fare just as well in my position. She would fare *better*, being the granddaughter of the Feyndaran queen. The court would not dare turn against her for fear of starting another war. Cerelia was planning this."

"I think you're wrong." Faye searched each of their faces in turn, willing them to believe her. Willing it to be *true*, if only so she did not have to see the pain on her friends' faces any longer. "For once, I think Calum's right. She's just trying to make it easier to negotiate. True, she overstepped her bounds, but she's willing to do that to get the Islands. She's manipulating you."

"And if she's not?" Tamriel asked, a sliver of fear sliding into his voice. "What if she's serious? What if she won't give me the troops I need unless I agree to marry Marieve? Where do we go from here? We have *no allies*."

Calum frowned. "We'll figure something out. My father still has bank accounts here. We'll withdraw his funds and use the money to hire mercenaries and swordsmen. With the Qadar, Daughters, and Cirisians on our side, we might win."

"*Might* isn't good enough. And we have no idea how long it will take to build up a large enough force to face Nicholas. How much will it cost to feed and clothe them, to sail them across the sea and march them all the way across the fishing sector?"

"Mercy and I can find a way to sneak into the castle," Faye suggested. "With the other Daughters, we can find and kill Nicholas. We may be free of the Guild, but we're still Assassins."

"No," Calum cut in before Tamriel could respond, pinning her with a stern look. "He knows you're with us, and he knows that if we were to act without an army, we'd send you in to kill him. He's a master general, remember? He plotted to steal the throne from Tamriel for weeks without anyone realizing it. He has to have protection around the castle."

"It's not impenetrable. We could find a way inside—"

He shook his head. "Even if you kill him, you still have to make it out of the castle alive and get the rest of us into Sandori. It would be the seven of you against all the soldiers and guards in the city, and as skilled as you are in combat, you're not making it out alive with those odds. Either we return with an army, or not at all."

A hush descended over the room. Faye stood helplessly in the middle of the room and watched Tamriel resume his pacing. Calum stared at his cousin with concern. Beside him, Mercy slumped forward and dropped her head in her hands as her siblings murmured comforting words. Akiva and the others lingered in the hall, awkward and uncertain.

Despite her bravado, Faye couldn't help the doubts that began to creep in. She had seen the gleam in the queen's eyes as she announced her conditions for helping Tamriel. It was the same gleam Mercy used to get when she knew she was going to win a sparring match.

Queen Cerelia knew Tamriel had no choice but to agree.

With this one condition, she'd secure her country's hold on the Islands as well as plant a member of her family on the Beltharan throne. She wasn't going to back down.

Mercy sat up, and Faye could tell by the devastation on her face that she had come to the same conclusion. Without a word, Mercy walked to Tamriel and took his face in her hands. "If she won't take no for an answer..." she said, her voice wavering. "If she won't give you the troops, you have to agree."

"No!" Tamriel said immediately, reaching up to grab her wrists. "I won't marry her. I love *you*."

"You love your kingdom, too, and your people need you. Listen to me, Tamriel," she blurted when he opened his mouth to argue, the words coming out in a rush. "Fight her with everything you have. Argue and negotiate and try to change her mind. But if she won't... If she demands this of you and will not back down... I want you to say yes."

"How can you say that?" He recoiled, stung. "What happened to standing up to the nobles together?"

"This is *different*. This isn't a matter of fighting prejudice—this is bringing the man who stole your kingdom to justice. How can you ask me to stand in the way of that?"

"Mercy—"

"You could forget about the kingdom," Calum interjected in a quiet voice. Mercy and Tamriel turned to him, glaring, and he held up his hands in surrender. "Look, this entire situation is shitty. I understand that. After everything you've been through, you deserve to be together. No one would blame you for turning your back on that court of vipers and choosing each other. You've sacrificed so much for Beltharos already, and look how the people repaid you."

"I am the *king*," Tamriel snarled. "I have a duty to my country, and I will see it through."

Calum shrugged and dropped onto one of the cushions,

crossing his arms over his chest. "I'm just providing suggestions."

Mercy turned to Tamriel. "You've given up so much for your kingdom. Now it's my turn to do the same. If regaining your throne means that I have to watch you marry her...I will."

"I won't do it. Even if Cerelia refuses to provide troops, I won't give you up. We'll find another way."

"You could stay on as his mistress," Cassia said. "Like Liselle and the king. He and Marieve would be married in name only. You could still be together."

Tamriel shook his head. "I swore Mercy would be my queen. I want her to rule by my side."

"Tamriel, *please*," Mercy begged. "You said it yourself—if we don't secure Cerelia's aid, we won't have any allies to turn to. You'll never get your kingdom back. I can't be the reason you give up your throne. *Please*, fight her with everything you have, but promise me you'll marry Marieve if there is no other option."

He reached up and gently brushed away the tears trailing down her cheeks. Faye's heart ached at the pain, devastation, and love on his face when he leaned down and kissed Mercy. Then he pulled back just an inch and breathed, "No."

She went rigid. "*No?*"

"I won't give you up for my kingdom, my love. I'm not giving you *or* my throne up." He let go of her and looked at Faye and the others. "Leave us, please."

Faye stood there for a moment, staring disbelievingly at Tamriel and Mercy, until Calum paused beside her and laid a hand on her shoulder. "Let's go," he whispered. "This is between them."

She took one last look at Mercy, her best friend, her sister, before turning and trailing after Calum and the others. When the doors softly clicked shut behind them, they stood there for a few moments, absorbing everything that had happened, before silently returning to their respective rooms.

32
PERCIVAL

Percival waited for Riona's footsteps to fade before taking off, careening around corners and running up the stairs, his heart pounding. Nicholas had figured out that he was helping the slaves, so he had to know that someone had been working with him—someone who had the freedom to come and go as she pleased.

He had to know about Celeste.

Percival flew around the last corner in a panic, startling the guards standing at the entrance to the king's chambers, and burst through the doors. He scanned the room with wild eyes. There she was—standing at the wardrobe, a wicker basket full of clothes braced on her hip.

Not missing. Not arrested. Not languishing in the dungeon.

Before she could even turn around, his feet carried him across the room. "You need to leave. You need to get out of the city." He grabbed the basket, tossed it aside, and took her hand, pulling her to the open doors of the balcony. "Do you have money? If you can hide out in the Church with

Lethandris, I can find a way to get some to you. Do you have somewhere to go? Some family? Friends?"

"Percival, wait!" Celeste twisted out of his grasp and snagged his arm, forcing him to face her. She gasped as she took in his crooked spectacles, the bruise blossoming across his cheek, the split lip. She didn't need to ask who had hurt him. "Why did the bastard do that to you?"

"He *knows*. Celeste, he knows about the slaves. He knows I helped them. He must be coming for you next—you and Hero and Ketojan. You need to warn them."

A shadow passed across her face. "I'll warn them, but I'm not fleeing, you fool. You think I'm leaving you alone with that vile man? The Creator himself couldn't tear me away."

"You're not listening to me," he said, imploring her to understand, to quit being stubborn for *five damn minutes,* and think about her own wellbeing for once. "He will kill you—I don't know how, and I don't know when, but I promise you he will make it painful. He warned me what would happen if I tried to help the elves. He warned me, and I knew what it would cost, and I put you in danger anyway. He will force me to listen to you scream and I can't—I can't do that, Celeste." Her name caught in his throat, a desperate plea. The panic inside him was a living, breathing thing, robbing him of every thought except getting her to safety. "I can't watch him kill you."

She shook her head, and the gesture made him want to grab her by the arms and shake her. "I swore to you that I would help the slaves escape. I don't break my word. Now shut up, take some deep breaths, and tell me what happened."

"Celeste—" he said helplessly, but she shoved a finger to his lips and guided him to the nearest chair. She pushed him onto the seat so she was standing over him, frowning down.

"Breathe," she commanded.

"But—"

"Shut up and breathe. In, two, three. Out, two, three. Do it."

He obeyed, taking in several lungfuls of air. It helped quell the panic, but—*damn her*—she should have been running, not attending him. Every second she spent in the castle was one too many.

"Now," she said, gently tilting his face up until he met her gaze, "tell me what happened."

True to her word, Riona had a healer sent to his room. The moment the man arrived, Celeste smiled at him, grabbed his medicine bag, and closed the door in his face.

She didn't interrupt once the entire time Percival explained. Her expression betrayed no hint of her thoughts as she wordlessly instructed him to hold a cool, wet rag to his bruised cheek, then set to work cleaning his split lip. She filled a small silver bowl with water from the faucet in the bathing chamber, and by the time he had finished speaking, the contents were tinged pink with his blood.

She sat back on her heels, having knelt on the floor to examine his stomach where Nicholas had punched him. The first question out of her mouth was not the one he had expected.

"Why do you put up with him?"

He blinked at her. *That* was what she cared about? What about the fact that the poor slaves they'd helped had been whipped and returned to their masters' estates? What about her own safety?

"I don't... He's my family. He's all I have. He's..." He faltered, fumbling for an explanation. Finally, he settled with, "Because I'm a coward."

She looked up at him sharply. "Because he has taught you

to fear him. Because he has spent your entire life making you think you're useless. Because he has fooled you into believing you need his approval to be worth anything."

Shame filled him. Those words—those truths—carved deeper wounds into him than his uncle's fists or blades ever could. Unable to face her, to see the pity he knew was on her face, he said, "You need to leave the city. It's not safe for you here."

"No."

"He's going to kill you."

"Then we strike before he has the chance."

Surprise rattled through him. "How do you mean?"

She leaned forward and rested a hand on his knee. A jolt shot through him at the touch. It struck him then that she had the most unusual eyes—pale green with rings of hazel around the irises. They weren't like Riona's blue, bright and startling. Their beauty was quieter, subtler, but no less stunning.

How had he not noticed them before? Now that he had, he couldn't stop staring.

"There's a poison," she whispered. "Gloriosa tansy. It mimics extreme inebriation in the victim before killing him. By the time Nicholas realizes what has hit him, it'll be too late. He'll be dead, and you'll be free to rule the kingdom until Tamriel returns to claim his crown."

He considered it. By the Creator, he considered it—his uncle stumbling and falling, unaware that he'd been poisoned; the feeling of the shackle falling away from Percival's throat, leaving him truly free for the first time. He imagined sitting on the throne, calling the soldiers hunting Tamriel back to the city, ruling justly and fairly until the rightful king came out of hiding to lead his people.

When he did not immediately object, she added, "We could take them all down—all the guards and nobles who betrayed Tamriel. They'll all be here in the castle for the royal wedding. Wine will be flowing. Everyone will be partaking. It would not be a difficult thing to ensure the right goblets get into the right hands. What date has your uncle set?"

"Two weeks from now."

Her expression turned thoughtful, a darkness he had never seen before slipping over her features. It was the same look his uncle wore when he was deep in thought, mapping out his next movements, plotting his next scheme. It scared him, and thrilled him, and made him sick to his stomach. So much could go wrong. A million little things could give them away, and yet...

And yet...

And yet...

"What do you think?" Celeste breathed, tilting her head in a challenge. With her kneeling on the floor before him, only a few inches separated their faces. Her remarkable eyes sparkled, drawing him in and sending him into an entirely different kind of panic.

"You could be hurt. You could be killed."

At any point during the next two weeks, Nicholas's men could come after her, and Percival would be powerless to stop them. He had never abhorred his inability to wield a sword more than in this moment. For her, he'd try. For her, he'd fight.

She smiled and reached under her skirt, into her waistband, up the loose sleeves of her blouse, behind her back. In a matter of seconds, she laid five small daggers out before him. "I'm not as helpless as you think. I can protect myself—and you, if need be. My damsel in distress."

He frowned at her attempt at levity. By the Creator, how he yearned to agree. How he yearned to see his uncle punished for his crimes. But if he did...he'd become a murderer. He'd have to live knowing he was responsible for the deaths of his uncle and countless nobles, and so would she. "You swore to Lethandris that you'd lead an honest life here. You'd be breaking your oath."

"You're stalling."

"I need to be absolutely certain you want to do this."

She looked at his bruise again, and her smile dropped. "After all this time, do you really doubt me?"

No. No, he didn't. He could see the conviction on her face, in the stubborn set of her jaw, in the arch of her brow. She had already done so much to help him. She had already risked so much for him and the runaway slaves.

He nodded. "Two weeks from today."

"On the day of your wedding," she said, and... Was that bitterness in her voice? Pain?

Before he could linger on the thought, on the way it made his heart stutter, his chest constrict, he jumped up and moved to the fallen wicker basket. He kept his back to her as he righted it and began picking up the clothes he'd strewn about the floor. He was going to marry Riona. Thinking about Celeste in that way was wrong, forbidden.

Then why—*why* did he do it so often?

When he was finished, he stood and turned to her, praying with everything in him that she had not sensed the turn his thoughts had taken. Her eyes—which, he realized with a start, had been watching him—darted to her knives, and she hurriedly began returning them to their hidden sheaths. Before she could put the last one away, he stepped forward and rested a hand on her shoulder, stilling her.

"Can you teach me?" he asked, nodding to the dagger. "Will you teach me to fight?"

Riona's guards eyed Percival with curiosity as he approached her room later that afternoon. Not once since she arrived had he visited her chambers in the guest wing; until she stumbled upon him and his uncle in the study earlier, every word they'd exchanged had been at the behest of his uncle at various banquets and feasts. The realization filled Percival with shame. Riona had left her entire life behind to marry a man who was little more than a stranger, and he had done nothing to make her feel welcome. He was angry at his uncle for betraying Tamriel, for forcing him onto a throne he didn't want, for arranging a marriage to a woman he didn't love, and he had been inadvertently taking it out on Riona.

He knocked on the door, and it swung open a moment later. Riona's eyes widened in surprise. Then she wordlessly stepped aside to let him in.

The soft swish of her ruby gown across the rug followed him to the center of the room, where he stopped and ran a hand through his hair before turning to her. "I'm sorry. I'm sorry for ignoring you. I'm sorry you had to intervene earlier. I'm sorry for—for being weak."

"Do not apologize." She nodded to the bruise on Percival's cheek, which Celeste had tried to hide under layers of cosmetics before leaving to speak with Hero and Ketojan. For the most part, it had worked, but a shadow still marred the right side of his face. Even so, there was no covering his split and swollen lip. "How many times has your uncle done that to you?"

"I've lost count."

Her expression turned sympathetic. "He is a cruel man. You do not deserve to be treated that way, regardless of your crimes."

He winced. "How much of our conversation did you hear?"

"Enough to know you've been helping the slaves behind

your uncle's back, and that you'll continue to do so regardless of what he says. Percival, you must stop this madness. I feel for the elves—I do, truly—but I fear for your safety. I fear for *our* safety. I'm to be your wife, and if the nobles discover what you've done, they won't hesitate to kill us the same way they did Liselle. Look what they did to Tamriel. For our sakes, please give up this dream of freeing them."

He studied the fear in her eyes, trying to reconcile the young woman before him with the rage-filled princess who had saved him earlier, the court-bred lady who had charmed the nobles, the girl who had spun in his arms and confessed to dreaming of becoming a dancer. It seemed impossible that they were all the same person. Then he remembered the cool, impassive mask Tamriel had always worn in the court, and it made sense. She'd lived in her uncle's court her entire life. She was practiced in hiding pieces of herself, in only revealing what parts she chose. They were complete opposites; Percival couldn't seem to keep his face from betraying every thought that passed through his mind.

If he and Celeste were successful, he'd need a queen like that at his side until Tamriel returned—*if* Tamriel returned. He may not be invited to many of his uncle's meetings with the council members, but he'd heard whispers that the deposed king vanished after the attack in Xilor. No one had seen him—not one soldier among the hundreds Nicholas had sent to hunt Tamriel and his allies down.

As much as he hoped Tamriel was off somewhere gathering a force to reclaim his throne, part of him feared that the king had been struck down during the attack in Xilor, that his body had been borne away by his allies for a private burial so Nicholas would not be able to defile his corpse.

Percival shoved the worries from his mind. Tamriel would return. Until then, Percival would do his best to rule in his friend's place—to do what was right for his people.

That started with a compromise.

"Very well," he said, and surprise flashed across Riona's face. She'd expected him to argue. He wanted to—he desired nothing more than to show his uncle that no amount of beating him would keep him from helping the slaves—but he had to consider Riona's safety. She had not asked to be dragged into this mess. Her future had been bartered away just as his had.

"I won't attempt to free any slaves, but I want a promise from you in exchange. Promise me that if Tamriel is killed, you will help me realize his goal of abolishing slavery across the kingdom. It doesn't have to be an immediate change," he continued when she opened her mouth to object. "It could take years. We'll have to start small—regulate the slave trade, punish the masters who mistreat their slaves—but if you want to defy my uncle and become the powerful queen your uncle's court never thought you could be, this is the way to do it. The nobles will fight it at first, but we'll stand together against them. I'll become the strong king you need at your side. We'll free the slaves, and they will worship you for it. I just need you to help me do what's right. Please, Riona."

Her expression had been shifting from wariness to curiosity as he spoke, but those last two words—the desperation in them—won her over completely. She nodded. "You have a deal. I promise."

The tension left his body. When he arrived, he hadn't been intending to ask this of her; he'd only wanted to apologize for what she'd heard earlier and to thank her for intervening. But as they had spoken, he'd recalled her words from that afternoon—*I do not intend to waste a second obeying your uncle's whims after I become queen*—and he'd seen an opportunity. He, Celeste, and Riona might never be able to best Nicholas in battle, but perhaps together, they could outmaneuver him in the court.

He offered Riona a grateful smile. For the first time, his dread at the thought of their marriage morphed into something different, something like hope. They did not love each other, but they had an understanding. For the good of the kingdom, he would be the king she needed, and she would be his queen.

He held out his hand, and she took it in her small, graceful one. They sealed their fragile, tentative alliance with one firm shake.

"Thank you," he said.

"It will be an honor to rule beside you, Percival Comyn," she responded.

When she let go and started toward the door to let him out, he took hold of her arm, stilling her. "I must beg one more favor of you. I need you to write to your king."

ॐ 33 ॐ
MERCY

Several days of unsuccessful negotiations passed. With each one, Mercy's fear that Tamriel might truly have to give into Queen Cerelia's demand grew. Every morning after breakfast, Tamriel and the queen sequestered themselves in a meeting room for hours. Having no duties to distract her from her worries, Mercy took to exploring the castle with Faye and her siblings. Every inch of the palace was opulently adorned: the walls covered in murals; the rooms filled with lavish furniture, priceless rugs, and tapestries; the halls lined with marble busts of previous Feyndaran queens. After a while, though, her awe wore off, leaving a bitter taste in her mouth. Every piece of finery served as a reminder of Feyndara's wealth—of the fact that Queen Cerelia could easily provide Tamriel the aid he needed.

Sensing her exceptionally foul mood one morning, Faye suggested sparring in the garden. Mercy begrudgingly agreed; she would much rather sulk and pace outside the meeting room, but she could do nothing to make the negotiations pass any faster.

As she slid her sheathed daggers onto her belt, her

thoughts returned to the night Queen Cerelia had announced her intention to marry Tamriel off to Marieve, and her chest constricted painfully. As much as it killed her to imagine giving Tamriel up, she would bear that agony if it meant restoring his throne. As much as she detested admitting it, Cerelia was right: his duty was to his country first and foremost. He was the king they needed. He was the king who would free the slaves and bring an end to the Cirisian Wars. She couldn't stand in the way of that. She *wouldn't*.

"You're thinking about Tamriel and Marieve again," someone said. Mercy turned to find Faye standing in the open doorway of her room, her arms crossed loosely over her chest. "It's written all over your face. You know, you are terrible at hiding your thoughts when you're angry." She looked down, shuffled her feet, then added, "About that promise you tried to make him swear... I thought you'd be overjoyed he refused you. He's not going to give in to Cerelia's demands."

"I am. Of course I am. But..." Mercy fidgeted with her sapphire ring. "But we'd already be marching on Sandori if Tamriel had just given in. Who knows how long these negotiations will go on? Who knows if Cerelia will even back down? Tamriel is locked away with her for hours each day, trying to reach a compromise, and *nothing's working*. Meanwhile, thousands of elves are suffering under their enslavement back home. They are being abused by their masters, and Tamriel would be able to stop it if he were on the throne. But he's not, and it's all because of me."

Faye's expression turned sympathetic. She crossed the room and stopped before Mercy, grasping her upper arms. "This is *not* your fault," she said sternly. "The only people to blame for the crimes exacted against the slaves are the scum who commit them. None of this is on your shoulders. Trust that Tamriel knows what he is doing. He has spent all his life surrounded by a court full of people who would have loved to see him and his father removed from power. Cerelia's nothing more than an old crone. He can handle her."

"She's an old crone with an *army*."

"And I bet she'll pledge her soldiers to Tamriel before the week is over." Faye slipped her arm through Mercy's and led her out of the room. "Tamriel loves you, and you love him. You are not going to give that up. I won't *let* either of you give that up. Before you argue that it's selfish to put each other before the kingdom, let me remind you how much you both have done for the people of Beltharos over the past few months. Do you think just anyone could cure a plague and defeat an army led by a bloodthirsty, blood-magic-wielding Cirisian and live to tell the tale? Do you think there is anyone else who could have taken down the Assassins' Guild after weeks of torture? I don't. I think you've more than proven yourself capable of being Tamriel's queen. The two of you were meant for each other; after everything you've been through, you've earned a little bit of selfishness."

Despite her worries, Mercy found herself smiling, her mood lifting. "Thank you, Faye." She stopped and pulled Faye into a hug in the middle of the hall. "I don't know what I would do without you. You've always been a better friend than I deserve."

Faye stepped back and flicked her braid over her shoulder, her lips curving into a teasing grin. "Maybe someday you'll find a way to pay me back for my wise counsel and unflagging support."

Mercy started toward the main doors of the castle, which had been flung open to allow a cool breeze to sweep through the great hall. Beyond them, the gardens spread out in a vast sea of green, narrow streams twining through the manicured lawn and between bushes laden with flowers. Without looking at her friend, she said, "Perhaps I could tell Kaius how you really feel about him."

"You—You wouldn't *dare*," she sputtered after a short, stunned pause.

"Although, I don't think I need to tell him. He's not blind, and you're not that good at hiding it."

Faye rushed after her, a flush rising on her cheeks. "He's a *friend*."

Mercy grinned, not bothering to respond.

Outside, Ino and Cassia were already sparring in a large patch of open grass just beyond the main doors. Mercy approached them, her dark mood temporarily forgotten, and examined her sister's stance as Faye trailed silently behind her. Her siblings had been talented yet untrained when she met them, but their skills had grown considerably in the months since. Cassia's form had improved. Ino, with his larger build, had learned how to strike harder to compensate for his size and slower speed. They moved across the grass in a whirl of leather armor and glinting steel. Matthias, lounging on the grass a few feet away, grinned and waved to Mercy.

Ino brought his sword down, straight toward Cassia's chest. She caught his blade with her own, then reached behind her back and pulled a dagger from her waistband, angling it under Ino's chin in one smooth movement. He dropped his sword, surrendering.

"You won."

She dropped her weapons, a look of triumph on her face. When she reached up to wipe the perspiration from her brow, a smirk tugged at Ino's lips. He lunged for her, and she let out a shriek when he crushed her in a hug and spun her around.

"Stop! You're *sweaty*!"

"So are you." He laughed. The sound was so rare coming from him that she couldn't help but smile. Mercy sat cross-legged beside Matthias, content to simply watch them. Faye settled on her other side.

At last, Ino set Cassia on the ground. She placed a hand on his arm to steady herself, dizzy from all the spinning. Ino bowed to Mercy, peering up at her with sparkling, mischievous eyes. "Any critiques, O Great Assassin?"

"I wouldn't advise picking your opponents up and *hugging* them."

"Well, they certainly wouldn't be expecting it."

"I wasn't," Cassia agreed, picking at the sweat-soaked collar of her tunic in distaste. "Please tell me you'll bathe before you hug me again."

"I do believe that lovely aroma you're smelling is of your own making," Matthias said. Mercy chuckled. *This* was what their life would become after Tamriel reclaimed his throne: joking, teasing, laughing.

Faye craned her neck and surveyed the vast gardens. "Where is Calum? I've barely seen him these past few days."

"He and the Strykers went into town right after breakfast," Cassia responded, nodding toward the gate. "Supposedly, a local weaponsmith has granted them use of his workshop, but I think they've just been using Drake's money to buy drinks for all the pretty young women at the nearest tavern."

"Whatever they're doing, I hope they're having fun," Mercy said, remembering the shock on Calum's face when he'd seen the Strykers in Cowayne. After what he had endured under his father's control, the old Calum—the charming, funny, sarcastic Calum—had been coming back slowly over the past few weeks, but nothing had seemed to heal him as much as his reunion with the Strykers. Just thinking of it made her smile. The Strykers were the family he had chosen, just like Faye and Mercy had chosen each other so many years ago.

Soft footsteps sounded on the grass behind her, and Mercy turned to see Lady Marieve and her cousin Alistair striding toward them. Marieve was clad in an exquisite gown of emerald silk. Her hair had been twisted and pinned into a cascade of curls down her back, showing off the long string of pearls around her neck and the emeralds dangling from her earlobes. She looked, Mercy noted with amusement, more like a work of art than a person—just another beautiful sculpture to decorate the halls of the castle.

She, Matthias, and Faye stood as Marieve and Alistair stopped a few feet away and dipped their heads in respect. They bowed in return, while Ino and Cassia picked up their weapons and returned to the castle to bathe and change. Matthias mumbled an excuse and jogged after them. Mercy couldn't blame him. She hadn't been able to look Marieve in the eye since the queen announced her demand that Tamriel marry her. If she did, she feared she'd do something irreversible—but *deeply* satisfying.

"I'm sorry for interrupting," Marieve said, watching Mercy's siblings walk away. "You looked like you were having a good time."

"We were. Your home is lovely," Mercy responded curtly, fighting to keep her voice from turning icy. "To what do I owe the honor of your company, my lady?"

Faye shifted, shooting Mercy a warning look.

Marieve twisted her strand of pearls around her long, thin fingers. Unbidden, an image of those graceful fingers cupping Tamriel's face and running through his hair filled Mercy's mind, and she promptly forced it—and the accompanying flash of jealousy—out of her mind.

She will not *win. Cerelia will not win,* she told herself, but her conviction waned a little more with each passing day.

"I want to apologize," Marieve finally said. "I see how desperate your king is to return to his country, and I see how much he cares for his people. I'm sorry the negotiations have dragged on for so long. The tyrant who sits on Tamriel's throne must be defeated and brought to justice for his crimes."

Mercy straightened a bit at that. "Does that mean you'll speak to your grandmother on our behalf? Convince her to give up this demand that he marry you?"

Marieve's brows furrowed. "What? No. No, of course not. What my grandmother said the other day was correct—he is a king and does not have the luxury of marrying for love. If she is going to pledge troops to him, she must ensure that our country gains something in exchange. She wants Cirisor, and having me on the Beltharan throne ensures that both our countries will honor their claims to the Islands. Such is the nature of politics," she said, seemingly oblivious to how patronizing she sounded. "I came to apologize for the pain this uncomfortable situation has caused you, and to assure you that I will make a wonderful queen for Tamriel. You needn't worry."

Faye's eyes widened, and Mercy stepped back, her anger flaring. She would give Tamriel up if it were the only way for him to reclaim his throne, but hearing Marieve speak as if it was an inevitability—like she was *entitled* to him—made Mercy's blood boil. Beside her, Faye's lovely face was impassive, the only hint of her rage in the shadow behind her eyes.

Mercy was glad Ino and Cassia had not left the swords behind.

"And where would I go once you became queen?" she asked, struggling to keep her voice even.

Alistair regarded her warily, but Marieve smiled, undeterred by Mercy's anger. "Considering what I've heard of your skills in combat, I suspect you would do well in the guard. Not in the king's personal guard, of course—we would not want the nobles to think you were still together—but you would have your choice in where you go. Perhaps Westwater would suit you. You could command a troop along the border."

Westwater. The farthest Mercy could get from the capital without leaving the country. She realized belatedly that Marieve wasn't oblivious—no, just the opposite: she was cunning, exactly like her grandmother. She would send Mercy away knowing she would never have to fear an attack from the former Assassin; if anything were to happen to Marieve— even if Mercy made it look like an accident—Queen Cerelia would send her army into Beltharos to reclaim the crown she had helped Tamriel win.

Mercy forced a tight smile. "How very thoughtful of you."

Just then, Tamriel emerged from the castle, lifting a hand to shield his eyes from the sun. He frowned when he saw Marieve and Alistair and started toward them. "What's going on here? What are you discussing?" he asked when he was near enough to sense the tension between the four of them.

Marieve bowed. "You, Your Majesty."

"Me? I'm flattered. Mercy, Faye, may I speak to you in private, please?"

Marieve and Alistair bowed again and started toward the castle. As soon as they were out of earshot, Mercy took a deep, calming breath and asked, "What do you need to talk to us about?"

"Nothing. You just looked about two seconds away from strangling Marieve, and I figured that would put a *slight* damper on our relationship with the queen." He forced a smile, but Mercy saw the fierce protectiveness in his eyes. He shot a dark look at Marieve and Alistair's retreating forms. "Are you okay?"

"I'm fine. But the sooner we get out of here, the better. I can't promise I'll be able to endure the company of that pretentious bitch much longer. How did your meeting with the queen go?"

His expression was answer enough. He opened his mouth to elaborate, but before he could say a word, his gaze lifted to something beyond her shoulder. "By the Creator..."

Mercy and Faye turned to see five Feyndaran guards on horseback pass through the gate at the edge of the gardens. A bronze-skinned elf was riding with the guard-commander at the front of the group. When he saw them standing in the middle of the garden, gawking at him, Kaius grinned and lifted a hand in greeting.

34

FAYE

Faye stared at Kaius in disbelief as he and the guards approached. She had not expected to see him until their return to Fallmond, but here he was, before her. *What in the Creator's name is he doing in Rhys?*

A smile tugged at her lips when he waved at her. She'd missed her friend in the week and a half they'd been apart. How many times during their journey across the sea had she scanned the deck, looking for him? How many times had she searched for a glimpse of tanned skin, the flash of a grin, the sparkle in his green eyes?

After they dismounted, the guards bowed to Tamriel, then two broke away and disappeared into the castle to alert their queen of the elf's arrival.

"What are you doing here?" Tamriel asked. "Don't get me wrong, I'm happy to see another friendly face, but I thought you'd be busy in the Islands."

"Nynev and I think it in our people's best interest to have someone from the Islands involved in the negotiations. We'd like a say in the future of our land, and as I've been made the new First of Odomyr's clan, I volunteered to come." Kaius glanced at Faye as he said it, and she dragged her eyes away, focusing on her hands. A pang of longing tugged at her heart. "Nynev remained behind to speak with the other Firsts about pledging fighters to your cause, Your Majesty. She'll be heading here as soon as training is under way."

"Eager to join the negotiations?" Mercy asked dryly. "How many people do we need to invite before we wear the queen down?"

"That's part of the reason, yes, but she also wanted to see you. She started crying when I told her you survived the Guildmother's abduction. Then she made me describe how you killed Illynor in excruciating detail...twice."

In her periphery, Faye saw her friend's face light up. She had never met the elf of whom they spoke, but the name snagged on something in her mind... When they were in Ellesmere, waiting for the troops to arrive, she had overheard Tamriel telling Mercy about what had happened to Nynev and her sister. She had stood down the hall from their room, tears welling in her eyes, as she listened to Tamriel describe how Niamh had given her life to kill Firesse and end the plague. She had wanted to comfort Mercy—her friend had been through so much already; she should not have had to mourn another person's death—but guilt had kept her rooted to the spot. Faye had fought in that battle on Firesse's side. She could have killed so many more of Mercy's friends. She could have been the one responsible for Mercy's grief, and the knowledge had left a sour taste in her mouth.

"It'll be good to see her again. How long has it been? Two months? Two and a half? I can't even keep track of the days anymore," Mercy said, frowning. "How is she coping with her sister's death?"

Sorrow flashed across Kaius's face. *Did he know Niamh?*

Faye wondered. "It has been hard on her, but having a clan to look after and recruits to train has helped. This wound will take a long time to heal, but she's tough. She'll—"

"And who, pray tell, is our newest guest?"

They turned to see Queen Cerelia striding across the grass, a handful of guards trailing behind her, but no family in sight. *Strange*. Every time Faye had seen the queen, she'd been surrounded by no fewer than a half-dozen members of her family. It felt odd to imagine them with duties of their own to attend.

Kaius and the guards who had accompanied him dropped into low bows. "My name is Kaius, Your Majesty. I come as a representative of the Firsts of the Cirisian Islands and as a member of King Tamriel's army."

She gestured for him to rise and, when he obeyed, scanned him from head to toe, taking in his Cirisian tattoos with a hungry gleam in her eyes. Anger flooded Faye, and she stepped closer to Kaius. The queen was a fool if she thought she could manipulate Kaius into giving her control over the Islands.

"Welcome to my home, Kaius of the Islands," Cerelia said with a regal nod of her head. "I look forward to learning more about your people. I shall give you some time to rest from your long journey, but I would like to speak with you before supper tonight."

"It would be my honor to oblige."

After the queen departed, the remaining guards helped Kaius empty his saddlebags and unload his pack before calling on a servant girl to take them to the guest wing. Kaius fell into step beside Faye as they made their way through the great hall. The memory of their quick goodbyes in Fallmond surfaced in her mind. He had stepped close and promised they would see each other again soon, his breath warm against her cheek as he whispered the words. Just before pulling back, he had reached out, grabbed her hand, and given it a quick squeeze.

She watched out of the corner of her eye as he admired the floor-to-ceiling murals. "It's nice to have you back," she said, low enough Tamriel and Mercy wouldn't be able to hear. Mercy teased her about Kaius enough as it was.

"Miss me?"

"Mercy did. Terribly. You're all she could talk about. Tamriel was quite jealous."

"Oh, I'm sure she couldn't get me out of her mind." Kaius shot her a crooked grin, and she pretended to be too absorbed in her surroundings to notice. Nothing had happened between them, and nothing ever would. Even if they survived the battle, they'd be going their separate ways once it was over—Kaius to Cirisor, and Faye to Fallmond. There was no point in giving in to the attraction she felt for him. At best, they'd only have a couple weeks together before leaving for their own homes. At worst...

She forced the thoughts out of her mind. They were friends and allies. Nothing more.

Kaius bumped her shoulder. "I missed you, too."

"She can't ask that of you. Is she mad?" Kaius gaped at Mercy and Tamriel, his eyes wide. As before, Tamriel had taken to pacing his and Mercy's bedroom, while Mercy helplessly watched on from her seat on the settee.

"I've been trying to negotiate with Queen Cerelia for days, and we're getting nowhere." Tamriel ran his hands down his face and let out a long sigh. "She doesn't even offer any other solutions. She just sits there and listens to me try and convince her to change her mind. It's like arguing with a rock."

"I suggested a way to get the army you need," Mercy said, and Faye's heart broke at the pain that flashed across her friend's face.

"No. I already told you, that is the line Cerelia may not cross. I am not giving you up to reclaim my throne."

"What other choice do we have? Believe me, I don't want you to marry Marieve either, Tamriel! But Nicholas needs to face justice for his crimes and that can't happen if you don't have an army!"

"We'll figure something else out," Kaius interrupted, his calming tone immediately soothing their distress. Mercy sagged against Faye, leaning her head on her shoulder, while Tamriel dropped to one of the cushions with an annoyed huff. "Cerelia wants the Islands more than anything. We're not going to give them to her, of course, but there must be some way to appease her. Maybe through a trade agreement? We don't have much, but we have plenty of natural resources."

Instead of responding, Tamriel merely shut his eyes and pinched the bridge of his nose. Faye wished she could help him in some way, beyond sympathetic looks and simple reassurances. Over the past several days, she had been wracking her brain trying to come up with a way around Cerelia's demand...and she'd come up empty. It didn't help that Cerelia wasn't budging. Negotiations required a give and take, yet the queen seemed not at all inclined to change her mind. She thought Tamriel would break, but Faye knew him better than that. He wouldn't give Mercy up for anything.

They discussed the negotiations for the better part of an hour. In truth, most of that time was spent sitting in silence, each of them considering—and discarding—multiple possible deals to make with the queen. She didn't want money. She didn't want trade. She wanted the Islands, and she was willing to destroy Tamriel and Mercy's relationship to get it.

When they finally dispersed to prepare for lunch, Faye followed Kaius into the hall, closed the double doors behind her, and let out a long, dejected sigh. "How are we going to get out of this mess?"

"I'm sure we'll find a way. We still have time. Nicholas might have even given up his search by now."

She shook her head. "He's like Mother Illynor—he's obsessive about gaining and keeping power. He's not going to rest until Tamriel and Mercy are dead, along with everyone who helped them. Then he's going to come for your people. We need to figure out a solution *now*."

"...We could fight without her. It would be risky, but we might be able to eke out a victory if we play our cards right."

"Not without losing the people we care about. I don't want to lose any more friends." *I don't want to lose you*, she almost said, but she bit her tongue before the admission had a chance to slip out. "You saw how much Firesse's war cost your people."

He flinched. "I know."

She moved closer to him, aching at the haunted look on his face. How many friends had he lost in the battle? How many clan members had he mourned? "After everything that has happened, are you ready to fight in another war?"

He was quiet for a few moments, then he murmured, "No. I'm terrified of what's to come. While I was in hiding in Sandori, trying to help those who had been injured in the fight, I prayed to the gods that I would never see another battle for the rest of my life. Alas, they had other ideas." He glanced at the tattoos coiling around his forearms and down his hands—the permanent reminder of his family, his home. "I don't want to fight, but I will do it because I know that is what is best for the future of my people. If I must give my life for them, I will do it gladly."

"Don't say that," she responded sharply, even as a part of her admired him for his selflessness and bravery. "You're not going to die."

"I hope you're right." He started toward his room—only two doors down from her own—and looked back at her before he entered. "I would truly miss the chance to get to know you better, Faye," he said before slipping inside.

She didn't see Kaius or Tamriel much over the next three days. They spent every morning in a meeting with the queen, and every afternoon sequestering themselves in the royal library or Tamriel's bedroom to discuss the negotiations. The lack of progress was driving them insane—Mercy most of all. To take her mind off everything, Faye enlisted the help of her siblings in distracting her. One day, they explored the city, marveling at the treehouses and the network of bridges that spanned from one platform to another. The next day, they joined some off-duty guards on a hunt in the forest, bringing back two deer and a boar for the evening's feast. The day after that, Mercy paced outside the meeting room while Faye tried—and failed—to talk her into wandering the gardens with her. Faye couldn't blame her. The more time passed, the more nervous they all became. Tamriel would fight Cerelia's demand with everything he had...but eventually, he would have no choice but to give in or give up.

That night, Faye was following the Strykers, Matthias, Ino, and Cassia across the garden when she caught a glimpse of someone beyond the rows of carefully-trimmed hedges. He was seated by the edge of one of the ponds, dragging a finger through the water. The moon was mostly obscured by clouds, yet even in the darkness, she recognized him.

"Find a carriage to hire," she called ahead to Calum. "I'll meet you at the gates in a minute."

"Don't take too long," Nerran responded with a crooked grin. "There's a lovely barmaid I've been eyeing, and I want to be there when she's finished for the evening."

"If she's wise, she'll be long gone by the time we show up," Amir retorted.

She left them to their friendly bickering as she wove through the hedges and crossed one of the small bridges spanning a stream. Kaius glanced up as she approached.

"Are you alright?"

He nodded. "Just thinking about the war. Part of me wants this whole mess to be over, while the rest hopes the battle never comes." The breeze snagged on Kaius's shoulder-length hair and sent a lock dancing in front of his eyes. He reached up, tucked it behind one pointed ear, then gestured to the grass beside him. "Care to sit with me?"

"As much as I would, Calum and the others are waiting for me. They've found a tavern for drinks and dancing, and I won't turn down a chance to get out of this Creator-forsaken castle. You should join us."

He glanced up at the sliver of the moon visible through the clouds. "I'd be missing a perfect night to brood. Besides, I don't think I'll be very good company at the moment."

"That's why you need a distraction." She smiled and offered a hand to help him up. "Come on. Have fun for once in your life."

Despite his somber mood, the corner of his mouth twitched upward at that. "You think I don't know how to have fun?"

"I haven't seen any evidence that you do."

Hearing the challenge in her voice, he grinned and

accepted her hand. Once he was on his feet, he slipped his other arm around her waist and smirked when her breath hitched. Only a few inches separated their faces. If he wanted to, he could kiss her. She wasn't entirely certain she would stop him.

He dipped his head and whispered into her ear, "If you would let me, Faye, I could show you just how wrong you are."

A tremor danced down her spine.

"Would you want that, Faye? Would you let me?"

Yes. Everything within her longed to say it, to give in, to feel his strong arms wrap around her and his lips move against hers. She wanted *more* than that...but she forced herself to remember the coming battle. She imagined him lying dead in the field, his beautiful green eyes staring sightlessly at the sky, his bronze skin pale and bloodied. She imagined him emerging from the battle unscathed and finding her that way, her long dark hair matted with blood. Neither of them deserved that heartache.

It's better this way. It's better if we're only friends.

He felt her stiffen and let go, taking a few careful steps back.

"I'm sorry," she said, wrapping her arms around herself to ward off the sudden chill.

"I understand." He gestured for her to lead the way to the gate. "After you."

Half an hour later, Calum found a table near the rear of the tavern large enough to seat all of ten of them. While he and the Strykers wandered toward the bar to order drinks, Cassia, Faye, and Matthias slid onto one of the benches, and Kaius and Ino claimed the one opposite theirs. Across the room, several tables had been cleared away to form a makeshift dance floor. A fast-paced, hearty folk song filled the room, too loud for conversation, and Faye tapped her foot to the beat. She had never seen dancing like this: fast and wild, the faces of the dancers flushed and exuberant as they swung each other around. They linked arms and spun, then broke apart, did a series of intricate steps, and repeated with a new partner. Faye grew dizzy just watching.

"These are on us," Calum announced when he and the Strykers returned with mugs and several pitchers of ale. He had to shout to be heard over the music. "We've been working on weapons for Tamriel, of course, but we've managed to pick up a few jobs here and there that allow us to indulge on occasion. After all, a king without his royal coffers is no better than us peasants!"

"To mediocrity!" Nerran chuckled, lifting his mug in a toast.

"Hear, hear!"

Faye laughed and claimed her own mug, enjoying simply being out of the castle, away from the politics of court life.

By the time they'd finished a few rounds of drinks, they had attracted a small crowd—mostly young ladies vying for the affections of Calum and the others. Calum, Kaius, and Ino remained polite, but did not indulge the lust sparkling in the girls' eyes. Conversely, Nerran and Matthias positively *adored* the attention. They grinned at the girls, chuckling when the young ladies melted at their charms, and escorted them one by one to the dance floor. Amir and Hewlin joined them for some dances, and Oren even partook of a few jigs.

"Well, sister, shall we dance?" Ino asked Cassia, who eagerly nodded and took his hand, her face flushed from the alcohol. He offered her one of his rare smiles and guided her to the dance floor, leaving Calum, Faye, and Kaius alone. Immediately, a group of three young women approached.

"The next song is a group dance," one said, "and we need three more people. Will you join us?"

Calum glanced at Faye and Kaius, raising a brow. "Shall we?"

Faye jumped to her feet, a little light-headed, and nodded. She had no clue how to do any of the dances, but she'd been watching, taking in the organized chaos. The few mugs of ale she'd consumed certainly helped to bolster her confidence as she followed the girls to the front of the room.

"I have no idea what I'm doing," she said to one of them.

"It's easy; you'll get the hang of it. Here, stand right here." She placed her hands on Faye's shoulders and positioned her to Calum's right. "Otsana, join them."

A red-haired girl took her place on Calum's left, then the rest of their small group lined up across from them, Kaius in the middle, and one girl on either side. The archer caught Faye's eye and grinned as the musicians began to play. Following Otsana's lead, they linked hands and began the dance. At first, Faye stumbled over the moves, uncertain and a little tipsy. She'd never danced like this in the Guild. They took a few steps forward, clapped their hands, and stepped back, stomping their feet as the music swelled. Otsana hooked her arm around Calum's, and they spun a few times before Otsana gestured for him to turn around and do the same with Faye. She grinned as he spun her so fast her feet nearly flew out from under her, letting out a wild, joyful laugh. As she turned, she spotted Ino, Cassia, and Matthias doing the same across the room, clapping along to the beat.

After a few more turns, the three of them formed a line again, standing opposite Kaius and the two young women. Although when they moved forward this time, Kaius and the girls lifted their arms to allow Faye, Calum, and Otsana to pass underneath. They were faced with a new group of three now—Nerran and two women who'd been working at the bar earlier that night. He winked at Faye before they began the steps anew.

They continued like that, clapping, stomping, spinning, continuing around the room, until the music fell quiet. Faye released Calum's hand and joined the dancers' wild applause, unable to keep the foolish grin from her face. She hadn't felt so light, so carefree, since she left her home eleven years ago. She was breathing hard, her face flushed, her tunic plastered to her skin. It was unbearably hot inside the tavern; every window was open, but what little breeze they let in offered no reprive from the heat of so many bodies. Across the room, she spotted Kaius and the young women with whom he'd been dancing drop a few coins into the box at the lute player's feet.

Calum followed her gaze to the archer, then wiped a few sweaty strands of hair from his brow. "Want to get some air?"

She nodded, allowing him to lead her through the room and out the front doors of the tavern. As soon as they emerged onto the cobblestone street, the cool night air wrapped around them, a welcome relief from the warmth of the room. A few people lingered near the doors, drinking, chatting, or simply taking in the fresh air. Calum guided her past them, then slumped against the wall, tipping his head back to stare up at the stars. His chest rose and fell quickly as he tried to catch his breath. Faye lifted her long braid from her neck, enjoying the kiss of the breeze against her skin. Several small shops lined either side of the road, their shutters latched tightly. A few of the treehouses above them glowed with soft, flickering lights, their windows open to allow the strains of music to drift in from the tavern.

She glanced toward the doors as another song began. Part of her yearned to join in, but she wasn't eager to return to the stifling room just yet. Instead, she replayed the few glimpses she'd caught of Kaius as they danced around the tavern, always just within sight, always just out of reach. The memory of his wide, dazzling grin filled her with warmth. Whether he would admit it or not, he'd needed to get out of the castle. He'd needed a night to forget about the uncertainty of their future, and she was glad she had been able to provide that. As temporary as it was, it was good to see him taking time for himself—not worrying about her, Mercy, Tamriel, or his people. Even if it was just for that night, he could set aside the weight on his shoulders and have fun.

"What's on your mind?" Calum asked, startling her out of her reverie. He'd turned toward her, his head cocked as he studied her. "You're smiling."

"Nothing," she responded, too fast.

"Liar." He crossed his arms, his lips twitching into a knowing smirk. "Could you possibly be thinking about a certain archer with dreamy green eyes?"

She was grateful it was too dark for him to see her blush. "You think his eyes are dreamy?"

"Listen, I may not be interested in men, but I'm not too proud to admit when one is handsomer than I am. As it doesn't happen often, I find it imperative to mark the occasion."

"Has anyone ever told you that you have a massive ego?"

"It matches the size of my—"

She slapped a hand over his mouth. "Don't you dare say it."

He swatted her away, laughing. "I was going to say it matches the size of my crossbow."

"That sounds like a euphemism," she said, grimacing.

"Maybe it is."

"By the Creator, Calum!" She chuckled, and he shot her a triumphant grin. "Have you no shame?"

"None at all. You know me. Anyway, it's been far too long since you really, truly laughed. It's good to see you haven't forgotten how." Every trace of humor faded from his face, replaced by concern. "Look, I did want to get some fresh air, but I also wanted to talk to you about Kaius. Are you truly going to keep pretending nothing is going on between you two? A blind man could see you two care about each other. You two shoot each other more sappy looks than Tamriel and Mercy do, which is saying something."

"It's...complicated."

"Nonsense. Kaius would swim across the Abraxas Sea, wrestle the Beltharan crown out of Nicholas's hands, and present it to you if you asked. Which reminds me—he deeply enjoyed humiliating me when I was Firesse's captive in the Islands, so if you could do me a favor and ask him to do something that will make *him* look like a fool for once, I would appreciate it."

She fixed him with a look.

"Ugh. You Assassins are so stubborn. We don't have long before we march on Sandori. One way or another, the negotiations are going to end soon. I say you spend as much time as you can with the people you love, because you never know when you're going to lose them. Creator knows I should have realized that sooner." His voice wobbled at the end of his sentence, and he looked down at his feet.

"Are you thinking about the noblewoman you loved?" she asked softly, remembering how hurt and shocked he had been when he'd found out about her death.

He nodded. "Her name was Elise," he murmured, his voice raw with love and pain. "I wanted to marry her. I would have done anything for her. We made so many stupid mistakes—so many stupid, *stupid* mistakes—and she lost her life because of it. Because *I* talked her into forging that damned contract on Tamriel's life. I will never forgive myself for that. Even now, I have nightmares of standing there in the Plaza, watching her be led to the executioner's block. I fight my way through the crowds, screaming her name, trying to get to her, to be with her... And I never make it there in time."

She rested a hand on his arm as he took a shuddering breath. "Calum..."

"Being here, surviving everything we've been through, is my punishment. For the rest of my life, I have to bear the knowledge that she'd still be alive if she hadn't helped me. I would give anything for just one more day with her. So—whether you want my advice or not—I think you should tell him how you feel. If, Creator forbid, something happens during the battle, you don't want to spend the rest of your days wondering whether you should have told him the truth."

She shook her head, even though she heard the truth in his words. Was it not selfish to indulge in her desire when there was so much more at stake? Was this pain not what she deserved after all the crimes she committed during the war? Perhaps if they both survived the battle, then they could explore what it would mean to be together. Until then...

"Let's go inside. I think another song is starting."

Before he could press her further, she turned and started toward the tavern. Just before she opened the doors, she heard Calum let out a long sigh and mutter, "Foolish, lovesick Assassins..."

She immediately found Kaius among the dancers, standing between Otsana and another girl he'd danced with earlier. They'd gathered into a large circle, linking their hands. He caught her eye and gestured with a jerk of his chin for her to join in. Calum's words still echoing in her ears, she smiled and obeyed. When she neared, he released Otsana's hand and claimed Faye's, drawing her into the circle. Behind her, the musicians began to play another jig. As one, they all rushed into the center of the room, crashing and colliding before dancing back. Faye couldn't fight the grin that sprang to her lips. When they rushed forward again, Kaius's grip tightened on hers so he wouldn't lose hold of her.

"You were right," he said in the midst of the chaos, shouting to be heard over the music and laughter. "I'm having fun, and it's all because of you. Thank you for inviting me."

She squeezed his hand, trying to ignore the flutters within her stomach. "I'm glad you agreed to come."

The sincerity of his smile melted her heart. "I wouldn't have missed it for the world."

❦ 35 ❦
PERCIVAL

Nicholas's eyes narrowed when Percival and Riona appeared, arm-in-arm, at the doors to the council chamber. Coming here, demanding their place at the council meeting, had been Riona's idea. Percival had not relished the thought of spending more time in his uncle's presence—especially after what had occurred between them in the study—but Riona had insisted. She did not want to waste any time in carving out her place among this court, she had said.

His uncle's flat stare weighed heavily on Percival. Self-conscious, he started to lift a hand to the bruise marring his right cheek. Before he could, Riona caught his hand and linked her slender fingers through his.

"Good morning, all," she said to the council, an easy smile on her full lips. Despite the intrusion, the advisors paused to offer her warm smiles and greetings. Percival stifled a snort as she led him to the table. Apparently he wasn't the only one who was affected by her beauty.

They claimed two chairs a few seats down from Nicholas, whose expression hadn't softened in the slightest. His good eye roved from Percival's bruised cheek, down his arm, and to their linked hands. His lips pursed. He was trying to decipher their intentions behind attending the council meeting, behind showing up uninvited, behind this display of affection.

"She is to be my queen soon," Percival said in answer to his unasked question. He kept his expression neutral, hiding his nerves. Every time he looked at his uncle, he saw Nicholas's fist swinging toward his face. "I thought she should know more about the kingdom over which she is to rule. More than that, it's boring being sequestered to the castle. Might as well do something productive while I'm stuck here."

The nobles murmured quietly amongst themselves, sensing the tension in the air. They didn't know the exact nature of Percival and Nicholas's relationship, but they had gathered enough from the few interactions they'd witnessed thus far.

Riona stared right back at Nicholas, her eyes narrowed. "I will remind you, my lord, that as your rulers, we do not need your permission to attend our own council meeting."

"No, of course not," he responded, seemingly unbothered by the barb. He leaned forward and studied the large map of Beltharos spread across the tabletop. Wooden figures marked the locations of the troops scattered across the fishing sector, converging along the king's highway and around Xilor, where the king was last seen. "We've had no sightings of the former king since the attack. While we know he did not perish in the battle, it's unclear whether Tamriel has abandoned his goal of reclaiming his throne—as unlikely as that scenario is, we must consider it—or he is under the delusion that he will be able to rally enough of a force to retaliate." He swept an arm toward the eastern edge of the map, where Feyndara would have sat had the paper continued. "Queen Cerelia may hate this kingdom, but she wants the Islands, which gives Tamriel a bargaining chip for negotiating for troops."

"*If* he made it past their shores," one of the council members said, his tone making it clear just how unlikely he considered the possibility, "could he have offered to withdraw his troops and cede the land to her in exchange for an army?"

Nicholas ran a hand along his jaw. As much as Nicholas was trying to hide it, Percival could tell he was frustrated by the entire endeavor. He had not planned on weathering such a drawn-out pursuit when he had decided to turn on Tamriel. He had expected to kill Tamriel and his allies and seize the throne uncontested. He had not foreseen Tamriel evading him at every turn. Hopefully, his eagerness to put an end to the threat to Percival's rule would make him careless.

And hopefully, his focus on the hunt for Tamriel would allow Percival and Celeste's plot to go undetected until it was too late.

"I cannot imagine he would hand over the Islands that easily, but if that was all that stood between him and gathering the army he needed to reclaim his throne, he would do it." Nicholas tilted his head, considering. "There's no point in pursuing him if he is going to lead his army straight to Sandori. He'll be delivering himself and his allies straight to our doorstep, and we'll be ready. This city has withstood sieges before. I'm going to call my troops back to the city, and we'll meet him in battle in the fields. How soul-crushing it will be for him to come so close to victory, and yet fall short when it matters most."

The entire time Nicholas spoke, Percival pretended to lavish Riona with attention—holding her hand, whispering in her ear, toying with the gold bracelets gracing her wrist—but he went still at his uncle's last sentence. Anger rushed over him. Had his uncle always been this cruel? He'd punished Percival with insults and fists repeatedly, but he had never acted with such malice toward anyone else until he turned on Tamriel.

Riona leaned over and, in a honeyed voice, whispered, "School your features. Keep glaring at him and he'll realize you've been paying attention." With her free hand, she reached up and brushed a curl from Percival's brow. "Remember, we're just here to put in an appearance. Now laugh."

He let out a forced chuckle, one he hoped the council members would mistake for embarrassment at Riona's flirtatious tone and coy grin. They'd needed an excuse to listen in on Nicholas's plans, and what better one than to play the roles in which his uncle had cast them? For now, they would be the perfect royals, a young, love-struck couple for the subjects to adore, while Nicholas pulled the political strings in the background.

"We'll work on that," Riona murmured.

Nicholas shot them an annoyed look. *Good.* "We cannot underestimate Queen Cerelia's contribution to Tamriel's army, which is why I have written to King Domhnall asking for Rivosi troops to join my own outside the city. By my estimation, they shall arrive shortly after the royal wedding."

Percival glanced at Riona sidelong, remembering too late to hide the concern flashing across his face. *If* Tamriel was alive, *if* he convinced Queen Cerelia to give him aid, *if* he returned to Sandori with an army at his back, he could have had a chance at defeating Nicholas's troops, but not with Rivosi soldiers to bolster the numbers.

Nicholas saw his expression and smiled. "Don't worry, Your Majesty. The deposed king may be coming for his throne. But if he does, we are going to take him down once and for all."

Percival rubbed his tired eyes with the heels of his palms as he approached the king's chambers. After the council members finished planning the impending attack, they began discussing the necessary arrangements for the royal wedding. Riona had responded with enthusiasm to many of their ideas—even going so far as to proudly show off sketches she had made of her gowns for the wedding and banquet—while Percival had played the dutiful groom-to-be. He'd listened intently, doted on his betrothed, and offered opinions on countless matters about which he could not have cared less. Who cared if the napkins were embroidered or lace-trimmed, ivory or beige? Who cared whether the food was served on goldware or silverware? (He had learned, after stating that exact sentiment, that gold was *always* the answer, according to three noblewomen who had gasped in horror, gaping as if he'd suggested they forgo the entire banquet and eat out of a trough instead.)

He jammed his spectacles on as he entered his chambers, then stopped mid-step when he saw the sleeping form atop one of the settees. Celeste was sprawled out on the velvet settee in the middle of the room, a blanket tangled around her legs, her hair a dark curtain that hung nearly to the floor.

He opened the door and peered into the hallway. "How long has the servant been here?" he asked one of the guards standing watch outside his chambers.

"An hour, Your Majesty. She insisted on waiting for you."

Percival glanced at Celeste, taking in the shadows under her eyes. Ever since they had decided to poison the nobles, she'd been spending her nights sneaking in and out of the castle—gathering gloriosa tansy, monitoring the patrol routes of the guards, and finding elves to help distribute the poisoned wine at the banquet. "Send for some food from the kitchen, please."

"Yes, Your Majesty."

"Thank you."

He closed the door and sat on the settee across from

Celeste, making as little sound as possible as he tugged off his doublet and unlaced his shiny leather boots. She shifted, her pale arm flopping over the side of the couch. A smile tugged at his lips as he returned his boots to the wardrobe and pulled a soft cotton shirt over his head. It was strange to see her so peaceful and relaxed, without a barb or clever quip perched on her sharp tongue; like finding a rose stripped of its thorns.

He rather liked her thorns.

A few minutes later, a servant arrived with a platter of eggs, buttery, cheesy potatoes, and slices of wine-poached pear. Percival accepted it from her and set it on the table in front of the settee before returning to his seat on the opposite couch. Celeste stirred at the scent of food. One eye cracked open. When she saw the platter, her lips parted into a small, sleepy grin. Then realization flashed across her face. She jerked upright, her cheeks flaming bright red when she noticed Percival sitting across from her, idly flipping through the pages of a book he'd borrowed from the castle library.

"I'm so sorry," she blurted, pushing a lock of hair behind her ear. "I didn't mean to fall asleep. I was just waiting for you, and, well..."

"Don't be embarrassed. You've been doing all the work to prepare for the, um, banquet." He closed the book and placed it on the table. "How much sleep did you get last night?"

"None," she muttered as she began eagerly shoveling eggs into her mouth. She moaned, her eyes flitting skyward. "If I could eat like this every day, I would never leave the dining room. How are you so skinny?"

"I'm not *that* skinny."

"*Please*. I can't see you unless I'm facing you head-on." She swallowed several bites of potatoes, then set down her fork and knife. "Are you ready to train?"

"Are you feeling up to training?"

In answer, she jumped to her feet and strode through the

open doors of the balcony, freeing two daggers from her sleeves as she went. He followed her outside, goosebumps rippling up his arms as the wind wrapped around him. She handed him a blade and then pointed to her chest.

"You want to hit right here, angling the blade up so it slides through the ribs and pierces the heart. If you hit bone, your dagger might get stuck, and then it'll get wrenched out of your hand during the fight. You'll be on your own against an opponent who is bleeding heavily and *pissed*. Now attack me." When he balked, she darted forward, slipped around him, and pricked his lower back with her dagger. "Got your kidney. Now you're dead. Attack me."

He turned and slashed, but she easily blocked the strike with the back of her arm. He tried to remember what she had taught him over the past few days—*Keep your weight on your toes, stand side-face, watch for the opponent's tells, anticipate where she's going to strike, never take your eyes off her blade*—but as he lunged forward, jabbing and slashing, everything became muddled. She moved too quickly for him to do anything except try to leap out of range of her blade. He didn't even have time to fix his stance before she came at him once more. The few times she slowed enough for him to strike, he pulled his swings at the last moment.

"You're afraid," she taunted, stepping back. She hadn't even broken a sweat. "You're afraid of hurting me."

He looked down at the dagger in his hand. "Of course I'm afraid of hurting you. We're fighting with real blades."

"Think I can't handle a few scratches here and there? Try again. I'll even go easy on you."

Frustration sparked within him. "Don't patronize me."

She grinned. "Let's see if you can hit me."

Again, she lifted her blade, and again, he lunged. She blocked every attack he attempted, be it a slash or stab or parry. His frustration mounted when he saw the teasing glint in her eyes. She was enjoying making a fool of him. She was *savoring* it, as she always savored making him squirm.

Well, two can play at that game.

He leapt forward with newfound ferocity, sweat pouring down his face and fogging the lenses of his spectacles. Nicholas's scowl flashed through his mind. Percival had tried so hard to live up to his uncle's expectations at their estate in Westwater. For years, he'd taken swordplay lessons every afternoon, and he had spent every evening going over the drills his tutor had shown him. No matter how much he trained, he invariably landed on his ass each time he faced off against an opponent. His tutor had seized the opportunity to save face by accusing him of not caring enough to learn how to wield a sword.

I'm trying! he had wanted to scream. *I'm doing my best!* Yet his best had never been good enough for Nicholas or his tutor —both of whom had given up on teaching him when he was fifteen.

His instincts took over as his thoughts roamed, anger clearing his mind. Celeste's blade slashed out, glinting in the sunlight, and he saw his opening. He twisted, hooked his foot around her ankle, and swept her legs out from under her. She fell flat on her back. He straddled her, pinning her legs down before she could jump to her feet.

"I won," he panted, angling his dagger at her chest exactly as she had demonstrated. He tried not to focus on the way the loose neckline of her tunic had slipped down, revealing a glimpse of cleavage, or the feeling of his thighs straddling her hips, or the way the sunlight hit her remarkable green eyes.

By the Creator, he *tried*.

"For once," she conceded, and he took immense pleasure from the pride in her voice. "But you need to practice more if you want to take on Nicholas and his men. I'm just a weak girl."

"Please," he scoffed. "There's nothing weak about you."

Celeste tilted her head, her dark hair spilling across the pale gray stone. Her lips curled into a mischievous smile that caused his breath to hitch. He was glad he was still panting from the fighting, otherwise she certainly would have heard it.

Her eyes dropped to his mouth. *Shit*. Perhaps she had heard it after all.

Celeste raised a brow and crooked a finger at him, beckoning him closer. His heart leapt into his throat, screaming, rebelling, as he leaned forward, unable to break this strange trance. *You're betrothed to Riona*, the logical, responsible part of his brain objected. *You swore that you would be faithful. You—*

You're falling in love with the wrong girl.

The revelation hit when their faces were only a few inches apart. It should have surprised him, unbalanced him, terrified him, but it didn't. He had been falling for a while. He'd suspected it before—he'd just prayed he was wrong.

She lifted her head and whispered into his ear, "You're right. I'm not weak. I am clever, though, and I told you one very vital tip you have failed to heed."

For a few moments, her words didn't sink in. Percival was too caught up in the brush of her warm breath against his cheek, the soft, teasing lilt of her voice, the arch of her lifted brow. The floral aroma of her perfume wrapped around him, and he knew it would still be clinging to his clothes when she left.

He didn't want her to leave.

He desperately, desperately hoped she'd leave.

His pulse thrummed unsteadily as he took her in, this sharp-tongued, wondrous creature. He wondered how it would feel to kiss her lovely, wicked mouth, to render *her* speechless and flustered for once. Then he felt a prick by his thigh, and he looked down to find her dagger hovering just over his crotch.

"I told you," she crooned as he cursed and scrambled off of her, "never take your eyes off your opponent's blade."

He let out a string of oaths, running his hands through his hair in agitation and mortification. She'd seen the way she affected him, and she'd played him for a fool. *Again*. It made him furious—so furious he trembled. She'd humiliated him, just like Nicholas always did.

Without looking back, he flipped the dagger over in his hand and offered it to her, hilt first. His voice was brusque, unfamiliar, when he said, "You're right. You won."

"Keep it. Just in case something goes wrong at the banquet."

Percival nodded, his arm dropping to his side. He focused on some point in the distance, clenching and unclenching his free hand, until his trembling eased. Creator save him from this cruel slip of a woman. He felt shaken, like the ground had just slipped out from under his feet, like he was trying to stay afloat in a stormy sea. They'd teased each other relentlessly, but she'd crossed a line by throwing his feelings back in his face. She had to know how guilty he felt for wanting her. She had to be aware of how hard it was for him to pretend to be enamored with Riona when his thoughts were consumed with her. She had to see it every time he looked at her.

Of course, that meant she also knew how deeply her mockery had cut him.

"Percival," she began, soft and apologetic. He didn't turn around, but he heard her take a few steps toward him. "I'm sorry. I didn't mean to—"

"Please don't say anything," he interrupted, staring out at the dark silhouette of the Howling Mountains in the distance. "Just go."

There was a beat of silence.

And another.

And another.

Then she said, "I was imagining it, too, you know. What it would be like to kiss you."

He heard the truth in her voice. That dagger between them had been a distraction—a desperate attempt to send all thoughts of want and desire out of their minds. It had worked a little *too* well. At least *she* had still been thinking straight enough to stop it before they did something they would regret.

He was marrying Riona. He had no right to want Celeste.

"Please, just go."

Silence stretched out for several minutes. When he finally turned around, he found that he was alone. He sat down, set the dagger she had given him on the ground at his side, and leaned against the balcony railing. Guilt wracked him. She had been right to put an end to...to whatever the hell just happened. He'd lost his mind. He'd let himself be swept away by desire, and she had saved him.

Percival—the coward that he was—had thanked her by throwing her out.

He'd find her later and apologize, he promised himself. He would make it up to her. They'd go back to teasing and mocking each other, they'd poison the nobles at the banquet, and they'd forget all about this cursed almost-kiss. Once Tamriel was again on the throne, they'd go their separate ways.

Friends. Just friends.

That was all he could afford to be with her.

36
FAYE

It wasn't until dawn that Faye and the others returned to the castle, exhausted and a little tipsy. Over the course of the night, Faye had lost track of how many rounds of ale they'd ordered. She had not drunk enough to lose control of her faculties, but even then, as their carriage clattered along through the garden, her head felt fuzzy, her body relaxed.

She pushed aside the lace curtain over the window and groaned when she saw the castle. Another day of unsuccessful negotiations. Another day of searching in vain for a solution that did not require Tamriel and Mercy to give the other up. Another day of a traitor sitting on Tamriel's throne.

Gentle snores filled the carriage. Matthias was slumped against one wall, his head lolling with every bump of the wheels, his arm wrapped around the shoulders of his slumbering sister. Ino regarded them with fondness in his tired eyes. When Cassia's scarf began to slip down, he reached up and gently adjusted it so it covered her mangled ear. He granted Faye a small smile before turning toward the window.

She looked to her left. Kaius was seated on the opposite

end of the bench, idly running a thumb across his lower lip while he stared out at the garden. The pale dawn light highlighted his profile—the strong line of his jaw, the high cheekbones, the edges of the tattoos coiling across his forehead and around his eyes. An ache filled her as she watched him, looking so pensive, so far away. *I say you spend as much time as you can with the people you love, because you never know when you're going to lose them*, Calum's voice whispered in her ear. *You don't want to spend the rest of your days wondering whether you should have told him the truth.*

Could she do it? Could she confess her feelings knowing they might lose each other in a few weeks?

The carriage rolled to a stop before the castle, cutting off her line of thought. Ino poked his brother in the ribs until he jolted awake, looking completely disoriented for a few moments before he realized where they were. An easy smile spread across his face. Cassia grumbled about having stayed out so late, but even she could not fight a grin when Ino reminded her how much she had enjoyed the dancing.

"Perhaps we could do it again before we return to Beltharos," she suggested as the carriage driver opened the door. "With Mercy and Tamriel, too. I think they'd enjoy having a night outside of the castle, away from the court and the politics."

"Creator willing, we won't be here much longer," Matthias muttered as he climbed out. Faye and the others followed him as the carriage carrying the Strykers rolled up behind theirs. Calum stepped out first, supporting a *very* drunk Oren.

"Someone overdid it last night."

"I'm fine," Oren mumbled. "Lemme go."

"Not a chance, mate," Nerran laughed, clapping Oren on the shoulder. "You should have known better to drink that much."

Oren dismissed him with a lazy wave of his hand.

Faye followed them to the guest wing, and Calum stopped a passing servant to ask for a pitcher of water before helping Oren into his room. One by one, her friends broke off and wandered into their respective rooms—no doubt to fall into bed and sleep off their drinks—until only Faye and Kaius were left. He thanked her again for inviting him, then paused just outside his door, a hand on the knob, looking like there was something else he wanted to say. Then he changed his mind and slipped into his room.

She started toward her room, but paused at the sight of the doors to Mercy and Tamriel's chambers. They were probably rising now, preparing for another day of unsuccessful negotiations. Both of them were trying to keep brave faces for their friends, but Faye knew the stress had been wearing on them; Mercy was agitated and short-tempered—even more so than when she'd been an apprentice at the Keep—and Tamriel seemed exhausted, his face haggard and drawn. While Faye and the others were out dancing and drinking, Mercy and Tamriel had been spending their time together, trying to figure out a way around Marieve becoming the queen of Beltharos.

Annoyance flashed through Faye. Queen Cerelia didn't care about Beltharos or the throne. She was a strong, powerful queen; clever and calculating. She knew that placing her granddaughter on the Beltharan throne was the best way to end the ceaseless Cirisian Wars and give the Islands some semblance of freedom, and she was going to rip Tamriel and Mercy apart to achieve it.

But...perhaps there was another way to tie the Feyndaran crown to the Islands.

Kaius was the First of a clan, as close to royalty as existed in the Islands. If he were to marry Marieve...

Her heart clenched in pain when the thought occured. If

he were to marry Marieve in Tamriel's stead, Cerelia would still get exactly what she wanted. Kaius would ensure that the fighting between Beltharos and Feyndara finally ceased; the Islands would be free—as free as Cerelia was willing to make them—and Kaius would be able to turn his attention to rebuilding the clans. With Nynev's help... With Tamriel's help... With Marieve's help... They could remake the war-torn Islands into a new country, a haven for the elves.

Faye took a step toward Kaius's room, then faltered. She had no right to ask him to give up his future and marry a woman he did not love. And yet she knew that if she suggested it, he would do it. He was that selfless. He cared that much about the future of his people.

Every smile, every flirtation, every tender moment replayed in her mind, sending waves of agony through her. She'd had crushes before. In the Guild, she and the other apprentices her age had admired the handsome young Strykers who accompanied Hewlin to the Keep every spring's-end. Despite Mercy's teasing, she had melted at every seductive grin or witty joke. It had felt good to be desired. With Nerran, it had felt good to forget about her fears for the Trial and lose herself in his lips, his arms, his bed. But he had been nothing more than a distraction.

Kaius... Kaius was so much more.

She didn't know exactly when she had begun to see him differently. During their journey to the Keep? Or after? When she had watched him, time and time again, put his people before himself? When he had come to comfort her beside her brother's grave?

Another memory surfaced; Kaius crouching before her in a dirty alley, his hands gently grasping hers as he cleaned the blood from her fingers. His eyes studying her, discovering all the secrets and weaknesses she had tried so hard to keep hidden. That may not have been the moment things changed between them, but it was the moment whatever changed had become irreversible.

Even so, she had pushed him away at every instance. She'd condemned them to this pain in an attempt to save them from grief and heartbreak after the battle. Calum was right. She'd been a coward. Rather than fearing what-ifs, she should have confessed her feelings long ago; she should have tried to enjoy what time they had left.

Now, she would never have the chance.

Kaius didn't say a word when he opened the door to her soft knock. He simply took in the devastation on her face, the tears brimming in her eyes, and stepped aside to allow her to enter. She crossed the room and dropped onto the armchair by the hearth. He followed her and sank onto the settee, watching her with concern.

It's better this way, she reminded herself. *Tamriel will claim his throne. Mercy will become queen. Nicholas will face justice. The Islands will be free.*

"Faye, what's wrong?" he finally asked.

Her heart—her traitorous heart—gave a painful tug at the sound of his voice. Had she been able to turn back time, she would have done everything differently.

She thought about Calum blaming himself for Elise's death—being forced to live with the knowledge that his crimes had led to her execution. *This is my punishment. This is what I get for killing all those people during the war, for not seeing how monstrous Illynor was, for not realizing how monstrous she had made me.*

It's better this way.

She summoned all her courage and said, "I think I know how to get Tamriel his troops."

When she finished explaining, Kaius simply stared at her. Emotions flickered across his face so fast she barely had time to register them: denial, defiance, anger, hurt, sorrow, disbelief. He was quiet for a few long, excruciating heartbeats, then...

"How can you ask this of me? Do you not care about me at all?" The pain in his voice nearly shattered her resolve.

I do. More than you know.

"Kaius, I'm so sorry," she responded, swiping at the wet trails her tears had left on her cheeks. She'd managed to speak without falling apart, but she had not been able to keep from crying. "You have every right to be angry—to be *furious*—with me. It's selfish of me to ask you to marry someone you don't love, and I won't blame you if you say no. But I don't see any other way for Tamriel to secure the troops he needs without giving Mercy up. We've been stuck in unsuccessful negotiations for almost two weeks with no progress. This way, the Cirisian Wars will end, Tamriel will reclaim his throne, and Cerelia will get what she wants."

"What about what *I* want?"

"You want what is best for your people. You will do anything for the ones you love." She hesitated, then confessed, "That's one of the things I admire most about you."

He stood and braced his hands on the mantle of the hearth, shaking his head. "Don't torture me like that, Faye."

"I'm so sorry," she said again, knowing it was not enough. Nothing she could say would lessen the impact of what she was asking him to do.

Her apology hung in the air between them. She wrapped her arms around herself and watched Kaius stare into the dark hearth, absorbing everything she had said. The silence stretched out to an eternity. Faye was half convinced he could hear her heart pounding against her ribs.

"...If I were to agree, Tamriel would have his troops within the week," Kaius eventually said, and Faye wasn't entirely certain whether he was speaking to her or to himself. "He'd be able to fight Nicholas and put him to justice. He'd be able to free the slaves. He and Mercy would be able to rule together."

He fell silent again.

One minute passed.

Then two.

Then three.

Finally, he turned to her, and she saw his answer in the sorrow in his eyes. "Very well. If that is what you think is best, and if Her Majesty agrees, I will marry Lady Marieve."

"No. You're not marrying Lady Marieve," Tamriel said, crossing his arms.

He was the first to recover from the shock of what Faye and Kaius had suggested. After Kaius relented, they'd gone straight to Mercy and Tamriel, interrupting their breakfast, and explained their idea. Mercy and Tamriel had sat and listened with growing horror, their eyes flitting from Kaius's somber expression to the tear stains streaking Faye's cheeks.

"Your Majesty, if it'll get you your army—" Kaius began.

The king frowned. "I can't ask you to sacrifice your future for me. Whether you will admit it or not, you two care about each other deeply. I will not let you give that up so I can reclaim my throne, when I am unwilling to do the same myself. There must be another way."

"We haven't come up with one yet," Faye said. "How much longer do you think we can wait for Cerelia to give in? Every day that we're stuck here is another day with that traitor ruling your kingdom, manipulating Percival, and hurting your people."

Tamriel's expression didn't change, but Faye could swear doubt flashed through his eyes before he blinked it away. He was desperate to return to his home, to protect and guide his subjects, and it was killing him to be stuck in these hopeless, endless negotiations.

"With all due respect, Your Majesty," Kaius added, "it's not your decision to make. It's mine. I will do this for you because I know this is what is best for both our peoples. If Her Majesty agrees, I will marry Marieve in your place so you and Mercy can rule together."

"I still stand by my suggestion that we poison them all," Mercy muttered. "We still have Tanni and the other Daughters. They can help."

"Yes, let's make an enemy of another country. We don't have enough problems as it is." Tamriel shot her a look, and she scowled.

"It's just a suggestion."

Tamriel turned to Faye and Kaius. "Are you sure this is what you want to do?"

Faye forced herself not to look at the archer as she nodded. She was fairly certain that if she did, she'd start crying again. Why had she pushed him away for so long? Why hadn't she just admitted to herself sooner that she cared for him? Why had she been such a fool?

"Yes, Your Majesty," Kaius said with a firm nod. His voice was tight, pinched, but Faye saw steady resolve in his eyes.

Tamriel sighed. "Then I must beg you not to do anything yet. Do not speak a word of this to anyone. Nynev will arrive tonight or tomorrow morning, and I want to give her a chance to come up with another solution before we say anything to the queen. Understood?"

Faye nodded again. "Thank you, Tamriel."

He shook his head. "It is I who should be thanking you both. Giving up those we love is never easy." Behind Faye, the doors swung open, and she looked over her shoulder to see a servant standing just beyond the threshold, waiting to escort Tamriel and Kaius to their meeting with the queen. The king sighed as he stood, seeming much older than his mere eighteen years, and followed Kaius to the door. "Let us pray none of us has to endure that pain."

37
TAMRIEL

As every morning, Queen Cerelia was already waiting for them, a teacup and saucer in hand, when they arrived in the meeting room. Whorls of steam danced in the air as she lifted it to her thin lips and took a sip, her stormy gray eyes roving over them from head to toe. A servant guided them to the couch opposite the queen, poured them each a cup of tea, then bowed to Cerelia before scampering off. The elf quietly shut the doors behind her, leaving them alone with the queen and the dozen guards lining the room.

"I trust you slept well, King Tamriel?" Cerelia asked, setting her cup and saucer on the marble table between them. She tilted her head and took in the dark shadows under his eyes. "Negotiations such as these are trying for us all, I assure you."

Tamriel bristled at the words, but he forced his face not to betray any hint of his irritation. Yes, he was certain these discussions had been *very* trying for her and her family. After all, they'd had to open their home to a group of strangers. That must have been *much* harder than having one's throne stolen, running for one's life, and negotiating for the future of three countries.

Beside him, Kaius scowled, but wisely kept his mouth shut.

"I beg you, Your Majesty, speak plainly," Tamriel said, being careful to keep his voice even. After the discussion he'd just had with Faye and Kaius, he was in no mood for games or clever tricks. "Do not insult my intelligence by feigning sympathy. You want the Islands, and I need troops. If you are willing, we can find a compromise that will benefit both our countries, and the people of the Islands. All I ask is that you do not force me to marry your granddaughter...as lovely and charming as she is," he added belatedly. "I love Mercy, and I intend to make her my queen."

"Would you grant Feyndara control over the Islands? Allow us to claim it as a territory?"

"We would be an independent people," Kaius responded, matching the challenge in the queen's voice with one of his own. "Belonging neither to Feyndara nor Beltharos, but trading with each."

The queen turned to Tamriel. "Suppose I agreed to your proposal. I give you your troops and allow you to return to your homeland without my granddaughter as your bride. I pull my soldiers from the Islands as a gesture of goodwill, of friendship. What is to keep you from sending your army to claim the Islands for your own kingdom once my men have left?"

"My word."

She scoffed. "We both know how little a person's word is worth. Look at how your own general turned on you. Look at how your Assassin broke her vow to the Guild. You cannot expect me to trust someone who has spent his entire life in that court of vipers. Creator only knows what tricks you've learned from those wretched courtiers your father allowed to walk all over him."

"With all due respect, Your Majesty, I would advise you to be careful how you speak about my father." A pang of grief shot through Tamriel. His father had not been a good king—he had always known that—but Ghyslain had tried to protect him from the court. He'd warned Tamriel that the courtiers would one day turn on him; it was not his fault that Tamriel hadn't listened. "Once I give my word, I do not break it. You would have nothing to fear from my army once I reclaimed my crown. Our countries could work together to rebuild the Islands; your granddaughter does not need a place on the Beltharan throne to achieve that."

"My granddaughter is not as weak or powerless as you think, Tamriel. Her presence in your court is exactly why I would not need to worry about your army. A marriage alliance between our countries would not only end these ceaseless wars, but Marieve would be able to act should you change your mind about the Islands—naturally, I would provide her troops of her own to accompany her to Beltharos...for her own protection, of course."

Tamriel bit his tongue to keep from lashing out at the obvious threat within her words. She would plunge his kingdom into more fighting if she did not approve of how his kingdom dealt with the independence of the Islands. Step one foot out of line, and Marieve would turn her soldiers on him and his people.

Kaius started to open his mouth, and Tamriel could tell by the look on his face that he intended to tell the queen about his and Faye's proposal. "Your Majesty—"

"*Not now*," Tamriel hissed, shooting the archer a sharp glare. *One more day,* he mouthed, and the archer nodded, frowning.

Queen Cerelia studied them. "What was it you were about to say, Kaius of the Islands?"

"Nothing, Your Majesty."

She raised a brow.

"These negotiations have gone on long enough," Tamriel said, drawing her attention to him, "and I've grown tired of sitting around talking while a traitor rules my kingdom. If you wish to have some say in the future of the Islands, we may meet here again tomorrow morning. If not, my friends and I will gather our belongings and be on our way to Beltharos."

Out of the corner of his eye, he saw surprise and disbelief cross Kaius's face, but he didn't look away from the queen. She'd pushed him beyond the limit of his patience. He was a king, and he would not let her manipulate him any longer.

If he had to, he would find a way to restore his throne without her help.

Cerelia pressed her lips into a tight line. Her gray eyes hardened, but did not offer him any hints as to what she thought of his announcement.

He held her gaze unflinchingly.

Finally, she stood, and all the guards snapped to attention. "That is unfortunate, Your Majesty. I wish you luck in the battle to come. May the Creator have mercy on you."

With that, she walked out of the room, heels clacking and skirts swishing on the stone floor. The guards filed out behind her, leaving him and Kaius alone. Tamriel shut his eyes and sagged against the back of the couch. Kaius let out a long breath, full of defeat.

"I know," Tamriel sighed without opening his eyes.

"We're going back to Beltharos."

"Yes."

"And you would rather risk all our lives than let me marry Marieve?"

"If Queen Cerelia doesn't give in by tomorrow morning,

we'll suggest it," he conceded, the words leaving a sour taste in his mouth. What kind of a king was he if he couldn't protect the people he cared for? Allowing Kaius to make this sacrifice was better than risking the lives of his friends in the battle, but he'd promised he would do everything in his power to keep Kaius from having to marry for politics.

Perhaps... Perhaps he *had* done everything he could. Perhaps it simply was not enough.

Dread coiled within Tamriel as he crossed the great hall. His conversation with the queen replayed over and over in his mind, and he cursed her for forcing him and his friends into this position. Had he just signed the death warrants of the only true allies he had left? Had he condemned them to a hopeless battle just so he wouldn't have to lose Mercy? Could he bring himself to march on Sandori knowing how many people would die in the fighting?

He was so absorbed in his thoughts, he didn't hear Lady Marieve calling his name until she was right beside him, glittering like a diamond. "Your Majesty, is it true you'll be leaving soon?"

"Yes, it's true." He frowned. Apparently, news traveled fast among the royal family. "I regret that the negotiations were not successful, but I cannot allow my kingdom to remain in the hands of that traitor any longer. I must return home."

Marieve glanced at the courtiers and servants moving through the vast room, on their way to various meetings, chores, and appointments, then gestured for Tamriel to follow her. Puzzled by her behavior—she certainly had not made any effort to seek him out in the past—he trailed after her through the halls until they found an empty sitting room. Marieve closed the door behind him.

"I didn't want what I have to say to be overheard by someone who will report back to my grandmother, for if she realizes that I've told you..." She bit her lip and fidgeted with the amethyst ring on her finger. "I snuck into my father's office last night and snooped through his desk. In it, I found orders for five thousand soldiers to be sent from various outposts across the country, and to amass here, just outside the city limits. The orders came directly from my grandmother. She has called in the army you need to reclaim your throne."

For a few heartbeats, Tamriel merely stared at her. He didn't know whether to be angry at the queen for assuming that he'd give in so easily, or glad that she would have been willing to offer him a thousand soldiers. "You're telling me I could have an army a thousand strong if I agree to your grandmother's demand that I marry you."

Marieve nodded. "Not just soldiers—ships, supplies, battering rams, trebuchets... Anything you need to infiltrate your city and win the battle, she will provide. That is how desperately she wants the Islands."

He forced down the bud of hope that bloomed within him. *A thousand soldiers...* "I will not marry you, my lady. I love Mercy."

"I know. And I promise you, if I thought there was another way for you to reclaim your kingdom, I would be offering it to you now. If you want to return to your home and bring that traitor to justice, you must go along with what my grandmother has asked of you. I will be a good wife, and a good queen, I swear to you."

He shook his head. "I appreciate you sharing this information, Lady Marieve, but I've told you my answer," he said carefully, fighting to keep a rein on his patience. Had he not made his stance on this issue clear enough? Without a doubt, she was only telling him of the queen's orders so he would accept the marriage. He started toward the door. "With all due respect, this conversation is over."

"My mother lost her life in the Islands," she blurted. "She was killed in an ambush by your father's men when I was a child, years after the supposed end of the last war."

Tamriel paused, the admission taking him by surprise. Her mother had served in the queen's army? That must be why Cerelia had been fighting so hard to gain control of the Islands; she, like so many of her people, had lost family to the war.

"It is no easy thing to watch your loved ones march to war," Marieve continued, pain in her voice, "and the wounds their deaths leave behind never fully heal. I want to save you from that grief, Tamriel. How can I allow you and your friends to march to a battle you have little hope of winning?

"We all must make sacrifices for our countries. My grandmother always told me being royal means giving up your own desires for the good of your subjects. For me, that's my freedom, my family, and the only home I have ever known. For you, that's Mercy. It will be painful to leave her, of course, but is it not a small price to pay for your crown? For the lives of your friends and soldiers?"

Tamriel's hands closed into fists, his back still to her. She was trying to manipulate him, just like her queen had. She was neither his friend, nor his ally. Still, her honeyed words touched the doubts that had been lingering at the back of his mind for days. Would it be better to live without Mercy, knowing she was alive because of Cerelia's soldiers, than to fight by her side and lose her in a hopeless battle? If it came down to it, would he give Mercy up to save her life?

He prayed he would never have to make that choice.

When he reached for the door handle, she blurted, "Your

Majesty, I've seen how fiercely you and Mercy have been fighting to stay together, how deeply you love each other. And while I know you will never feel the same way about me, I will be a good wife. I can be the queen your country needs."

He glanced back at her—this glittering gem, this poised, perfect courtier—and there was no doubt in his mind when he said, "*Mercy* is the queen my country needs."

The double doors to his chamber were open when he arrived at the guest wing, excited chatter spilling out into the hall. A smile spread across his lips, chasing his dark thoughts away, when he recognized one of the voices.

Mercy, Faye, Matthias, Cassia, and Ino were all seated around the low table in the center of the room, listening in rapt attention as Nynev described her return to the Islands. They were all so absorbed in the story that none of them noticed Tamriel at first. He leaned against the doorframe, arms crossed loosely over his chest, and simply watched. When Nynev left Sandori to take over Firesse's clan, he had not known if he would ever see her again. He hadn't realized until that moment just how much he had missed having her and Niamh around.

After a few minutes, the huntress looked up and paused mid-sentence when she saw him. His grin grew when she jumped to her feet and nearly ran Faye over in her haste to greet him.

"Mercy filled me in on everything that has happened since we parted," Nynev said as she pulled him into a fierce hug. He embraced her just as tightly. When he'd first met the tough, outspoken huntress, he had not imagined befriending her. Yet she and her sister had left the Islands, healed his people, defended his home, and placed themselves in the path of blades meant to stop his heart. He would never forget that. "I'm sorry to hear of your father's passing. I know things between you were...difficult, to say the least, but no one should have to watch a parent pass in such a violent manner."

"Thank you, Nynev." He pulled back and guided her to where Mercy and the others were sitting. "Are you faring well, everything considered?"

"I should be asking *you* that question. You look like hell."

He grimaced. "I'll admit, I did not miss your unfailingly brutal honesty."

"The courtiers speak in enough riddles as it is. I've no time or energy for such games."

Mercy turned to him. "Kaius told us what you said to the queen. If you decide it is time to end the negotiations, we will stand by your side. We could leave for Beltharos as early as tomorrow, if you wish."

Tamriel looked at each of them in turn: Nynev, his stubborn friend; Faye, his unlikely ally; Kaius, his former enemy; Matthias, Cassia, Ino, his steadfast supporters.

Mercy, his love, his savior, his future queen.

He took her hand, lacing his fingers through hers, and nodded. "Tomorrow, if the negotiations fail, we will sail home."

38
MERCY

"This place reminds me of Sandori," Nynev said as they crossed one of the bridges in the garden. She stared down at the water and watched a school of fish pass below them, their orange and white scales glimmering in the late afternoon sunlight. All across the manicured lawn, guards roamed, servants attended their chores, courtiers strolled, children pranced and played. A peal of high-pitched laughter spilled out from somewhere to their right, near the edge of a pond. Even into autumn, flowers bloomed on the bushes lining the walkways, bobbing in the breeze. It was peaceful, calm.

Which was to say, nothing at all like Sandori.

Mercy raised a bow at her friend. The huntress had been unusually quiet since Kaius told them about Tamriel's ultimatum for the queen. "Like Sandori? How so?"

"So much beauty hiding so much ugliness. Everything is so fake. The people. Their kindness. The gods-damned *trees*," she spat, wrinkling her nose at a hedge pruned into the shape of the Creator's holy eye. "Even they have been twisted into something they are not. I hate all of it."

"Then I am doubly grateful you decided to come. We'll have to be each other's impulse control. I'm afraid I'm unable to inhabit the same room as Cerelia without saying some decidedly undiplomatic things."

"Ha. I wish you would show that selfish bitch of a queen just how fearsome the future queen of Beltharos truly is. She'd hand over her troops in a heartbeat." Nynev tugged at a stray thread on the hem of her tunic, the action betraying her nervousness and impatience. The two emotions had been Mercy's constant companions since she arrived.

She shook her head. Every morning for the past week, Tamriel had tried to convince her to join the negotiations, claiming that it was her right to have a say in the future of Beltharos. She retorted by listing all the ways in which she could murder Cerelia—and therefore get them all killed—before the queen's guards could even bat an eye. That response, coupled with the wicked grin on her lips, was usually enough to silence his objections. As it was, she could barely endure the court dinners every night without being tempted to hurl her knife at the queen. "I'm not to be trusted to keep my temper around her."

"And you think I'm any better? My father used to claim my tongue is sharper than any sword."

"We'd level the whole castle if we faced her together."

"Good. We'd take out the entire royal family in one fell swoop. I don't see the downside."

They neared the gate just as it swung open. A company of twenty-or-so young men rode through, one after another, bows and quivers slung over their shoulders. Mercy and Nynev paused at the end of the cobbled path to watch them spill across the greenery and slide from their saddles, chattering amicably. Mercy recognized a few from around the castle. They must be off-duty guards. If the carts attached to some of the horses, each carrying loads covered in stained tarps, were any indication, they'd gone on a hunt.

"Speaking of the royal family," Nynev muttered, jerking her chin toward the handsome lord in their midst. Alistair dismounted, a shock of black hair falling over his brow, and lifted a hand in greeting when he spotted them. Mercy offered him a polite nod, nothing more. Nynev narrowed her eyes and sauntered over to him, appraising the large deer secured to the back of Alistair's stallion.

She frowned at her findings. "A buck, sloppily struck down. The arrow lodged in his ribs and only pierced a single lung. I'd bet my bow you had to chase him down for a long while before he finally fell."

The lord's brows furrowed as he watched her study his kill. He shot Mercy a look that said, *Who the hell is this stranger and why is she speaking to me so brazenly?* She lifted a shoulder in a shrug. Nynev had never blunted her words for anyone, be it commoner, prince, or king. She certainly wasn't going to start now.

"I do not believe I've had the pleasure of making your acquaintance." His voice was polite, but there was no masking the subtle barb in his words. Nynev's eyes flitted to him for the briefest of moments before she continued circling the buck. Exasperated, the lord said, "I would like to know who you are, and why you find my hunting skills so lacking."

"Not lacking as much as offensive." Nynev pointed to another wound in the buck's stomach. The blood dribbling out of the hole was fresher there, still shiny and wet. "You let the poor thing suffer before you killed it."

His expression softened then, a hint of shame coloring his fair cheeks. "The pain it felt beyond the first wound was unintentional. For that I am sorry, and I shall endeavor to strike true next time."

Nynev nodded, satisfied by his response, and returned to Mercy's side. Alistair studied the tattoos coiling around her temples and across her high cheekbones. "You must be the huntress my grandmother mentioned. Nynev, is it not?"

"It is."

He offered her a slight bow, which seemed to charm her. At the very least, it played to her ego—a wise move on Alistair's part. He'd seen the confidence in the way she'd swaggered up to the cart, and decided to indulge her. "I have a great deal of respect for your people. My father has served as Protector of the Islands for as long as I've been alive, and I will take up the mantle when he is no longer able to do so."

Wrong thing to say. Mercy saw it in the slight tensing of the huntress's shoulders, the embers that flared in her eyes as she regarded the young man before her. Lord Justus had sent wave after wave of Feyndaran soldiers into the Islands, both during and after the most recent bout of the Cirisian Wars. Countless Cirisians had lost their lives after being caught in the fighting. Even worse, the soldiers, bored and grumpy after spending so long in the Islands, had invaded the camps and committed unspeakable acts on the young women who lived there.

Mercy watched all these responses spring to her friend's tongue; by now, she knew Nynev well enough to sense when she was preparing to draw blood. She reached out to lay a hand on Nynev's shoulder in warning, but before she could, the huntress cocked her head, brushing off the comment. "Then you must be Alistair. Forgive me, is it Prince or Lord?" she asked with feigned respect. "I can't keep all these silly court titles straight."

"Lord, as it's a queendom. I cannot take the throne, so I shall serve my country in other ways."

"I see," Nynev responded, turning away from him in a clear dismissal. Mercy fought the smile that surfaced at the lord's bewildered expression. She doubted he'd ever been dismissed by an inferior before. "Mercy, shall we retire to the castle? I'm weary after my long journey, and I'd like to swipe something from the kitchen on the way back to my room."

"We shall," she replied, perpetually amused by her friend's ability to sidestep court decorum, to cut straight to the quick. That was, perhaps, what she had missed most about Nynev: this savage, biting sort of charm.

Nynev linked her arm through Mercy's and led her along the path back to the castle. Before they made it out of earshot, Nynev called back, "Find me before supper and I'll teach you the *real* way to take down a buck, *your lordship*."

Mercy shook her head, chuckling, as they left Alistair and the others staring after them. "How do you do that? How do you twist your words like that? I could use that trick in the court."

"Tell you what: survive the battle, and I'll teach you." Nynev's pace faltered a second after she said it; both their minds drifted back to the problem at hand—how to secure Tamriel his army.

Mercy looked over her shoulder at the walls surrounding the castle and the forest visible in the distance. Tamriel had told them last night about the information Marieve had shared. It was hard to imagine five thousand soldiers marching to the capital at this very moment, setting up tents and preparing supplies just outside the city proper. Those soldiers were the key to winning back Tamriel's throne, and they all knew it. They could fight without them—they could *win* without them—but it would be a hollow, death-filled victory.

Tamriel had given the queen an ultimatum. Less than twenty-four hours from now, they'd be preparing to sail to Beltharos. The only question was whether they'd have troops at their back when they did.

39
FAYE

Faye's dagger cleaved the air, whistling, as she twisted and slashed low.

We're going back home.

She advanced on light feet, her blade reflecting the light spilling in through the wall of windows before her.

We're going back to Beltharos.

Three quick arcs of the weapon—one angled up, beneath her imaginary opponent's breastplate and into his gut; another on a diagonal, into the vulnerable flesh of his underarm, left vulnerable by a gap in the plates covering his arm and shoulder; and the final one straight across his throat.

We're going to leave Kaius behind.

She whirled around and hurled the dagger at the wardrobe against the opposite wall. It was heavier, clumsier, than her usual throwing knives, but she'd been well taught. It flipped end over end before thudding into one of the wardrobe's wooden doors, its handle quivering from the force of the throw. Three throwing knives followed shortly thereafter.

Faye paused and wiped at the sweat beading on her brow. It had been too long since she practiced her drills; she'd been neglecting them for fear of the memories they would bring flooding back. The war. The Keep. The battle with the Daughters. She'd been able to keep them at bay while she'd practiced; once she'd felt the weight of the dagger in her hand, muscle memory had taken over, narrowing her focus to a razor's edge. Now, that concentration slipped, and images of blood-soaked bodies and eyes devoid of life flashed through her mind. Faye grabbed one of the bedposts to steady herself, gripping the post so tightly her fingers began to ache, and took a few long, deep breaths. Gradually, the memories began to fade. They left her shaky, a slight quiver in her knees, but at least she did not fall apart like she had in Cyrna so many weeks ago.

Good. You're doing good, she told herself, repeating it over and over until she began to believe it. She'd sworn to Tamriel that she would fight in his army, and she couldn't do that if she was unable to bear the sight of blood. Much more of it would be spilled before he was once again king of Beltharos. A few more weeks of fighting, and then she'd be free to return to Fallmond. Until then, she would strive to continue making progress. She would not fail her king.

Faye turned to retrieve her knives from the wardrobe, only to find Kaius standing in the doorway of her bedroom, watching her. His hand was still clasped around the door handle.

"How long have you been standing there?"

"Since you decided to turn the wardrobe door into wood chips. The queen is going to kill you for that."

"She can afford a new one."

She crossed the room, pulled the blades from the door, and set them on the desk beside her leather armor. He'd seen the way the drills had affected her, the way the memories had flooded her mind. He'd watched her banish them without his help.

She could do this. She could leave him behind. She didn't need him to comfort her any longer.

"Faye, you've hardly looked at me since this morning. I miss you. I miss the girl I danced with at the tavern last night."

By the Creator, had that only been last night?

"I'm sorry," she said, and she meant it. Before, she had pushed him away out of cowardice. Today, she was doing it out of necessity. Come tomorrow morning, should the queen agree, Kaius would be betrothed to Marieve. Come tomorrow morning, he would no longer be hers to desire.

He stepped into the room and shut the door behind him. Without a word, he walked to her and tipped her chin up with two fingers, his brilliant green eyes capturing hers. A storm of tumultuous emotions swept over her: sadness, longing, desire, grief, regret...and something deeper, something *more*. A shuddering breath escaped her. The edge of the desk dug into the backs of her legs as she leaned against it.

"Can we pretend, just for a little while," he murmured, "that tomorrow will never come?"

A dangerous, dangerous smile tugged at her lips. Without pausing to allow herself to think it through, to consider how much more it would make tomorrow hurt, she kissed him.

He let out a low sound of surprise, of joy, of desire. In a heartbeat, she was wrapped in his strong embrace, his lips moving with hers, his hands tangled in her long hair. Her heart pounded in her chest. A bloom of happiness, of complete and utter *rightness*, unfurled within her.

This.

I want this.

I want him.

She deepened the kiss, teasing his tongue with her own, and he responded in kind. He blindly reached out and knocked the weapons and armor off the desk before lifting her up so she was perched on its surface. His fingers trailed down her side, teasing the slip of bare skin where her shirt had ridden up, and sparks raced through her.

Kaius pulled back, just an inch. "This is wrong," he whispered, his voice raw, breathless.

She tilted her head, savoring the sight of him awed and flustered. "Do you want to stop?"

"By the gods, no."

Then he claimed her mouth again. She cupped his face as his hands trailed down her thighs and hooked behind her knees. He wrapped her legs around him so they were chest-to-chest, hearts racing in time with each other.

Kaius broke away to press a line of kisses down her neck. She tipped her head back, letting out a soft gasp when his lips brushed the skin right above the neckline of her shirt. He looked up at her, his crooked, joyful smile warming her to her core. "May I see you, Faye? Truly see you?"

She plucked at one of the ties on his tunic. "Don't be greedy."

He laughed and pulled his tunic over his head, revealing flawless bronze skin, the toned muscles of his torso and stomach, the Cirisian tattoos swirling across his collarbone and down his arms. He went completely still as she lightly traced one of the vines coiling around the curve of his shoulder, admiring the beauty of the artwork. *He* was a work of art, in a way that this castle and its occupants could never hope to achieve. His perfection was in the way he loved, in the way he gave, in the way he mourned. He was gentle hands, kind smiles, and knowing eyes. He was *everything*.

"You're so beautiful," she told him, still running her fingers along the tattoo. It was there, in those swirling, graceful lines, that he held his heart. This tattoo was a mark of his freedom, of his home, of a boy's dream to escape his chains. It was the memory of his people's history, of the elves they'd lost in the wars, of the promise he'd made to protect the Islands.

"You're so beautiful," she said again.

He reached up to grasp her hand, his smile turning tender. "I was just about to say the same about you."

She guided his fingers to the top of the line of buttons on her shirt. Together, they undid them one by one, until she, too, was topless before him. Neither of them seemed to breathe for a few moments, simply drinking the other in. Faye felt strangely jittery. She'd had experiences with young men before—she'd gone *further* with young men before—but never like this. Not with her heart laid as bare as her flesh.

He watched her.

She watched him.

And then he said, "I love you, Faye Cotheron."

And it felt like her heart was going to burst from her chest when she responded, "And I love you, Kaius."

He kissed her again, but not like before. This time, it was soft, a brush of lips against lips, a hand caressing her cheek, another cupping her breast. It wasn't hungry, or desperate, or frenzied. It was him pulling away to whisper in her ear, it was his breath on her cheek, it was her losing herself in the wonder that was *him*.

When her fingers dropped to the laces at the waistband of his pants, he lifted her up, carried her to the bed, and gently laid her across the mattress. He leaned over her, one hand braced on either side of her head. "Do you want to do this, Faye? It's going to make it harder to say goodbye."

She beamed up at him, somehow, impossibly, loving him more for trying to spare her feelings. But Calum had been right. Even if they only had this one day together, she would not trade it for the world. "We'll just have to pretend that we're not going to say goodbye."

So they pretended.

And pretended.
And pretended.

She woke curled in his arms. At first, she didn't allow herself to think it anything more than a dream; it was too magical, too wonderful, too impossible, what had happened between them. Then she felt her back pressed to his chest, the warmth of his skin soaking into her, and she knew that he was really, truly *there*. His soft breaths tickled her bare shoulder, sending a flutter through her heart. She laced her fingers through his. Her eyes remained closed, because there, in the shelter of his arms, there was no Feyndaran queen. There was no traitor sitting on a stolen throne. There was simply a young woman, and the man she loved.

The man in question shifted, murmuring something unintelligible in his sleep, and rolled closer to her. She could feel his heart pounding a steady beat against her back.

Eventually, her eyelids fluttered open. The sky through the windows was streaked with shades of pink and orange, the sun low on the horizon. It had to be dusk. She was still too exhausted to have slept an entire night.

A flash of pain shot through her. Soon, they'd have to rise and go to dinner. She'd have to sit with Kaius and the others among the courtiers, while the queen reigned over them all from her lofty throne at the head of the table. She'd have to watch Marieve waltz into the room and claim her seat across from Mercy and Tamriel, still believing herself to be the future queen of Beltharos. She'd have to endure the pitying looks her friends were sure to direct at her and Kaius.

But not now. Not yet.

Gently, she eased herself out of his embrace with a silent promise to return shortly. By the Creator, she would spend a lifetime in his arms if she could. But sunset had always been her favorite time of day, and with the spectacular riot of color sweeping across the sky, she wanted to mark this one. She wanted to remember every part of this moment: Kaius lying in her bed, the silken sheets tangled around him, his face made soft and peaceful by sleep. She let herself soak in the sight for a few heartbeats before slipping out of bed and pulling on the first crumpled piece of clothing she found on the floor—Kaius's tunic. It fell to the tops of her thighs, loose and airy. It smelled like him, too—something sharp and clean and wild, like the Islands.

Draping her long hair over her shoulder, she walked over to the balcony and leaned against the railing, smiling to herself as she took in the sunset. The dwindling rays of sunlight bathed the garden in an orange glow. They flickered and shimmered on the still surface of the pond where she had found Kaius the night before.

Drifting voices drew her attention to a large patch of grass along the side of the castle, a fair distance from her balcony. A series of targets had been set up along a stone half-wall, and there Nynev stood with Alistair, Mercy's siblings, the Daughters, and a handful of guards. Faye couldn't make out the words, but it was clear from the bows and the way Nynev was gesticulating that she'd gathered them for an archery lesson. Most of them—Mercy's siblings and the Daughters—were lounging on the grass, staring up at the clouds. The guards milled about, hands on their bows or swords, more concerned with their lord's safety than learning. Only Alistair seemed to be listening in rapt attention, nodding along to whatever Nynev was saying.

As Faye watched, the young royal stepped forward, aimed, and loosed an arrow. It sailed through the air and landed just to the right of the bull's-eye. Immediately, Nynev snatched it from the target, marched up to him, and poked him in the chest with the point of the arrow as she repeated her instructions. He plucked the arrow from her fingers and tried again.

And again, he fell just short of the bull's-eye. Or, more accurately, just to the *right* of the bull's-eye.

Now, Nynev picked up her own bow and nudged Alistair out of the way. She nocked an arrow, paused to give him some advice, then let it fly. It hit the first target dead in its center. She did it again with the second target, then the third. Bull's-eye. Bull's-eye. When she reached the one on which Alistair had been practicing, however, she didn't hit the center.

She split his arrow straight down the middle.

Even Faye was awed by the huntress's skill. She could strike down any creature from a mouse to a man, but to be *that* precise... It was beyond anything Faye could hope to achieve. She doubted even Mercy could do it, although she would never say it to Mercy's face.

Nynev turned to Alistair and performed a theatrical bow, which the young lord didn't even seem to notice. His attention was still fixed on the arrow she had buried in the target. Behind him, Matthias and the others clapped, and Nynev bowed again. Faye couldn't make out their expressions from this distance, but she was certain the huntress graced Alistair with a cocky grin as he picked up his bow and stepped forward once more.

The wind caught a lock of Faye's hair and sent it dancing in front of her face. She frowned as she pushed it behind her ear. It had grown nearly to her hips over the past several months, but part of her balked at the thought of cutting it. Trytain and the other tutors had always insisted she crop it like the other girls—a braid as long as hers was easy to grab in a fight, they'd reminded her—but she had refused. As a child, her mother had often sat her on the edge of the bed each morning and plaited her hair, humming an off-key folk tune while her fingers raked through Faye's thick locks. After Faye arrived at the Guild, she had let the girl she'd been die, but she had not been able to bear cutting her braid. It was the one bit of comfort, of home, that she had allowed herself to keep.

Most mornings, Fredric had sprawled across the mattress beside her and doodled on scraps of paper. Once, though, he had taken it upon himself to try and braid Faye's hair while their mother was otherwise occupied. The unfortunate outcome had been a snarl that looked vaguely like a plait, and a knot near the nape of her neck that was so tangled it had needed to be cut out. Faye chuckled at the memory.

A soft noise from inside her room drew her out of her reverie. She turned to find Kaius ambling toward her, rubbing one eye with the heel of his palm. His hair was loose around his face, the imprint of the pillowcase still pressed into his cheek, and his pants were slung low on his hips. His hand dropped to his side as he offered her a sleepy, lovesick smile. Warmth bloomed within Faye, her cheeks flushing. For so long, she'd been so focused on *not* letting her feelings for Kaius show, she didn't know what to do—what to *say*—now that everything was out in the open. All she knew was that she would do anything to stay in this moment, to keep tomorrow morning from arriving and ripping him away from her.

Maybe, she reminded herself, *we won't have to say goodbye.* There was still a chance Queen Cerelia wouldn't accept their proposal...but Faye didn't allow herself to linger on the thought. Tamriel needed the queen's troops, and if Faye had to give up the man she loved to ensure that, she would.

Kaius tilted his head, a knowing look crossing his face. Before Faye could say a word, he walked across the balcony and wrapped her in his arms. She closed her eyes and rested her cheek on his tattooed shoulder, splaying her hands across his bare chest. His heart beat a steady rhythm under her fingers. She tried to take comfort in the feel of his pulse; it was yet another reason he should be the one to marry Marieve—if he were to be her husband, he would remain here at court while Faye and the others marched to battle. He wouldn't die in the fighting. He'd survive. He'd *live*.

He shifted, just enough to lean down and kiss her. As his mouth moved softly, tenderly, with hers, every argument she'd been repeating to herself crumbled. Her heart cracked. If she could, she would never let him go.

He pulled back, and it took her a moment to open her eyes and take in the darkening sky just behind him—the reminder that they had, at most, hours left together. She felt a jagged, raw wound open up inside her. When she looked up at him, she saw the same pain reflected on his face. He pressed his forehead to hers.

"I don't want to marry Marieve," he whispered, the words full of misery and anguish. He said it like a confession—like it was a callous, selfish thing to wish to marry for love. "I don't want to lose you."

She reached up to cup his cheek, and he leaned into the gentle touch. "I don't want to lose you, either."

But—

She didn't have to say it; they both knew the *but* was there, dangling in the air between them. They didn't want to do this, but they would for Tamriel and Mercy, for Beltharos, for the Islands. They would make this sacrifice and bear this loss, because that was who they were: a woman who had given up everything to become an Assassin, and a man who would do anything to help his people. Their duties were to their homes and their friends.

Faye reluctantly backed out of his embrace. She turned to the railing and stared out across the garden, trying to ignore the ache in her chest. The sun had already begun to dip below the horizon; half the sky was still streaked with the pinks and oranges of sunset, while the other half twinkled with bright stars. She swallowed the lump in her throat and forced out, "We're late for supper. The others will be wondering where we are."

"Forget about supper. Stay here with me." He swept her hair aside and kissed her neck. "I want to spend as much of this day as possible with you in my arms."

She turned around and pulled him into another desperate, passionate kiss, the taste of her tears mingling with the taste of his lips. He tugged her close, one hand slipping around her waist, the other skimming her bare thigh and toying with the hem of her stolen tunic.

Tomorrow, Tamriel, Kaius, and Nynev would negotiate with the queen one final time.

But for now, she held him tightly, her teeth grazing his lower lip, her heart swelling, breaking, and bursting, as she let herself pretend tomorrow would never arrive.

40

PERCIVAL

Percival jumped at the sharp knock on his chamber door. He cursed as tea sloshed over the rim of his cup and splattered on the hem of his cotton sleepshirt. He barely had time to set the cup and saucer on the table before Nicholas barged into the room, scowling.

"You're not dressed?"

"I just woke up, and my servant hasn't arrived yet," he responded mildly, forcing down the pang of worry that shot through him. He and Celeste had stayed up until the early hours of the morning going over the plan for the attack at the banquet, then she had left to ensure the helpers she had enlisted for their plot were prepared. Usually, when she left in the middle of the night, she returned around dawn and collapsed on the settee opposite Percival's for a few hours' rest.

He glanced at the balcony, telling himself she was just finishing the last touches—speaking to Lethandris, gathering her helpers, stashing her vials of poison. She'd be here soon.

She'd better be here soon.

"She'd better be here soon," Nicholas grunted. "We're running on a tight schedule as it is."

He walked to the wardrobe and pulled out the doublet the royal tailor had delivered two days ago; a beautiful work of gold thread and black silk damask. He laid it across the back of the nearest armchair, then set a pair of black trousers next to them. "We'll be leaving for the Church in an hour. The High Priestess will wed you and Riona, and then you'll present your queen her crown," he said as he turned back for a pair of shiny leather boots. "Get dressed."

"Yes, Uncle." Percival jumped up and moved behind the settee to change into the pants. As he tied the leather laces at his waist, his uncle studied him, taking in his tousled hair, slightly askew glasses, and the faint shadows hanging under his eyes.

"Have you not been sleeping well, Percival?"

"Just, um, nervous."

"You and Riona have certainly warmed to each other these past couple weeks. You could barely keep your eyes off her at the last council meeting." Although his tone was nonchalant, Percival heard the hint of suspicion underscoring his uncle's words. He and Riona might have fooled the council into thinking that they'd fallen for each other, but his uncle wouldn't be tricked so easily. "You care for her. What is there to be nervous about?"

"Regardless of my feelings for her, I'm not eager to have all that attention on me again. I barely made it through the coronation, and that was in front of a fraction of the people who are going to show up today." He let out a tight laugh, fidgeting under his uncle's heavy stare. So that was why Nicholas had come: not to reassure him or encourage him, but to interrogate him.

Well. He may be suspicious of Percival's sudden change of heart, but he'd never expect his timid, bookish nephew to plan something like what he and Celeste were about to unleash.

Nicholas scoffed. "With her at your side, no one's eyes are going to be on you, nephew. All you have to do is endure the ceremony and banquet, then get to work making lots of little heirs." Then he added, "You *do* know how heirs are made, don't you?"

Ears burning, he snatched the fresh tunic Nicholas extended, then turned and shucked off his sleep-shirt. "I know how it's done. I'm not a child."

A heavy hand on his shoulder stilled him. "What's this?"

Percival glanced down at his arm and found a dark bruise blotting his pale skin. He winced. Celeste had been growing bolder in their training.

"How did you get this bruise, Percival?"

His mind scrambled for an excuse. He wasn't permitted outside the castle, so he couldn't claim to have gotten it somewhere in the city. He couldn't admit to training without drawing more suspicion and putting Celeste in danger.

Settling on the only explanation he could think of, he shot his uncle a glare and said, "It must have happened when you hit me so hard you knocked me out of my chair."

Never mind that two weeks had passed since then. Never mind that the bruise on his cheek had all but faded. Never mind that this one was clearly fresh.

The door swung open then, saving him from spilling the clumsy words tangling at the tip of his tongue. Relief swept over Percival when Celeste entered, but it morphed into panic a heartbeat later. Did Nicholas know that Celeste was the one who had helped him sneak runaway slaves out of the city? Two weeks ago, he'd been certain of it, but nothing had happened in the days since. No guards had come to clap her in chains and drag her off to an execution.

Nicholas's good eye flitted to her, annoyance flashing

across his face. "Mind the time, girl. We've a schedule to keep."

She dropped into a low curtsy. If she was surprised to find Nicholas in Percival's chamber, her expression didn't show it. "My apologies, my lord. It won't happen again."

"It had better not. Arrive late again, and you'll find yourself begging for scraps in Beggars' End."

"Yes, my lord."

Nicholas rolled his eyes and left the room, sidestepping Celeste—still in her curtsy, head bent toward the ground—and closing the door behind him. As soon as his footsteps faded down the hall, she rose and rushed over to Percival.

"I'm so sorry I'm late. What did he want?"

Percival shook his head as she helped him slip his arms into the doublet, then began working on the trail of tiny gold buttons spanning from his collar to his navel. "Just kept implying that there was something behind the way Riona and I have been acting lately. He's suspicious, but I'm certain he doesn't expect anything like what we're about to do." Guilt rose within him at the thought of killing so many people, but he forced it down. The nobles and guards they were targeting tonight had turned against Tamriel. This was retribution. This was *justice*. "What took you so long? I was worried about you. Did something go wrong?"

"No, no, everything's fine. It's no small task to plan the murder of several dozen courtiers, you know. Sometimes it takes a while to get everything ready."

When she started to turn away, he grabbed her hand, and she froze. "Promise me you'll be careful. If you're caught—"

"I promise, Percival." She tilted her head back to look at him, and he saw her smile falter when she realized how close they stood. Only a few inches separated their faces. If he wanted to, he could kiss her.

Oh, how he wanted to.

He released her and took a jerky step backward, turning away and quickly finishing the last of the buttons. Things had been tense between them since that day on the balcony. He had tracked her down a few hours later and apologized, but it hadn't set everything right. Quite the opposite, in fact—he hadn't been able to look at her without thinking of that almost-kiss. He knew it haunted her, too. Every time they trained on the balcony, she was strictly professional, touching him only when she had to correct his stance or adjust his grip. Once, he had slipped past her guard and ended up standing a few inches from her, his blade angled at her throat. Her expression had transformed, softened, as she stared up at him. By some miracle, he'd managed to stagger back before he lost his mind entirely. She had cleared her throat and pretended nothing had happened, and they had continued their lessons.

Thus, they'd reached a shaky equilibrium, poised on a knife's-edge between friends and something more.

He couldn't stand it.

At present, an awkward silence stretched out between them. *Creator save me,* he wordlessly implored. He was marrying Riona today. They may not love each other, but he would not disrespect her or dishonor their marriage vows by taking another woman to his bed.

When he turned back to Celeste, she held out his boots. She watched him slip them on, tucking the dagger she had given him into the leg, then helped him wrangle his unruly curls. The entire time, she didn't meet his eyes.

It was safe. It was necessary. It was agonizing.

"My helpers will be wearing slave sashes just like mine," she eventually said, fidgeting with her slave sash. She was careful to keep her voice low so the guards couldn't hear her through the doors. "They'll slip in with the rest of the crowd after the coronation, get the drinks from the kitchen, and then bring the poisoned ones to the targets. All you have to do is stay with Riona and charm the nobles. Just to be safe, you might not want to drink the wine."

"Understood. Where will you be? With the kitchen staff as we planned?"

She nodded. "I volunteered to help serve the dishes, so I'll be in the throne room. If you need to get word to me, just give a message to any slave wearing these." She turned, showing off the pins holding up her high, braided bun. Each one was decorated with a small silk bloom of Winter's Lace.

"Got it." When she turned around, he held out his arms and did an exaggerated spin. "How do I look?"

"Like a king."

Had he imagined it, or was that disappointment in her eyes?

"Let me be the first to congratulate you on your wedding day, Your Majesty. Riona is...a lucky woman. I hope she knows that."

She pivoted on her heel and practically sprinted to the door.

"Celeste, wait—"

He hurried after her and caught her arm just as she reached for the door handle. "I have something for you. Please, don't leave just yet."

She studied him warily.

He walked into the king's bedroom, opened the top desk drawer, and grabbed the gift he'd stashed there. Her eyes widened when he returned and presented her with a velvet box. "For you. As a thank-you for everything you've done for me. And for being a friend when I had none."

"Percival..." When he smiled and nodded encouragingly, she opened the lid. Her mouth fell open in surprise. "By the Creator, what did you do?"

She lifted the necklace from the box. The pendant was

made of swirls of silver filigree sculpted into twisting branches and blooming flowers. Nestled in the center of every bloom was a shimmering peridot. She twisted it, admiring the way the gemstones caught the light.

"Green," he said, grinning at her awestruck expression. "Your favorite color."

"You remembered?"

"Of course I did."

She thrust the necklace at him. "I can't accept this. Are you *joking?* What am I supposed to do with this?"

"Wear it. I'd assume that's what one does with necklaces, although I cannot speak from experience." His grin widened. It was nice to be the one surprising her for a change—to see *her* at a loss for words. "It's a gift. I hope you'll overlook the fact that I had to ask another servant to purchase it for me. Asking you to do it would ruin the surprise."

She returned the necklace to the box and hugged it to her chest. "Thank you, Percival."

He gathered his courage and confessed, "In another life, it would be you standing at that altar. Not Riona."

She gaped at him. Before she could respond, someone rapped on the door, startling them both. "Your Majesty, the carriage has arrived to take you to the Church," a guard called.

His stomach twisted into knots. His *wedding*. Soon Riona would move into the queen's rooms on the other side of the king's chamber. They'd be ruling the kingdom together until Tamriel returned or they managed to overthrow Nicholas, but that could take years—years of pretending to be in love, of making and raising heirs, of playing puppet while Nicholas controlled the kingdom.

He sighed and started toward the door.

"I'll see you after the ceremony, Your Majesty," Celeste said as he reached for the handle. His confession still hung in the air between them. It was obvious she didn't know how to respond to it, and he could accept that; he'd simply needed to get it off his chest. He'd needed her to know how much he cared for her, how far he'd fallen.

"Thank you for everything, Celeste."

He left her standing in the middle of the room, hating every step that carried him away from her.

🌿 41 🍂
TAMRIEL

Tamriel and Mercy were already dressed, wide awake and somber, when someone knocked on their door just before dawn. Tamriel opened it to find Faye and Kaius standing there, both wearing grave expressions. Wordlessly, Tamriel stepped aside to allow them to enter. As they moved past him, he exchanged a look with Mercy, remembering the conversation they'd had earlier that morning:

Everything is going to change today, Mercy had murmured, rolling onto her back to stare up at the canopy over their bed. She had been flipping a small object over and over in her fingers; in the darkness, he hadn't been able to make it out at first. Then it had caught the soft moonlight drifting into their room, and he had realized it was the sapphire ring he'd given her—the one that had belonged to his mother.

I know, was all he had said. It was all he could *think* to say as he propped himself up on one elbow and rubbed his tired eyes. Yesterday, he'd given Queen Cerelia an ultimatum; this morning would be their last opportunity to negotiate. One way or another, Tamriel was going to face Nicholas's army. If he had to do it without Feyndaran forces, so be it. He would not marry Marieve.

There were few things he would not do for his kingdom, and giving up Mercy was one of them.

Now, though, he couldn't help but feel a stab of pain as Faye and Kaius sat on the cushions in the center of the room, the low table between them. Nor could he ignore the guilt that flashed across Mercy's face. Faye and Kaius had not come to dinner last night, and it had not been difficult to imagine why. Tamriel frowned, wishing there were some other way to secure Queen Cerelia's aid. He shouldn't have had to ask this sacrifice of his friends.

"Are you sure you want to do this?" Mercy asked softly, laying a comforting hand on Faye's shoulder.

"For you?" Faye responded, forcing a brittle smile. "Try to stop me."

Kaius nodded. "As much as it pains me, I would rather marry a woman I do not love than see you march to war without an army. If marrying Marieve means a better chance of you all surviving the battle, I will do it."

"What's this about marrying me?"

They all looked toward the open door, where Marieve was standing with a brow raised at Kaius. For once, she was not dressed in her usual finery; instead, she wore a loose gown of burgundy silk, her hair falling freely around her shoulders, not a pearl or gemstone in sight. The effect was disarming. She looked like an entirely different person—no longer simply a product of her grandmother's court. It struck Tamriel that she was even younger than he had originally thought; she couldn't have been more than sixteen years old.

Kaius, Mercy, and Faye stood and bowed. Marieve dismissed their show of respect with a flick of her wrist, then focused on Tamriel. "I wanted to speak with you once more before you left to negotiate with my grandmother. You wish me to marry Kaius in your place? You must know this will not work. My grandmother will never agree."

An idea struck Tamriel then. It was a long shot, but if he could convince Marieve to speak to her grandmother on his behalf, Cerelia might just give up on forcing a marriage between them. The queen had to be growing desperate; Tamriel hadn't been bluffing when he told her he would leave without an army. If he sailed home today, she would lose her one chance to negotiate for the Islands.

"No, she won't," he agreed, "unless you speak to her first, my lady. Tell her of our proposal. You may be able to convince her to change her mind."

Marieve scoffed. "Have you learned nothing in your time here? My grandmother doesn't change her mind."

He stepped closer. "Your grandmother doesn't care about placing you on the Beltharan throne; she's just trying to ensure that both our countries have a say in the fate of the Islands. Despite my vow to pull my troops from Cirisor, she is convinced that once she stands down, I will send in my army to reclaim the land. She does not trust me enough to take me at my word, but she *does* trust you.

"If you and Kaius were to marry—you acting in Feyndara's best interests, and Kaius acting in those of Beltharos and Cirisor—you could help the Islands heal from the damage wrought by generations of war," he continued. "You could create a haven for the elves, be one of the leaders of a brand new nation. No more soldiers would have to die. No more innocent Cirisians would be caught in the fighting." He leaned in and softened his voice, turning yesterday's admission back on her. "No more young girls would lose their mothers to war."

Out of his peripheral vision, he saw surprise flicker across Mercy's face. "Your mother was a soldier? I thought she died protecting Princess Nymh from an attack on her life."

"That was her sister. My mother was a soldier in Her Majesty's army, one of the best," Marieve said, her expression tender, love and grief mingling in her eyes. "She met my father when she leapt in front of a blade to save his life. Despite all the healers saying she would not survive the night, he insisted on overseeing her treatment and nursing her back to health. As soon as she was fit enough to travel, he placed her on the saddle before him and rode to Castle Rising. The day they arrived, they were married."

Mercy and Faye regarded Marieve with identical awed expressions—Faye at the romance of the tale, Mercy at the bravery and selflessness Marieve's mother had shown. "She sounds like a great woman," Mercy said. "I'm sorry for your loss."

"Thank you." Marieve looked once more at Tamriel, a smile gracing her lips. "I couldn't stop thinking about her after I heard that you planned to make the Islands an independent country. I think she would have liked you. She wanted to bring peace to Cirisor. After the war ended, she left Rhys to patrol the Islands and protect the Cirisians from your father's troops. She always wished she could do more to aid them."

"She may not have been able to help my people," Kaius said, speaking up for the first time since her arrival, "but *you* can. The Islands need protecting. We lost many people to Firesse's war, and we'll lose more in the battle to come. With your help, we can rebuild the clans and establish trade with Beltharos and Feyndara. We'll be able to do everything your grandmother wishes without tearing Mercy and Tamriel apart. Your mother's sacrifice would not be for nothing."

"My grandmother will never agree to it," Marieve repeated, although a sliver of doubt had crept into her voice. "She wants the land for herself."

"As soon as we secure passage to Beltharos, we'll be sailing home," Tamriel reminded her. "The chance for negotiating will be long over. If Her Majesty truly wants to end the war, she will hear us out. This is her only opportunity to end the war peacefully. Please, speak to her on our behalf."

Marieve studied her hands, weighing everything they'd said.

Tamriel glanced at Mercy. Her expression was stony, but there was no hiding the desperation in her eyes, the tension in her body. If Queen Cerelia would not compromise, they would leave without an army. He wouldn't back down. He and Mercy had been through too much to lose each other now.

At the low table, Faye lifted her head and locked eyes with Kaius. Pain flashed across her face as Kaius gave her a small, sad smile.

"Very well," Marieve finally said, drawing their attention back to her. "I will speak to my grandmother, and if she agrees, I will marry Kaius in your place, Your Majesty."

Relief flooded him. "Thank you, my lady."

A shadow passed through Faye's eyes, but she blinked it away, schooling her features into a mask of neutrality. Tamriel had seen the look on her once before—when she had met him outside Sandori only a few weeks ago. She'd kept her expression blank as she described how Mother Illynor was torturing Mercy, but nothing could have hidden the terror and desperation that had lurked beneath her words. Tamriel had not fallen for the façade then, and he didn't fall for it now.

Mercy leaned closer to her friend and placed a hand on her arm.

Kaius dipped his head in respect. "It would be my honor to marry you, Lady Marieve."

"The honor is mine. I'm sorry for the pain this causes you," she replied, glancing at Faye. Tamriel's brows rose. Apparently, he and Mercy had not been the only ones to notice Kaius and Faye's absence from supper the night before. Marieve was more observant than he had given her credit for. "It's admirable that you are willing to give up the person you love for your king."

"For our king *and queen*," Kaius corrected.

Faye nodded. "There is nothing we would not do to help them defeat Nicholas and claim their thrones."

"I cannot promise that I will be successful, but I will tell my grandmother what you have said. Come to your usual meeting room after breakfast. We will meet you there."

"Thank you for this, Lady Marieve," Tamriel said.

She nodded. "We do not know each other well, Your Majesty, but I can tell from the love and loyalty you inspire in your friends that you are a great king. While it would have been my honor to serve as your queen, Mercy is the woman you should have at your side. I will do everything in my power to convince my grandmother to agree to your proposal."

She shot one more sympathetic look at Faye and Kaius, then stepped into the hall and pulled the door shut behind her.

True to her word, Marieve and Queen Cerelia were waiting in the meeting room when Tamriel arrived. The queen was seated in the middle of the couch, regal and poised as ever, and Marieve stood a few feet away, her hands clasped in front of her. Guards lined every wall of the room. Tamriel tried to catch Marieve's eye, to gauge whether she had been successful, but she lowered her gaze to her hands.

His stomach sank.

The queen tilted her head. "You've brought company."

He nodded. After Nynev had failed to appear after breakfast, he had sent his guards out looking for her, then invited Mercy and Faye to join him and Kaius for their final meeting with the queen. "I hope you do not mind, Your Majesty. As the decision we make today affects all of us, I thought it wise to include them in the negotiations."

She grinned and gestured toward the couch opposite her. "The more the merrier. Please, be seated. We have much to discuss." She waited until they all took their places—Tamriel in the center, Mercy and Faye on either side of him, Kaius standing by the arm of the couch—before continuing. "My granddaughter has told me what you discussed this morning. She made quite an impassioned plea on your behalf…and I am inclined to agree to your proposal."

Tamriel eyed the queen warily. After nearly two weeks of negotiations, it couldn't be this simple. Cerelia had to have some trick up her sleeve.

Just as he thought it, Marieve stiffened almost imperceptibly. Her eyes, full of sympathy, flitted to his face before dropping back to her hands. His blood turned cold.

"Of course, I have another condition," Cerelia said as the tension in the room rose. "Think of it as a show of goodwill between our countries—a way to prove to our people that there is trust between us, that we shall be ushering in a new era of friendship and unity."

"What is it?" Tamriel asked. Beside him, Mercy bristled with anger. It poured off her in waves, and her eyes burned with the desire to wipe the smirk off the queen's face. He wasn't entirely sure he would stop her if she tried.

Before she could say a word, the doors swung open, and they all turned to see Nynev and Alistair stride in, Atlas and the other guards on their heels. "Apologies for our tardiness, Your Majesty," Nynev said, dropping into a low bow before the queen. "I left for the city at dawn, and it still took me ages to find your grandson."

She turned to Tamriel and the others. "I overheard your conversation this morning, and I can't allow any of you to give up the people that you love. That's why I've asked Alistair to marry me in Tamriel's stead. And"—she beamed at the queen—"he has agreed. If it pleases Your Majesty, we will marry and serve the Islands for both Beltharos and Feyndara."

The queen peered up at her grandson, her usually smug expression faltering. "Is this true, Alistair?"

"It is, Your Majesty. As you well know, I have trained all my life to take up the mantle of Protector of the Islands once my father passes into the Beyond. But I can do more for the elves by being there—in Cirisor, working on your behalf. Nynev and I will help the Cirisians recover from the fighting that has plagued their land for generations, and when the time comes, Marieve can take my father's place as Protector of the Isles."

For a moment, the room was silent, every one of them considering the words still hanging in the air. Tamriel cursed himself for not thinking of it sooner. He detested asking any of his friends to marry purely for political gain, but it would have saved Faye and Kaius the heartbreak of thinking they would be forced to say goodbye in a few days.

Mercy rose and approached the huntress. "Nynev, do you truly mean this?"

Nynev smiled. "My sister made a sacrifice for the good of your kingdom. Now is my turn to do the same." She leaned close and whispered, just loud enough for Tamriel to make it out, "Not that it's much of a sacrifice to marry a handsome young lord."

"If you wish to marry in Tamriel and Marieve's places," the queen finally said, "then so be it. Should King Tamriel agree, we will pull our troops from the Islands and establish the land as an independent country. Alistair will act in the interests of Feyndara, and Nynev will act in those of Beltharos."

"We will be acting in the interests of the *Islands*," Alistair corrected politely.

Tamriel blinked at Cerelia, disbelieving. "You will provide the troops I need to reclaim my kingdom? And leave me free to marry whom I please?"

"Yes, if you agree to my condition."

Marieve flinched.

He steeled himself. "Which is?"

"I've heard so many terrible stories of what happens to elves in your country. Even those who are elven-blooded are at risk of being harmed or killed by the vipers in your court." She looked from Tamriel to Mercy. "Your children will look human, but they will be half elf. It is only fitting that they learn about their heritage in a land where their people have not been enslaved, tortured, and killed for generations. I would like you to allow me to oversee your firstborn child's education here in my home until he or she comes of age to ascend the throne."

Rage—sudden and blinding—swept over Tamriel. After all this, she still had the gall to make demands of him? Of his and Mercy's future children? "Absolutely not."

"Rest assured, Your Majesty, I only want what is best for both our countries. Your child should know what life is like for elves on both sides of the Abraxas Sea. You cannot tell me honestly that life for elves and the elven-blooded will become any easier in the next few decades. They may lose their chains, but there will still be prejudices to combat, old wounds that need healing. A place as volatile as your capital city is not fitting for a young child's development."

"Should we be lucky enough to have children," Mercy said, her voice laced with a dangerous, deadly calm, "we will protect them with our lives. You cannot claim to be willing to do the same."

The queen held up her hands. "In my home, that will not be necessary. Whose people killed and defiled Liselle Mari? Whose capital was attacked by Cirisians? Whose throne is currently held by a traitor? Rhys is safe. As I said before, entrusting me and my family with the education of your firstborn would prove to our people that there is no bad blood between our countries. If they see their sovereigns working together—allies, *friends*—all past indiscretions will be forgotten. Beltharos, Feyndara, and Cirisor alike would benefit from that unity."

Tamriel opened his mouth to argue, but paused when he noticed Mercy and Faye exchanging meaningful looks. A short, silent conversation seemed to pass between them. Then Mercy walked around the back of the couch and leaned forward to whisper in his ear. "We're not even married yet. Let's take back the kingdom, then we'll fight this battle."

He turned to look back at her, shocked that she would even consider agreeing to the queen's demand. "She is *not* getting our firstborn."

"Of course not." A wicked smile tugged at Mercy's lips. Something cruel and twisted flashed through her eyes, so quick Tamriel was certain no one else saw it. "She won't live long enough to take our child from us."

The promise of violence in her tone sent goosebumps rippling up and down his arms.

"Well?" Queen Cerelia asked, raising a brow. "Have we reached an agreement, Your Majesty?"

Tamriel looked to each of the others in turn. Marieve was gnawing on her lower lip, her eyes flitting from Tamriel to Cerelia and back. Nynev stepped closer to Alistair, standing by her decision. Faye was glaring at the queen, one hand lingering by her hip—no doubt ready to pull a throwing knife, should she need it. The fingers of her other hand were threaded through Kaius's.

Mercy set a hand on his shoulder and lifted her chin, a defiant set to her jaw. Seeing her standing there, staring down the queen, regal and beautiful and fierce, bolstered his confidence.

He turned to Queen Cerelia. "We have, Your Majesty."

❧ 42 ☙
PERCIVAL

Percival's stomach clenched when the double doors of the Church swung open. The musicians in the corner of the room began playing a soft melody as the nobles seated in the pews twisted to catch a glimpse of their future queen, their whispers filling the room. While their attention was diverted, Percival wiped his sweaty palms on his trousers. *Everything will be fine. Just have to make it through the ceremony. Then...*

Then the banquet.

Then the murders.

Two Rivosi guards strode down the aisle and claimed their places at the bottom of the dais steps. They were clad in shining silver armor, elaborately decorated swords and daggers sheathed at their hips, and the Rivosi royal crest—a dragon in flight—was proudly emblazoned on their breastplates. Two more followed them, and two more followed *them*, stationing themselves at regular intervals down the entire length of the aisle. When they had all taken their places, Lord Winslow walked to the dais, bowed to Percival and the High Priestess, and sat on the first pew beside Nicholas, beaming all the while.

The music swelled when Riona appeared.

Percival could swear everyone in the room sucked in breath at her beauty.

Her gown, crafted of blue-green silk, hugged every curve of her body as she walked down the aisle. The golden threads woven through the bodice gleamed in the sunlight spilling through the tall windows lining the room. The collar was open, baring her shoulders, collarbone, and elegant neck, which dripped with more gold necklaces than Percival could count. A cloak of the same blue-green silk tumbled from the back of the dress into a long train lined with pale pink silk and trimmed with elaborate embroidery. When she lifted her chin to smile at Percival, the gold dust across her lids sparkled.

With every pew she passed, the nobles stood and dropped into low bows. One by one, they did this, until she arrived at the base of the steps of the dais. The music crescendoed as Percival descended on shaky legs, took her hand, and guided her to her place before the High Priestess.

When the music softened once more, the High Priestess bade the attendees be seated. Her voice carried through the room as she launched into a story about the undying love between the Creator and his bride, Osha. As the nobles listened, enraptured by the romantic tale, Riona caught his eye and squeezed his hand. It was a small gesture, but it did wonders to ease his nerves. They were allies. They'd sworn to do everything they could to take down Nicholas and reclaim their futures. That was more binding, more sincere, than any marriage vows they could exchange.

Percival stole a glimpse over the High Priestess's shoulder. Lethandris was lined up against the back wall with the other priestesses, dressed in the robes of the Church. She gave him a shallow, almost imperceptible nod of encouragement, pity flashing across her face. Did she know about his feelings for Celeste?

He pushed thoughts of her away. By the Creator, he was marrying another woman *right this second!*

Not once during the ceremony did he allow himself to glance at his uncle. He was certain that if he did, Nicholas would see every emotion running rampant within him: his discomfort at being the center of attention, his hatred for the heavy crown atop his head, his longing to be standing there with a different girl—one with a teasing glint in her eyes and a wicked, barbed tongue.

At the High Priestess's bidding, Riona shared her vow first, a promise to rule beside him and remain faithful to him. Percival followed, a small burst of pride filling him when his voice didn't waver or his tongue stumble over the words. Then they exchanged rings.

And just like that, they were married.

"You may kiss your queen, Your Majesty," the High Priestess said.

His heart hammering in his ribcage, he stepped forward, pulled Riona into his arms, and kissed her. The nobles jumped to their feet and cheered as she twined her fingers in his hair and parted his lips with her tongue, causing him to let out a sound of surprise. She was a good kisser, he had to admit, but nothing stirred within him at the embrace—not the way it had when he had almost kissed Celeste earlier. When they broke apart, he wrapped her in a hug and whispered, "You're good at playing the lovestruck new bride."

"And you're a better kisser than I had expected."

They turned to the nobles, hands clasped between them, and let the shouts and cheers spill over them. Percival accepted them with smiles and nods, while Riona grinned and flashed the diamond and ruby ring he had given her. Several noblewomen swooned over the sparkling gemstones.

After several minutes, the High Priestess lifted a hand to silence the cheers. "If you would kneel, Your Majesty," she said to Riona, gesturing to the top step of the dais. Percival released her hand and stepped back as she obeyed, sweeping aside her train and kneeling on the stone, her head dipped forward in respect. The High Priestess pulled a vial of holy oil from the pocket of her gown and drew the Creator's holy eye on Riona's forehead.

"Riona Nevis, henceforth to be known as Her Majesty Riona Comyn"—Percival inwardly flinched at the change in her name—"do you swear to aid your husband in governing your subjects fairly in accordance with the laws of Beltharos?"

"I swear it."

"Do you promise to protect, guide, and provide for the people of your kingdom, in times of prosperity and in times of adversity, to the best of your ability for as long as you are able?"

"I do."

"Will you to your power ensure justice and mercy be executed in all your judgments, and, as the Creator himself once did, strive to rid your country of those black of heart and foul of deed?"

At this, Percival's attention turned to his uncle. Nicholas's face was unreadable, hard as eudorite, but Percival knew the addition of the latter phrase rankled him. It seemed the argument Percival had overheard so many weeks ago after his own coronation had not dissuaded the High Priestess from sneaking subtle jabs at Nicholas's character into her oration.

"I shall," Riona vowed.

A priestess stepped forward, a velvet pillow bearing a smaller version of the king's crown in her hands, and offered the crown to Percival. He picked it up—a stab of envy shooting through him when he felt how much lighter it was compared to his—and gently set it atop Riona's head. The rubies set into the gold matched the wedding ring on her finger.

"It is my great honor to present your queen, Her Majesty Riona Comyn, wife to the twenty-fifth sovereign of the great country of Beltharos," the High Priestess announced as the musicians began a new, joyous melody. "May your reign be prosperous, your life long and joyful, and your heart full of courage, Your Majesty."

Riona rose to the cheers of the nobles and courtiers, the movement sending flecks of light throughout the room and onto the high, arched ceiling. In the pews, Lord Winslow and Nicholas were standing and clapping. If Percival had thought the Rivosi lord could not look any more proud of his charge, he was wrong. The man positively glowed as he regarded Riona. Beside him, Nicholas was also fixated on the new queen, but with the same slightly suspicious look as he'd worn this morning in Percival's chamber.

The sight spurred Percival to motion. He stepped forward and joined Riona on the top step, protectiveness sweeping over him. While they had agreed to revolt against Nicholas in the future, he'd been careful to keep her in the dark about his and Celeste's plan for the banquet. Should anything go wrong, he didn't want her harmed.

Riona smiled and clasped his hand, batting her lashes at him coyly. He grinned and planted another kiss on her lips. The cheers swelled anew when he pulled back, took her other hand, and kissed her knuckles, right above her wedding ring. Let the nobles think they were happy. Let them think they were the perfect, lovesick royal couple they pretended to be. That charade would be shattered soon enough.

It was just past midday when Percival and Riona were ushered out of the Church and into a grand carriage surrounded by royal guards on horseback. Nicholas and Lord Winslow clambered in behind them and settled on the opposite bench. At a shout from Rhiannon—one of the many guards who had been chosen to escort the carriage back to the castle—the driver snapped the reins and the procession began. Carriages carrying various members of the king's council clattered along behind them as they made their way through the winding streets and into the Sapphire Quarter. The Church bells pealed, signaling the conclusion of the ceremony. People lined the streets and leaned out of upper-story windows to catch a glimpse of their new queen.

Flowers flew through the air, landing atop the royal carriage and dropping to the streets. Young women admired Riona's gown—what little they could see of it through the window—and jostled one another for a closer look. Young men admired Riona's beauty and shot Percival envious looks. Children sitting atop their parents' shoulders chattered excitedly, only to giggle shyly when Riona and Percival waved to them. Through it all, Nicholas did not say a word; he merely leaned back against the wall of the carriage, a slight smirk on his lips as he watched Riona and Percival play the parts he'd crafted for them.

Of course, some people were not so enamored of their new royal family. For the most part, they hid it well, but Percival still caught a few frowns and scowls amidst the crowd spilling over the sidewalk. Most came from the elven slaves Tamriel would have freed had he been allowed to return to the city. Percival wished he could speak to them, *comfort* them, but he didn't even know if his and Celeste's plot was going to work. More than that—he didn't know if Tamriel was even *alive*.

By the time they arrived at the castle gates, Percival's cheeks were aching from holding a smile for so long. When the carriage rolled to a stop, he let the smile drop for a few blessed moments as the driver clambered from his seat, rounded the carriage, and opened the door, offering a hand to help them down. When Percival emerged, his hand still linked with Riona's, the crowd gathered in the intersection cheered wildly.

Nicholas moved to Percival's side and gestured to the castle gates. "Shall we, Your Majesties? Do remember to make it look like you're enjoying yourselves."

"With your nephew as my husband, how could I not?" Riona asked, sweeping past him and dragging Percival along with her. Their guards—a mix of Riona's Rivosi guards and Nicholas's Beltharan ones—trailed them through the gates and across the castle grounds.

As much as Percival resented being forced to marry for politics, he had to admit the council members had outdone themselves in planning the celebration. And the slaves, who had actually *done* the decorating, had executed their tasks beyond anything he had expected. Stakes lined either side of the gravel carriageway, strands of colored glass ornaments forming an archway all the way to the castle steps. Garlands of multicolored blossoms twined around the stakes and up the banisters of the stairs. While the main banquet tables had been set up in the throne room, small tables laden with pastries and treats were scattered around the gardens. A platform had been erected before the castle steps, upon which several musicians were playing a lively, jaunty tune that resounded across the grounds.

The eager revelers spilled through the gate behind them

as they approached the castle. As they passed a table, Riona reached out and swiped a small caramel-covered cake, plucking one of the roasted pecans off the top and holding it up to Percival's lips. "Pretend to enjoy the celebration, Your Majesty," she whispered, low enough for only him to hear.

For the next few hours, they moved from conversation to conversation, charming nobles and accepting words of congratulations. Percival was careful to steer Riona away from the servants wandering the grounds with platters of wine goblets. He searched the grounds for a glimpse of Celeste—if only to settle his nerves and reassure him that everything was going according to plan—but there were too many people, too many faces, too many courtiers vying for his and Riona's attention. She was inside, at the banquet, he reminded himself.

Even so, his nervousness mounted as the afternoon gave way to evening. He and Celeste had agreed that their helpers would wait until later in the evening to circulate the poisoned goblets—giving the revelers time to drink enough regular wine that the effects of the gloriosa tansy wouldn't be noticed until it was too late—but still, he grew anxious as the sun started to sink below the western horizon. One of the helpers could be caught putting poison into the drinks. One of the innocents here could grab the wrong goblet. Someone might—

He forced the thoughts from his mind. Dwelling on his worries wasn't going to do any good. Celeste had planned the attack down to the minute.

Nothing would go wrong.

Percival guided Riona to the patch of grass before the musicians' platform, and together they joined the dancing couples. Percival let the music sweep over him, wash away his concerns, as he spun Riona under his arm. She grinned at him, the gold beads in her braids flashing in the light of the lanterns scattered across the castle grounds. The celebration was far from over. Percival had no doubt that if not for his and Celeste's attack, it would last well into the next day...or perhaps even longer.

When the song ended, a gaggle of pink-faced children ran up to Riona and asked her for a dance. She laughed as they tripped over one another to bow and curtsy and babble whatever nonsense their courtier parents had instructed them to say to a royal. Taking their hands, she led them to the center of the makeshift dance floor and formed a circle, the six of them spinning and twirling and giggling. Percival retreated to the castle steps, leaning against the banister as he surveyed the celebration.

More people than he could count filled the castle grounds, dancing, eating, drinking, chatting. Some wandered the hedge mazes with their friends or their children. Some admired the glass ornaments dangling over the carriageway. Some had formed a half-circle around four stakes planted in the grass, watching several guards hack away at straw-filled dummies suspended from hooks, the fabric skin painted to resemble Cirisian tattoos. Through it all, servants slipped through the throngs of people carrying platters of drinks or desserts. His eyes latched onto those with the small white buds pinned in their hair. Soon, this merry celebration would come to a bloody end, and all he could do was wait.

"Enjoying the party?" Nicholas said, startling Percival. He looked up to see his uncle standing a few steps above him, nodding toward the castle grounds.

"I think 'party' is a gross understatement."

"Only the best for my nephew and his lovely bride. Come now, let's have a toast. Show them all just how happy you two are." He descended the remaining few steps and slung an arm around Percival's shoulders, dragging him toward the musicians' platform. Nicholas swiped a goblet from a passing slave, dragging Percival along too quickly for him to see if the young woman was wearing Winter's Lace blossoms. He bounded onto the platform, lifting his glass high as the musicians abruptly ended their song. The sudden quiet drew the attention of the revelers.

"A toast to our king and queen!" he roared, hauling Percival onto the platform beside him. When he spotted Riona in the gathering crowd, he held out a hand and pulled her up, as well. "Long live King Percival and Queen Riona!"

"Hear, hear!" the nobles shouted, lifting their goblets. Percival and Riona exchanged perplexed looks. Was Nicholas acting like this because of gloriosa tansy? Percival hadn't smelled wine on his uncle's breath when he'd slung his arm around his shoulders, but why else would he be so uncharacteristically joyful?

Then he spotted a slave pushing her way through the edge of the crowd, trying to get to him. Her expression was that of fear, of horror, her face as pale as the white blossoms pinned in her hair.

"As it is our king and queen's first day ruling together," Nicholas shouted, "why not mark the occasion by having them hold court? I've been told the guards arrested a few traitors earlier today, and they are in need of sentencing."

Dread filled Percival as a half-dozen guards led Hero, Lethandris, and Ketojan—each clapped in chains at their ankles and wrists—out of the castle and down the stairs. *What the— How did the guards find them?* His terror must have been showing on his face, for Riona stepped closer to his side, her brows furrowing as she glanced from him to the prisoners. Whispers rose from the gathered nobles.

"These three are responsible for the escapes and attempted escapes of several dozen slaves," Nicholas yelled over the growing noise of the crowd. "They stole your property! They freed your valuable investments! They corrupted King Tamriel and convinced him to help them sneak runaways out of the city!"

Percival's heart pounded as the nobles shouted over one another, demanding the prisoners' executions. Riona set a hand on his shoulder, but the touch didn't register as he watched his friends stumble over their heavy chains. *No! No, no no!*

Creator only knew how long Nicholas had waited to make him pay for every little defiance over the past few days. He wouldn't reveal that Percival had been helping them free slaves—not now that the people of Sandori were embracing their new royal family—but he would force Percival to watch his friends be executed.

Percival grabbed his uncle's arm and hissed, "You cannot do this."

"I warned you what would happen if you tried to help the slaves. You brought this on yourself." Nicholas ripped his arm out of Percival's grasp and turned to the crowd. "The traitors even sent an agent into the castle—my *home!*—to try and sway my nephew to their side."

Nicholas looked over his shoulder as the doors to the castle swung open again. For a moment, Percival stood frozen, his blood rushing in his ears. *No. He cannot be talking about... He cannot mean...* Then he saw Lethandris's eyes lift to the front of the castle, and her face crumpled in defeat.

He turned slowly, unsteadily, to see Rhiannon and three other guards lead Celeste down the castle steps. Her hair had fallen from its bun and now hung in a tangle of pins and loose curls, some of the white blossoms splattered with flecks of crimson. She'd lost her slave sash and her lace dress was slashed and bloodied, but, aside from a bloody nose and a bruise on the right side of her jaw, she looked relatively unharmed. He didn't doubt she'd made good use of every one of her five daggers before she was caught. Her chains clanked against the stone as Rhiannon dragged her down the last few steps and marched her through the crowd, dumping her at the foot of the platform. A swift kick to the back of her leg sent her to her knees.

On instinct, Percival stepped forward, but Riona yanked him back. "Do not move a muscle if you do not wish to join them," she warned as the other guards pushed Hero, Lethandris, and Ketojan to their knees beside Celeste. "Give me a moment to think."

"Thieves!" someone in the crowd shouted.

"Hang 'em!"

"Send them to the executioner's block!"

Ketojan's expression was stony, stubborn. Silent tears trailed down Hero's cheeks, but she did not flinch at the insults the nobles and courtiers hurled at her. They'd always known the risks of freeing the slaves. They'd always known something like this could happen. Lethandris stared down at her hands, mouthing the words of what Percival assumed was a prayer. She was still clad in the formal robes she'd worn at the wedding. Beside her, Celeste stared up at Percival, an apology in her eyes. He realized then that she was wearing the necklace he had given her. Her shoulders were slumped, curled in as if to protect her from the crowd's demands for her execution. Despite her terror, she shot a glare at Nicholas, then mouthed something to Percival. She had to repeat it twice before he finally understood:

Do not yield.

It sounded like a goodbye.

"No—" he began, but Riona's grip on his shoulder tightened in a warning. His mind raced. He could get them out of this. He could. Somehow. There *had* to be a way.

Nicholas lifted a hand, and the crowd's insults and jeers

quieted. He turned to Percival and Riona, a triumphant grin on his face. "What do you say, Your Majesties?" He gestured to the four stakes planted in the grass, where several guards had taken down the Cirisian dummies and were now setting stools below them. Nooses hung from the hooks, swaying slightly in the breeze. "Shall we have a hanging tonight?"

43
PERCIVAL

"Shall we have a hanging tonight?"

The words rang in Percival's ears as the crowd roared, a sea of faces twisted in rage. Panic closed a fist around his throat. *NO. Nonononono. This cannot be happening.*

Nicholas smirked at him over his shoulder, out of sight of the nobles. Even if they'd been able to see it, they wouldn't have noticed; they were too busy hurling insults and half-eaten pastries at the four prisoners kneeling before the platform. Celeste lifted her arms to shield herself from the projectiles. A small cake exploded against the back of her head and left a smear of icing in her hair. The sight made Percival's blood boil, morphing his fear into fury.

Nicholas turned to Riona. "What shall be done to these criminals?"

Bastard. Lying, manipulative bastard, Percival seethed. He eyed the sword strapped to his uncle's belt. There was no way he could get to it in time to pull it from its sheath, not before his uncle rammed it through his chest—or worse, turned it on Celeste and the others. He still had the dagger

Celeste had given him, but even with all his training, it would be useless against his uncle's sword and brute strength. *Think of something!* He needed a distraction. He needed a plan. Anything would be better than simply standing there, gaping.

"Hang them!" someone shouted, and several members of the crowd echoed the demand.

Riona lifted her chin, fury in her eyes as she gazed at Nicholas. "Surely this can wait until tomorrow, my lord. There is no need to taint our wedding day with bloodshed."

"You are the queen now, Your Majesty. You swore an oath to uphold the laws of this kingdom. What better way to begin your rule than by proving to your subjects your dedication to your subjects?" Nicholas responded, a challenge glittering in his good eye. "Would you disappoint them by denying them this spectacle?"

"They can live with disappointment for one day." She turned to Rhiannon. "Send the prisoners to the dungeon and ensure that they are watched by Rivosi *and* Beltharan guards. We will deal with them tomorrow."

Rhiannon looked at Nicholas, who shook his head. "Get the prisoners to their feet," she commanded the other guards. Percival's stomach lurched as they yanked his friends up and pushed them toward the nooses.

"No!" He whirled on Nicholas, seething. "Your queen has given you an order! Their deaths will not mar this celebration!"

Before them, the crowd—the *mob*—parted to allow the guards and prisoners to pass. Celeste bucked and thrashed, trying to free herself from her captor's grasp. Hero and the others fought as well, to no avail.

Amidst the chaos, Percival's eyes found the servant who had tried to warn him. She was standing in the middle of the sea of nobles, a small wooden object in her hands.

Percival recognized it a heartbeat before all hell broke loose:

Crossbow.

He grabbed Riona's arm and yanked her back, shielding her with his body as something whizzed through the air. Someone gasped, and he turned to see Nicholas staggering away from the edge of the platform, a bolt protruding from his chest. He pressed a hand to the wound and blood began leaking through his fingers.

Screams erupted from the crowd. Several nobles sprinted for the cover of the hedge mazes, and the musicians tripped over their instruments as they scrambled out of the way. Rhiannon and a handful of guards rushed toward the platform as Nicholas stumbled and dropped to his knees. One drew his sword and plunged it through the servant's gut. She crumpled, her blood pooling on the grass.

"Find your guards and don't leave their sides," Percival told Riona, pulling the dagger from his boot. He ran to his uncle and ripped the sword from the sheath on Nicholas's belt.

Riona shouted his name as he leapt off the platform. It didn't occur to him to check that Nicholas was dead. The gloriosa tansy would finish him off soon enough, if the poisoned wine had indeed reached him as Celeste had planned. All his attention was focused on getting Celeste and the others to safety. His blood rushed in his ears, muffling every sound except his heart screaming, *Save them! Save them! Save them!* When he passed the dead servant, he tucked his dagger into his boot and swiped the crossbow off the ground. It was no longer than his forearm, with six small bolts stored in notches just below the limb of the weapon.

Five guards surrounded his friends. Seeing Percival racing for them, Ketojan slammed his head into one guard's face, causing him to stumble backward, his hands flying up to his broken nose. Hero leapt in front of Lethandris, shielding her as the guards unsheathed their swords. Celeste twisted, swept one man's feet out from under him, and wrapped the chain connecting her wrists around his neck. As soon as he went limp, she rifled through his pockets until she found a ring of keys. Percival arrived just as the cuffs around her ankles fell to the ground.

"Some friends you have here," Percival panted as he positioned himself between her and the three remaining guards. To his right, Ketojan had followed Celeste's lead and looped his chain around the neck of the guard with a broken nose.

"Some timing you have," she grunted. As soon as the shackles on her wrists fell away, Percival tossed her the crossbow.

"We don't wish to harm you, Your Majesty," one of the guards yelled. "Lay down your weapon and return to the castle."

He slashed out with his sword, not bothering to respond. He'd already revealed his true loyalties to the court; at this point, he'd be lucky if he survived. The servant had bought him an opening, and he wasn't going to waste it. She'd given her life to save his friends. He would do the same, if necessary.

He parried and blocked as the guards struck, while Celeste scrambled to her feet and loaded a bolt. She tossed the keys to Hero and aimed the crossbow at one of the guards. The trigger clicked, then the woman slumped to the ground, a bolt sticking out of her skull.

More guards rushed out of the castle, spilling down the steps. Rhiannon, who was kneeling over Nicholas with her hands pressed to his wound, jerked her chin toward Percival and his friends. The guards swarmed the garden. *Shit! Shit, shit, shit!* They were heavily outnumbered.

"You need to get out of the city!" Percival yelled to

Celeste, never taking his eyes off his opponent's blade. By some miracle, he managed to break through one guard's defense and shove his sword through the man's chest.

"What about you?"

"I'll—I'll figure it out."

"Come with us." Another body thumped to the ground, a bolt sticking out of one of the chinks of her armor, providing them a momentary reprieve from the fighting. Celeste turned to him, her eyes wild, her hair a mess. Blood was splattered across her face and neck, coating the peridot necklace.

He shook his head, his heart leaping into his throat as more guards approached. "I can't. I swore to Tamriel that I would serve the kingdom. I need to hold the throne until he returns—*if* he returns." He glanced at Hero and Lethandris, relieved to see their chains lying in a heap on the grass. Then he looked to the platform. His stomach sank when he saw Rhiannon sling Nicholas's arm over her shoulders and pull him to his feet. *He's alive.* The servant's bolt had injured him, but it had not killed him.

"Leave now. Find Tamriel," he implored Celeste. "He must be alive. He must be coming for his throne. Find him and tell him everything about my uncle's plans for the battle."

"Percival—"

"I'll buy you time. Now *GO!*" he roared, lifting his sword as the first of the guards reached them. Celeste was wise enough not to argue further. He didn't look back, but he heard her urge the others on. Several of the guards raced after them. The rest encircled him, blades glinting in the lantern light. The sun had already gone down. *Good.* The darkness would give Celeste and the others the cover they needed to lose the guards and get out of the city.

"Arrest my nephew!" Nicholas shouted from across the gardens, right before Rhiannon helped him stumble into the castle. His voice was thick with pain, but there was still power in it. He was weak, and he must have lost quite a lot of blood, but he was going to live. Percival was certain of it. Monsters like Nicholas were not so easily defeated.

He spun, his blades outstretched. A few of the guards regarded him warily, others patronizingly, as if he were nothing more than a child playing with a toy. No matter. He didn't need to kill them; he just needed to keep them from pursuing his friends for as long as possible. "Stand down! Your king commands you to lower your weapons!"

None of them did. Of course. They were on his uncle's payroll.

Still, he fought them as long as he could. Every time one stepped forward to clap him in chains, he lunged, slashing out. Sometimes, he rent flesh. Most times, *his* flesh was the one being sliced open. Before long, he was staggering, growing fatigued, bleeding from dozens of nicks and gashes. Eventually, he fell to his knees, the weapons slipping out of his grasp. He sucked in lungfuls of air as the guards pressed in around him. One leveled the point of his sword at Percival's throat.

Through the press of their bodies, he spotted Riona being escorted into the castle by a mix of Beltharan and Rivosi guards. She glanced over her shoulder and met his eyes, her own wide with terror, before she disappeared through the doors.

In front of the platform, bodies littered the grass, mounds of shining silks, shimmering damasks, priceless brocades. Nobles—the ones Celeste's helpers had been instructed to target with the poisoned wine. Percival recognized Dunstan and Jocasta Astley among the slack faces, as well as Corinne Burgess and Landers Nadra. His son, Leon, was kneeling at his father's side with a girl his same age, tears rolling down their cheeks.

At least one thing went right tonight, Percival thought, but the sentiment brought him little comfort.

Someone closed shackles around his wrists. Cuffs on his ankles followed.

"Sorry about this, Your Majesty," one of the guards muttered. Percival lifted his head just in time to see the pommel of a sword swinging toward him. It cracked against his skull, sending stars shooting through his vision, right before everything went black.

44
MERCY

Three days later, they were ready to set sail.

Marieve had been right about her grandmother's orders: soldiers had begun arriving outside Rhys's city limits a day after Tamriel and Cerelia had signed the document outlining the details of their agreement. The forces quickly numbered into the hundreds, then to the thousands. Every day, Mercy and Tamriel had accompanied General Cadriel to the army camp, where makeshift barracks had been constructed to house the soldiers. Tanni and the other Daughters—who had kept mostly to themselves since their arrival in Feyndara—had opted to stay in the camp and teach the soldiers tricks for breaking through chinks in Beltharan armor. Meanwhile, Calum and the Strykers had enlisted the help of Tamriel's guards and Mercy's siblings in crafting additional weapons and supplies.

Mercy was standing at the end of the dock, staring out at the glittering waves of the Abraxas Sea, when she heard footsteps approach from behind. She looked over her shoulder and smiled at Tamriel. He was dressed in a simple cotton tunic and fitted trousers—far from his usual court attire—and the breeze snagged on a strand of hair that had fallen from the leather tie at the nape of his neck. She turned toward the sea. A moment later, he slipped his arms around her waist, resting his chin on her shoulder.

"We're going home," he breathed, his voice hopeful and light. "I can't believe after all this time, we're finally going home."

"Neither can I," she whispered, lacing her fingers through Tamriel's. She had lost track of the days while they were on the run. When they arrived in Feyndara, it had come as a shock to learn that almost a month had passed since Nicholas's attack. She hadn't wanted to believe it at first. They had spent a month evading Nicholas's soldiers, gathering a ragtag army, sleeping on hard ground, and hunting for food—all while they should have been celebrating their victory over the Guild.

Fortunately, the time away had brought good things, as well. Mercy's broken ribs no longer ached, her fingers were healed, and all the sparring with Faye and her siblings had helped restore the muscles she had lost due to malnourishment. Faye's side was puckered and scarred from the wound she had received at the Keep, but it no longer hurt her to fight. Calum, with the help of the Strykers, had begun to return to the charming young man she had met so many months ago.

Even so, none of them would ever be the same person they were at the start of the summer. Despite everything they'd endured, Mercy was glad of that. The cold, ruthless Assassin she had been was dead, and in her place stood the future queen of Beltharos.

Mercy turned, linking her hands behind Tamriel's neck and pulling him into a kiss. "Let's go reclaim our kingdom," she murmured as she leaned back, and he grinned.

"As you command, my love."

Someone cleared his throat. They looked back to find Kaius, Faye, Calum, and Mercy's siblings standing at the bottom of the gangplank of the nearest ship. The Daughters, the Strykers, and the guards had already embarked; Mercy could hear their laughter drifting over from the deck.

"Ready to go, Your Majesties?" Calum called, lifting a brow. "Or are you just going to stand there admiring the view?"

"We'd already be on the sea if *someone* hadn't taken so long getting dressed this morning," Tamriel retorted, humor glittering in his eyes.

"I was finishing some work on my armor. Either way, I resent having to wake up at this ungodly hour."

"I resent having to spend the next week on this ship with your ugly mug for company!" one of the Strykers shouted.

Mercy laughed, while Tamriel merely smiled and gestured to the gangplank. "After you, my friends."

Just as Mercy and Tamriel were about to follow them onto the ship, a line of carriages appeared from around the corner and rolled to a stop near the shore. Queen Cerelia and her family stepped out, each clad in finery save for General Cadriel, who had donned an ornate breastplate and strapped a sheathed sword to his hip. The armor was only for show, of course, since they wouldn't arrive in Beltharos for another week. Mercy had to admit, however, that he cut a striking, impressive figure for the soldiers. He bowed to his mother, pressed a kiss to her cheek, then swept his daughter up in a hug that lifted her clear off her feet. When he set her down to exchange farewells with the rest of his family, Marieve turned away to wipe tears from her eyes.

Nynev ran down the pier and pulled Mercy and Tamriel into a tight hug. "I wish I could come with you. It feels like I've only just arrived and you're already marching off to war."

"You have your own battles to fight here in Rhys, I'm sure," Mercy said as she backed out of the embrace, her eyes drifting to the queen. "Has she started making plans for the wedding yet?"

"Oh, I'm sure she did the moment you all arrived. The sooner we're married, the sooner she gets to start exerting control over the Islands." She grinned. "Or so she *thinks*. Now go before she tries to speak with you."

"We will, but... Will you be happy with Alistair?" Tamriel asked, brows furrowing with concern. "I appreciate what you did, but I don't want you to be miserable because of me."

"Do not worry about me, Your Majesty. Whatever consequences come of my choices, they are mine to bear. I offered to marry him to secure your army and ensure the end of the fighting over my home. If that is what it takes to bring peace to my people, I will do it proudly." Mercy was surprised by the affection on Nynev's face as she gazed at her betrothed. She looked almost...*enamored* with the young, handsome royal. "We may not know each other well, but we've spent the past few days discussing my duties on the Islands and his duties at Castle Rising. We will make it work. He is sweet and kind, in addition to being devoted to establishing Cirisor as its own land. I could do a lot worse."

Mercy stepped forward and clasped the huntress in another hug, aching at the thought of parting so soon after being reunited. "Take care, Nynev."

"Don't sound so forlorn. We'll see each other soon, I promise. Alistair and I will visit you in Sandori and we'll shower each other in wedding gifts." Nynev squeezed her back just as tightly, a smile in her voice. "Do you think we could lug one of those nice downy mattresses back to the Islands? Shockingly, sleeping on the ground lost its appeal after spending so much time in the castle's guest rooms."

"I'm sure something can be arranged," she responded. Her smile faltered as Queen Cerelia marched toward them. "Do you think she has spotted us? Can we make a run for the ship?"

"I thought you weren't afraid of the queen."

"I'm afraid of what I'll do to her if she dares patronize us one more time," she muttered, her fingers drifting toward the twin daggers sheathed at her hips. The orange and red gemstones in the hand guards sent flecks of colored light across the pier as she, Tamriel, and Nynev bowed to the approaching queen.

"Thank you again for opening your home to us and providing us troops, Your Majesty," Tamriel said when they straightened. "Despite our...disagreements, I am grateful for the aid you have given us. Please rest assured that I will do everything in my power to see your people home safe."

"I'll be eagerly awaiting news of the battle, King Tamriel. Good luck, and may the Creator watch over you both. I am interested to see what kind of rulers you two become."

"Thank you, Your Majesty," Tamriel and Mercy replied in unison. Beyond the queen's shoulder, Mercy spotted Lady Marieve making her way toward them, arm-in-arm with her father.

Queen Cerelia bade them farewell, then turned to exchange a few final words with her general. While they spoke, Marieve slipped away and gestured for Tamriel, Mercy, and Nynev to follow her a little farther down the dock.

"Your Majesty, my lady, I wanted to wish you luck in the battle to come. If I did not have my own duties here—and if I were of any use with a sword—I would be fighting with you at my father's side. Alas, as it is, I fear I would be more hindrance than help," she said with a slight smile. "Please, if you have need of anything, do not hesitate to write. You may have no great love for my grandmother, but I hope that you will consider me, at least, a friend."

"Of course," Tamriel said, dipping his head slightly.

"Thank you, my lady." Mercy offered the royal a tight-lipped smile and dipped her head in respect. She didn't care much for Marieve, but the girl *had* spoken to the queen on their behalf. Without her, they likely wouldn't have been able to convince Cerelia to provide them troops.

Even so, she'd not forgotten Marieve's suggestion to ship her off to Westwater upon their return to Sandori. She certainly wouldn't forget about it anytime soon.

Mercy and Tamriel boarded the ship and joined their friends at the railing. Nynev waved to them, beaming, as the soldiers moved to their places across the ship. Tears trailed down Marieve's cheeks as her father began shouting commands, preparing the ships to sail. The other members of the royal family watched with steady, even gazes as the ships cast off.

Before Mercy knew it, they were out on the open water. When Feyndara's shore faded into the distance, she tipped her head back and breathed in the salty sea air. They had a week of sailing and a long march ahead of them, but for now, they could let down their guards. They'd secured what they'd needed. They had an army.

And yet, they had no idea what they would face when they crossed the Abraxas Sea. Would Nicholas have troops waiting at the shore, ready to attack before they even had a chance to dock? Or had he pulled his men back to the capital, expecting Tamriel to mount an army against him? Mercy didn't know Nicholas well, but she was sure the general wouldn't rest until their heads were staked upon the city walls.

The thought sent a chill down her spine, and she forced it from her mind. They hadn't heard from Seren Pierce, which meant—*hopefully*—nothing had changed. They would be joined by the Cirisians and Qadar at Fallmond, further bolstering their numbers. Hopefully, it would be enough.

We're going to win, Mercy told herself as Tamriel reached over and clasped her hand. *We* have *to win.*

45
PERCIVAL

Consciousness dragged Percival back slowly, first with nothing more than a series of sensations: exhaustion, dizziness, agony, a pounding headache, and a wet, damp chill that had settled deep within his bones. He was sore in more places than he had thought were physically possible. The slightest movement sent pain shooting through his body and a wave of nausea churning in his stomach.

He opened his eyes to pitch blackness. He blinked hard, trying to focus on something beyond the throbbing in his skull. Something nagged at him—something had happened to land him in this pathetic, enervated state—but all he could think about was how the world was spinning around him.

He was vaguely aware of lying on cold, hard stone. He rolled onto his back and let out a weak groan. Some parts of his doublet stuck to him, the fabric crusted to his skin, while other parts felt warm and slick. He ran his fingers over his arm, sucking in a sharp breath when they brushed a deep gash just below his shoulder. The pain cut through some of the haze in his mind, drawing him back to himself. How long had he been bleeding?

Percival remembered facing off against the guards and being struck by their swords. Most of the cuts had clotted—that much was obvious from the stiffness of his clothes—but some of them continued to bleed; the one in his arm in particular. He would probably need stitches...not that his uncle would send a healer down to tend to his injuries. Judging by the clamminess of his skin, he'd been in the dungeon for quite a while. How long had it been since the banquet? A day? Two?

Percival wiped his bloody fingers on his trousers—also ruined—then reached up and gingerly ran them over the goose egg protruding from the back of his head. The edge of the pommel had cut him. His curls were plastered to his skull, coated in dried blood. The feeling sent a shudder through him.

It took him a long time to stand; he had to keep pausing whenever he moved too fast, the world tilting beneath his feet. He staggered blindly through the darkness, his uninjured arm outstretched, until he slammed face-first into a cold iron bar. An expletive burst from his lips. His Creator-damned arm had gone straight between the bars of his cell.

"*Shit*," he muttered, rubbing away a drop of blood where the bridge of his spectacles had cut into his nose. He grasped the bars of what he assumed was the door to his cell, goosebumps rising across his flesh. "Celeste?" he croaked, his throat dry as old parchment. "Hero? Ketojan? Lethandris? Are you in here?"

No answer. No sounds at all save for his rasping breaths and the pattering of water droplets somewhere to his left.

Had they made it out of the city? They would be in the dungeon with him if they had been caught...unless they had been executed upon capture.

An image of Celeste hanging at the end of a noose, her peridot necklace replaced by one of rope, flashed through his mind. He stumbled to the rear of his cell and crumpled, bracing his hands on his knees as he fought the bile rising in his throat. There was nothing for his stomach to expel, but it still tried. He sank to the floor and retched a couple times before collapsing onto his side.

As he lay there in the darkness, he comforted himself with the knowledge that the nobles who had betrayed Tamriel were dead. Nicholas was likely alive; he had survived the shot to the chest and had not, as far as Percival had seen, consumed any poisoned wine. Perhaps Celeste's helpers had not been able to get close enough to give him one of the drinks laced with gloriosa tansy. Perhaps he had simply chosen not to take part in the drinking. It mattered not, he supposed. Nicholas was alive, and Percival was in a cell. Riona was somewhere in the castle, probably being fretted over by Lord Winslow and her guards. Celeste was gone.

What would happen to him?

Again, all he could do was wait—for an interrogation, for a trial, for an execution, for a savior...

So he closed his eyes, drew his knees in close, and waited.

46
FAYE

The stars were shining brightly overhead, a vast blanket spreading as far as the eye could see, when Faye emerged on the deck one night. She nodded a greeting to the soldiers manning the ship as she approached the railing. This late, the sea was dark as ink, the reflection of the night sky rippling over the waves. She could just make out the silhouettes of the ships following theirs.

The first few days of their journey had been relatively easy —they had helped man the ship; discussed the battle strategy with General Cadriel; and taken turns sparring or playing cards with the soldiers in their spare time. After a while, however, the reality of their situation began to sink in. Even if they won the battle against Nicholas's army, they would lose friends and family. No amount of training or planning would protect them from a well-aimed blade or arrow. Any of them could die.

She slipped her fingers under the hem of her tunic and brushed the puckered skin of her newest scar. It wasn't an arc or line like all her other ones—no, Mother Illynor's spiked mace had taken chunks out of her flesh. The scars pebbled the entire left side of her stomach, pulling tight whenever she moved too far or too quickly.

Footsteps sounded behind her, and she let her hand drop from the wound. When the footsteps halted, she turned, and her heart leapt when she found Kaius standing there. He was leaning against the mainmast, his hair loose around his face, his arms crossed over his chest. She must have woken him when she'd climbed out of her hammock.

"I thought you might want to talk," he said. "We haven't had much time to ourselves since we cast off. I've been missing you."

She offered him a faint smile. "We might have to sneak off for a good long while once we're back in Fallmond."

Between all the chores and planning, she and Kaius had barely exchanged two words since leaving Feyndara. The one time they had managed to slip away unnoticed, they'd been discovered not fifteen minutes later in an alcove below deck by a very embarrassed, *very* flustered young soldier. Kaius had merely glared at the soldier as he babbled whatever order General Cadriel had sent him to deliver. Faye had not heard a word of it; she'd been too busy covering herself with her discarded tunic and trying not to blush from head to toe. As soon as the soldier left, she and Kaius had locked eyes...then promptly burst out laughing.

Judging by the crooked smile tugging at Kaius's lips, he was remembering their misadventure, as well. He joined her at the railing and wrapped an arm around her. The warmth of his body seeped through the blanket, chasing away the chill left by the sea breeze. "So," he murmured, dipping his head to kiss the side of her neck, "what's keeping you up?"

"At the moment? You."

He shot her a knowing look. "Nice try. What's *worrying* you?"

"Just...everything. I'm terrified of the battle to come.

What if I freeze up again? What if all that blood—" She stopped. "I don't want to think about it. You've comforted me enough these past few weeks."

"That just means I'm now an expert at it." When she didn't immediately respond, he set his hands on her hips and turned her around, forcing her to look up into his brilliant green eyes. They glimmered in the dark as he searched her face. "Did you freeze up during the battle at the Keep?"

"No, but—"

"Did you freeze up when you stumbled upon soldiers attacking those elves in Cyrna?"

"No, but—"

"You are so much braver than you think, Faye. You will do anything to help the people you love. By the gods, you didn't even know those women in Cyrna, yet you didn't hesitate to protect them. That's what I love most about you." Warmth bloomed within her as he spoke. She closed her eyes and leaned into his embrace. "You're not weak, Faye. You're human. The wounds left by Mother Illynor will take a long time to heal, but if you choose to fight, I will be by your side through it all."

Her throat constricted at the love, the promise, in his voice. "I don't want to lose you."

He kissed her forehead, and she felt him smile against her skin as he said, "You have too little faith in my skills, my love."

They stood there in silence for a while, listening to the occasional creaks of the ship, the soft footsteps of the crew manning the deck, the lapping of the waves against the hull. Faye wrapped her arms around Kaius's waist, linking her fingers at the small of his back. For a moment, she let herself believe they were the only people in the world.

After a few long, peaceful minutes, she tipped her head back to gaze up at him. Something about this night—about their discussion—made her want to confess everything to him. She lowered her voice, trying to soften the blow of the words, as she said, "After the battle in Sandori, I hated you for everything you did for Firesse."

He flinched, pain and guilt flashing across his face. Whatever he had been expecting her to say, that wasn't it.

"But I was wrong," she continued, reaching up to cup his cheek before he could turn away. It was too dark to see the rush of blood to his cheeks, but she felt his skin burn with shame. "You and I have both made terrible mistakes and committed unspeakable crimes. Even though I knew you regretted them, I flung yours back in your face the entire time we rode to the Keep. I accused you of not caring—of not trying to do what was right—even as you and your people risked your lives to save my best friend. What you said on our journey was true: I was furious at myself for following Mother Illynor's orders, and I took it out on you because it was easier than facing what I had done. I'm so sorry for the way I treated you."

He opened his mouth to interrupt, but she barreled on, needing to get everything off her chest. He had to know how much he meant to her. "When we were in the Forest, I realized just how wrong I was about you. Time and time again, you risked your own safety for your people, for Mercy, for her family, and for me. You allied with Tamriel in the hopes of securing freedom for the slaves and winning independence for your home, knowing full well you might not survive the battle with the Guild. You were willing to give up *everything* for the future of your people. It amazed me. *You* amaze me. You are kind, clever, smart, strong, *fearless*—"

"Faye—"

"You are everything I hoped to become when I joined the Guild. You've seen how hurt and broken I am, and never once have you made me feel lesser because of it." A lump rose in her throat. She stared up at Kaius through the tears welling in her eyes, trying to read his expression. She had never spoken so openly, so candidly, before—even to Mercy. "Mother Illynor saw my anger and twisted it into something monstrous. You make me remember who I was before that hateful creature, who I can be again... If you'll have me, I will spend every day for as long as we have left trying to be the person you deserve."

Holding her by the waist, he leaned down and kissed her. A jolt of desire shot through her when his fingers slipped below the hem of her shirt and grazed her skin. Her heart pounded, so full of love and joy that she feared it would burst. It belonged to him—completely, eternally; it had since the night he'd brought her back to herself in Cyrna.

His lips parted against hers as she ran her hands down his bare chest, feeling his pulse beating as erratically as her own. He had heard the unspoken promise in her words—the promise to not only fight for their friends, but for a life after the battle.

"Faye," he breathed. He gently wiped away a tear trailing down her cheek. "You are already perfect in my eyes. I love you exactly as you are."

"I'm so sorry for the way I treated you."

"Forgiven," he murmured, leaning down to claim her lips again. "Completely forgiven."

47
MERCY

With over five thousand soldiers at their backs, it took them three days to ride to Fallmond. They had docked just north of Cowayne—far enough from the town to avoid their ships being spotted by any nearby troops—and splashed through the shallows, carting food, weapons, armor, and other supplies to the shore. In addition to two dozen wagons, Queen Cerelia had given them three battering rams for the battle. While General Cadriel and the soldiers had struggled to drag the battering rams through the shallows and onto the sandy shore, Tamriel's guards had donned plain clothes and ridden off to Cowayne in search of news regarding Nicholas and the false king. What they recounted upon their return had been troubling—Riona and Percival had been married; at the banquet, someone had poisoned all the nobles who had betrayed Tamriel; and Percival had gotten himself arrested for trying to save the lives of four slave-sympathizers.

Tamriel's face had gone white as a sheet when he heard the last part. The raven's note that had brought the news to

Cowayne had not specified the names of the prisoners, but Mercy had been certain two of them were Hero and Ketojan. Nicholas had made no efforts to hide his hatred of the slaves. He must have gone out of his way to find the people who had helped them escape. No one in the market had heard whether the four prisoners had survived, but knowing Percival had tried to save them had given Mercy newfound respect for Tamriel's old friend.

Now, she sagged in her saddle when Faye's childhood home appeared before them, relief flooding her at the sight of the tents dotting the land. Kaius's fighters had arrived, and they had come in droves. There were more tents than she could count, and she suspected there were more in the valley behind the house. When she looked back at Kaius, he grinned. He and Nynev had done well finding recruits.

Mercy ran a hand along Blackfoot's neck as Tamriel stopped their small party at the edge of the property. Due to the size of their army, they had left General Cadriel and the troops to make camp on the outskirts of town. The only people who had accompanied Mercy and Tamriel to Faye's home were the royal guards, Mercy's siblings, Calum, the Strykers, Faye, and Kaius. Mercy dismounted, and Blackfoot swung his head around and nuzzled her with his velvet-soft nose.

"I missed you, too," she said, gently working a tangle out of his mane. The demon-horse—as Faye liked to call him—had *not* been happy after spending weeks in Cowayne's stables, but he had thawed immediately after Mercy had presented him with a sugar cube from the ship's store. "You know you'd be less grouchy if you had let the stablehands take you out of your stall every once in a while, instead of snapping at everyone who came near. We even paid them extra to exercise you."

He snorted and turned away.

Someone shouted something in Cirisian, and elves flooded out of the tents, bathing their group in warm welcomes. Kaius exchanged quick words with an archer, then turned to Tamriel, beaming. "Five hundred elves are ready to fight for you, Your Majesty. Half came from the Islands, and the other half are runaway slaves who heard of our work in Cyrna and Xilor. It seems word of your intention to free the slaves is still spreading. According to Ciaran"—he nodded to the elf at his side—"more runaways are arriving every day. Seren Pierce also managed to secure soldiers from the Fitzroy and Clancy noble families."

As he spoke, Mercy searched the crowd for the slaves they had saved in Xilor. When she spotted them, she was delighted to see each of them proudly bearing the tattoos of various Cirisian clans on their faces and arms.

Tamriel gaped at the size of the crowd surrounding them. "They've all come to fight for me..." he said with disbelief. "Me—a Myrellis king—after everything my people have done to them."

"Cassia was right. Tell them of your plans, give them a chance to fight for their freedom, and they will follow you," Kaius said, his grin growing larger. "You have given them hope, Your Majesty."

Across the field, Faye's parents rushed out of the house, the apprentices close on their heels. Faye dropped Kaius's hand and whirled, opening her arms just in time for Arabelle to tackle her in a hug. Indi and Zora joined the embrace a heartbeat later. Faye's parents wrapped their arms around all four of them.

"We've missed you, little lamb," her father said, his voice muffled. He stepped back and affectionately ruffled Arabelle's hair. "This one has been worrying about you since the moment you left. I don't think a day went by that she didn't ask when you were coming home."

"They freed you?" asked a voice from Mercy's left. She turned to find Atlas and Julien standing with Seren Pierce, Nerida, and their slave. Liri stood a few feet away in a simple tunic and fitted pants, a dagger sheathed at her hip. For the first time, she wasn't wearing her slave sash.

The elf smiled at Atlas. "Yes, your parents freed me shortly after you left, and I've been training with the Cirisians since they arrived. I'm going to join His Majesty's army."

"You don't have to fight," Nerida responded, fixing her former slave with an imploring look. "You could stay here with Pierce and me. I don't want to see you hurt."

Liri shook her head. "I still have friends in the capital. I have to do this for them."

"We must march soon," Tamriel was saying to the crowd when Mercy turned her attention back to him. "Our army is growing too large to sustain for long, and the more time we spend here, the more time Nicholas will have to prepare for the battle."

Ino stepped forward then. "We haven't seen any of Nicholas's soldiers since we docked, which means he has likely ordered them to return to the capital. He knows that we're coming, and he has the advantage of hiding behind the city walls, but—"

"Unfortunately for him," Matthias cut in, flashing a cocky grin, "those walls will not protect him and his men for long."

Tamriel turned to one of the Cirisians. "Have Duomnodera and the other Qadar arrived yet?"

The elf shook her head. "She sent word that it took longer than expected to convince the other High Mothers to pledge warriors to your cause. They should arrive the day after tomorrow, at the latest."

"Very well. As soon as they arrive, we'll march." The crowd parted before him as he approached Faye's parents. Both gaped when he bowed to them. "I have said it before, but it merits repeating: I am beyond grateful for the aid you have shown me and my friends. Your kindness will never be forgotten. Once I have reclaimed my throne, it will be my privilege to grant you anything you desire in repayment for your help."

Faye's mother smiled at him. "It is our honor to serve you, Your Majesty. You have shown us—as you have shown every person here—that you are the king Beltharos needs. You are kind, just, and honorable, and we are proud to call ourselves your subjects."

Matthias cupped his hands around his mouth and shouted, "Long live King Tamriel!"

The cry was quickly picked up by the Cirisians. Tamriel let out a surprised laugh and turned in a slow circle, taking in the sea of hopeful faces surrounding him.

Cassia moved to Mercy's side and said, loud enough to be heard over the cheers, "This may be his army, but they've pledged to fight for you both—their king and their queen." She regarded Mercy warmly, slung an arm around her shoulders, and pulled her close. "I once told Liselle she was mad for believing anyone could save the elves of this country, but you've proven me wrong. I'm so glad you did."

Mercy shook her head and leaned into her sister's embrace. "We haven't won yet."

"We *will*," Cassia insisted. "Nicholas won't see it coming."

Mercy fell silent. There was no point in arguing—not when they might only have a few more days together. As she watched Tamriel turn around once more, awe and wonder on his face as he listened to the elves cheer, she allowed herself a moment to believe her sister was right.

After dinner, she found Tamriel standing outside the house, fading sunlight staining his tanned skin a deep gold. He ran a hand through his hair and let out a long breath as he surveyed their makeshift camp. Most of the elves had already retired to their tents for the night, but a few were seated in a semicircle near the field, chatting in their strange tongue. Others had taken to washing down and brushing the horses or crafting arrows with the Strykers.

Mercy didn't say a word as she approached Tamriel, following his eyes to the three apprentices climbing the large, gnarled tree near the bank of the river. Arabelle's knees were hooked over one branch, her hair hanging in a thick curtain as she dangled upside down.

He reached over and laced his fingers through Mercy's.

For a few minutes, they merely stood there, hand-in-hand, listening to the apprentices laugh. Faye's mother was working in the kitchen with Cassia and Liri, washing the dishes left over from their meal. Through the open window, Mercy and Tamriel could hear them singing an old folk song.

Finally, Tamriel whispered, "I'm terrified of what the next few days will bring."

"I am, too. So much is going to change."

When he turned to her and grabbed her other hand, she was surprised to see the raw, vulnerable look on his face. He stepped close to her, their breaths mingling in the cold nighttime air. "You and I—we've made a court worth ruling, a court of some of the bravest people I've ever had the privilege of knowing. Everyone here has pledged themselves to our cause because of what we stand for. Not because of my royal surname or the depth of my family's coffers. They are willing to fight and die for us because they trust us. Until I saw it with my own eyes, I couldn't have imagined this was possible. I can still hardly fathom it."

He leaned down to give her a soft kiss. "It's all because of you, my love. I never could have done any of this on my own." He ran his thumb over the sapphire ring on her finger. "You're going to make a wonderful queen. It will be my greatest honor to rule beside you."

❧ 48 ☙
PERCIVAL

The scraping of iron hinges woke Percival from a light, fitful sleep. He scrambled to his feet and lifted a hand to shield his eyes as a swath of light cut through the darkness, momentarily blinding him. The movement caused the wound near his shoulder—which had finally clotted—to pull tight. Pain shot down his arm.

"Who's there?" he called, his voice dry and rasping.

He squinted as a dark form neared his cell door. His eyes began to adjust to the light flooding in from the hall, allowing him to see well enough through the cracked lenses of his spectacles. A guardsman in heavy armor stood before him, a keyring dangling from his belt, and a sheathed sword at his hip. The sudden, desperate urge to reach through the bars and grab the weapon filled Percival. Could he get close enough to seize the blade, take down the guard, and free himself?

Percival took a half step forward and grit his teeth as agony nearly sent him to his knees. He was weak, hungry, and dehydrated. Even if he could somehow overpower the guard, there were countless more in the castle. He wouldn't be able to fight them all. Even if he somehow made it to the escape tunnel, what would he do after that? Flee to the countryside and leave Riona to Nicholas's mercy?

No. His uncle may have forced him to become king, but he had made a vow to protect this kingdom and its people. For all he knew, Tamriel was dead. Someone had to lead the country in his place, and Percival would die before he allowed his uncle to take the throne. If the rightful king wasn't coming to bring Nicholas to justice, the responsibility fell to Percival.

He took another step toward the door, and the guard tensed, a hand going to the grip of his sword. "Put your back against the far wall, Your Majesty. I've brought you food and water."

Percival didn't move. "Tell me," he said, fighting to keep his teeth from chattering from the dank chill of the dungeon, "is my uncle preparing my execution?"

"Put your back against the far wall, Your Majesty."

"Did the prisoners escape? The ones I freed?"

"I shall ask you one more time, Your Majesty. Stand against the far wall, or I shall leave with your food. Your choice."

Percival begrudgingly retreated to the rear of the cell. The guard crouched by the door and set a roll of bread, a few strips of dried meat, and a cup of water on the floor. Without a word, he straightened and started toward the door.

"Wait!" Percival blurted, rushing across the cell. He nearly knocked over the water in his haste. "As your king, I command you to release me. Take me to see my queen."

"Her Majesty is under house arrest," the guard said as he turned around. "Your uncle has named himself regent until you stand trial."

"House arrest? But she's innocent. She had nothing to do with the prisoners' escape."

"She is also awaiting trial for acting as your accomplice. Your uncle found evidence that she aided you and the prisoners in the attempt to free those slaves a few weeks ago."

"Evidence that Nicholas *fabricated!*" he said desperately. That had to be the case; she hadn't known anything about the poisoning. "He's trying to frame her for the crime so he can take the throne! Can't you see that?"

The guard shook his head. "I'll return with more food in a day or two, Your Majesty."

"Don't leave! I am your king! I command you to—"

The door clanged shut, plunging him into darkness once more. Percival spat a curse and slammed the side of his fist against the nearest bar of his cell, causing the iron to ring. He sank to the cold floor and groped blindly for the water, downing it all in a few large gulps. It was gone far too soon. Then he started on the bread and meat, his stomach aching, and considered everything he'd learned.

Nicholas had finally seized the throne for himself. Now that he had no need for a puppet, he wouldn't hesitate to send his own nephew to an early grave. The thought shouldn't have hurt Percival as much as it did. Nicholas had broken a generations-old vow when he turned on Tamriel; the fact that he was willing to sentence a member of his own family to death should not have come as a shock. And in some ways, it didn't: Percival had known for a while that his uncle was a monster, and that it was only a matter of time before he would tire of playing puppet master. But a small part of him remembered the rush of joy he used to feel whenever he earned one of his uncle's rare smiles. A part of him still looked at Nicholas and saw the ghost of the father he had lost so many years ago.

He dropped his head in his hands. He needed a plan if he was going to attempt to escape. Nicholas was going to kill Riona, too, all because she was unlucky enough to get dragged into the middle of this mess. He must find a way to help her; he would never forgive himself if Nicholas hurt her.

Familiar blue-green eyes flashed through his mind, and his heart lurched. *Celeste.* She would have started plotting her escape the moment she regained consciousness. Hell, she would have found a way out of this Creator-damned cell long ago...but she wasn't here, and Percival didn't have her skills or ingenuity.

He moved to the rear of the cell and curled up tightly, trying to conserve what little heat he could. At this rate, the cold would kill him well before his uncle did. He had no idea how long he'd been locked away down there. A few days? A week? He didn't even know if it was day or night. The only thing that was certain was that he had to come up with an escape plan, and soon. If he stood trial before the court, it would already be too late. Nicholas would do everything in his power to ensure Percival was given a death sentence.

An eternity later, the guard returned.

Percival lifted his head as the light once again cut through the darkness. The sickly-sweet stench of vomit hung in the air and on his breath; as desperately as he had tried to fight the sickness rising within him, his stomach had purged itself of the unexpected meal sometime after the guard had left. He'd gone too long without eating to stuff himself so suddenly—although *stuffing himself* was being rather generous considering the meager amount of food he had been given. It would not have sustained even a child for long.

His stomach rumbled as he watched the guard set more food and water down by the door of the cell. It was the same fare as last time: bread, meat, water. As soon as the guard backed well out of reach and nodded to him, Percival staggered to the front of the cell and snatched up the food. He forced himself to eat slowly. He couldn't afford to lose any more strength.

The guard cleared his throat and said, "Are you feeling ill, Your Majesty?"

Percival took a gulp of water and nodded toward the rear of the cell, where the puddle of half-digested food was still blanketed in shadow. "No, but I was earlier."

"I mean as in an illness, Your Majesty. You're shivering, but there is a sheen of sweat across your brow. And your eyes are...glazed."

"Oh." Percival wrapped an arm around himself to try and control the tremors wracking his body, to no avail. His fingers brushed the gash in his upper arm, and he winced at the pain that rippled through him. He squinted up at the soldier. "My... My arm. It got a nasty cut at the banquet. Could be an infection. Would my uncle permit a healer to tend to me?"

"I'll ask, Your Majesty."

With that, the guard left again. Percival huddled there in the dark, his back pressed to the bars, his arms wrapped around his knees, his wound throbbing. All the other cuts had healed well, but this one was the longest and the deepest. Since no one had come to stitch his wounds, he had ripped off part of his doublet and fashioned it into a makeshift bandage, but the once-fine fabric was now coated in grime from sleeping on the floor of the cell. He untied the makeshift bandage and gingerly touched the gash. It was too dark to see, of course, but he could feel the heat emanating from the infected skin.

Of course, he thought bitterly. *Because there weren't enough things going wrong already.*

Percival let his head fall back, and it hit the bar behind him with a dull thud. He doubted Nicholas would allow a healer to attend him. If his uncle cared about his health, he would have sent a healer down immediately after the banquet. He just hoped the infection didn't spread too quickly. He would need all his strength if he was to escape from his cell, find Riona, and confront his uncle.

"Your Majesty."

The voice dragged Percival from sleep. Sometime after the guard left, he had curled up at the back of his cell, drifting in and out of consciousness for Creator only knew how many hours. A groan slipped out as he rolled over and forced himself to sit upright. He blinked up at the familiar figure, backlit by the light from the hall. "Have you brought a healer?"

"Uh—no, Your Majesty. Your uncle did not deem one necessary. I've been ordered to monitor your condition and provide you some supplies from the healer's store."

Percival's vision adjusted to the light just in time to see the guard toss something into the cell. He reached out to catch it, but it bounced off his palm and hit the floor, unfurling as it rolled. It was a linen bandage. He let out a defeated sigh and close his eyes. *So much for a clean bandage.* A smaller voice whispered, *I'm going to die in here,* but he shoved the thought aside. He was going to find a way out. He just needed more time.

Glass clinked against stone. Percival's eyes opened, his brows furrowing as he watched a small bottle roll across the floor, coming to a stop when it hit the toe of his left boot.

"Use that to clean the wound," the guard said, nodding to the bottle. "It will slow the spread of infection for a short while. I'll return tomorrow to check on you."

"Tomorrow," Percival repeated thoughtfully. As the door swung shut, he grabbed the bottle, poured some of the thick herbal mixture onto his fingers, and gently applied it to the gash in his arm. The wound was covered in a jagged, uneven scab which cracked and oozed at his touch. Fire spread from his shoulder to his fingertips as the medicine began to work, so sudden and shocking, he couldn't help the gasp of pain that escaped him.

He examined the bottle as best he could in the darkness. It was tiny—only about the length of his index finger—but it could work for a weapon. He flipped it over and smashed the bottom against the floor. By some miracle, it broke, but didn't shatter. He felt along the edge of the broken glass, being careful not to cut himself, then used the makeshift bandage he had discarded to sweep the leftover shards into the next cell. Hopefully, the guard wouldn't see them when he returned.

Percival wrapped his arm in the linen bandage, then lay down once more, hiding the bottle between his body and the wall. He had no idea when the trial would take place, but the sooner he acted, the better.

He had to escape *tomorrow*.

49
FAYE

Shouts from the valley behind Faye's childhood home drew her attention around noon the next day. She tucked her throwing knives into their sheath—the Strykers had replaced the ones she had lost during the attack in Xilor, as well as made her a new sheath that held ten rather than her previous six—and set the whetstone down by her feet. Beside her, Kaius rose, his brows furrowing as he gazed in the direction of the commotion.

"Duomnodera and the others should know better than to make so much noise," he muttered, frowning.

Faye scanned the riverbank until she found Mercy and her siblings. They'd been washing clothes and preparing bandages for the battle, but now they stood side-by-side, blades and bows in hand.

"Do you think it's Nicholas's soldiers?" Faye asked Kaius. Around them, the Cirisians paused in their tasks and grabbed weapons. A few moved closer to Kaius, ready to defend him at a moment's notice.

He shook his head. "I set watchmen on the hills. The

patrols would have seen them coming from a mile away. In any case, it doesn't sound like troops. Listen."

She did, and after a moment, she understood what he meant: the shouts weren't accompanied by the sounds of a battle. It sounded more like two people...arguing.

"I wouldn't have *had* to come if you had some semblance of self-control! Or some sense of self-preservation! Have you even thought about all the trouble you'll be leaving for your king when you get yourself killed?"

"You saw me with a bow—you know I can handle myself in a fight. You, on the other hand—"

"Don't you dare start that again! Lords aren't meant to be fighting battles. We have duties to the court—"

"Damn you and your court! I never should have let you come along! I'd have left you on the ship if I hadn't known your wretched grandmother would flay me alive for abandoning you."

Tamriel stepped out of the house, Calum, the Strykers, and Faye's parents on his heels, and shot Faye a questioning look. She shook her head. She recognized the voices, but she had no idea how their owners came to be at Fallmond. The last time she'd seen them, they were standing by the dock in Feyndara, watching their ship depart.

"*Abandoning me*," the man scoffed. "I'm not helpless. And watch the way you speak about my grandmother! She's your queen now, too."

"The day I call her my queen is the day I let her take the Islands! *Over. My. Dead. Body!*"

"Well, you're making it awfully easy for her at the moment, aren't you? Continue like this and soon enough, it *will* be over your dead body."

Out of the corner of her eye, Faye saw Mercy sheathe her twin daggers. Her siblings did the same. They, too, had recognized the voices.

Not two minutes later, a royally-pissed-off Nynev appeared at the mouth of the valley astride a tall black mare. Alistair, his face flushed with anger, trailed after her on a chestnut stallion. Faye could hardly believe what she was seeing, even as Nynev turned to snarl something insulting about the Feyndaran queen over her shoulder. A dozen Cirisians surrounded them, one half wearing weary, annoyed expressions, the other half looking about ready to murder the huntress and the young lord. They must have escorted Nynev and Alistair through the valley.

Faye, Kaius, Mercy, and Tamriel met them at the edge of the property. Nynev released her horse's reins and slid off the saddle, running the last few yards to them.

"Marital bliss," she said to Mercy and Tamriel, dropping into a breathless bow before them. "Look what you have to look forward to."

"We're not married yet," Alistair objected, still a few yards back. "And if you'd only listen—"

"Nynev, what in the Creator's name are you doing here?" Tamriel cut in, utterly baffled by their sudden appearance.

"What, did you think I would leave you to fight while I sat in that pretty castle and ate pastries all day long? I'm here to help you win your crown."

"The queen let you leave?" Mercy asked as Alistair dismounted and joined them. Anger radiated off him, but he had the grace to look embarrassed at the audience their shouting had attracted.

"Not exactly—"

"I caught her sneaking out of the castle in the middle of the night," Alistair interrupted, shooting her a sidelong look. "Considering she had her bow and quiver slung over one shoulder and a bag of supplies over the other, it wasn't hard to figure out where she was going. She's lucky I didn't call the guards—a kindness for which she has not once thanked me, might I add. If my grandmother found out she was trying to run away, she'd have figured Nynev was breaking your deal and called her troops back to Feyndara."

Nynev opened her mouth to retort, then scowled and grunted, "Thank you."

"All I ask is that you think things through before you go charging head-first into battle," he responded, exasperated. "If you get killed, the truce between Beltharos and Feyndara will be ruined. They'll go back to warring over the Islands, and your people will be caught in the middle of the fighting, just like they have been for years."

Faye glanced at her friends. Mercy and Tamriel were watching the exchange with varying degrees of bewilderment; Tamriel seemed at a loss for words. Kaius had given up on the entire conversation and turned to speak in Cirisian with the elves. Nynev and Alistair appeared to be two seconds away from doing *something*—although Faye was not entirely certain whether that *something* involved tearing out the other's eyes or tearing off the other's clothes. She suddenly felt sorry for the crew that had taken the lord and the huntress across the sea. She couldn't imagine being stuck on a ship with them for a day, let alone an entire week.

"I understand the stakes," Nynev replied quietly, an edge to her voice. "Do not think I made this decision lightly. I am fighting for the freedom of the slaves, as well as for my friends' right to rule. If it will ease your mind, know that I will do my best not to get killed." After a pause, she softened her tone and added, "Next time, I promise to tell you before I go charging headfirst into battle."

"For the Creator's sake, *please* tell me there won't be a next time."

"I fought with Tamriel against Firesse, I will fight with him against Nicholas, and should he ever have need of me again, I will be by his side. If that is a problem, you should not have agreed to marry me."

Alistair blinked a few times, startled and impressed by her proclamation. She lifted her chin, daring him to argue.

Finally, he said, "No, it's not a problem. But I'm going to have to practice a lot more with my bow if I want to be worthy of fighting beside you."

She beamed at him. "I might be able to teach you a thing or two."

"Well, uh, now that that's settled," Tamriel began, having recovered from his surprise, "perhaps you could fill me in on the story of how you got here. I believe I've missed quite a few details."

"You heard the basics," Nynev said, looking like she had momentarily forgotten they were there. "There's not much more to tell. We snuck out of the castle, hired a ship to take us across the sea, and rode as hard as we could to Fallmond in the hope that you had not yet marched to war. Thankfully, we spotted the Feyndaran army camp from a distance and were able to avoid the patrols. If Cadriel finds out Alistair is here, he'll send him back to Feyndara."

"No, he'd murder me on the spot," Alistair muttered.

"You're lucky he didn't hear you shouting," Mercy said, crossing her arms. "Is that all you two have been doing since you set sail?"

For the first time, Nynev's cheeks flushed bright red. Faye wasn't sure which detail was more surprising—that the sharp-tongued huntress was blushing, or that the young lord failed to meet any of their eyes, his expression turning sheepish. So, *fighting* was not *all* they had done during their journey. Faye felt another wave of pity for the poor sailors. And she'd thought *she and Kaius* were insufferable.

Mercy grimaced. "Creator's ass—forget I asked." She

turned to Tamriel. "Were we that obvious when we first fell in love?"

He nodded, fighting a smile. "I'm afraid so."

"Oh, stop already," Nynev chastised, but without any bite behind the words. In fact, her grin was larger and brighter than Faye had ever seen it.

Kaius exchanged a few final words with the Cirisians before they departed, shooting more dark looks at Nynev and Alistair as they left. He fell into step beside Faye as Tamriel led their small group toward the house.

"I should have known Nynev wouldn't let us fight on our own, even with an army at our backs," Kaius said, watching Nynev run across camp and throw her arms around two Cirisians with her clan's tattoos. "She can be reckless and stubborn, but she's loyal, and a good archer. Can't say I'm surprised she risked the queen's fury to come here. Even I would have been tempted to run if I'd been left behind."

"That's just because you wouldn't be able to tolerate the queen for more than a day," Faye teased. "You'd brave the Howling Mountains if it meant you didn't have to spend one more day in her court."

He caught her hand and laced his fingers through hers. "If it would have given me another day with you, yes, I would have." He offered her a brief smile, then turned to where Nynev stood, chatting with the elves she had embraced. By the house, Alistair was speaking with Mercy and Tamriel, probably filling them in on the details of their journey. His eyes never strayed from Nynev, although she did not seem to notice his attention. "What is surprising, however, is the lord's arrival. He hadn't struck me as the hero type."

"Hopefully he's skilled with a sword. I appreciate that he wants to protect Nynev, but I can't imagine letting him fight with us will do wonders for Tamriel's relationship with the queen. We'd be better off tying him up and shipping him back to Rhys."

Kaius nodded. "I'll have Nynev and him join my archers. They'll be close enough to the action that they won't feel useless or coddled, but far enough that they won't be in as much danger as the rest of us." After a thoughtful pause, he added, "If anything goes wrong, we never saw them. They snuck into General Cadriel's camp and fought with his troops—that way, all Cerelia's anger will be directed at him, not us. Got it?"

"Got it."

As Tamriel, Mercy, Nynev, and Alistair made their way into the house, she and Kaius returned to the oak tree at the edge of the property, under which they had been sitting before Nynev's arrival. She picked up the whetstone and one of her throwing knives, letting the rasping of the blade against the stone fill the quiet. Around them, the Cirisians returned to their tasks—taking inventory, crafting arrows and bolts, sharpening blades, helping Faye's father tend the field. Their soft, lilting language danced in the air. Most of it sounded like lovely, melodic nonsense to her, save for the few words and phrases Kaius had taught her on the ship.

It was hard to stomach the thought that many of these people would not be alive by the end of the week. Tamriel might have the numbers to take on Nicholas's army, but they'd be approaching from the fields, vulnerable to arrows, bolts, and cannon fire from the city walls. During Firesse's attack, Faye and the other Daughters had been kept well away from the bulk of the fighting, but she had seen the aftermath of the battle when she had snuck Calum out of the city. Fires had raged among the outlying houses, flecks of still-burning ash falling from the sky and piling up on the streets, and the fields had been pitted with craters from cannon fire. The worst part had not been the bodies—it had been the *lack* of bodies. All that had remained of Firesse's fallen soldiers were unidentifiable body parts strewn across the grass, too thoroughly obliterated to be raised by her blood magic.

It had taken Faye an eternity to walk across that field. After a while, she had simply gone numb. All that had kept her from falling apart completely was the knowledge that she needed to get Calum as far from the city as possible if she wanted a chance at freeing Mercy from the Guild.

The memory caused bile to rise in her throat. She shut her eyes and sucked in deep breaths until the nausea passed, exactly as she had in Feyndara. It took a while, but she eventually managed to subdue the tremors wracking her body. She had no idea when she'd begun to tremble.

When she opened her eyes again, she found Kaius watching her, concern plain on his face. He had shifted closer to her while she had been caught in the flashbacks, but remained silent, allowing her to make her way back to reality on her own. Although it pained him to see her like this, they both knew she had to learn to deal with the memories on her own. After all, she might not have the luxury of him standing by her side for much longer.

Duomnodera and her warriors arrived not two hours later. Faye took a quick count of the scaled creatures. There were at least thirty of them, possibly closer to forty; it was difficult to get an exact number, considering they were nearly identical. The only distinctions lay in the patterns of their scales and the lengths of their horns, but even those differences were so subtle as to be negligible.

Duomnodera led her warriors toward Tamriel, dropping into a low bow before him. The Qadar behind her grumbled but did the same. Faye suspected the proud creatures despised having to bow to any human, even if he *was* a king. She couldn't imagine Illynor bowing to anyone.

"Apologies for our late arrival, Your Majesty," Duomnodera said, her voice so similar to the Guildmother's that it sent a chill down Faye's spine. "I gathered as many warriors as I could, but some of the High Mothers were wary of sending their people across the sea. We're ready to march when you are."

And that was how, an hour and a half later, Faye came to be standing before her parents, exchanging tearful goodbyes. Tamriel, determined to face Nicholas's army sooner rather than later, had immediately ordered them to pack up camp. With most of their supplies already stowed in packs, saddlebags, and supply carts, they had made quick work of disassembling the tents and preparing the horses for the long ride to Sandori. They only had a few hours of daylight left, but with the Cirisians' night vision, they'd be able to ride well into the night. With a host of this size, the sooner they reached Sandori, the better. They didn't have the resources for a lengthy march across the country.

"I'm so proud of you," Faye's father said as he wrapped his arms around her, his voice muffled by her leather armor. She clutched him back just as fiercely, breathing in the familiar scent—of earth, of soap, of *home*—that clung to him. He released her, then reached up to brush away the tears trailing down her cheeks. "If we could, your mother and I would be right beside you on that battlefield."

She offered him a shaky smile. The little girl within her, the one who had run away and given all this up, desired nothing more than to remain here with the family she'd left behind. Yet her father had been right when he told her of his dreams for her future. This would always be her home, but her duty called her to serve her king and queen. "I know, Papa. I love you."

"I love you, too, my little lamb."

She turned to her mother, who had watched their exchange with a mixture of pride and sorrow on her face. "Mama—"

Before she could say more, her mother clasped her in a tight hug. "Come back to us, Faye," she whispered.

She had to fight to speak past the lump in her throat. "Always, Mama. I promise. And I'll be expecting a fresh blackberry pie waiting for me the next time I see you."

Her mother laughed as she backed out of the embrace. "I'll make you as many blackberry pies as you desire."

She hugged them each one more time, then forced her feet to carry her to where Kaius was waiting with the horses. He handed her Nightstorm's reins, and she climbed onto the saddle, comforting herself by running her fingers through her mare's thick mane. A few feet away, Mercy and Tamriel exchanged farewells with Seren Pierce and Nerida. They, along with Arabelle and the other apprentices, would be staying here in Fallmond. Arabelle, Indi, and Zora had protested vehemently to this, but Faye and Mercy had not budged on the issue. If Faye had her way, the girls would never bear the weight of having taken a life.

She glanced back, her eyes roaming over the ragtag army behind her. Countless elves, Daughters, and Qadar were lined up across the property, all the way to the valley. They'd march through Fallmond and join General Cadriel's troops on the king's highway. To her left, Atlas hugged his parents, then joined the rest of the royal guards at the front of the line with Tamriel and Mercy. Just behind them were Mercy's siblings, then Calum and the Strykers, then Faye and Kaius. Nynev and Alistair were somewhere among the Cirisians, probably praying General Cadriel wouldn't notice them. Alistair had even gone so far as to paint Cirisian markings onto his face and arms.

Kaius climbed onto his horse, reached over, and gave Faye's hand a quick, reassuring squeeze. *We'll make it through this,* the gesture said.

By the Creator, I hope we make it through this, she thought.

From the front of the company, Tamriel scanned the long line of soldiers, his expression solemn, his posture confident. He'd grown into quite the gifted leader, so different from that terrified prince who had cowered before Aelis months ago. She felt a sudden, overwhelming rush of gratitude that Mercy had broken her oath. She couldn't imagine how different their lives would have been if she had gone through with her contract.

"Ready?" Tamriel finally asked, his voice carrying over the land.

They all nodded.

As ready as we'll ever be, Faye thought, tightening her grip on her horse's reins.

"Then let's be off."

⚝ 50 ⚝

PERCIVAL

Percival's hand tightened around the neck of the broken bottle when he heard the dungeon door swing open, the scraping of the ancient iron hinges grating on his ears. As before, he lay on his side, hiding the makeshift weapon with his body.

"Your Majesty?" the guard called.

Percival didn't answer. He didn't dare. The light slanting in from the hallway cast the guard's long, distorted shadow on the wall; it was this Percival watched, waiting for the man to step into the cell to check on him. His body trembled so violently he couldn't seem to stop. His limbs felt frozen, but he knew if he were to touch his forehead, he'd find it burning. His ragged and torn clothes were damp with sweat, and the gash in his arm ached worse than ever before.

The healer's medicine hadn't worked.

He gripped the bottle tighter. He had one chance to escape. If he ruined it, he and Riona were as good as dead.

"Your...Majesty?" the guard repeated, a note of concern in his voice. When Percival still did not respond, he muttered an oath and approached the cell door. Metal clanged as the guard flipped through keys on the keyring. Once he finally found the right one, he unlocked the door, pushed it open, and ran to Percival. "By the Creator, he'll have my head if I let the king die before the trial," he muttered as he dropped to his knees on the grimy floor, heavy armor clanking. "Never mind that he's the one who said not to send a healer down."

A hand closed around Percival's upper arm—the uninjured one, thank the Creator. As the guard rolled Percival onto his back, he thrust the broken bottle upward, into the first bit of exposed skin he saw.

Hot blood sprayed across his face, making him gag. Percival scrambled to his feet as the guard's hands flew to his throat. "Oh, shit!" he gasped as he realized where he'd struck the man: straight in the jugular—a fatal hit. The guard ripped the broken bottle out of his neck, and blood spurted from the wound with every pump of his heart. "Shit, shit, shit!"

He hadn't meant to *kill* him. By the Creator, he *hadn't* meant to kill him. He'd only intended to wound him, to catch him by surprise. He'd only needed an opening to escape.

"I'm sorry!" Percival blurted, rushing forward and setting his hands on the guard's neck, trying to stanch the bleeding. Dimly, distantly, he knew he couldn't save the man's life. There was nothing to be done. He'd be dead in seconds. "I'm so sorry! It was an accident!"

Blood—more blood than he could have ever imagined—spurted out of the gash, coating his hands and the cuffs of his sleeves. With one great shudder, the life left the guard's eyes. He went limp, his head lolling, eyes open and unblinking. Percival released him and crawled backward until his back hit the wall. Horror and shock warred within him.

He couldn't tear his gaze from the body. He hadn't gotten a good look at the guard before, but now, with the man's face tipped toward the door, it was evident that he had been young, perhaps only a few years older than Percival. Guilt clawed at him. He'd never killed before—not with his own two hands. He had never watched someone take his last breath. Until now. To know that this young man lost his life because of *him*, because of a foolish *mistake*...

Percival sat there for several long minutes, simply staring at the body. When he finally stood, his legs were weak, both from the lack of food and the shock of having taken his first life. He stumbled toward the guard, being careful to avoid the dark puddle spreading across the dungeon floor, and closed the man's sightless eyes. His stomach churning, he wiped his hands on the guard's tunic, then pulled the ring of keys from the guard's belt and the sword from its sheath.

He eased the dungeon door open and peered into the hallway. As far as he could see, it was empty. He strained, listening for the sound of footfalls, and was met with only silence. As he crept down the hall, the escape tunnel a few corridors down called to him. It would be so easy to slip away, but he couldn't do that to Riona or Tamriel. He owed it to his king to remove the traitor on the throne. If he died trying, so be it. It was better than being executed in front of the entire court.

His injured arm burned as he climbed the stairs. He'd have to use the sword with two hands, but even then, he wouldn't be able to fight for long. His uncle's guards outnumbered and outmatched him.

He reached the landing and stepped into the hall, his heart hammering in his chest. The corridor in which he stood was far enough from the main body of the castle that, for now, he was alone. To get to the guest wing, he'd have to pass through the great hall.

In all honesty, it was a suicide mission.

There was no cover in the hall, no furnishings to hide behind should a guard suddenly round the corner, so his only option was to race toward the great hall as quickly and quietly as he could. It wouldn't be long before someone realized the guard he had killed was missing, and the dungeon was the first place they'd check. Not to mention, he'd left a trail of blood behind him—his skin and clothes were covered with it.

He slipped through the first doorway he saw, finding himself in one of the many unused sitting rooms scattered throughout the castle. It was filled with settees, armchairs, and low tables, each one covered with a cloth and a fine layer of gray dust. He set his sword on the ground, pulled the cloth off the nearest armchair, and scrubbed at the blood covering his face, chest, and arms. It didn't do much in the way of cleaning him, but at least now he was dry enough that he wouldn't track blood everywhere he went.

I should have made Celeste teach me more of her tricks, he thought as he returned to the hall, listening for the thud of heavy boots on the stone floor. He recalled the ease with which Celeste had come and gone all those times they had plotted in his chambers. Of course, she had never walked through the castle covered in gore. Even *she* might've had difficulty sneaking out unnoticed, but he didn't doubt she would have found a way. She had constantly surprised him with her skills. Honestly, if she had told him she could walk through walls, he might have believed her. She made it look *that* easy.

He ignored the pain that accompanied the thoughts of her as he neared the great hall. She and the others had to be searching for Tamriel and his army right now. Percival would see them again soon. He *would*. He refused to acknowledge the possibility that they might not have escaped the city.

They were *alive*.

By the time he was only a few corridors from the great hall, his heart was pounding so hard he could barely hear anything but the rush of blood in his ears. The lack of guards troubled him. Even if his uncle had not thought him capable of besting the guard watching over his cell, Percival should have encountered at least one patrol by now.

"—marching to the capital. Scouts saw the elves a few days ago."

As soon as the words reached him, Percival jerked to a halt. The voice was coming from the next hall and quickly growing closer. Percival searched for cover to no avail. Then, just as two guards rounded the corner, his eyes landed on a small door set into the wall behind him, the wood so aged and gray it nearly blended into the stone. An old servants' passage. He ran to it as the guards drew their swords.

"STOP!"

"PUT DOWN YOUR WEAPON!"

Stuck. The damned door was *stuck*.

He slammed his uninjured shoulder into the door until it flew open, the hinges squealing, then darted inside and raced down the dim hall. He didn't pause to consider where he was going; he needed to lose the guards before finding Riona. Luckily, the Creator seemed to be on his side, for once. The walls were narrow, barely wide enough for two people to stand abreast, and the only light came from narrow gaps in the bricks every dozen yards. It was nearly as dark as the dungeon, which meant that while he wouldn't be able to see where he was going, the guards wouldn't be able to see *him*.

The hinges shrieked again. His palms grew slick as he blindly ran down the hall, heavy footfalls echoing behind him. That was one more advantage, he realized: he could hear the guards, but they couldn't hear him.

When the hall split, he chose to go right, trailing a hand

along the wall in an attempt to orient himself. In the darkness, it was nearly impossible to tell how far he'd gone or where in the castle he might be. Somewhere, there had to be stairs to the king's chambers. If he could find them and get to Nicholas...

"You go left, I'll go right. He can't have gotten far," said a voice behind him.

His heart leapt into his throat. The guards had reached the fork, so they weren't far behind. Percival shoved the thought of confronting Nicholas out of his mind. Even if he could navigate this labyrinth, he wasn't strong enough to get past his uncle's guards. Percival wouldn't stand a chance.

As he plunged deeper, taking every turn at random, the words he had heard earlier finally sank in. Only one person would be marching to the capital with elves right now, and that was Tamriel. He must have gathered an army. He must be coming to reclaim his kingdom.

The realization bolstered Percival's confidence. Nicholas would not sit on the throne for long. Tamriel would bring him to justice, and he would pay for his crimes with his life.

A line of light appeared in the distance, like the crack under a door. He pushed himself faster, ignoring the protests of his exhausted muscles and the pain shooting down his injured arm. Only one guard was pursuing him now. He sounded further away than before.

When Percival reached the door, he steeled himself before pulling it open, grimacing at the wail of screeching hinges. He blinked against the sudden light and lifted his sword on instinct. For all he knew, he could have just stumbled into the guards' barracks.

When his eyes finally adjusted, he realized he had emerged at the end of the guest wing. He sent a quick, silent *Thank you* up to the Creator, then immediately rescinded it when he saw the half-dozen Beltharan guards standing watch outside Riona's door. He didn't have time to wonder where Riona's usual guards were before the Beltharans unsheathed their swords and advanced on him.

"Lay down your weapon, Your Majesty," one called. "You're clearly hurt. Put down your sword and no further harm will come to you."

Behind him, the door to the servant's passage swung open, and out stepped one of the guards who had been pursuing him. Fear turned Percival's blood cold. He was surrounded. What had he been thinking, trying to run? He should have known better than to believe he would be successful in getting Riona out of the castle. If his uncle were here, watching this mess unfold, he'd laugh until he cried. Nicholas had been right about one thing: Percival had no mind for strategy.

"I'll say it again, Your Majesty: lay down your weapon. Cooperate, and we will—"

There was a *thunk*, then a cry of pain and surprise.

Percival whirled to see Riona standing in the middle of the hall, a pile of books in her arms. He watched in disbelief as she hurled one at a guard's head. The man dodged it, unlike the first guard she had hit, who was still dazedly rubbing at the bruise blooming across his temple. She caught Percival's eye as she threw another one, a heavy tome that looked like it could do quite a bit of damage, and mouthed, *Run!*

He didn't waste a second. As she distracted them, he darted through the gap between two bewildered guards and sprinted to her. He grabbed her hand and dragged her down the hall behind him. "Come on."

"Lord Winslow—"

"He'll be fine. He's not my uncle's target. You need to get out of the city and back to Rivosa." He gasped for breath as they raced around the corner. The guards were not far behind. The distraction had bought them time, but not enough. "Where are your guards?"

"Sick. I think Nicholas had them drugged."

The bastard. Death by an executioner's axe would be too kind an end for Nicholas Comyn. He should suffer as much as they had.

"There's a tunnel under the castle. It'll take you outside the city walls. Once you get to Rhenys, you can hire a carriage to take you home."

"Come with me."

He shook his head. By the Creator, he would love nothing more than to leave this wretched castle behind, but his body was aching worse than it ever had—more than he'd thought was possible. "My arm's infected, and I'm already exhausted. I'll only slow you down."

"But—"

"The guards will catch us and ship us back here for our trials. Don't make everything I've done today mean nothing. You *have* to get out of here." He squeezed her hand. "Promise me."

"...Fine. I promise."

They hurtled through the great hall, startling the guards and servants they passed. Nicholas and Rhiannon were there, too, speaking with the other guard who had chased him into the servants' passage. Thick bandages were wrapped around Nicholas's chest where the crossbow bolt had struck him, but he was standing on his own, no hint of pain on his face. "STOP THEM!" he bellowed, his voice reverberating through the room.

"They're going to kill us," Riona said, her voice tight with terror.

"They were already going to do that," he responded, pushing their pace even faster. Black spots began to bloom in his vision, but he couldn't risk slowing down. He needed to get Riona out. He needed to get her to safety.

When they reached the stairwell, Percival released her hand. "Take a right, then the second left, then go through the third door on your right. The tunnel will take you to the eastern side of Sandori, outside the walls. I wish I could help you more."

She surprised him by pulling him into a tight hug. "You've already helped me more than you know. You're a good man, Percival. It would have been my honor to be your wife." She released him and glanced over her shoulder, her eyes widening when the first few guards appeared at the end of the hall.

"Go on. I'll do what I can to stall them."

She gathered her skirt in one hand and ran. He turned his back to her and lifted the sword as the guards approached. He would do anything to ensure she made it out of the castle. It was his fault she was here, after all. He should have fought his uncle harder, should have insisted on delaying the wedding. He couldn't have her death on his hands, as well.

I'm sorry, Tamriel, he thought when he spotted his uncle among the guards. *I tried to stop him, but I failed.*

He didn't doubt that Tamriel would win the battle, but he wouldn't live to see the rightful king take his throne. If he didn't die here, his uncle would certainly waste no time in arranging his trial.

His knees started to tremble. Black spots bloomed and burst in his vision. Blood oozed from the gash in his arm; the jagged scab had torn open at some point.

I don't want to die.

The thought came to him, sharp and clear, through the haze of pain clouding his mind. It was such a simple, obvious thing. The threat of death had been hanging over his head for weeks, but right now—for the first time—he didn't feel like a pawn in his uncle's game. Nicholas had underestimated him. He had not expected that Percival would figure out a way to escape from the dungeon. For so long, his uncle had been two steps ahead.

Not anymore. The game would end now.

He lifted his sword and met the first guard's blade.

51
TAMRIEL

Tamriel squinted against the bright sunlight, frowning, as three Cirisian scouts on horseback appeared in the distance. Kaius had sent archers ahead on the king's highway to keep an eye out for Nicholas's soldiers. So far, they'd seen no one, and the fact irked Tamriel to no end. Nicholas was mocking him by allowing his army to march unimpeded across the kingdom. Of course, he was glad that his enemy's troops had not struck yet, but that only meant Nicholas was saving his army's strength for the attack at Sandori. He was planning to strike them down in one swift blow, rather than draw out the war. Utilizing the city's defenses was a good tactic—it was what Tamriel would have done, had their roles been reversed—but he shuddered to imagine what other tricks Nicholas might have in store. He hadn't become the greatest general in the last century by fighting with honor.

Once the scouts were near enough that Tamriel could make out their faces, he realized they weren't alone. Mireia and Ilya each shared a saddle with a young elven woman. The other horse carried an older human and a skinny, white-haired elf.

Tamriel jerked his horse to a stop so quickly Akiva's stallion nearly slammed into his. His eyes had to be playing tricks on him.

One glance at Mercy's face told him he had not made a mistake.

Without exchanging a word, they spurred their horses to a gallop. Tamriel's heart leapt as his horse's long legs ate up the distance between him and the friends he had feared he would never see again. In his periphery, he saw a wide smile break out across Mercy's face.

In what felt like no time at all, their two parties met. Tamriel tugged on the reins and dropped from the saddle at the same time Hero and Ketojan did. They immediately threw their arms around him. Their voices overlapped as they spouted a thousand things at once, speaking so quickly Tamriel only managed to catch bits and pieces.

"We thought we'd never see you again!"

"—told everyone you were dead—"

"—preparing for a battle, calling in an army—"

"—whispers that you were freeing slaves—"

"—*knew* you'd come back!"

"And I should have known you two would be alright," he said as he drew back.

Their heads hadn't been staked to the city wall, but ever since Nicholas's attack, Tamriel had been terrified that they'd been killed alongside Cassius and his other supporters. Even so, he had not realized how much he had truly missed them until this moment. With the chaos that had ensued after Nicholas's betrayal, he'd had no time to mourn them. But now, knowing they were alive nearly sent him to his knees with relief.

To his right, Lethandris climbed down from Ilya's horse

and hugged Mercy. The brown-haired elven girl who had been riding with Mireia hovered at the priestess's side. Out of the four of them, she looked the worst for wear: the bottom of her tattered lace dress had been torn to make bandages for the cuts on her arms, and a few greenish-yellow bruises marred her nose and one side of her jaw. Darker bruises coiled around her thin wrists. Tamriel spotted identical bruises on Hero, Ketojan, and Lethandris as well.

"What in the Creator's name happened to you?" he asked, turning to Hero and Ketojan. Fury rushed over him. "It was Nicholas, wasn't it?"

"He tried to have us killed, Your Majesty," the brunette said, her expression darkening. The elf touched the ornate peridot necklace hanging just below her collarbone. "Percival saved our lives. He fought the guards so we could escape and find you."

"*He* fought the guards?" Mercy asked doubtfully. They'd seen Percival try to attack his uncle back in Sandori. Percival had many skills, but even he would be the first to admit swordplay was not one of them. "How did he manage that?"

"I taught him. I'm excellent with all manner of blades—and I'm an even better instructor."

"Seems to me you're a bit cocky, too."

"Merely honest."

Mercy's lips spread into a smile as she examined the girl with newfound respect. Although they'd only just met, Tamriel had a strange, sudden sense that they would get along extremely well. There was a hint of violence about her. Perhaps it was something in the way she stood, proud and tall, despite her disheveled appearance. It reminded him of when he'd first met Mercy.

The girl turned and bowed to him. "My name is Celeste, Your Majesty. Percival sent us here to tell you what we know of Nicholas's plans for the battle. How much have you heard about the state of the capital?"

"Not much. We only returned from Feyndara a week ago."

She looked over his shoulder at the approaching army. Because of the heavy supply carts and battering rams, they'd been making slower time than Tamriel would have liked. He detested every day the traitor sat on his throne. Nicholas wouldn't have control of the kingdom for long, however. They would arrive at the outskirts of Sandori by midday tomorrow, at the latest.

"How many soldiers do you have?"

"Nearly six thousand," he said. More runaway elves, eager to earn their freedom, had joined the ranks during the march from Fallmond. Many had joined their masters on hunting trips or had taught themselves how to fight. Others—the young and untrained—had agreed to aid the army by staying out of the battle and serving as healers. "Do you know how many are in Nicholas's army?"

"I don't know exact numbers—he was always careful to discuss the specifics of the attack in private, where I couldn't eavesdrop—but I do know he called all the soldiers who had pursued you back to the capital. I'm sure you figured that out already. And there's...something else." She faltered, biting her lower lip, and Tamriel watched the blood drain from her face. Apprehension filled him. He looked to Mercy, then to Hero and Ketojan, as Lethandris stepped forward and laid a hand on Celeste's arm.

"What is it?" he asked, fear for his soldiers flashing through him. Had he led them all this way for a slaughter?

She took a deep breath, then began to explain.

That day, they didn't stop to make camp until well past midnight. Once their tent was pitched, he and Mercy lay together on their shared bedroll, their blankets doing little to stave off the nighttime chill. She shivered in his arms, her cold hands curled in the fabric of his tunic. For a while, they whispered to each other in the darkness, discussing tomorrow's battle and easing the fears they didn't dare voice in front of the others. After Mercy fell asleep, Tamriel slipped out of the blankets and stepped outside. Around him, the camp was nearly silent; they were all exhausted from riding for so long, and they'd need all the energy they could get for the battle. Akiva and Atlas stood watch over his tent, but they were well out of earshot, seated around a low-burning fire to keep themselves warm.

He tilted his head back and stared up at the sky. It was clear and completely cloudless, revealing a blanket of twinkling stars and a bright full moon hanging low on the horizon. The sight filled him with sorrow. The possibility that this could be the last nighttime sky he would ever see was almost too much to bear.

He wasn't ready to die, but neither was he foolish enough to believe that everyone he cared for would survive the battle. That *he*, who was Nicholas's primary target, would live beyond tomorrow.

What Celeste had told them earlier hadn't left his mind. Weeks ago, Percival had gone to Riona Nevis and asked for her help in defeating Nicholas. After she agreed, they wrote to the king of Rivosa and described each of Nicholas's crimes in detail, then begged the king to send his army to Sandori. Not knowing whether Tamriel was alive and gathering troops of his own, they had foreseen two options: the Rivosi army could join the battle and fight alongside Tamriel to return the crown to its rightful owner, or they could bring Nicholas to justice and establish Percival and Riona as the new sovereigns in Tamriel's stead. Because they feared that Nicholas could somehow intercept the letter, one of Riona's guards had snuck out of the castle, ridden to Rhenys, and dispatched a raven from there.

The problem was, they had no idea whether King Domhnall had listened to their pleas. They'd suspected Nicholas would write to Domhnall as well, entreating him to send an army—which he did. They had then learned at a council meeting that Rivosi troops had been dispatched to Sandori, but whether the soldiers were going to fight for Riona or Nicholas remained uncertain. Riona and Percival were the queen and king, but Nicholas was a respected general, and the head of the Comyn fortune. King Domhnall would've had little doubt that Nicholas truly held the power of the crown. Had he believed his niece's claims and sided with her? Or had he been eager to ally himself with Nicholas after learning how swiftly and easily he had claimed the Beltharan throne?

They wouldn't know until they reached Sandori. Celeste, Hero, Ketojan, and Lethandris had left the city before the Rivosi troops arrived. As far as they knew, Percival was dead, awaiting execution, or confined to the castle. Regardless, he wouldn't be any help. No matter which side the Rivosi army took, their involvement would shift the tide of the battle. Victory might have been well within Tamriel's grasp against Nicholas's army alone, but they'd be vastly outnumbered if they had to fight Rivosans, as well.

Tamriel turned in a slow circle, surveying the sea of tents surrounding him. The canvas seemed to glow under the moonlight, some weathered and worn, some bearing Feyndaran crests, some—like those of his guards—bearing the crest of his family. He reached into his pocket and touched the piece of paper he had stored there, one of three identical copies. Of the two others, General Cadriel carried one, and Faye's parents held the third. It was a simple document consisting of a few lines of writing: his final wishes should he perish in the battle, and his naming of Mercy as the heir to his throne. He trusted her more than anyone. With or without him, she would be the queen Beltharos needed.

Should they both perish...

He let go of the paper and returned to his tent. A sliver of light cut across the dark interior, illuminating Mercy's sleeping form. Moving quietly to the bedroll, he lay down beside her and took her into his arms once more, gently brushing aside a stray curl that had fallen onto her forehead. Her beauty struck him anew, and a rush of love swept over him, so sudden and acute it took his breath away.

"I love you, Mercy," he whispered. "Forever and always."

He closed his eyes and tried to pray. *Creator, if I don't make it through this, watch over her. Protect her and her family. Help her be happy.* A sharp, annoyed sigh escaped him as the words fell flat. He was no good at praying. How could he possibly express everything she meant to him, everything he wanted for her, in a few sentences?

She shifted, burying her face in his neck, and mumbled his name. The sound brought a smile to his lips.

He kissed the top of her head, finally giving in to exhaustion. The last thing he thought before he fell into a deep and dreamless sleep was, *Please let me have a life with the woman I love.*

52
MERCY

No one spoke much that morning. By dawn, their belongings were packed, meager meals eaten, and horses prepared for the last leg of their journey. Mercy fidgeted in her saddle as she rode beside Tamriel at the front of the host. In a few short hours, they'd be fighting for their lives. She glanced at Tamriel for what felt like the millionth time that morning. He'd been quieter than usual; even Calum had given up on trying to lighten his mood after a few witty quips had failed to elicit so much as a smile. She didn't blame him. Even if they emerged victorious, he'd carry the weight of his soldiers' deaths for the rest of his life. So many of them were civilians. So many of them had only basic training with a blade or bow...and yet they were willing to march to war for him.

Tamriel had been staring straight ahead ever since they set off, his dark eyes fixed on the horizon as if he could already see Sandori in the distance. He'd been playing the confident king well these past few days, but with the battle looming so close, he let all pretense fade. A muscle in his jaw worked. His knuckles were white around his horse's reins. He still sat tall in his saddle, his shoulders squared, but it was more from stress than confidence; he was so tense Mercy didn't think he could slouch if he tried. She was glad Faye and the others were riding behind them. They couldn't see the darkness that kept flitting across his face.

"Tamriel," she said softly, and he started, drawn out of his thoughts. "We're going to bring Nicholas to justice. The traitor will not sit on your throne for much longer."

He offered her a tight smile, one that didn't quite reach his eyes. "*Our* thrones."

When she frowned, unsettled by the sadness in his voice, he reached over and grabbed her hand, giving it a reassuring squeeze. They were both aware of how much was at stake, how much they had to lose—and that was why they were going to fight like hell to keep it. They'd come too far to fail.

They lapsed into silence for a long time, their joined hands hanging between them as they rode side by side.

She scanned the rows of elves until she spotted Faye and Kaius in their midst, riding close to Hero and the others. Hero, Ketojan, and Lethandris would be working as healers during the battle, watching over the younger volunteers and aiding any who were injured outside the city walls. Even though they wouldn't be directly involved in the fighting, it was still a dangerous job. They'd have to brave the arrows and cannon fire to bring wounded soldiers in from the fields. Celeste had volunteered to join the battle, and had scavenged a handful of daggers and a set of leather armor from General Cadriel's supply wagons. Most of the troops were outfitted with swords and gleaming steel armor, but Celeste's experience as a thief made her more suited to light weaponry. Since she was good in close quarters, she'd be one of the people climbing the ladders and taking out the guards atop the city walls.

When they were only an hour from the capital, General

Cadriel joined them at the front to discuss last-minute details of the attack with Tamriel. Mercy half-listened, too nervous to think about much more than the battle awaiting them. She may have been trained by some of the best assassins in the world, but she was still only one woman. *We've been through worse odds than this,* she reminded herself, echoing the words she had said to Tamriel so many weeks ago, *and we've emerged victorious every time. We can do it again.*

It felt like no time at all passed before Sandori appeared in the distance. Mercy could make out the gilded spires of the castle, the dark outline of the city walls, and the smudges of burned houses spilling across the land. Outside the city limits, white tents bearing the Beltharan royal crest dotted the fields, exactly as they had when Mercy and Tamriel had returned from the battle with the Guild. Beyond them, soldiers were lined up in even rows on what would soon become a pitted, blood-soaked battlefield. Atop the city walls, flashes of light reflected from the soldiers' armor as they took their places at cannons or along the crenellations. As Mercy studied the troops, she realized there were no Rivosi banner men among them. King Domhnall's army should have arrived by now. Where in the Creator's name were they?

She could tell by Tamriel's expression that the same thought had crossed his mind. He turned to General Cadriel. "Keep an eye on our rear. Nicholas could have ordered the Rivosi troops to flank us." He jerked his chin to the scouts they'd sent ahead, who had returned only moments ago and reported immediately to their general. "Did they see anything?"

"Nothing, Your Majesty. Perhaps the Rivosans were merely delayed. Still, we'll be careful. We won't make the mistake of underestimating Nicholas Comyn."

As the general rode off to get his men into position,

Tamriel started shouting orders to the archers, preparing them to attack. Kaius gave Faye a quick kiss before joining his people, relaying Tamriel's commands in Cirisian for those who didn't speak the common tongue. Faye touched her lips as she watched him ride away. Then she straightened, pulled two throwing knives from their sheath, and rode over to Mercy's side. Together, they watched the archers line up along one side of the field, Nynev and Alistair somewhere in their ranks.

"All that training in the Guild," Mercy mused, "and yet I never expected anything like this to happen. Who could have foreseen us sitting here, free of Illynor and the tutors, fighting to save a kingdom?"

Faye shook her head. "You were right about one thing, though. Do you remember what you said to me when you found me burning my wedding dress all those years ago? After I told you why I ran away?"

The memory of Faye's tear-streaked face filled her mind, and she nodded. "I told you that when we were full-fledged Assassins, we would hunt down monsters like the man who tried to make you his bride. That it would always be you and me."

Her best friend, her oldest friend, guided her horse closer to Blackfoot, then reached over and grasped Mercy's hand. "You and me," she murmured, giving her fingers a tight squeeze. "Always."

Mercy spotted movement to her right, and turned to find Cassia, Matthias, and Ino riding up to her, helms on and blades unsheathed. On her other side, Calum and the Strykers were spread out beside Faye. Calum's massive crossbow was in his hands, a quiver of bolts slung across his back, and a sword was strapped to his side. When he noticed her gazing at him, he grinned and winked. She rolled her eyes, unable to keep a matching grin from spreading across her lips.

Cocky bastard, she mouthed to him.

He pressed a hand to his heart as he rode over to her. "Don't be cruel, princess," he said when he reached her side. "You'll hurt my feelings."

"Try not to die. I hate to admit it, but I might actually miss you."

His mouth dropped open. "Why, Mercy, I believe that's the nicest thing you've ever said to me."

"Don't let it go to your head."

"Too late. I'm now even more insufferable than I was before, and it's all your fault."

She opened her mouth to respond, but the clomping of hooves drew their attention back to the troops. Tamriel and his guards joined them just as General Cadriel approached, a determined look on his face. "The troops are in position, Your Majesty. We'll march on your order."

Tamriel looked to Kaius, who confirmed that his archers were ready with a nod. Then he turned to Duomnodera, whose warriors had formed a tight circle around Tamriel, Mercy, and the others. They were armed with every manner of weapon: swords, daggers, crossbows, maces, spears, even flails.

"Then let the battle begin," Tamriel said. He turned to the archers and cried, "Nock!"

As one, they pulled arrows from their quivers and fit them to their bow strings.

"Aim!"

They lifted their bows, razor-sharp arrowheads flashing in the sunlight. Across the battlefield, Nicholas's archers did the same. Mercy reached for the shield strapped to her saddle. Out of the corner of her eye, she watched her friends grab theirs. Behind Nicholas's army, soldiers scrambled to load cannonballs into the barrels lining the city walls.

"Loose!"

Everything happened in a blur. One moment, Mercy was sitting in her saddle, her shield raised over her head, listening to the twang of bows and the whistle of arrows cutting through the air. Mere heartbeats later, arrows rained down upon them. Terror jolted through Mercy as screams erupted from both armies. Some arrows hit nothing but grass. Others found exposed flesh and chinks in armor. Somewhere to Mercy's right, a horse shrieked as an arrow buried itself in its side, having found a gap in the horse's plate mail.

Tamriel shouted again, and the archers fired a second volley, then a third, then a fourth. Nicholas's army matched them volley for volley, until Mercy lost count of how many times she and Blackfoot had narrowly avoided being hit. Men and women on both sides continued to fall. The cannons fired every so often, sending a spray of earth over Mercy and the others, but they did not strike any of Tamriel's soldiers. The traitors were firing warning shots, trying to intimidate Tamriel into surrendering. *Look how easily we could blow your soldiers to bits,* they seemed to say. *Look how easily we could destroy you.*

If anything, the taunts made Tamriel even more furious.

Every trace of fear and sadness had left his face, replaced by a dark look that promised a violent end for those who dared stand against him. He ordered the archers to fire until their quivers were empty, then lowered his shield and unsheathed his sword. He lifted it high in the air for all to see. "CHARGE!"

The archers darted out of the way, rushing back to the supply wagons to grab the ladders, as Tamriel's army advanced. The pounding of thousands of hooves filled the air. The Feyndaran soldiers swarmed around them, their horses thundering across the battlefield, and enveloped Mercy and the others in the ranks. Adrenaline flooded her veins. Blackfoot kept pace with Tamriel's horse as they rushed toward Nicholas's troops. Here, in the midst of so many soldiers, it would be harder for Nicholas's men to strike the king, especially with the Qadar serving as a shield. Behind them, soldiers pushed the three battering rams across the field, grunting with the effort of maneuvering them across the uneven grass. Mercy and the others had to clear enough of a path for the rams to reach the gate. The sooner they breached the city, the better.

Nicholas's army charged, and the two sides met with crashes of steel and cries of pain. Even with all the soldiers the archers had taken out, they were fairly evenly matched. The arrival of the Rivosi army would tip the scales, but Mercy was terrified to find out with whom the king decided to ally.

A young man on a massive stallion broke through the line of Qadar and barreled toward Mercy. His sword arced for her, but she jerked Blackfoot's reins, ducked low, and slashed one of her daggers across the stallion's neck as he charged past. Hot blood splattered across Blackfoot's side, and the man fell from his saddle as his horse crumpled. Cassia finished him by plunging her sword through his stomach. Mercy opened her mouth to thank her sister when a cannonball went hurtling through the air. It crashed into a group of soldiers to her right, hitting both Tamriel's soldiers and Nicholas's, and sent ravaged body parts flying. Blood and dirt speckled Cassia's new scarf. Bile rose in Mercy's throat, and she just barely had time to drag her eyes away before she found herself facing yet another soldier.

They kept coming, over and over and over. She took one down with a strike to his neck, then another with a deep gash to his sword-wielding arm, then another by plunging her twin daggers into his horse's flank. Every time she killed one, she found another blade swinging her way. One strike glanced off the chainmail covering her arm, and she sent a silent thanks to Tamriel for giving her such strong armor.

It wasn't long before she was soaked in blood, and she had no idea how much of it was her own. She had no memory of being wounded, but even if she had been struck, she was too focused on cutting her way toward the gates to notice the pain. Blackfoot was uninjured; Queen Cerelia had provided them several sets of armor for their horses. He was still standing, still charging forward, snapping and stamping at anyone who dared get too close.

She twisted in her saddle, realizing she had not seen Tamriel for several minutes. Her heart stopped, seizing with fear. "TAMRIEL!" she screamed, her words drowned out by the sounds of battle. Her ears rang from the cannon fire.

"TAMRIEL!"

She turned Blackfoot around, searching desperately for him, but all she found was chaos. She couldn't even make out the faces of most of the soldiers surrounding her; they were either wearing helms or splattered with blood.

The battering rams were closer now, making their way through the clashing armies. As she watched, a cannonball smashed into one and shattered the frame, rendering it useless. The soldiers wheeling it across the battlefield stumbled backward, shielding themselves from the large, deadly splinters with their arms. Two fell and did not rise again.

Behind them, the archers had armed themselves with swords and daggers, and were carrying long ladders into the fray. When they reached the city wall, they'd climb up and try to take down Nicholas's men from the ramparts—but they still had to make it through the clashing armies and maze of houses on the city's outskirts.

Mercy turned to find a sword swinging straight at her face. She yanked Blackfoot's reins with one hand and lifted the dagger in her other. Before their blades could meet, a throwing knife buried itself in the soldier's eye, and he tumbled off his horse with a cry of agony. Mercy whirled and found Faye a few feet away, she and her horse coated in blood and flecks of dirt from the cannon fire.

"Have you seen Tamriel?" Mercy shouted over the din of the battle. At first, she thought Faye couldn't hear her, but then her friend jerked her chin to her left. Mercy breathed a sigh of relief when she spotted Tamriel fighting alongside Calum, the Strykers, and Duomnodera. The Qadar had closed ranks around him, taking on several of Nicholas's soldiers at a time in an attempt to keep them from breaking through to the king.

A wave of arrows fell around them, several nearly striking Tamriel and the others. Nicholas's archers were firing from atop the city walls, not caring whether they hit Tamriel's men or their own.

"We have to—" she started, but another round of cannon fire cut off her words. The cannonball sailed through the air and crashed into another battering ram, breaking it into pieces. Only one remained.

"WHAT?" Faye yelled.

"THE CANNONS!" She pointed to the city walls, and Faye nodded. They had to take down the cannons and distract the archers. Any one of those arrows could find its way to Tamriel's heart.

Faye glanced back and pointed a throwing knife at one of the approaching ladders. Kaius was at the front, fighting one-handed while bracing the weight of the ladder on a shoulder. "Go on! I'll stick with Tamriel!"

Mercy didn't hesitate. As soon as a gap in the chaos opened, she dug her heels into Blackfoot's sides and plunged through it. In her periphery, she saw Cassia, Ino, and Matthias galloping after her. Relief transformed Kaius's face when he spotted them approaching.

"We'll hold the soldiers off!" Mercy shouted, and he nodded. "Get to the wall!"

Together, she and her siblings cut a path through the soldiers, intent on nothing but breaching the city's defenses. If the cannons took out the last battering ram, at least they could open the gate from within the city—but that meant climbing the tall, unguarded ladders and risking being struck down by an arrow. If she failed, they'd be trapped, picked off one by one until Nicholas deigned to make an appearance.

Coward, Mercy seethed, fury fueling her attacks. Being a well-respected general, she had expected him to lead his army, but he had yet to grace them with his presence. He probably wanted to let his soldiers tire Tamriel and his army out before he joined the fight.

"Where are you, you traitorous bastard?" she muttered.

They finally burst free of the fighting soldiers. With Kaius and the others close behind, they made their way through the abandoned streets outside the city. The walls seemed taller than she remembered them, an excruciating climb several stories high. A few archers noticed their approach and began firing down at them. One of the runaway slaves holding the ladder crumpled, an arrow's white fletching sticking out of her chest.

Finally, they reached the city wall. Mercy held her shield over her head as the archers continued firing down at them. Her siblings did the same, while Kaius and the elves propped the ladder against the wall. The hooks on the end caught on one of the gaps in the crenellations. Kaius began scaling the ladder first, several elves following. Worry gnawed at Mercy as she watched them ascend. One of Nicholas's soldiers hurled a dagger straight down, trying to dislodge the elves. Kaius jerked to the side, but not far enough. The dagger slashed through his leather bracer and carved a deep gash in his forearm, causing him to hiss in pain. Blood dripped from his elbow as he climbed.

Mercy dragged her eyes away. The sight of other ladders going up along the length of the wall offered a modicum of relief, but it didn't stop her heart hammering against her chest. With every pulse, it screamed, *Tamriel, Tamriel, Tamriel.* He could be dead, and she wouldn't know until the battle was over...if she lived that long.

She dropped from Blackfoot's saddle, gave him a reassuring pat on the neck, then began climbing the ladder. *Stop the cannons. Take down the archers. Open the gates.*

Nothing else mattered.

Cassia, Matthias, and Ino climbed up after her. By the time she reached the halfway point, the old wounds where Drayce Hamell's arrows had struck her began to ache. She ignored it and pushed herself faster. Kaius and another elf had already made it up to the top. She looked up just as one of them tossed an archer over the wall. His arms pinwheeled wildly as he plummeted, and she tore her eyes away just before she heard his body crunch against the cobblestone.

Mercy allowed herself the briefest glance back at the battlefield. She couldn't make out individual faces from where she stood, but she spotted several Qadari warriors clustered together in the middle of the clashing armies. Tamriel couldn't be far away. The good news was, they were slowly forcing Nicholas's troops back, closer to the city. The last battering ram had made it beyond the edge of the fighting and was now rolling at a steady—albeit slow—pace toward the gate. Its sides were splattered with blood.

When she reached the top of the ladder, she hauled herself over and onto the battlements, immediately drawing her daggers. The wall was only a few feet wide, which made for cramped fighting conditions. Kaius and the others were already engaged with several archers. They moved so fast their blades were mere flashes of silver. Some of Nicholas's archers died from a wound, but many more simply were thrown over the side of the wall, painting a gruesome picture across the street far below. Mercy turned to help Cassia over the top of the ladder just as a horn sounded from somewhere further down the wall, its call echoing through the empty streets and spilling over the battlefield below.

"What is that?" Cassia asked, clutching Mercy's hand tightly.

"I don't know." She frowned. They weren't lucky enough for Nicholas to be sounding a retreat. They hadn't even made a dent in Nicholas's numbers.

Then she spotted movement down below, and the pieces fell into place. Matthias and Ino joined her and Cassia on the battlements, and they gaped down at the previously empty streets as hundreds of people emerged from the houses that had been destroyed in Firesse's attack on the city. They were clad in full armor, and Mercy didn't need to see the crests emblazoned on their breastplates to know they were the Rivosi troops King Domhnall had sent.

Her heart sank. Domhnall had sided with Nicholas.

"Why make them hide?" Matthias hissed. "Why only have them join the fight now?"

Mercy opened her mouth, but Ino answered for her, his voice grim. "Because he wanted Tamriel to think he had a chance at winning. He wants to crush our spirits before he kills us all."

As the Rivosi troops ran toward the battlefield, pulling their swords from their sheaths, another deafening boom split the air. It was so loud that it rumbled through the bricks below Mercy's feet. Ino grabbed her elbow, steadying her, as they watched a cannonball hurtle through the air toward Tamriel's army. Soldiers dove out of the way as it slammed into the last battering ram, destroying the frame and half the wheels.

Cassia flinched. Matthias let out a string of curses, while Ino unsheathed his sword and started toward the soldiers, murderous fury rippling off of him. Mercy stood there for a few heartbeats, so full of rage she couldn't stop staring at the ruined battering ram. Then she pivoted on her heel and strode after Ino, twisting her twin daggers into one double-bladed staff. There was a gate release somewhere on this wall, and she was going to cut down every soldier in her path until she found it.

❧ 53 ☙
PERCIVAL

A low, rumbling *boom* startled Percival awake. Reverberations shuddered through the stone floor below him, and his eyes flew open to pitch blackness. *The dungeon.* He scrambled to a sitting position and let out a sharp hiss of pain. Every inch of his body hurt. He was certain that if he could see himself, he'd find his fair skin underscored with deep bruises and scabbed cuts. He reached up to fix his crooked spectacles and started at the sound of jangling chains. His wrists were bound by two heavy cuffs; he hadn't noticed their weight at first, too distracted by the pain shooting down his injured arm. An exploration of his torn sleeve revealed a crusted, bloodied bandage and a still-oozing wound. The skin around the gash felt warm, although not as inflamed as it had been when he'd escaped. The infection wasn't completely healed, but for now, all that mattered was that he was alive.

By the Creator, I'm alive, he thought with a shaky, relieved laugh. *At least for a short while.*

He hesitantly reached out and ran his hands over the floor, steeling himself for the feel of the guard's dried blood.

He found only cold stone. They'd placed him in a different cell to await his trial. Why Nicholas's men hadn't killed him after his little display of heroics outside the stairwell, he had no idea. He couldn't remember much of that day. After Riona had slipped from his view, he'd fought as hard as he could, but he hadn't lasted long. Exhaustion had overtaken him before the guards had. He just hoped he had managed to buy her enough time to reach the tunnel.

Percival staggered to his feet and moved to the door of his cell, his chains clanging. "Riona! Are you in here?"

No response. He chose to believe that meant she had made it out of the city and was now on her way to Rivosa. Hopefully, Lord Winslow and her guards had managed to escape, as well. He prayed they would find each other. Nowhere in Beltharos was safe for her right now, and it would take at least a week for her to reach the border. The road was dangerous for a young woman traveling on her own.

A series of booms rumbled through the dungeon, and this time Percival realized what the sound was: cannon fire. A battle was raging outside the city walls. Whether Nicholas's forces were facing Tamriel's army or King Domhnall's—or both—he didn't know. He only hoped he would live long enough to witness his uncle brought to justice.

Through the door, he heard the muffled sounds of fighting. His brow furrowed. Had the troops already breached the castle? Surely the cannons wouldn't be firing if Tamriel and his soldiers had made it past the city's defenses. Something heavy thudded against the door, then it swung open with a bright burst of light from the hall. Percival threw up a hand to shield his eyes as a body flopped to the ground, blood spilling from the gaps in its armor. Then it was dragged into the hall by someone he couldn't see.

"Who's there?" he called, his heart pounding. If the troops had made it to the castle, the battle had to be almost over. They just needed to find his uncle and put an end to his tyranny. "Your Majesty? Mercy?"

"Try again," said a voice with an elegant, melodic accent. "I made a vow that I would help you defeat your uncle. You cannot believe I would run off and leave you to the mercy of his treacherous court."

Percival's mouth dropped open as Riona stepped into the room, lifting her skirts so they didn't drag in the trail of blood left behind by the body. Three guards followed her into the dungeon. One rushed forward with a ring of keys, and Percival watched in astonishment as he unlocked the cell door and removed Percival's cuffs.

"What are you *doing* here? I thought you were on your way home!"

"Saving you, of course." Her mouth pressed into a thin line as she studied the various cuts and bruises marring his face. He glanced down and found more peeking through the rips in his ruined doublet and trousers, the fine clothes he had worn for their wedding now little more than rags. "Can you run?"

"I can fight."

She shot him a dubious look, but instead of arguing, merely gestured for him to follow her into the hall. "I was afraid you were going to say that," she said as they made their way toward the stairs. "If you insist on facing your uncle, my guards and I will stand with you."

"But how are you still *here*, in the castle?" he tried again, and she let out a huff of annoyance, as if that detail wasn't the least bit important.

"I made it outside the city and hid, waiting for the guards to move on and search elsewhere. It took a day and a half, but eventually Nicholas or Rhiannon must have decided the hunt for me could be postponed until after the battle. I was planning to sneak in tonight, but when I heard the cannon fire, I figured now was as good a time as any to find you and Lord Winslow." As she spoke, they rounded the final corner and found Lord Winslow and the rest of the Rivosi guards waiting at the bottom of the steps. The lord was wide-eyed and pale, his hair sticking up in every direction, and the guards were splattered in blood. "Luckily, four of my guards were being tended to in the infirmary. I sent one ahead to Lord Winslow and the others, then took the rest to rescue you. Any more questions?"

He shook his head, still a little shocked by her sudden appearance. Part of him feared that she was nothing more than an apparition conjured by his fevered mind, that he'd wake up curled on the dungeon floor with her name on his lips.

Riona ran the last few steps to Lord Winslow and pulled him into a quick hug. He barely had time to put his arms around her before she backed out of his embrace and turned to her guards. "Ian, Wendell, escort Lord Winslow to Rhenys and await word from me. Sell these if you need money." She pulled off her gold and emerald earrings and dropped them into one guard's hands. "If you do not hear from me in a week's time, return to Innislee and tell the king what has transpired."

"Don't be mad, my lady," Winslow interrupted, stepping in front of Riona. "We must all get out of this city. This is no place for a woman of your birth. As soon as the battle is over, Nicholas Comyn will have you both arrested and executed."

She shook her head. "Lord Winslow, I am the queen of this kingdom. Until Tamriel Myrellis claims his throne, it is my duty to protect his people from the tyrant who stole the crown. I will not see you harmed in the process. Ian, Wendell, there's a tunnel a few halls down from here that will lead out of the city. Do you remember the directions?"

They both nodded.

"Take Lord Winslow and leave. Creator willing, we'll see you soon."

Before the lord could protest again, Ian and Wendell took hold of his arms and pulled him down the hall.

As soon as they were out of sight, Percival and Riona followed the remaining guards up the stairs and through the halls, their pace so quick Percival could barely keep up. Every so often, his hunger and fatigue got the best of him, and the floor began to slip out from under his feet. Each time, Riona's hand was there to steady him. Her brows pinched in concern. "Are you sure you want to fight?" she whispered.

He nodded, trying to ignore the jolts of pain shooting down his injured arm. "I need...I need to see my uncle pay for his crimes. I'm not going to sit here while you go out and face him yourself. Are Tamriel's troops or your uncle's attacking? Did you see banners when you were outside the city?"

She shook her head. "I didn't see. I'm sorry."

When they arrived at the armory, Riona rushed inside and started searching through the chests lining the walls, tossing sheathed daggers and quivers of arrows over her shoulder. After a few minutes, she turned to him and shoved a metal breastplate into his arms. "Put this on."

While she continued searching, the Rivosi guards helped him strap on a suit of mismatched armor; the breastplate Riona found was narrow enough through the ribs to fit him, but they had to search through three more chests before they found enough pieces to cover his long, thin limbs. When he was finally finished, they secured a belt with a sword and dagger around his hips. He looked down and frowned at the gleaming silver armor. He felt like an imposter, a stablehand playing at knighthood.

Then he turned and spotted Riona. She stood across the room, her priceless silk gown traded for a suit of armor. Her long braids spilled out from under her helm, the gold beads shimmering. The sight stunned him. She had sworn that she would stand against Nicholas with him, but neither of them had imagined it like this. The few times they'd discussed it, they had pictured their overthrow of his traitorous uncle far in the future, after years of careful political maneuvering.

"Do you know how to use those?" he asked, nodding to the daggers strapped to her hips.

"Do you know how to use that?" she countered with a raised brow, gesturing to the sword at his side.

He did, but not with his entire body aching and one arm burning with infection. He'd barely held his own long enough for Riona to escape the other day. Despite that, he said, "Well enough to wield it against my uncle. If you and your guards can get me close, I'll do my best to take him down. Do you know where he is?"

She looked to her guards, and one answered, "He left the castle as soon as the battle began. I believe he's overseeing the attack from Myrellis Plaza, Your Majesty."

Percival frowned. It was unlike his uncle not to be leading the charge. Even with so much at stake, Nicholas would never shy away from a battle.

"One last chance to change your mind," Riona said, joining him by the door. "Are you sure you want to do this?"

He pulled his sword from its sheath, testing its weight. "The Creator himself couldn't stop me."

54

FAYE

Faye's ears were ringing so much from the cannon fire that she almost didn't hear the horn blaring from the city walls. As the soldiers around her faltered, distracted, Faye took the opportunity to grab her last throwing knife and hurl it into the throat of the nearest enemy soldier. He fell with a gurgle, clutching his throat. A second later, a sword swung toward Nightstorm's chest, but Faye whipped her dagger out and blocked it before it could slice through her mare. The soldier's eyes widened in shock as the blade severed his head from his body.

"FAYE!" someone cried, and she turned her horse to find Tamriel pointing toward the city gate. No—not toward the gate, which was still closed, but to the soldiers emerging from the abandoned houses on the outskirts of the city. Rivosi soldiers, Faye realized with a start. Domhnall had allied with Nicholas. The traitor had positioned the Rivosi soldiers here to trick Tamriel into thinking their numbers were even—that he had a chance of victory.

She dug her heels into Nightstorm's sides, galloping

through the chaos until she was close enough to Tamriel to shout, "Should we retreat?"

His reply was cut off by the fire of another cannon. As they watched, openmouthed, the cannonball sailed over their heads and crashed into the frame of the last battering ram. Faye's stomach sank. She prayed Mercy and the others had made it to the top of the city wall. She squinted against the bright sunlight, searching for a glimpse of Mercy or Kaius, but she was too far away to make out any details.

Tamriel shouted something to her.

"WHAT?"

He rode closer and grabbed her arm, pointing to the edge of the battle. The Rivosi soldiers were streaming into the chaos, swords unsheathed, and slashing at—at *Nicholas's* soldiers.

She gaped at Tamriel. "They're on our side?"

He nodded, his eyes bright with renewed confidence. "They deceived Nicholas!"

"How many do you think there are?" she shouted.

Tamriel scanned the battlefield, trying to make a count. "Enough to turn the battle in our favor." Panic flashed across his face. "Where's Mercy?"

Faye pointed to the ladders propped against the city wall. There must have been a half dozen set up already, and more going up as they spoke. The king flinched when a body went tumbling off the battlements.

"Creator, watch over her," he muttered.

"Watch over us all," Faye amended.

Three soldiers broke through the Qadars' line and rushed toward them. Faye dropped from her horse's saddle and lifted her dagger, positioning herself in front of Tamriel. Out of the corner of her eye, she saw Calum and the Strykers fighting a group of enemy soldiers, their faces and bodies coated in blood she hoped was not their own.

The first soldier sprinted toward her, his sword angled at her face. Her heart hammering in her chest, she knocked his blow aside, slipped behind him, and shoved her blade through the gap in the armor behind the man's knee. He crumpled, letting out a cry of agony that she swiftly cut short. She straightened, shoving a strand of hair that had fallen from her braid out of her face. The remaining two soldiers were circling Tamriel. He parried one, but the other darted in and cut a long gash through his horse's flank. The horse screamed and collapsed, tossing Tamriel from the saddle in the process. Faye dashed to him, leaping over fallen bodies and slipping on slick patches of blood. How had the king managed to get so far away so quickly?

One of the soldiers drove the point of his sword down, straight at Tamriel's exposed neck, and Faye hurled her dagger at him. It wasn't as precise as her throwing knives, but it hit its mark. The man fell onto Tamriel, his sword narrowly missing the king's jugular. Tamriel shoved the body off and scrambled to his feet just as the other soldier lunged.

Faye grabbed a random sword from the ground, but before she could make it to Tamriel's side, an arrow pierced the enemy soldier's eye. He staggered, his expression contorted in pain and horror, before toppling face-first to the ground. Faye ran to Tamriel. "Are you hurt?"

He bent down and grabbed the helm that had been knocked off his head when he'd fallen from his horse. "Just sore. I'll be fine."

He turned to his horse, which was still lying on its side, its flank spilling blood. The gash was so deep Faye could see the bone. Tamriel knelt beside it and ran a gentle hand along its neck, trying to calm the terrified creature. Pure grief shone in his eyes as he murmured something Faye couldn't hear over the din of battle. Then he rose and cut the animal's throat, ending its suffering. Its pained shrieks quickly faded to silence.

A handful of Rivosi soldiers appeared to their right. Faye stepped in front of Tamriel and angled her sword toward the strangers. King Domhnall may have sent his army to fight for Tamriel, but that didn't mean they'd let him live. She wouldn't put it past the Rivosi king to kill Tamriel so Riona could remain on the throne.

The leader slung his bow over one shoulder and lifted his empty hands. Eyeing Faye's sword, he slowly reached up and removed his helm, revealing dark skin and striking blue eyes. "I've come to help you," he shouted over the fighting. "Do you remember me, Your Majesty?"

Tamriel's brows furrowed, then recognition flashed through his eyes. "Prince Domhnall?"

The Crown Prince of Rivosa, Faye realized. She'd learned of him and his four siblings back at the Keep, but she had never expected to meet a member of the Rivosi royal family. The eldest son, Prince Domhnall II, had been serving as general of the Rivosi army for the past five years.

The prince glanced at the shattered husks of the battering rams. Countless bodies surrounded them, dismembered by the cannonballs or gouged by splinters. "Do you have a plan for getting into the city now that your battering rams are—"

A cheer rose from the city walls, cutting off the rest of his question. They all turned to see the gate swinging open. Faye couldn't fight the grin that spread across her face. Mercy and Kaius had done it. They had fought their way past Nicholas's men and opened the gates.

Tamriel turned to Prince Domhnall. "It seems so."

From somewhere across the battlefield, General Cadriel shouted, "ADVANCE! Into the city!"

Prince Domhnall and his men unsheathed their swords. "I

must go lead my men, Your Majesty," the prince said to Tamriel. "Good luck."

And then he was gone, lost in the chaos.

Faye grabbed Tamriel's arm and dragged him toward her horse. His army was already racing through the streets, footfalls echoing off the abandoned houses as they rushed toward the gate. He and Faye would be lost in the current unless they took Nightstorm. "Come on. We have to find Nicholas."

As soon as he was seated in the saddle, she climbed up behind him. She freed her bow and quiver from where they were strapped to her saddle while he shouted orders to Duomnodera, then to Calum and the Strykers. Within seconds, they closed ranks around Tamriel and Faye. Despite Mercy and Kaius's efforts, there were still archers atop the walls. They fired down at the soldiers streaming through the city gate.

At a kick of Tamriel's heels, Nightstorm burst into a gallop. Duomnodera and a half-dozen warriors rode ahead, shoving through the crowd. Calum and the Strykers trailed behind them. Nerran and Hewlin were pale and bloody, but alive. Amir and Oren were nowhere to be found.

Calum caught her concerned look and shouted, "Amir was hit by an arrow. Oren took him back so Hero and Ketojan could tend to him." His expression was deceptively calm, but Faye saw the panic in his eyes. The Strykers were his family, even more so than Mercy and her siblings. For his sake, she hoped they would all survive. He'd lost far too much already.

She was about to respond when her eyes landed on a crumpled body at the bottom of the wall, bones sticking through bloody bronze skin.

Kaius!

Her heart stopped. The entire world stopped. The arrow she'd nocked slipped out of her slackened grasp and clattered to the street.

Tamriel, feeling her tense, glanced over his shoulder. "Faye? Something wrong?"

She couldn't answer. Her eyes were locked on the corpse, terror turning her blood to ice.

Someone gripped her arm tightly, hard enough to bruise. She jumped, startled and found herself staring into Calum's face. He was riding alongside Nightstorm, so close his leg brushed Faye's. "It wasn't him," he said, his voice low and steady. "It wasn't Kaius."

"I *saw* him." She twisted in the saddle, trying to catch another glimpse of him, then realized they'd already passed through the gate. Tamriel and the Qadar were charging down the main road toward the castle, a sea of Rivosi and Beltharan soldiers surrounding them. Nicholas's men were standing atop some of the buildings, firing crossbow bolts down at the army.

"*Listen to me*," Calum snapped, his fingers digging into her upper arm. "That wasn't Kaius. The tattoos were different. It wasn't him. Do you understand?"

Faye sucked in a few quick, sharp breaths, and nodded. She hadn't seen the body well enough to make out his tattoos, but she trusted Calum. Kaius wasn't dead. He *wasn't*. Calum shot her one more concerned look before releasing her.

Her hands shaking, she nocked another arrow and loosed it at one of Nicholas's archers. It sailed through the air and punched through his leather armor. The man collapsed, the crossbow slipping from his hand and tumbling to the street below.

At the end of the block, Akiva and Atlas careened around the corner and gestured wildly to Tamriel. "THE PLAZA!" they shouted over the pounding of armored feet and the clomping of hooves. "HE'S IN THE PLAZA!"

Tamriel dug his heels into Nightstorm's sides, spurring her even faster. "Faye! Are you able to fight?"

"Y-Yes." Faye loosed another arrow and took down the next crossbowman they passed. She had promised to fight with Tamriel and Mercy. She wouldn't let them down. "Let's not keep Nicholas waiting."

55
TAMRIEL

Tamriel's blood pounded in his ears as he guided Nightstorm through the winding streets of his city. Crossbow bolts whizzed past, catching some of his soldiers in the chest, the neck, the face. Bodies thumped sickeningly against the cobblestone as his archers shot crossbowmen from the rooftops. Behind him, Faye still trembled —although not as hard as she had been. Even so, she didn't falter once as she loosed arrow after arrow at Nicholas's men. To Tamriel's right and left, Calum, Nerran, and Hewlin did the same.

All the windows they passed were shuttered up tightly, and Tamriel imagined his citizens huddled in their rooms, listening to the sounds of men and women dying just outside their homes. The thought made him sick. He wished he could tell them it would all be over soon.

A few yards ahead, Duomnodera gestured to her warriors. Half of them fell in position after her and rode ahead toward the Plaza, swinging heavy maces and flails at every enemy soldier within arm's reach. The remainder formed a wedge before Tamriel and Faye and pushed through the fighting.

Bolts clattered against their scales and fell harmlessly to the ground, and Tamriel sent a silent thanks up to the Creator for their nearly impenetrable scales.

They had nearly reached the Plaza. Tamriel unsheathed his sword, gripping it with white knuckles, and Faye withdrew more arrows from Nightstorm's saddlebags.

"TAMRIEL MYRELLIS!" a voice roared, echoing through the streets. "I HAVE SOMETHING THAT BELONGS TO YOU!"

Tamriel gritted his teeth at the sound of Nicholas's voice. Even now, after being deceived by the Rivosi troops, the bastard was cocky. Tamriel hoped Nicholas's arrogance was all a show to keep his soldiers' morale high. The general was skilled, but Tamriel doubted he had anticipated that King Domhnall's troops would betray him.

Hope sparked within Tamriel. The three battering rams Queen Cerelia had granted him had been destroyed, and yet his troops had still been able to breach the city's defenses, thanks to Mercy, Kaius, and the others. Without the advantage of the city walls and Rivosi soldiers, Nicholas had to be panicking.

They turned the corner and rushed into the Plaza, the Qadar still in tight formation around him. Tamriel's eyes immediately found Nicholas amidst the fighting soldiers. He stood near the fountain, surrounded by a host of royal guards, but he wasn't alone. When Tamriel saw who stood in front of Nicholas, a blade to her neck, his stomach dropped.

Faye went absolutely still. "Mercy."

Mercy.

One of Nicholas's arms was around her waist, pinning her to his chest, and the other held a dagger to her throat. There was a gash in the side of her head. Her curls were wet and shiny with blood, but her eyes were alert, burning with fury. If she died today, Tamriel knew she would go to her grave with that look on her face. She wouldn't let Nicholas see so much as a hint of fear.

He looked up. Crossbowmen lined the rooftops surrounding the square. Half of their bolts were trained on Mercy, ready to pierce her chainmail armor should she make the slightest move. The rest of the marksmen aimed at Tamriel as he halted Nightstorm on the edge of the Plaza, his Qadari warriors forming a protective barrier around him.

Mercy's gaze met Tamriel's, and she slowly shook her head, gravely. He understood the meaning behind the gesture; she wanted him to attack and reclaim his throne, even if it cost her life.

Not a chance.

"Surrender, traitor," Tamriel snarled at Nicholas, his voice carrying across the square. Out of the corner of his eye, he saw Duomnodera and her warriors silently emerge on several of the surrounding rooftops and quickly dispatch Nicholas's crossbowmen. They dumped the bodies on the square below, then picked up the fallen crossbows and fired on the remaining archers. More of Tamriel's soldiers—a mix of elves, Rivosans, and Feyndarans—spilled into the Plaza. "You've lost the Rivosi army and we have you surrounded. Lay down your dagger, release Mercy, and accept defeat."

Nicholas tilted his head thoughtfully. "I must admit, you've fought well, Tamriel. Much better than I had expected. Much better than my coward of a nephew could ever hope to do. Unfortunately for you, my men were able to capture quite a few of your friends."

He nodded to Rhiannon, whom Tamriel hadn't noticed amidst the fighting soldiers. She led several soldiers from the fray, dragging several chained prisoners alongside them. Tamriel's chest seized when he spotted Kaius, Matthias, Ino, and Cassia, as well as a handful of Cirisians.

Nicholas's lips curled into a cruel grin as his soldiers lined

Kaius and the others up beside Rhiannon. "Order your army to retreat, renounce your claim to the throne, and your friends will live. Refuse, and you will watch every one of them die."

"He's bluffing," Calum hissed, riding up to Tamriel's left. "Don't trust him."

Tamriel nodded, seething. Nicholas wasn't a fool; he was well aware that he was outnumbered. He was playing his last hand, and Tamriel knew his former general was lying. This war wouldn't end until one of them was dead.

Now, to get Mercy and the others out of Nicholas's grasp...

"Friends, soldiers," Tamriel called, addressing the troops filling the Plaza, enemy and ally alike. A few of Nicholas's soldiers regarded him warily, their eyes darting from the traitor to their rightful king. They had betrayed Tamriel, but he would offer them clemency if it meant saving the lives of those he loved. He lifted his chin and surveyed the troops—his subjects. "I did not return to Sandori for a slaughter. I intend to reclaim my crown and bring the traitor who stole my kingdom to justice, but that does not mean you must die. None of you must watch another friend, brother, or sister die today. Hand over your weapons and surrender peacefully, and you will receive mercy."

Several soldiers exchanged cautious looks, murmurs rising throughout the ranks. Nicholas whipped around, dragging Mercy along with him, and bellowed commands as a handful of men and women sheathed their swords and fell to a knee. None objected as Tamriel's soldiers stripped them of their weapons and led them out of the Plaza. It wouldn't do much to tip the scales further in Tamriel's favor, but it helped nonetheless.

He glanced up at Duomnodera, and a shake of her head confirmed his fear: neither she nor her warriors had a clear shot on Nicholas. There was no guarantee they would be able to strike him down without hurting Mercy. If the bolt didn't kill him on impact, he'd slash Mercy's throat and drag her to the Beyond with him. Tamriel couldn't risk it. He would find a way to save her and the others—he just needed a little more time to *think*.

Again, Mercy met his eyes and nodded, her expression imploring. He ignored her. *It will not come to that,* he told himself as Faye tensed behind him. *I will not sacrifice her.*

He could order his soldiers to attack. They had greater numbers. It would be over quickly, and they might manage to wrest some of his friends away from Nicholas, but he would cut Mercy's throat the second Tamriel made a move. Kaius and the others would follow. It was selfish, but Tamriel wouldn't give them up for his kingdom.

Nicholas's shoulder. Celeste had revealed to them that Nicholas's shoulder had been wounded at the banquet following Percival's wedding. If Mercy could take advantage of the still-healing injury, if she could slip out of his grasp...

"I warn you, Tamriel," Nicholas said, cutting through his frantic thoughts. "I am not a terribly patient man, and your hesitation will cost you. Rhiannon, if you will."

Rhiannon nodded to her men, and the soldiers behind the Cirisian prisoners plunged their swords through the elves' backs. Their leather breastplates split like tissue, gut-wrenching cries spilling from their lips. Kaius let out a roar of fury as his people fell, lifeless, to the soldiers' feet.

"I will give you one more chance to surrender," Nicholas called. "How many lives are worth your kingdom? Are you willing to watch your lover die so you can sit on the throne once more?" He nicked Mercy's neck with the blade. Tamriel's vision turned red with rage as a drop of blood rolled down her throat and disappeared below the edge of her chainmail. "Mercy will be the last to die. I'll make both of you watch as I slaughter what remains of her family."

As he spoke, a soldier shoved his sword through Cassia's back. Mercy went completely still, her face turning bone white, before she let out a cry that sounded more animal than elven. The soldier behind Cassia twisted his sword, eliciting an agonized scream from her, then pulled out the blade. Matthias and Ino lunged for their sister, but the men holding their chains yanked them backward as Cassia slumped to her knees. A trickle of blood spilled over her lower lip. Mercy swayed as she watched her sister fall and suck in her last, labored breath. A heavy, shocked silence swept over the square at the pure, raw grief in her sobs. Tamriel's heart broke.

"You'll pay for that, you bastard!" Matthias roared. He jumped to his feet and slammed his forehead into the nose of the soldier holding his bonds. More rushed forward to subdue him, blades unsheathed. Beside him, Ino and Kaius took full advantage of their captors' distraction. They tugged sharply on their chains, pulling the soldiers holding them off balance, and ripped the swords from the men's hands. They ran to Matthias's side, brandishing their blades at the soldiers who immediately swarmed them.

Tamriel stood in Nightstorm's stirrups. "ATTACK!" he shouted to his troops. To Duomnodera and the other Qadar on the rooftops, he cried, "When you have a clear shot, *FIRE!*"

He dropped into the saddle and dug his heels into Nightstorm's sides, steering her straight toward Nicholas and Mercy as enemy soldiers rushed them, forming a shield of bodies against the crossbow bolts. Faye sent arrow after arrow whizzing past him, trying to clear the way ahead. The Qadar who had escorted them to the Plaza spread outward, maces swinging, crunching and shattering bone. Calum,

Nerran, and Hewlin drew their swords and plunged into the fighting.

"I'm out of arrows," Faye said. "Go after Nicholas. I'll get the others, and we'll be right behind you."

He caught a flash of silver in his periphery—Faye drawing the dagger at her hip—before she dropped from the saddle, rolled, and sprang to her feet. Without a moment's hesitation, she began cutting a path toward where Kaius and the others stood back-to-back, struggling to fight in their chains.

Tamriel gritted his teeth, the echo of Mercy's sobs filling his ears. By the Creator, he would do *anything* to keep from hearing those sobs again. He would have faced a thousand armies to keep her and her family safe...but he'd failed her.

He scanned the sea of armored bodies until he spotted Mercy's black chainmail. She'd somehow escaped Nicholas's grasp and claimed a fallen soldier's sword. As Tamriel watched, struggling to push Nightstorm through the fighting, she slashed low, but the traitor blocked her strike and shoved her backward. She stumbled over a dead soldier's outstretched arm before righting herself, just in time to block Nicholas's next attack. Tamriel could hardly bear to watch. Mercy may have been trained by the Guild, but Nicholas was at least two heads taller and three times her weight—all muscle. Watching her sister's death had left her rattled, too. She was trembling so hard Tamriel could see it from across the square.

"Faster, Nightstorm," he implored the horse, jerking the reins as a sword arced out and nearly caught the mare's side. Every time Nicholas attacked Mercy, terror shot through him. All it would take was one misstep, one miscalculation on Mercy's part, for Nicholas to cut her down.

He looked up at the Qadari warriors on the rooftops. Their bolts whizzed through the air, taking down soldier after soldier, but none of them reached Nicholas. Mercy was still too close. They wouldn't risk hitting her.

"I'm coming, Mercy," Tamriel breathed, his grip on his sword growing slick. Where in the Creator's name was Celeste? General Cadriel? Nynev? The Daughters? "Hold on a little longer, my love. I'm coming."

❧ 56 ☙
MERCY

Mercy blinked hard against the sweat stinging her eyes, lifting her sword just as Nicholas's swung toward her face. Their blades met and locked, the impact sending reverberations down her arms. She grimaced at the twinge of pain that shot through her chest and down her side. Earlier, she had fought as fiercely as she could across the city wall, but the enemy soldiers had eventually overwhelmed her, Kaius, and the others. Her old wounds were protesting from so much exertion.

Even so, that pain was nothing compared to the agony gripping her heart. Every time she blinked, she saw the soldier's blade tearing through her sister's back. Matthias was still raging at Cassia's death; she'd lost sight of him, but she could hear him shouting over the clashing steel. She didn't dare look over to see if he, Kaius, and Ino had managed to gain the upper hand against their captors. All her attention was trained on Nicholas. One slip, and she would die. He was stronger and taller than she, but luckily, she was faster—an advantage made greater by the fact that he wore heavy plate mail and she only chainmail.

She pushed hard against his sword, her arms shaking with the effort. The flicker of pain that flashed across his face sent a small surge of satisfaction through her. His shoulder was still healing from the bolt that had struck him at the banquet. She could do this. She just needed to hold him off until Tamriel and the others reached her. She wasn't foolish enough to think she could best him on her own.

Without warning, she ducked below their locked blades and slipped behind him. He turned, but not fast enough. Spying a dagger on the ground, she swiped it up with her left hand and slashed across the back of Nicholas's thigh, right below the edge of the cuisse. She straightened as he let out a howl of pain and frustration. The movement caused the world to tilt beneath her. She tucked the dagger into one of the empty sheaths on her belt—her beautiful Stryker-made daggers had been confiscated by Nicholas's soldiers earlier— and gingerly touched the wound on the side of her head. It wasn't very deep, but it was long, and it was bleeding a *lot*. She would need stitches.

When Nicholas started limping toward her, she climbed onto the wall of the fountain, searching for Tamriel or Faye or Kaius—anyone who could help her defeat Nicholas.

"I should have killed you when I had the chance," Nicholas snarled, one hand pressed to the gash in the back of his leg. "I wanted to see the look on Tamriel's face as he watched you die. I won't make the same mistake again."

"I don't intend to give you the opportunity." Her voice came out more steady and sure than she felt. She took a few steps back along the rim of the fountain, being careful to stay out of the range of his sword. If she could lure him up there with her, the Qadar would have a clear shot to take him out. It wasn't the humiliating public execution she had envisioned for him—the execution she would have savored—but all that mattered now was killing him before anyone else she loved died.

She looked for her friends again, her heart pounding. *Please, please, please. Someone, help me.*

Tamriel was still halfway across the Plaza. Enemy soldiers kept swarming him, advancing in such great numbers that they were able to break through the Qadars' defenses and surround him. It was all he could do to keep them from dragging him off Nightstorm's saddle. In between attacks, his eyes met hers, wide and terrified. Then another handful of traitors barreled toward him, and the connection was broken. To Mercy's immense relief, Faye and Kaius appeared out of nowhere and helped Tamriel fight the soldiers off.

To her left, Ino and Matthias were fighting the men who had held them hostage. A few cuts marred their faces and arms, but they kept slashing, striking down enemy soldiers and cutting through the thinning ranks. Mercy's training had paid off; they were holding their own, even while shackled. They occasionally used their chains as weapons, in addition to their swords. As she watched, Ino grabbed hold of his chain and swung it into Rhiannon's face, shattering her nose. She let out a cry and dropped her sword, her hands flying up to her broken nose. Matthias seized the opportunity to slash her throat.

Mercy took another step back as Nicholas approached the fountain's wall. She lifted her sword, her arms shaking, and prepared to fend off another attack. Out of the corner of her eye, she saw Duomnodera and the Qadar take aim. *A little farther.* He needed to be fully atop the fountain's rim, in plain sight of the Qadar.

"Uncle!" shouted a voice from somewhere to her right. "End this madness now!"

Nicholas paused. Mercy cursed silently as he set his foot back on the ground and turned toward the source of the outburst. A group of soldiers in Rivosi armor were fighting their way through the enemy ranks. Mercy frowned, puzzled. Most of King Domhnall's troops had remained on the battlefield with the remainder of Nicholas's army.

Understanding dawned when she spotted the two people in the Rivosans' midst, clad in suits of mismatched armor. One was a woman with beautiful dark skin. The other, taller one—

"Percival?" Mercy gasped. Her eyes dropped to the bloody sword in his hand. After his pitiful attempt to kill Nicholas upon their return to Sandori, she had never expected to see him wielding a sword again. She wouldn't have trusted him not to somehow impale himself with it. For once, Mercy was glad to be wrong. She'd never been happier to see Tamriel's old friend.

Nicholas's lip curled. "Nephew. How kind of you to join us."

Percival pushed through the fighting soldiers until he was facing his uncle, just out of reach of his blade. The dark-skinned woman—Riona Nevis, Mercy realized—stood beside him, glaring at the traitor. "You're going to get everyone killed!" Percival yelled. "Do you not see that you've already lost? Lay down your sword and accept defeat!"

"The battle will be over when Tamriel is dead. And look— here he comes."

Tamriel had broken free of the enemy soldiers and was now riding Nightstorm at a gallop through the chaos. Blood dripped from his sword, and murderous fury burned in his eyes as he glared at Nicholas. He looked absolutely terrifying, bearing down on them so fast, slashing aside or riding down the soldiers who tried to block his path.

While Nicholas's back was to her, Mercy slashed out with her sword. Percival moved at the same time. His strike was clumsy, slow and uncertain, but it distracted Nicholas enough for Mercy to carve a deep gash in his arm. Nicholas whirled with a hiss of pain, switching his sword to his other hand, and lunged at his nephew and Riona.

"I did this for our family, you fool," Nicholas snarled, easily dodging the arc of Percival's sword.

"No, you did this for *you*. You, and your massive ego."

Riona danced on the balls of her feet at Percival's side, glancing uneasily between Percival, Nicholas, and her guards. When the opportunity presented itself, she took a few swings at Nicholas, but it was obvious by her stance and grip on her sword that she had only a fundamental knowledge of how to wield it. Still, Mercy had to admire her courage. She and her guards could have fled the city and returned to Rivosa. Instead, they had remained to fight for the true king of Beltharos. Riona glanced at her guards, searching for support. The Rivosans who had accompanied her were all engaged in combat, trying to keep the enemy soldiers from rushing to Nicholas's aid.

Mercy jumped down from the fountain's wall and drew the dagger from the sheath at her hip. Her vision grew fuzzy around the edges, but she ignored it as she stalked toward Nicholas. Tamriel was almost upon them. He deserved this kill, but that didn't mean she couldn't make Nicholas suffer until Tamriel arrived.

While his attention was locked on Percival and Riona, Mercy flipped her dagger's grip, lunged, and buried the blade into Nicholas's side, just below the edge of his breastplate. He howled in pain as blood poured from the wound. He swung his injured arm back and hit Mercy with his gauntlet so hard she saw stars. She released the dagger still buried in Nicholas's side and staggered back, blinking hard in an attempt to clear her vision. Another wave of blood leaked out of the cut on her head and trickled down her ear.

"You bitch," Nicholas snarled at her, slashing again at his

nephew. When Percival stumbled backward into Riona, narrowly avoiding a deep gash across his gut, Nicholas turned on her. He advanced quickly in spite of the injury to the back of his leg. Crossbow bolts flew through the air, but none got close enough to hit Nicholas. Duomnodera and the others must have been worried about hitting Mercy, Percival, and Riona. She wished she could order them to just take the shot, but even if they could hear her over the fighting, they wouldn't disobey Tamriel. She wanted to scream, to shake Tamriel. Any one of them would give his or her life to restore his throne. He *had* to win the battle.

"The Guild's greatest Assassin," Nicholas sneered, taking one step forward for every step she retreated. "All those rumors, all those stories about Illynor's ruthless elf, and look at you—barely able to stand on your own. You may be skilled at striking from the shadows, killing innocents, but you're nothing compared to a true warrior. It's pitiful. Still, I must commend your—"

Steel crunched, and his eyes widened when he looked down at the crossbow bolt protruding from his chest, just above his heart. It had punched straight through his breastplate. His expression contorted in shock and disbelief as he gingerly touched the blood-slick point of the bolt. Mercy lowered her sword and looked over his shoulder. Only one person she knew had a crossbow strong enough to break through steel.

Sure enough, Celeste and Calum were standing on the opposite side of the fountain, the massive limb of the weapon obscuring the elf's face. Celeste shoved it into Calum's hands and dashed along the fountain's wall as Nicholas fell to his knees, a low moan escaping him.

Percival let out a sharp breath when he saw her. "Celeste! By the Creator, you're alive!"

"I am, and the others are, too. All thanks to you. But you

don't look well at all." She jumped off the fountain and started toward him, then spotted Riona at his side and stopped mid-step. A flicker of emotion flashed across her face, but she blinked it away. "Are you hurt?"

"I'll be fine," he said, a stubborn set to his jaw.

Mercy doubted it, but his tone made it clear he would hear no argument. Now that she had a chance to really look at Percival, she realized his skin was pale and slick with sweat. His eyes glimmered with fever. *What in the Creator's name happened to him since Celeste fled the capital?* Despite whatever ailed him, he stood tall, staring down at his uncle with hatred plain on his face.

"You...missed...my heart," Nicholas grunted through gritted teeth. He tried to push to his feet, but swayed and dropped forward, bracing himself with a hand on the blood-slick ground. His other hand went to the wound in his chest in a vain attempt to stanch the bleeding.

Mercy walked up to him, ripped the dagger from his side, and leveled the blade at his throat. "She hit you exactly where she intended," she said as Tamriel broke through the last line of soldiers and dropped from Nightstorm's saddle. His heavy boots splashed through puddles of blood as he stormed toward the man who had stolen his throne. "It's time you faced the king's wrath."

57

PERCIVAL

Percival watched, breathing hard, as Tamriel marched up to Nicholas. Now that the adrenaline of the fight had begun to fade, he could barely manage to stay standing. A headache pounded behind his eyes. Shivers wracked his body. He was fairly certain the wound in his arm had ripped open during the battle. At this rate, it was never going to heal properly. He'd be lucky if he retained full use of his arm. Even so, standing here, witnessing his uncle kneeling before the king he had betrayed, was worth it.

Nicholas sucked in a sharp, pained breath and pushed himself up so he was looking Tamriel in the eye. Blood poured out of the gash in his side and over his breastplate where the bolt had pierced him.

Tamriel glanced at Mercy, holding a dagger to Nicholas's neck. "Are you hurt anywhere besides your head?"

She ran her fingers over the gash in her scalp, shoving bloody hair out of her face. "A few cuts, but nothing that won't heal."

Around them, the battle still raged. No one had yet realized that Nicholas had lost. Riona's guards were still locked in combat with enemy troops, trying to fight their way back to their lady. Calum was standing atop the fountain's wall and shooting crossbow bolts at Nicholas's soldiers. Percival ached to reach for Celeste, to feel her palm in his, but he didn't dare. Under duress or not, he'd married Riona. Still, he could hardly believe that Celeste was here, was *alive*. He'd hoped desperately that she had survived her flight from the capital, but part of him had feared he would never see her again.

Beside him, Riona was scowling down at Nicholas. A rush of gratitude and affection filled him. Few foreigners would go into battle for the king of another land, and yet she had done it without hesitation. He gently tugged the sword out of her shaking hands and slipped it into the sheath at her hip. "Riona," he murmured. "Thank you."

She merely nodded, her striking blue eyes roving over the dead soldiers surrounding them.

Mercy stepped back, sheathing her dagger, and Tamriel angled his sword at Nicholas's throat.

"Ever since your attack," the king said with a sharp, cruel edge to his voice, "I've imagined what it would be like to stand here, before you, and watch you die for your crimes. I trusted you, Nicholas. I made you my general, and you turned my own army against me. You ordered the deaths of my friends, my courtiers, my supporters. You stole my kingdom and sent soldiers to hunt me down." The king's eyes narrowed. "And yet, as much as I would savor the opportunity to bring you to justice and end your miserable existence, your death is not mine to claim."

Percival stared at Tamriel in shock as he turned and proffered his sword, hilt first. "Percival, the honor is yours."

On the ground before him, Nicholas turned his head slowly, a sneer tugging at his mouth. "Him? He's a coward. He doesn't have it in him to kill me."

Mercy grabbed the crossbow bolt in his chest and twisted,

eliciting a roar of agony from Nicholas. Hearing it, the enemy soldiers around them faltered, suddenly realizing that the battle had been lost. Their weapons clattered to the cobblestone as they turned toward their fallen leader. Mercy released the bolt and snarled, "Your nephew has shown more bravery than you ever have, you bastard."

Tamriel stepped closer, still holding out his sword. "Percival..."

His hand twitched, aching to take hold of the weapon. To his left, Celeste moved closer, not quite touching, but offering silent support nonetheless. Every fiber within him desired to grab the sword and plunge it into his uncle's gut. How satisfying it would be to watch the life fade from his uncle's eyes. How utterly right it would feel to listen to him take his last breath knowing his coward of a nephew was the one who had sent him to his grave. After everything Nicholas did to him, it would be a fitting end to his life.

Then his mind drifted back to the dungeon, to the feeling of shoving that broken bottle into the guard's throat, and his stomach twisted. He remembered how horrible it had felt to witness the young man claw helplessly at the hole in his neck, blood spilling over his fingers.

It had been a mistake. An accident. Percival wasn't a murderer.

Nicholas had manipulated him, insulted him, mocked him, and forced him onto a throne—and into a marriage—he didn't want. Nicholas had beaten him. He would have killed Celeste, Hero, Ketojan, and Lethandris to punish Percival for his disobedience. He would have sentenced Percival to be executed if he'd had the chance.

Despite every cruelty and thinly veiled barb, he had not managed to break Percival.

And Percival would not sink to his level now.

He looked at Tamriel and shook his head. "Go ahead, Your Majesty. This moment belongs to you."

Let him claim Nicholas's death, Percival thought. *He deserves it.* Everything he had done was to bring them to this moment. He had prayed every night that Tamriel was alive. He had risked his life time and time again to undermine his uncle's authority. And now, with Nicholas's death, this nightmare would finally be over. For the first time in his life, he would be free.

"I knew you wouldn't be able to do it," Nicholas said, a patronizing chuckle escaping him. He didn't look away from Percival, even as Tamriel approached and angled his sword at his throat. "You're a coward. A gutless fool. You could have been a *king*, and instead you chose to serve this man—this *child*—who will bring about the downfall of our great kingdom. You—"

Tamriel's sword cut through the air, a flash of silver, and blood sprayed as Nicholas's head was severed from his body. Percival forced himself to watch as his uncle's corpse swayed once, then crumpled.

Percival went numb.

He dimly registered Tamriel wiping the blood off his sword, shoving it into his sheath, then turning and wrapping his arms around Mercy. The king's voice carried across the square as he commanded his soldiers to apprehend the remainder of Nicholas's army and send word of their victory across the country. Percival stood there, a faint buzzing filling his ears, as men and women rushed past him in search of healers.

Someone touched his arm. He looked down and found Celeste lingering at his side, her brow creased with worry. He shot a quick glance at Riona—as far as Riona knew, Celeste had been his servant and friend, nothing more—but her eyes were still fixated on the stump where Nicholas's head had been.

A jolt of surprise went through him when he spotted a flash of pale green peeking out from below the neck of Celeste's leather armor. "You're wearing the necklace I gave you."

She reached up and touched the ornate pendant. "I never took it off. Percival, are you alright?"

It was an absurd question, and she knew it. As awful as his uncle had been, he was the only family Percival had ever had. There had been a few moments of joy, of pride, among the darkness of his childhood, and he had clung to those memories as a drowning man clings to his last breath. A small part of him had refused to admit that the man who had once been a father to him was gone. He'd been so desperate for a parent who loved him that he had been willing to endure Nicholas's moods and insults for the slightest hint of affection.

And now...

Now, all his family was gone.

They regrouped at the castle. No one said much on the walk there, save to offer each other a few quiet words of comfort. They were all exhausted, emotionally and physically. The battle was over, but there was much left to be done. The slaves had to be freed, the traitorous soldiers punished, the damage to Sandori and Xilor repaired, the king's council replenished...all while mourning the deaths of those who had fallen in battle.

Mercy let out a cry of relief when she saw Blackfoot grazing near the castle steps, blood-splattered but uninjured. She released Tamriel's hand and ran to her stallion, throwing her arms around his neck. Tamriel grinned at the sound of her laughter, tears of joy slipping through her lashes.

Percival trudged along at the rear of the group, trying to ignore the concerned looks Celeste kept shooting him. She walked beside him, leaving several feet between them. The distance felt like miles, an impassable chasm. How cruel of the Creator to reunite them now, after his marriage to Riona.

When they reached the top of the steps, Percival paused and leaned against the railing, staring out at the city his uncle had nearly destroyed. He heard Mercy and Tamriel pass through the tall double doors and into the castle, but he didn't follow.

Riona stopped and rested a hand on his shoulder. "Do you want to talk about anything?"

He shook his head. "Just need to think."

She hesitated, then nodded and trailed her guards into the great hall.

As soon as the doors swung shut behind them, Percival rested his elbows on the railing and dropped his head into his hands. Because of his uncle's arrogance, stubbornness, and pride, so many people had lost their lives today. So many had been corrupted by the promise of coin or prestige.

"What are you thinking about?"

He jumped. Turning back, he found Celeste standing just beyond the castle doors, frowning at him. He had thought she'd gone inside with the others.

She started toward him. "Please talk to me. I have no idea what happened to you since the banquet, and it's terrifying me. You look like you're about to keel over."

The image of the guard he had killed flashed through his mind again, making his stomach roil. "I just...need some time to sort everything out."

How desperately he wanted to reach out and pull her close, to hold her in his arms and kiss those full, lovely lips.

His hands closed into fists at his sides. He had made Riona a promise that day in the Church. They were friends, nothing more, but he wouldn't break his vow to her...even if it killed him to let Celeste go.

She read his thoughts on his face. Those remarkable eyes, the ones that had captured and captivated him so many times, dropped to her hands. Today, they would exchange no mocking quips, no flirtatious jests. "I wish things could have turned out differently, Percival," she whispered, touching the peridot pendant. Then she turned on her heel and strode into the castle, leaving him alone.

After several minutes, he wandered into the great hall. Riona and her guards stood off to one side, speaking quietly to one another, and Percival tried not to glance at Celeste as he crossed the hall to join them. Mercy's siblings were there, too; they'd been separated in the fighting. Matthias sat in the middle of the floor, Cassia's body cradled in his arms. A slender river of blood wended its way across the tile floor. As Percival approached, Ino knelt beside his younger brother and wrapped an arm around his shoulders, letting Matthias lean against him as he broke down in sobs. Percival's chest constricted at the sight. Ino's expression was haggard, his eyes empty as he stared at some point in the distance. There was a shallow gash in his chest, but he didn't seem to notice. He just kept comforting his brother.

At the rear of the room, Tamriel and Mercy were embracing. The king murmured something in her ear—something Percival was too far away to hear—then she pulled back, wiping the tears from her splotchy face, and nodded. Mercy sank to her knees beside her brothers. Her slender, nimble fingers trembled as she grabbed one end of Cassia's bloodstained scarf, which had started to unravel, and wrapped it the way Cassia had always worn it. When she let out a shuddering, hiccuping sob, Tamriel crouched beside her and pulled her close.

"I'm so sorry for your loss," Percival finally said, his voice low and miserable. He hung his head. "I should have done more to stop my uncle. I should have—"

"He's dead," Mercy interrupted, looking up at him with red-rimmed eyes. "The Creator will see that he suffers for his crimes. His deeds are not your responsibility."

Percival started to argue, but a shout from outside cut him off. They all turned as the doors swung open and a group of people spilled into the great hall. Faye and Kaius were clinging to each other, bloody and battered but alive. They rushed over to Mercy and her siblings as soon as they saw Cassia's body. A Cirisian woman, a young man with Cirisian marking painted on his face, and a middle-aged man in fine armor followed them inside.

Tamriel rose and started toward them. "General Cadriel—"

The general held up a hand. "You must call for the healer. One of your men—"

"Tam!" Calum cried as he and Nerran stumbled inside, Hewlin's arms slung over their shoulders. The older man's face was nearly as gray as his beard. The front of his tunic had been slashed open, and although Nerran had stripped off his shirt and pressed it to the wound, Hewlin's blood had already soaked the fabric. "Tam, we need a healer. Healer Tabris—"

"Is no longer here," Celeste interrupted, already running to meet them. "But I can help. Keep pressure on the wound; don't take that shirt off it or he'll lose too much blood. There's an unused meeting room two halls down from here. Lay him down on the table. You two"—she pointed to a couple of Riona's guards—"go down to the infirmary and get the healer. I'll do what I can until he arrives, but he's going to need to sew the wound. And you," she said, pointing to another guard, "I need you to find Hero, Ketojan, and Lethandris. They're in a healer's tent outside the city, just beyond the battlefield. If they can spare a set of hands, have one of them sent here to help."

At a nod from Riona, they ran off to complete their tasks. Celeste looked back at Percival once before following Calum, Nerran, and Hewlin into the hall. After they disappeared, the Cirisian woman helped Mercy to her feet and pulled her into a tight hug.

"I'm so sorry, Mercy," she said, her voice muffled by Mercy's armor. "I'm so, so sorry. I wish I could have done something to help. Alistair and I barely made it off that battlefield."

Beside them, General Cadriel shot a warning look at the young man—Alistair—then turned to Tamriel. "The remainder of Nicholas Comyn's forces have surrendered and turned over their blades, Your Majesty. Prince Domhnall and his army are holding them outside the city, where they await your judgment."

"Domhnall is here?" Riona gasped. "I hadn't expected His Majesty to send... Never mind. It doesn't matter. I must speak with my cousin and send word of our victory to my king." She bowed to Tamriel and led the remainder of her guards out of the castle.

Cadriel bowed low before Tamriel and Mercy. "It was an honor to fight beside you, Your Majesty. My lady." He frowned sadly at Cassia, still in the cradle of her brother's arms. "We lost family and friends today—and we shall never forget their sacrifices—but allow me to be the first to congratulate you on your victory. The throne of Beltharos belongs, once again, to its rightful ruler."

∻ 58 ⩫
TAMRIEL

Your Majesty, as you have requested, I've begun compiling a list of those who lost their lives in today's battle. Of course, it will take time to gather the names of all the dead, but here I've written those of the people closest to you. May the Creator have mercy on their souls, and may they find peace eternal in the Beyond.

Cassia Mari

Kova Avalynn

Akiva Lawland

Amir Bellmere (of the Strykers; died in the healers' tent from wounds sustained in battle)

Tanni (of the Assassins' Guild)

Wren (of the Assassins' Guild)

If I may speak plainly, Your Majesty, I know you will carry the weight of their deaths for the rest of your life. I hope, however, that this knowledge will ease your burden: they would not have followed you into battle if they did not believe wholeheartedly that you are the king Beltharos needs—and that Mercy is the queen who must rule beside you. It is evident in everything you do that you care for your *people more than any king or commander I have served, and it has been my privilege to fight for you. I am certain Akiva and the others would say the same.*

Your faithful guard and friend,
Atlas LeClair

❦ 59 ❦
MERCY

Cassia's death had not been a dream.

By the Creator, how she had prayed it was a dream.

A heavy weight rested on her chest as she stared up at the ceiling of the king's bedchamber, exhausted after a restless night. Her fists curled around the silk sheets, and she tried to focus on the sunlight slanting in through the windows as she fought the sob building in her throat. Cassia was dead. Mercy never should have let her siblings follow her onto the city wall. She should have spotted the soldiers rushing onto the battlements sooner, should have placed herself between them, should have found a way to get them back down the ladders or into the city. If she had, Cassia would still be alive.

Liselle. Dayna. Adriel. Mistress Sorin. Cassia.

How many more people could she bear to lose? How many more pieces of her heart could be torn away before there was nothing left?

After the battle, her injuries had been tended by Healer Tabris—who, after hearing the news of Tamriel's victory, had left hiding and rushed straight to the castle—and then she and Tamriel had retreated to the king's chambers. They'd barely had enough energy to strip off their bloody armor, change into a fresh set of clothes, and collapse onto the bed. Mercy had expected to fall asleep in seconds. She would have welcomed the reprieve from her grief. Instead, the moment Tamriel's arms had wrapped around her, she had broken down. She had cried until she fell asleep, and he had held her the entire time, occasionally whispering in her ear or kissing her tears away.

Now, she lay on the down mattress alone. She ran a hand across Tamriel's side of the bed and found a note on his pillow, scrawled in his familiar hand. There were matters of state to which he had to attend, he'd written, and she was welcome to send for him should she desire his presence.

A faint, teary smile spread across her lips. She didn't doubt that he would drop everything to rush to her side, but she wouldn't be so selfish as to drag him away from his duties. They had known how much they stood to lose when they decided to go to war with Nicholas. They had lost family and friends in the battle, but it was time to be strong for their kingdom. Grieving had to wait.

So she would be strong—for Cassia, for her parents, for Liselle...for everyone who had sacrificed themselves so she and Tamriel could live.

Mercy rose slowly, grimacing at the pain that shot through her skull, and dressed in a lightweight tunic and pants she found in the wardrobe across the room. She was fairly certain they belonged to either Tamriel or Percival, but she didn't care. They fit, and they weren't soaked in blood, unlike the pile of armor and clothes still crumpled in the corner of the room. Their coppery stench made her sick to her stomach.

In the sitting room, she found a platter of cheese and

meat, a bowl of fruit, and a pot of cold tea. Despite her lack of appetite, she forced herself to eat until the throbbing in her head lessened. How long had it been since she last ate? Twenty hours? More? The cooks had promised to send food to their room yesterday, but she and Tamriel had fallen asleep before the servants bearing their meal had arrived.

Atlas and Julien were waiting for her outside the king's chambers, dressed in the lightweight leather armor the royal guards favored when patrolling the castle grounds. Julien's eyes widened when he saw the thick layers of bandages wrapped around her head, but he merely offered her his arm —which she declined—before he and Atlas led her down the stairs and through the great hall. On the way, they passed several rooms that had been repurposed into makeshift infirmaries for the injured soldiers. In one, Hero and Ketojan were working side by side in perfect sync, as comfortable tending soldiers as they had been nursing sick elves in Beggars' End. The knowledge that they had survived the battle sent a wave of relief through Mercy. She wasn't as close with them as Tamriel, but even so, she'd come to care a great deal for them.

As they approached the throne room, Mercy studied the portraits of past Myrellis rulers. The place where the painting of Ghyslain and Elisora had once hung was still empty, but it wouldn't be for long. Beside it spanned several yards of empty wall. Soon, a painting of her and Tamriel would hang there— and one day, portraits of their children and grandchildren would follow. The hope that accompanied that thought made her steps a little lighter.

They passed through the double doors, and Mercy smiled when she saw Tamriel sitting on the throne, his father's—now *his*—diadem nestled among his curls. This was where he belonged. This was where he should have been since they returned from the Guild. This was the strong, confident king she had imagined he would one day become...only now, a smaller, yet no less ornate, throne sat beside his.

A small crowd surrounded the dais: the High Priestess, General Cadriel, Prince Domhnall, several commanders from the Beltharan, Feyndaran, and Rivosi armies, and the few remaining members of the king's council. Seren Pierce and Nerida, along with Arabelle and the other apprentices, would be arriving before the week's end to oversee the city's repairs. Faye, Kaius, and the rest of Mercy's friends lingered on the edge of the crowd. It was a shock to see them wearing finery again; for so long, they'd been limited to armor and the few clothes they had gathered during their journey. With them were Nynev and Alistair, as well as several runaway slaves and Cirisians from the troops Kaius and Nynev had gathered.

Tamriel was so absorbed in his discussion with the council members, at first he didn't notice her approach. As she and the guards neared the edge of the crowd, Faye turned and grasped Mercy's hands. "How are you doing?"

Mercy shook her head and searched the room for her brothers. When she saw them, her heart broke. They were standing together against the far wall, their eyes downcast, their expressions more devastated than she'd ever seen. For so long, the only family Ino, Matthias, and Cassia had had were each other.

"I'm here for you," Faye whispered. She released Mercy's hands and pulled her into a tight hug. "We'll make it through this, I promise. You and me—always. Remember?"

Mercy nodded, remembering the night she had learned of the death of Faye's brother. She had said almost the exact same thing to Faye then, and she had meant it. They were sisters in every way except blood. They'd been through a lot over the past several months, but every hardship and every fight had made them into the people they were today.

When she stepped back, she realized silence had fallen

over the throne room. The council members parted before Tamriel as he walked to her, a small smile gracing his lips. "I was hoping you would show up," he said when he reached her. He took her hand, stepped close, and whispered, "I've been waiting for you. It's time I fulfilled a promise I made long ago."

He led her to the dais, toward the two thrones. "I know you're not technically queen yet, but I don't care. I want you at my side when I address the court. This victory was as much your doing as mine." They climbed the steps, and he nodded to the smaller of the two thrones, waiting for her to claim it as her own. "My father had this made for my mother when she became queen. I had Atlas and Julien retrieve it from storage for you."

Her heart swelled as she took her seat before the court, and Tamriel settled on the throne beside hers. Their joined hands hung between them. With his other hand, Tamriel reached into an inner pocket of his jacket and pulled out a scroll. He searched the sea of faces until he found his cousin. Calum met his gaze with a wide, proud grin.

"After Nicholas Comyn's betrayal, I was left without a throne, without a crown, and without an army," Tamriel began, his voice carrying through the massive room. "I had nothing, save for the people who stood by my side. Together, we traveled across the kingdom, spreading the word that we were gathering an army and that we would accept any slave willing to join us in battle. I did not ask that they forgive the crimes that have been committed against their people for generations. I did not ask them to fight for me because I was the rightful king. All I asked was for them to trust me. If they fought for me, I swore, my first deed as king would be to release them from the bonds of slavery."

The courtiers gaped at Tamriel in disbelief. A few—just a

few—glanced away and smiled. Pride bloomed within Mercy's chest as she looked past the nobles and spotted her friends' joyful expressions. Nynev's eyes were bright with excitement. Kaius and Faye had joined the Cirisians at the edge of the crowd, and Faye was nodding along as Kaius translated for the elves who didn't speak the common tongue. He couldn't seem to stop grinning. Percival, who was standing with Riona and her guards, beamed up at Tamriel. Mercy was surprised he had managed to attend; he still looked a little faint from the infection in his wounded arm.

Mercy found her brothers among the elves, delighted to find that the excitement had temporarily drawn them out of their grief. They regarded her and her king with equal parts sorrow and pride. She knew what they were thinking—the same thing had been running through her mind since Tamriel began to speak:

Cassia should be here. She should be sharing this victory.

As soon as she thought it, a soft, familiar voice whispered in her mind, *I am.*

Her jaw dropped. *Cassia?* Across the room, her brothers gaped at her. Had they heard Cassia, too?

I'm here, sister. A gentle, invisible hand brushed across her cheek, and Mercy leaned into her sister's touch. When she spoke again, the words were faint, barely discernible: *I'm so proud of you. Thank Tamriel for me.*

Mercy's heart clenched as Cassia's voice faded. She bit her lip to keep the tears welling in her eyes from falling. The last thing she needed right now was to fall apart in front of her future subjects.

"I have had the privilege of knowing some extraordinary people," Tamriel continued, raising his voice to be heard over the murmurs rising from the nobles. "They fought for the slaves' freedom until their dying breaths. Although Liselle and Cassia Mari did not live to see their efforts come to fruition, their courage and selflessness will never be forgotten." He looked over at Mercy and grinned. "As king of Beltharos, it is my duty and honor to declare that from this day forth, every person held as a slave within this country is now and forever free."

60
FAYE

Tamriel opened the scroll and tried to elaborate, but a cacophony of shouts cut him off. Nynev and the others let out loud cheers, whooping and laughing and hugging each other. Tears of joy trailed down the cheeks of the runaway slaves. Faye grinned at Kaius, amused by his efforts to hide the triumph on his face from the courtiers.

At the front of the room, the courtiers began speaking over one another, arguing and demanding an explanation. Faye noticed Tamriel's grip on Mercy's hand tighten, but his charming, confident smile didn't falter as he and Mercy attempted to calm the nobles.

"I know it will take time to implement this change, but it is for the good of every person in this kingdom that—"

"As the king of Beltharos, his word is law. The city guards, as well as the Beltharan army, will consider anyone who breaks this law in open rebellion of the crown, and—"

Their words were quickly lost in the chaos. Faye reached under the hem of her tunic for the small dagger she had tucked into her waistband that morning. She tensed for a fight, fearing that the nobles would soon abandon their objections in favor of violence, but a hand on her arm stilled her.

"Wait," Kaius said. "This is their battle, not ours. They were well aware how the nobles would react to hearing this news, and they must learn to navigate the court on their own if they are to rule. They will face many more challenges in the years to come."

Faye followed his eyes to the dais. Atlas, Julien, and several of Riona's guards had formed a line in front of the steps, their hands on the grips of their swords as they regarded the nobles with wary looks. It should have offered Faye some comfort that they were armed while the nobles were not, but at this moment, all she could think about was the horrible way Ghyslain's council members had slaughtered Liselle. The drawing of Liselle's desiccated corpse filled her mind, but this time, it was Mercy hanging from the castle gates.

"Trust me, Faye," Kaius said, raising his voice to be heard over the cheers of the elves surrounding them. "I promised Tamriel that my archers and I would aid him in abolishing slavery from his kingdom—we will stand by his side the moment he calls on us—but he and Mercy made a decision long ago to stand together against the court. Today, they're daring to do something of which Ghyslain and Liselle could only dream. They will weather this storm, and all the ones that come after it, as they have so many times before."

He's right. Slowly, reluctantly, Faye released her grip on the dagger. Over the past few months, Mercy and Tamriel had been through so much pain and heartache, yet they'd managed to endure it all. They had survived betrayals, Assassins, plague, and war. And now, they were going into battle again, for the good of their kingdom. Faye had no doubt they would emerge victorious.

She turned to Kaius, and his smile grew as she slipped her

arms around him. "They did it. They really, truly did it."

"*We* did it, my love." He reached up to tuck a strand of hair behind her ear, letting his fingertips lightly trail down her cheek. "I always knew you were strong enough to overcome the terrors plaguing you, my brave, beautiful warrior."

His words caused a memory to surface—one she'd been trying desperately to forget. "I saw you—during the battle... dead. I mean, I thought it was you, and I... I panicked. More than panicked. I froze," she stammered, the horror of those few excruciating minutes flooding her. "I thought all my fears over the past several weeks had come true. I thought... I thought I'd lost you."

"Lost me? I told you before, you have too little faith in my skills." He kissed her, then added, "Besides, I never could have deprived you of the pleasure of my company."

She snorted. "You've been spending too much time with Calum. You're starting to sound like him."

"Oh, by the gods— Forget I said anything."

He let go of her, and Faye laughed at the disgust on his face. Despite both being dedicated to restoring Tamriel's throne, Calum and Kaius had never mended the rift that had grown between them in the Islands so many months ago. For Tamriel and Mercy's sake, they'd gotten along as well as could be expected during their journey, but Faye suspected their mutual dislike would never disappear completely. Too much bad blood lay between them.

She started to respond, but was distracted when several nobles brushed past her and walked toward the door, grumbling. At the front of the room, Atlas and the other guards relaxed, letting their hands drift from their swords. Tamriel and Mercy grinned at each other. A shadow of grief still hung behind their eyes, but for now, they'd fulfilled their promise to Cassia, declared slavery illegal, and braved the court as king and soon-to-be-queen for the first time.

Once the last of the council members had left, the High Priestess stepped forward and asked permission to approach the king. At a nod from Tamriel, the guards moved aside to allow her to pass. Faye watched as she climbed the steps, exchanged a few quiet words with Tamriel and Mercy, then dropped into a low bow before them.

"Please, Your Majesty, I beg your forgiveness for crowning another in your stead," she said softly. "I wanted to deny Nicholas Comyn control of the kingdom—I told him that you were the rightful king of Beltharos until he could prove that you had passed into the Beyond—but I could not endanger my priestesses by drawing his ire. Still, I did what I could... I refused to give Percival Comyn and his wife the blessing of the Creator when I performed their coronations. They may have sat on the throne, but they were never true monarchs."

"Rise, High Priestess," Tamriel responded. "Percival already told me how you defied his uncle. You did what was necessary to protect your priestesses. There is nothing to forgive."

She thanked him and bowed once more before leaving the room. As soon as she disappeared through the double doors, Riona—who had been standing near the far wall, a thoughtful expression on her face—glanced at Percival before hurrying after the High Priestess. Percival, deep in conversation with Calum and Prince Domhnall, didn't appear to notice his wife's departure.

Faye scanned the jubilant faces around her. At the front of the room, Mercy and Tamriel descended from the dais to join their friends in celebrating the day's victory. The Cirisians and runaway slaves encircled them immediately, cheering and lavishing praise upon the king and his future bride. Mercy let out a startled laugh as Matthias scooped her up in a tight hug. Ino bowed to Tamriel, smiling through his sorrow.

Faye turned back to Kaius, who was watching the entire scene with pride shining in his beautiful green eyes. "My people are finally free," he breathed, as if the full impact of Tamriel's pronouncement hadn't truly hit him until that moment. "Part of me thought I'd never live to see this day. There will be so much work to do... Thousands of elves left without homes, without money or jobs, but...they're finally free.

"However, now that I am a First, I must return to Cirisor and help rebuild the clans. I have no doubt that elves will flock to the Islands once they learn that they have been freed, and I must be there to welcome them, as Firesse and her clan did for me when I first arrived." He faltered then, fear flashing across his face. "After everything Firesse did...I will understand if you do not wish to return with me. It would pain me greatly to be away from you, but if you wish to remain here with Mercy, or in Fallmond with your family, I will visit when I can."

Love for him rushed through her. Even now, after everything they'd been through, he was still trying to protect her. She linked her hands behind his head and pulled him into a kiss. "Where you go," she whispered against his lips, "I go."

He leaned back, just a few inches, and searched her gaze. "Are you sure? Your family—"

"I will visit them, but my father was correct when he said I don't belong on that small farm any longer. It's not my home, and it hasn't been for a long time." She looked toward her friends. "And Mercy... She's my best friend, my sister, but she doesn't need me to protect her anymore. I can do more for her and Tamriel by helping you and the other elves rebuild the Islands."

He beamed at her. "I can think of no one I'd rather have by my side."

61
PERCIVAL

Hours later, Percival was a few feet from his room in the guest wing when he heard the squeal of iron hinges behind him. He turned just as Riona stepped into the hall, dressed in a silk gown with her long braids hanging loose around her face, devoid of their usual gold beads. Strangely, her only piece of jewelry was the eudorite pendant she never took off. No gold, no lace, no priceless gemstones... The effect was startling. He had never seen her look so...unadorned.

"Where did you go earlier?" he asked. "I turned around to speak with someone, and when I turned back, you were gone. And why are you dressed like that?"

"I needed to speak with the High Priestess about us—our...situation. Will you come in?"

As he followed her into her bedchamber, he noted the lack of guards posted outside her door. Even with Nicholas dead, he was surprised that her guards would leave her unattended.

"They're loading my belongings into a carriage," she said, catching his confused expression, and that was when he noticed the chests stacked against the far wall. One of the wardrobe's doors hung open, and he glimpsed an array of bright, shimmering fabrics within. "Simple clothes make for easier traveling, and they keep one from being targeted by highwaymen. My cousin, Prince Domhnall, thinks it would be best if I return to Rivosa. Now that King Tamriel once again has control of his kingdom, I have no real purpose here. That's why I wanted to talk to you."

She sank onto the couch and gestured for him to join her. Once he was settled, she turned to face him, her striking blue eyes pinning him in place. "Neither of us was happy about being forced into this marriage, but we've grown close these past few weeks, and I consider it a privilege to call you a friend. Now, I must know plainly: is there a possibility of our relationship becoming anything more than platonic? Can you imagine yourself falling in love with me?"

Percival opened his mouth, faltered, and closed it. How in the Creator's name could he answer those questions after all she'd done for him? She hadn't asked to be sent here, manipulated into a forced marriage, and turned into a tyrant's puppet. She had risked her life for him and his people, despite being a stranger in a foreign kingdom. Now, whether they liked it or not, they were bound by their vows. And yet he couldn't bring himself to lie to her.

"I do not doubt that you would have been a wonderful wife and queen," he confessed, the words coming out in a rush, "but I won't lie to you. I love someone else. I didn't mean for it to happen—I tried to fight it, to ignore it—but I fell in love with her nonetheless. And I need you to know we never did anything. Nothing happened between us, I swear it."

Her only reaction was a slight pursing of her full lips. No shouting. No shock. No anger. When she finally spoke, all she said was, "It's Celeste, isn't it?"

Simply hearing her name sent a dagger through Percival's heart. "How long have you known?"

"I've suspected it for a while. Your face lit up every time she walked into the room, even if she never so much as glanced your way. At first, I thought it was just a passing fancy, but I realized how wrong I was at our wedding banquet. You risked everything to save her life. It wasn't difficult to see then how much she meant to you."

"I would have risked everything for you, as well," he responded, thinking back to the day he had escaped from his cell. Once the blackness had begun to creep into his vision, he had been certain he was going to fall unconscious. He hadn't expected to wake up, but it hadn't mattered, because he had known that Riona was safe and free.

A small smile tugged at Riona's lips. "Your uncle was wrong about you, Percival. You're a good, kind, selfless man." She looked away then, one hand rising to touch her mother's eudorite pendant. "That's why I left the throne room early to speak with the High Priestess. We discussed the wedding, and I persuaded her to annul our marriage—if you agree, of course. She said because our vows were exchanged under duress, and never consummated, our marriage is not binding in the eyes of the Creator. After she issues the proper documents, you and I will each be free."

For a few heartbeats, he was so stunned he didn't know how to respond. "You... You did that for me?"

"Of course I did. Even if she had not agreed to annul the marriage, I would not have held you to your vow. You deserve to be with the woman you love." Her fingers tightened around the pendant. "I will be departing for Innislee tomorrow, but before I leave, I want you to know... I understand why you said you cannot love me. However, if things had turned out differently—if we had remained on the thrones...I do not think I could have said the same."

It took him far longer than it should have to decipher her meaning. When he finally understood, he gaped at her, but she barreled on before he could attempt to string together a reply. "When my guards return, I will have one of them send word of our decision to the High Priestess. She will issue the proper documents for the Church's records and send copies to you—here—and to me in Innislee. In the morning, I will leave for Rhenys and continue to Rivosa after I collect Lord Winslow."

"You're not going to stay for the wedding?"

She shook her head. "Prince Domhnall will remain here with the army while his soldiers are being tended by the healers, but I have duties to attend in my king's court. Not to mention, I've missed my home and my family. It'll be good to see them again. Someday, I would like you and Celeste to visit my home in Innislee."

"We would be honored to." Percival rose and started toward the door, then paused and turned back. "Riona," he said softly, "do you love me?"

At first, she didn't say anything. She simply crossed the room and stopped before him, her eyes searching his face, her smile laced with sorrow.

Then she stepped forward, rose onto her toes, and kissed his cheek. "Last I heard, Celeste was working in the infirmary with Hero and Ketojan. You should go to her."

Percival's thoughts were still a jumble as he walked down the hall toward the makeshift infirmaries. The soldiers with the gravest wounds had been brought to the castle, and Percival could hear their cries of pain through the closed doors he passed.

Unconsciously, his hand drifted to the wound in his arm.

The entire time the healer had been cleaning, stitching, and bandaging it, he hadn't been able to bring himself to look at it. The stench of the infection, coupled with the lingering shock of witnessing his uncle's death, had turned his stomach. The healer who had tended to him had chastised him for fighting, warning him that it was unlikely the damage he had wrought on the muscle would ever completely be repaired, but Percival had brushed the man's words off. He had already assumed as much. When he responded that he would have fought for his king even if he had lost the entire arm, the healer had merely muttered something about him being headstrong—although his tone implied he would have rather said *foolish*. Then he had handed Percival a jar of a strong, herbal ointment, instructed him to keep the wound clean, and moved on to his next patient.

Percival wandered down two more halls before he found the room in which Celeste was working. The door was ajar, and he leaned against the frame as he peered into the gap, not wanting to disturb her or the soldiers. Judging by the empty bookshelves lining the room and the desk pushed against the far wall—which was now cluttered with bottles of tonics, poultices, tinctures, jars of dried herbs, rolls of bandages, and various medical equipment—the room had once been a study. Now, though, it was crammed with cots. Hero and Ketojan had helped the royal guards bring them in from the makeshift infirmary in the End after they had run out of furniture in the other rooms of the castle.

Celeste stood in the middle of the room, murmuring comforting words to a soldier as she unraveled the bandage around his arm. She was clad in a simple tunic and pants, seemingly oblivious to the bloodstains splattered across the cotton, and her long hair had been braided and coiled into a bun at the nape of her neck. A few cots away, a healer Percival didn't recognize was tending to a gash in a young man's leg.

The soldier whimpered as the last layer of the bandage fell away, revealing fresh stitches, but Celeste's reassuring smile didn't falter. She continued speaking to him as she opened a stoppered bottle and began gently dabbing medicine onto the wound. The soldier gritted his teeth so hard the tendons stood out in his neck. His hands closed into fists around the lightweight blanket draped over his legs, and he didn't release them until Celeste finished wrapping his arm in fresh bandages.

Watching her work, so calm and confident, Percival marveled again at the miracle that was *her*.

His brazen, shameless, sharp-tongued Celeste.

He entered the room and quietly closed the door behind him. She was so absorbed in her duties that she didn't notice him until he was nearly beside her, carefully picking his way through the crowded room. When she spotted him, she straightened, brushed a stray strand of hair from her face, and offered him a weary smile. Judging by the faint shadows under her eyes, she hadn't slept at all since the battle.

"I want to help," he whispered, trying not to wake the slumbering soldier to his left. "What would you like me to do?"

A healer arrived to relieve them an hour later. Percival wrapped an arm around Celeste's shoulders as they stepped into the hall, and she sagged against him, so tired she didn't object to his sudden proximity. They made it to the end of the hall before he stopped, frowning.

"Where do you live? Do you stay with the rest of the servants here in the castle? I know you're not technically a slave, but..." He shut his mouth before he could start to ramble. "Where do you sleep?"

"I have a small place in Guinevere's Square, near the university, but I haven't been there in weeks. Too much to do. Too much time on the run. Just get me a carriage and I'll find my way."

"Nonsense. You're nearly asleep on your feet. You can stay in my room tonight."

"Your room?" She blinked up at him with a crooked smile, a faint glimmer of mischief dancing in her tired eyes. "At least buy me dinner first."

He laughed, then responded, "I have lots of work to do now that half the council is dead. I doubt I'll be sleeping tonight."

"Still, what will your *wife* think?" she asked, the word coming out low and bitter. "I doubt Riona would care for my sleeping in her husband's room. People talk, you know."

He shook his head. "She's not going to be my wife for much longer. She spoke to the High Priestess and convinced her to annul our marriage."

"You're...not going to be married any longer?"

He nodded.

A smile spread across her lips, and she slipped an arm around his waist. "Good. That's...good."

Neither of them spoke the rest of the way to the guest wing. When they reached his room, he guided Celeste to the bed before crossing the room and closing the door. "If you'd like to change, feel free to take anything from the wardrobe. I'll find a servant and have some food sent from the kitchens."

"Thank you."

When he returned ten minutes later, he expected to find her asleep. Instead, she was perched on the edge of the mattress, her hair hanging in loose waves to her waist. She wore nothing but a long sleep-shirt that reached to the middle of her thighs. His eyes dropped to her bare legs, and he became painfully aware that she was in *his* room, sitting on *his* bed, wearing *his* clothes. He had slept in the sitting room of the king's chambers with her before, of course, but that had been when the possibility of them having a future was nothing more than a desperate, impossible dream. Now, it was all he could think about.

His heart hammered in his chest. By some miracle, Celeste didn't notice him staring. She was too distracted studying the peridot necklace in her hands.

After a few moments, she looked up at him. "When you gave this to me, you told me that in another life, I would be the one standing on that altar with you. Did you really mean that?"

Percival had to bite back a laugh. Did she really have to ask? Could she not see the truth every time he looked at her? He crossed the room and took her hand, closing their fingers around the pendant. "I meant it with all my heart," he said softly, "but I never thought I would have the chance to do this."

He leaned down and kissed her. She let out a soft, surprised sound, then reached up and cupped his face with her free hand. The feel of her lips on his, the taste of her sharp, wicked tongue, stole his breath away. *She* was the woman he loved. *She* was the woman he should have married.

Celeste broke the kiss and leaned back, just enough for her unusual eyes to captivate him for the thousandth time. Exhaustion still lingered in their depths, but there was something more—something he had glimpsed before. He hadn't allowed himself to hope it was anything more than a figment of his imagination.

"I love you, Percival Comyn," she whispered, offering him a grin that made his heart stutter. "I don't believe I've ever had the chance to tell you."

"No, I don't believe you have." He kissed her once more,

then tugged the necklace out of her hand and set it on the bedside table. "You should rest now. I have a feeling you will be needed in the infirmary soon. And since when do you know how to heal?"

"I'm full of surprises."

He grinned. "That you are." At a nudge from him, she slipped under the silk sheets, her eyelids fluttering shut as soon as her head hit the pillow. He sat on the edge of the bed beside her and brushed the hair from her face. "I must go back to work. There is much yet to be done, but once Tamriel and Mercy are firmly in control of the kingdom, I'll have to return to my family's estate in Westwater. Will you... Will you come with me?"

She cracked one eye open and smiled at him. "Are you joking? You couldn't make it a day without me."

⚜ 62 ⚜
MERCY

When Mercy arrived at the council chamber early the next morning, she found Tamriel sitting alone at the head of the large table, rubbing his eyes with the heels of his palms. Countless papers and reports were scattered before him. At the sound of the doors swinging shut, he leaned back with a long, weary sigh and blinked up at her.

"You look exhausted," she said as she sank into the chair next to him. He immediately grabbed her hand and laced his fingers through hers.

"Why, thank you for that. You look beautiful, as always."

"I *meant* that you should have woken me. I would've helped you with some of this. Soon enough, it'll be my kingdom, too."

"I know—don't think I don't trust you with this, because I do—but I wanted you to get as much sleep as you can. You kept tossing and turning last night. Were you dreaming of Cassia or the Guild?"

"Cassia."

Hearing her sister's voice the other day had left her

rattled, but relieved. It was comforting to know that at least in some way, her sister was here with her, although it didn't make her death any easier to bear. Mercy wished they could have spoken longer. The silence following those few precious seconds had been jarring, like losing Cassia all over again. Mercy had wanted to curse the Creator for mocking her. Why allow Cassia such little time in the In-Between when Liselle had managed to fully materialize several times? Why take yet another family member from her, after she has already lost so much?

Of course, the Creator had not deigned to answer. She should've known better than to think there would be some explanation. If there was anything she had learned over the past several months, it was that the Creator cared little for her.

If he did, he wouldn't have stolen everything from her.

Or...almost everything.

Tamriel squeezed her hand, sensing the dark direction her thoughts had taken. "I know nothing I can say will ease the pain of losing her, but I'm here for you. Matthias and Ino are here for you. Cassia gave her life so we could change this kingdom for the better." When she nodded, unable to speak around the lump building in her throat, he leaned forward and kissed her temple, just below the edge of her bandage. "Do you want to talk about your dream?"

She shook her head. As soon as she had fallen asleep, she'd found herself wandering the castle halls alone, searching in vain for her family. She would catch a glimpse of a slate-gray form—the curve of a shoulder, the flash of a smile—but when she spun, no one was there. Twice, she had spotted a figure at the other end of the hall, but it turned the corner and disappeared from view before she could make out who it was. Each time, she had run after it, begging it to wait... But each time, she had turned the corner and found herself in yet another empty hall.

Alone again.

"I don't want to think about it," she murmured, her heart aching.

Tamriel rose and rested his forehead against hers, being careful not to brush the gash by her temple. They remained in that position, silently comforting each other, until a sharp knock sounded on the council room doors. Tamriel muttered an oath.

"I know we went through all this work to reclaim the kingdom, but do you think it's too late to give it back to Percival?" he asked in a weak attempt at levity. He stood, brushed the wrinkles out of his doublet, and returned to his chair. "Come in."

One by one, the remaining members of the king's council filed into the room. Mercy spotted Edwin Fioni and Porter Anders among them, but she didn't recognize any of the other faces. They were all minor nobles—men and women who had not been staunchly in support of Tamriel or Nicholas. They settled into the seats around the table. Over half of them remained empty.

Over the next few minutes, more people joined them: Percival, Faye, Kaius, Atlas, Julien, Matthias, Ino, Nynev, Alistair, and several commanders from the royal guard and the Beltharan army. Mercy had expected to see Calum, but Faye leaned over and whispered that he was still in the infirmary with Nerran, watching over Hewlin. The leader of the Strykers had lost a lot of blood, and Healer Tabris was still unsure whether he would survive.

The Daughters—Hanna, Nerine, and Theodora—were the last to arrive. They leaned against the wall near the double doors, blades sheathed at their hips, arms, thighs, and probably a dozen other places Mercy couldn't see. A few council members glanced at them uneasily, and Mercy had to fight a smirk. Tamriel had been wise to invite them.

"Thank you for coming," Tamriel began, shuffling the papers in front of him into a neat pile. "First, it is my honor to introduce you all to the new Master of the Guard, Atlas LeClair."

Atlas bowed at the king as the council members applauded politely. A few exchanged wary looks, having no doubt heard the rumors of Atlas being a so-called *Unnatural*, but they were wise enough not to voice any complaints to his face. That, or they'd noticed the large sword hanging in the sheath at his hip and decided it was best not to anger him. At his side, Julien beamed, grinning from ear to ear.

"Atlas has served the guard faithfully for years," Tamriel continued, smiling at his old friend, "and has been a member of my royal guard for the past several months. He has risked his life for me, for my subjects, and for this kingdom. I can think of no one who deserves the post more."

Atlas bowed once more, beaming, before stepping back and resuming his post at the door.

Tamriel looked to Mercy, allowing her to take the floor. She turned toward the council, preparing her words carefully. She was not yet queen, nor did she hold a noble title, so it felt strange to be sitting there, addressing them as if she were their equal. As if she were their *superior*.

"In addition to Atlas's promotion, there has been one more change to the guard: Hanna, Nerine, and Theodora have enlisted and will serve as members of our personal guard."

When she nodded toward the Daughters, one of the council members sputtered, "But they're assassins! Murderers! You would have them serve the very king they attempted to kill?"

Nerine's eyes narrowed.

"It is true they served Illynor," Mercy responded, "but she is dead now, and her Guild is obsolete. They were nothing more than soldiers carrying out their commander's orders. If you wish to see them punished for their past crimes, by that same logic, we should punish every soldier who fought for Nicholas. Would it not be wiser to spend our time and resources on repairing the damage to the city? Would it not be more beneficial to treat this time as a period of healing for the kingdom?"

"Once Illynor was defeated, they surrendered and peacefully turned over their weapons," Faye added. "They have sworn a solemn oath to protect His Majesty and Mercy."

Theodora stepped forward then and dipped her head in respect. "His Majesty offered us mercy when he would have been justified in slaughtering us. We will not betray the trust he has placed in us."

"This is all well and good," another council member interjected, scowling, "but I've come here to learn how you plan to implement the freeing of the slaves. I've invested hundreds of aurums in my slaves. Families all across the kingdom have invested money in their slaves. We *rely* on them. Are we now to lose those investments? Are we not to be compensated for the loss?"

Several of the nobles grumbled, most echoing similar complaints. Percival, Faye, and the others responded, voicing their support for the king's ruling. Mercy was surprised to see Porter Anders and a few of the nobles arguing in favor of the slaves' freedom.

"Foolish decision—"

"Should have happened a long time ago—"

"—bring about the ruin of the kingdom—"

"—an entire industry, a *trade*—"

"People aren't products to be bought and sold."

"I may not agree with His Majesty's decision," Porter

Anders was saying, raising his voice to be heard over the others, "but he is the king, and his word is law—"

Tamriel rose and waited for the council to fall silent. He kept his expression carefully neutral, but Mercy could tell how hard it was for him to remain diplomatic. After two years of risking his life helping slaves escape from the capital, he was impatient to free them. "As I said before, this change will take time to implement. I have already ordered ravens to be sent to each city with the news that the slaves are now free, and dispatched soldiers to ensure that the law is followed. You are certainly welcome to keep the elves on as *staff*, provided that they are paid a fair wage, treated humanely, and are working under a mutual agreement. As for your...*investments*," he said, unable to keep a hint of disgust from slipping into his tone, "I will not insult the elves by placing a price on their freedom; they are people, not property. You have certainly benefitted immeasurably from the work the slaves have done over the years, far beyond your initial payment. I will not hear another word about compensation."

A few council members objected. One started to mutter an insult under his breath, but shut his mouth when Mercy shot him a sharp glare.

Tamriel met her eyes, grim and determined. As he had said, this was only the beginning: they still had to figure out how to house all the elves left homeless, arrange education and apprenticeships, set up a fund to support former slaves until they found jobs or learned trades... It would be a long, uphill battle, but it was one Mercy and Tamriel were more than willing to fight.

"This is folly," someone muttered. Mercy whipped her head around, eyes narrowing, and pinned the council member with a harsh look. He continued whispering to the man sitting on his left, unperturbed. "He's worse than his madman of a father."

Mercy's temper flared. Tamriel's expression didn't change, but she was certain he had heard everything. She started to rise, a barb on her tongue, but Tamriel cut her off before she could speak.

"My father and Liselle worked for years to secure the slaves' freedom," he said, a warning in his voice. "They dared to try and improve the lives of the slaves—to treat them as true citizens of this kingdom—and they were successful until my father's council members, the men who were sworn to serve and support him, murdered Liselle in cold blood. They *butchered* her. They *defiled* her. Is that an appropriate punishment for trying to help the slaves? Were Drake and the other council members justified in what they did?"

He looked to each council member in turn. Porter Anders and several of the men around him met Tamriel's eyes, clearly impressed by the new king. Others stared down at the table —still not happy, but not arguing, either.

"I am not my father," Tamriel continued. "I've learned from his mistakes, and I will not tolerate violence. This kingdom has endured enough destruction, and now is a time for healing. Over the next several months, we will work to ensure that slaves across Beltharos have been released from their chains, that they have homes and jobs, and that they are treated as subjects of this kingdom. With your help, we can ensure that this transition goes as smoothly as possible."

Percival rose and bowed, Matthias and Ino following suit a moment later. "You have my support, Your Majesty."

"And mine."

"And mine."

One by one, Faye, Kaius, and the others stood and pledged their support to Tamriel and Mercy. Porter Anders and several other nobles followed their lead. A few stumbled over the words, their expressions dark, and Mercy made a mental note to keep an eye on them. She caught Hanna's eye and jerked her chin toward the grumbling nobles. Hanna offered a subtle nod, sensing her thoughts.

After several minutes, only two nobles had yet to stand and bow—Edwin Fioni, and a young woman Mercy recognized, but didn't know by name. When all eyes turned to them, they made a point of pushing their chairs away from the table, rising, and striding to the council room doors. Atlas and Julien moved to block their exit, but Tamriel waved them off.

"Fioni and Merrin, I have not dismissed you. Take your seats."

The woman—Merrin—paused, but Edwin merely turned, offered Tamriel a stiff bow, and said, "I will not support this, Your Majesty. It's not right. Elves were meant to serve humans. They are not meant to be our equals."

A few seats down, Nynev snapped, "But we're good enough to fight for you, aren't we? My sister sacrificed herself to save this city. You stand here today because she gave her life for you. She was worth a thousand of you bigots."

"Nynev, control your temper," Tamriel cut in, shooting her a sharp look. When she shut her mouth, anger still burning in her eyes, Tamriel turned back to Fioni and Merrin. "You are free to leave, but know that in doing so, you forfeit your places on this council. Now, more than ever, we must stand united."

Again, Merrin hesitated, glancing at Fioni to gauge his response. He merely shook his head. "I'm sorry, Your Majesty. I cannot support this. It's unnatural. The Creator made elves to serve his Creations, not to be their equals. I cannot be a part of this. I beg your forgiveness."

Tamriel scowled, but nodded. The nobles bowed to Tamriel, but before they reached the doors, the king turned to the former Daughters and said, "Hanna, Nerine, Theodora, escort Fioni and Merrin to their estates and see to it that their slaves are removed from their households. Inform the elves that they are welcome to work and live here in the castle as long as they wish. As for you"—he turned a cold, angry glare on Edwin and the woman—"try to impede them in any way, and you will be stripped of your noble titles. You have openly defied the law, and there is no place for dissenters among my nobility."

Merrin's jaw dropped. For the first time, fear flashed across Edwin's face. He regarded Tamriel as if only now realizing that the young man standing before him was no longer the cold, distant prince he used to know. Hanna and the other Daughters took a step forward, and he scurried into the hall, Merrin close on his heels. The assassins bowed to Tamriel before sauntering out after the nobles.

As soon as the doors swung shut behind them, the king gestured for the rest of the council to be seated. Under the table, out of view of the others, he gripped Mercy's hand tightly. It was the only outward sign of the tension running through his body.

He offered the council members a smile that didn't quite meet his tired eyes—a smile crafted long ago for the court. These past few days had been the hardest on him. Between trying to appease the court, cleaning up after the mess Nicholas had made of the kingdom, dealing with the armies still stationed outside the city, and attending all the other duties required of a king, he'd barely slept.

Mercy worked with him when she could, but at times she felt like more of a hindrance than help. She was still learning about ruling a kingdom, while Tamriel had been born and bred for this life. It was going to take a long time to become confident in leading the country, but she and Tamriel would figure it out together. The first part, the most important part, was uniting the council. The nobles may still be wary of the changes to come, but in securing their support, Tamriel and Mercy had taken the first step to granting the slaves the freedom they deserved.

The freedom they'd *earned*.

"Now that that unpleasantness is over," Tamriel said, leaning forward, "let's get to work."

63
PERCIVAL

After dinner, Percival stood at the top of the stairs that led to the halls below the castle, steeling himself for the scent of dank, earthy air. The stench brought back memories of the time he had spent in the pitch-black dungeon, bleeding, freezing, and starving, waiting to be dragged before the court. He had learned after the battle that his and Riona's trials had been set for the next day. If Tamriel's army had been delayed just one day, they would not have been alive to see his victory.

Riona...

They had exchanged quick goodbyes before the council meeting. After their discussion the day before, there wasn't much left to say—or, rather, there had been *too much* to say. Percival couldn't figure out how to properly express to her how grateful he was for everything she'd done for him. He had tried—by the Creator, he had tried—but she had simply smiled at him, handed him the ring he had placed on her finger at their wedding, and reminded him that they were only saying goodbye for a short time. They would see each other again, she had promised, when he and Celeste one day visited Innislee.

At the mention of Celeste, he had glanced away, still unsure how to discuss her with Riona. After leaving his room the night before, he had worked in the empty council chamber until he'd fallen asleep in the early hours of the morning. By the time he had returned to his room for a change of clothes, Celeste was gone, once again at work in the infirmary with Hero and Ketojan. She had made the bed, tucking the sheets under the mattress so tightly he had almost convinced himself the memory of her lying there was nothing but a dream. Then he had found the note she'd left on the pillowcase, one sentence scrawled across the paper:

I can't wait to go to Westwater with you.

Don't feel guilty, Riona had said before her departure. *After everything your uncle put you through, you deserve to be happy.* Then she had hugged him, climbed into the carriage with her guards, and left. He had stood at the top of the castle steps and watched her carriage clatter along the main road until it passed through the city gates.

Now, Percival forced himself to walk down the stairs, trying to ignore the panic that swept over him when he emerged into the cool, dimly-lit corridor. He trained his eyes straight ahead as he passed the door of the dungeon and continued through several unfamiliar halls. When he arrived at Ghyslain and Liselle's tomb, he found the door ajar. Inside, Tamriel was standing between the two caskets, his hand resting directly over the place where Percival imagined the late king's heart would be.

Tamriel looked up at him, not appearing the least bit annoyed at the interruption. He removed his hand from the casket lid and lowered it to his side. "At first, when I heard you coming, I thought you were Mercy. Then I realized that if you were Mercy, I *wouldn't* have heard you coming," he said with a wan smile. "Did she send you to find me after I didn't show up to dinner?"

"No, but she's the one who told me to look for you here. I hope you don't mind the intrusion. Are you...okay, Your Majesty?"

"Please don't start calling me 'Your Majesty.' Do it in front of the court if you must, but not in private. We're beyond honorifics, my friend." The king cast one more look at his father's casket, then joined Percival in the hall and closed the door behind him. "I just needed some time to think everything through. It feels like I've been moving non-stop since the battle with the Guild. Before that, actually. I don't think I've gotten a full night's rest since I met Mercy—and I doubt I'll get another anytime soon. At least here, it's quiet."

Percival trailed him across the hall and into another room. This one didn't hold a casket, just a settee, a few rows of bookshelves, a desk with various pieces of jewelry, and what looked like several paintings covered in dust cloths. These things had belonged to his mother, Percival realized as he lingered at the threshold, watching the king carefully pick his way toward the paintings. This room didn't hold a body, but it was as much a tomb as the one they had just left.

A sickening thought suddenly occurred to him, and he choked out, "My uncle— The...uh, heads— I was never allowed outside of the city. When you returned, were the heads still...?" He couldn't bring himself to finish the question. The horrible memory of the heads staked above the city gate filled his mind. He would never forget the sight.

Tamriel nodded. "They were still there. I gave some of Nicholas's highest ranking commanders the pleasure of returning them to their bodies." His tone said enough about the state the heads had been in after sitting out in the open for so long. A shudder went down Percival's spine. "If I were as cruel as your uncle, I would've had the heads of the

497

commanders staked there once they finished. Sometimes, I'm tempted. As far as Mercy is concerned, they deserve it... But I'm tired, Percival," he sighed, his shoulders slumping. "I'm tired of fighting. I'm tired of *hating*."

Tamriel dropped onto the settee, sending a cloud of dust into the air. "As it is, they'll be stripped of their rank and sent to work in the mines in Blackhills." He glanced at Percival over his shoulder. "Are you sure you don't want to stay here in the capital? I need a new Bacha now that Cassius is...well..."

Percival took a few steps into the room, trying not to bump into any of the furniture. "You know that I will always support you and Mercy, but I have an estate back in Westwater. There are families there who depend on my forces to protect them from Rivosi raiding parties. I can't just abandon them. Now that I'm the head of my family, the responsibility falls to me."

"I understand. Just know that the offer stands, should you change your mind. I'll have to find someone to fulfill Cassius's role, but you will always be welcome here."

"Thank you, Tamriel."

The king stood and grabbed one of the paintings, gesturing for Percival to follow him. Together, they climbed the stairs to the main floor of the castle and made their way to the hall of portraits just outside the throne room. Tamriel removed the dust cloth and revealed a beautiful painting of King Ghyslain and Queen Elisora. The late king was beaming, looking happier than Percival had ever seen him, and the queen gazed back at him fondly. A shimmering gold gown clung to the queen's rounded belly, heavy with child.

Tamriel hung the painting on the hook still sticking out of the wall, then stepped back to look at it. "I've always loved this painting of them," he breathed, more to himself than to Percival. "When I was younger, I imagined that they had this perfect life, this perfect marriage. I hated Liselle for coming between them, and I hated the Creator for taking my mother from me. I imagine you felt the same way about the deaths of your parents, did you not?"

Percival nodded, remembering his visits to their graves. When he was a child, Nicholas had occasionally taken him to their family plot in Westwater and told him stories about his parents. He used to enjoy those days; he liked to hear about his father's and uncle's childhood adventures. He had laughed at the tales of his father turning into a stuttering fool around the beautiful young woman who later became his wife.

As he grew older, however, and endured more of his uncle's barbed comments and thinly-veiled insults, he began to resent the Creator for stealing his parents from him. He loathed the fact that the Creator had left him in the care of someone so cruel, so manipulative, when he'd once had two parents who loved him.

Eventually, he stopped visiting their graves, but he had never forgotten the stories.

Tamriel studied the portraits surrounding them, full of the solemn faces of Myrellis kings. Then he turned to Percival. "Celeste told me about how you tried to free those slaves."

Shame filled him. "It didn't make a difference. They were caught before they made it to the Islands, and they were whipped because of it. I didn't help them at all."

Tamriel's brows rose, surprise flashing across his face. "Percival, you *tried*. You defied him every chance you had. That's more than most would do in your position."

"Celeste exaggerated."

"Perhaps, but that's only because she adores you. She also told me about your plans to take control of the kingdom if I died. You and Riona were going to outmaneuver Nicholas, turn the court against him. As glad as I am that we all survived the battle, I know the kingdom would have been in very good hands with you as its king. You would have led my people well."

Percival blinked at him, shocked by the praise. Tamriel loved his kingdom almost as much as he loved Mercy. Hearing that he would've trusted Percival to rule in his stead meant more to him than he would have expected. "Thank you. Although I must say, I'm also glad that it didn't come to that. Saves me the headache of having to deal with court politics. I've endured enough to last a lifetime."

"I understand completely. But you know, there is one good thing to come of all this. One bright light amid the death and destruction."

"What?"

A wide grin spread across Tamriel's face. "Now I get to marry the woman I love."

❧ 64 ☙
MERCY

ONE WEEK LATER

Mercy had just finished breakfast when a knock sounded on the door of the king's chamber. Before she could respond, Faye, Celeste, Lethandris, and Nynev spilled into the sitting room, already chattering excitedly over one another. They were each dressed in a beautiful gown, from shimmering silks to embroidered damasks to delicate laces. A handful of servants trailed behind them, a gown draped across one's arms.

"You're getting married today!" Faye sang as she dropped onto the settee beside Mercy and wrapped an arm around her shoulders. "I can't believe it!"

Mercy grinned at her, excitement fluttering in her stomach. They had rushed preparations for the wedding, foregoing a grand ceremony at the Church in favor of a small, intimate affair in the throne room. Mercy couldn't care less about the location, the number of guests, the decorations, or any of the other details the council members had inquired about. All that mattered was that she would finally be marrying her handsome, brave, wonderful Tamriel.

Before the Trial, she never would have imagined that anything like this was possible.

Celeste set several pots of cosmetics on the small table before her and frowned at the faint shadows under Mercy's eyes. "Have you not been sleeping well? I could have given you Ienna oil from the healers' stock."

"Very tactful, Celeste," Lethandris whispered. "That's what every bride wants to hear on their wedding day—that they look tired." Then, to Mercy: "You look lovely."

She waved them off. In truth, she hadn't slept much that night. For the first time, though, it had been anticipation, not nightmares, that had kept her up.

"What does it matter?" Nynev called from the other room. "She and Tamriel certainly aren't sleeping tonight."

"Oh, by the Creator, I do *not* need to think about that right now," Faye retorted. "Time to get ready, Your Soon-To-Be-Queenliness."

While the servants were busy building a fire in the queen's chamber, Celeste applied a light layer of cosmetics, then Faye and the others helped Mercy into her gown. She ran her hands over the smooth silk, admiring the way it slipped between her fingers, and grinned at her reflection in the floor-to-ceiling mirrors. The front of the dress was simple—floor-length and sleeveless, with a modest V neckline—but the back was open to the base of her spine, crisscrossed with fine strands of pearls. The silk was a deep, striking sapphire blue—the same shade as the gem in the ring Tamriel had given her.

"When you described the dress to me, I was afraid it was going to look plain," Faye confessed as she began combing through Mercy's wild curls. She was careful to avoid the gash in the side of Mercy's scalp, which was healing well, but still rather tender. Thankfully, she'd been cleared to remove the bandages two days ago. "But now that I see it on you... It's perfect. You look stunning, Mercy."

"Faye, are those tears in your eyes?" she teased. She turned to look at her best friend, but Faye grabbed her shoulders and forced her to face forward...which would have worked, had the room not been lined with mirrors.

"Don't be ridiculous."

"They are *absolutely* tears," Celeste said.

Faye whirled on her, baring her teeth in a snarl. "I haven't forgotten my Guild training."

Mercy shook her head. "If you're going to kill each other, do it tomorrow."

"They'll still be hungover from the celebration," Nynev called. "Next week may work better."

"I'm not helping them *schedule* it."

"You'll be our queen. Doesn't that make us your responsibility?"

Mercy groaned, but she couldn't fight the smile that broke through. She couldn't seem to stop smiling, even as Nynev and the servants dragged her into the queen's chambers and attacked her hair with metal combs they had heated in the fireplace. Once her hair was stick straight and glossy—courtesy of a lightly perfumed oil the servants applied after they finished their work—Lethandris plaited her hair into a single long braid and coiled it into a bun at the nape of her neck. Faye then tucked pearl- and sapphire-encrusted pins into her hair.

Once they had finished, Faye dismissed the servants. She covered Mercy's eyes and guided her into the sitting room. "Take a look," she whispered, then stepped back so Mercy could see her reflection.

Her breath caught. The gown fit her perfectly, and the deep blue silk complemented her tanned skin and dark hair. Celeste had covered the shadows under her eyes with powder, then swept a shimmering gold pigment across her lids to brighten the hazel flecks in her eyes. She marveled at the transformation. She still looked like herself, but...polished. Beautiful.

Regal.

"You would put Marieve to shame," Faye said, tears once again welling in her eyes.

"You would put *Riona* to shame," Celeste amended.

A few minutes before they had to leave, Mercy strode into the king's bedchamber and returned with one of her Stryker-made daggers. The day of the battle, Nynev had returned to Myrellis Plaza and picked through the bodies until she found the soldier who had confiscated Mercy's daggers. Mercy had let out a decidedly un-Assassin-like squeal when Nynev had presented them to her.

As the others watched, she sat on the settee, lifted the hem of her skirt, and strapped the sheath to her calf. When she stood, the fall of her gown perfectly hid the bulk of the weapon. She shot them a wicked grin as she stepped into the hall. "One can never be too careful."

Matthias, Ino, and Calum were waiting for them outside the throne room, deep in conversation. When they heard Mercy and the others approaching, they turned, brows rising.

Calum whistled. "Love, if you didn't have Tamriel completely under your spell before today..." He shook his head. "Tam's a goner."

"He's going to forget his vows," Matthias agreed.

Ino wrapped her in a tight hug. "You look beautiful," he whispered in her ear, his voice thick with emotion. "I wish the others had lived. Mother and Father would be so proud of everything you've done. If they could see you now, their precious Bareea..." He stepped back and took her hand, forcing a smile. "Liselle and Cassia would have been so jealous of your dress. They'd be begging for ones just like it."

"Because of them, we're here today," she reminded him, squeezing his hand. Of the three of them, he was the one who had taken Cassia's death the hardest. He was the eldest, the protector. He, Matthias, and Cassia had been together for decades, ever since they were separated from Dayna and Adriel as children. For so long, they'd had no one but each other. Losing her had broken his heart.

"I know. It's just...hard to get used to her being gone."

"Hey," Matthias said gently, resting a hand on Ino's shoulder. "I miss them as much as you do, but you do realize this is a wedding, don't you? The only tears allowed today are tears of joy."

"We know," Celeste said. "Faye has already cried twice."

"I didn't *cry*—"

Lethandris moved between them, fighting a grin. "The musicians have begun to play, which means it's almost time to start. Come on, let's go inside."

She and Nynev led Faye and Celeste into the throne room, leaving Mercy alone with Calum and her brothers. Through the open doors, Mercy could hear music and the buzz of conversation from the excited guests. A nervous, excited jitter ran through her.

"Just so you know, there's still time to back out of the wedding," Calum teased, a crooked grin on his lips. "You don't have to marry him just because he saved your life about a hundred times. I'm fairly certain you're even now."

She rolled her eyes. "Shouldn't you be traveling with the Strykers right now? Or working in a blacksmith's shop somewhere?"

His grin grew wider. "You can't get rid of me that easily, Sis. Hewlin is still recovering, so our little band of Strykers isn't going anywhere anytime soon. I'll be doing Cassius's work until Tamriel appoints a new Bacha. Maybe once this whole mess concerning the slaves is settled, I'll travel around with them some more, but for now, you're stuck with me."

"Creator save us all."

He opened his mouth to respond, but the music swelled, cutting him off. "Ah. That's your cue." He moved aside and made a deep, theatrical bow. "After you, princess."

"You're not coming?"

"I've already missed my chance to join the guests. I'll slip in after you get to the dais. Everyone's eyes will be on you, anyway."

Ino and Matthias each took one of her arms. Mercy sucked in a breath, her heart pounding and her stomach fluttering, before nodding once. Together, they walked into the throne room.

She had a vague sense of hundreds of eyes on her—even for a *small affair*, the throne room was nearly full to bursting—but everything else fell away the moment she saw Tamriel. He stood before the High Priestess on the top step of the dais, dressed in shining leather boots, black trousers, and a doublet the same shade of sapphire as her gown. The gold embroidery along the collar and cuffs shimmered faintly under the light streaming in through the massive window behind the thrones. He was her dashing prince. Her brave king. Her love.

And he was staring at her as if she were the most beautiful woman he had ever seen.

She practically floated all the way to the dais. When they

reached the bottom of the steps, Ino and Matthias released her arms, bowed, and then took their places among the guests. She lifted her skirt and climbed the steps until she stood face-to-face with Tamriel. The music swelled once more, and he beamed as he took her hands.

"Ladies and gentlemen of the court," the High Priestess began once the music faded, "we gather here for the wedding of King Tamriel Myrellis and Mercy Mari, and the coronation of our new queen..."

The High Priestess was halfway through a story about the Creator and his bride when Mercy spotted a flash of gray in her periphery. Her grip on Tamriel's hands tightened as the memory of her recurring nightmare filled her mind—the one in which she chased the ghosts of her family through the castle, only to find herself alone again and again. His expression immediately transformed from dreamy, lovestruck bliss to concern. When she turned her head, just enough to look toward the back of the room, he followed her gaze.

Behind her brothers, behind their friends, behind the council members, behind the nobles, Mercy saw them:

Her family.

Dayna's face was exuberant. She grinned up at Mercy and Tamriel and slipped an arm around Adriel's waist, resting her head on his shoulder. Adriel pulled her close and kissed her temple. Beside him, Liselle's form wavered, little more than a silhouette, but Mercy was able to make out enough to see her lift her hands to her chest, right over her heart.

And to her right—happy, lovely, wonderful Cassia. She looked exactly as she had before the battle. The scarf she had worn the day she died was wrapped around her head, and her tunic and leather breastplate were undamaged. If not for the fact that her skin and clothes were all a dull, slate gray, Mercy might have thought she'd come back from the dead.

They're here.

She turned forward and met Tamriel's eyes. They shone with joy as the High Priestess finished her story and asked him to recite his vow.

"For so long, I was terrified of falling in love," he began. "I saw how broken it left my father, and I was certain that it would lead to nothing but my own destruction. Then I met you, and I realized that I was *absolutely right*. Loving you destroyed the cowardly, cold prince I used to be and turned me into the king I am today—a king determined to do right by all his subjects. You taught me to stand and fight for what I believe in, my amazing, fearless, warrior, and I cannot wait for you to become my wife, and my queen."

Her heart swelled. She could feel the weight of her family's eyes on her as she said, "Until I came here, I thought I was alone in this world. I was angry, hateful, and cruel, and I hurt the people closest to me while trying to prove my worth to the monsters who had tormented me all my life. That all changed when I met you. You saw all my flaws, and you loved me anyway. You turned me into a better person—a person I never would have imagined I could become. You've completely changed my life, and I cannot believe that I am fortunate enough to spend the rest of it with you."

A priestess carrying a velvet cushion stepped forward, and the High Priestess picked up the two simple gold bands sitting on top of it. The first, she handed to Tamriel. "Your Majesty, King Tamriel Myrellis, do you take Mercy Mari to be your wife from this day forth, to love her wholly and completely, in prosperity and in poverty, in this life and the Beyond?"

"I do," he said as he slipped the ring on her finger, right above the sapphire ring.

"And Mercy Mari, do you take King Tamriel Myrellis to be your husband from this day forth, to love him wholly and completely, in prosperity and in poverty, in this life and the Beyond?"

"I do," she said, placing the ring on his finger. She glanced toward her family as she repeated, "In this life and the Beyond."

65
TAMRIEL

Tamriel was still in shock, still marveling at the beauty of the woman before him and the miracle that was this moment, when the High Priestess said, "Then it is my privilege to pronounce you husband and wife. You may kiss."

Before Mercy could do anything, he cupped her cheeks and pulled her into a kiss. His love. His bride. His *wife*. A cheer rose from the guests as Mercy reached up and laced her fingers behind his neck. He knew some of the nobles still resented the thought of their king marrying an elf, but he couldn't care less. He loved Mercy, and he wouldn't let any of them hurt her the way they had Liselle.

They turned toward the guests, and Tamriel couldn't keep the wide, foolish grin off his face as he turned toward their friends, right at the front of the crowd: Ino, Matthias, Calum, Percival, Celeste, Faye, Kaius, Nynev, Alistair, Lethandris. Seren Pierce, Nerida, and Faye's parents were there as well, having left Fallmond as soon as they learned of the victory against Nicholas. Arabelle, Indi, and Zora stood with Liri, the LeClairs' former slave, and bounced with excitement. Even

Hero and Ketojan had been able to leave the infirmary long enough to attend the ceremony. Affection rushed over him. Over the past several months, these people had become his family.

At the back of the room, the ghosts of Mercy's family flickered and began to fade. Mercy's grip tightened on his hand, and he knew that she had seen it. *Stay a little longer,* he silently implored them. Mercy had lost so much. She deserved to have her family with her today.

The High Priestess lifted a hand, and the cheers began to quiet. "If you would kneel, please, my lady," she said to Mercy. Tamriel moved back as Mercy knelt on the top step and closed her eyes. The High Priestess accepted a vial of holy oil from the priestess who had presented the rings, then drew the Creator's holy eye on Mercy's forehead.

"Mercy Mari, henceforth to be known as Her Majesty Mercy Myrellis, do you swear to aid your husband in governing your subjects fairly in accordance with the laws of Beltharos?"

Tamriel's chest swelled with pride as she said, "I swear it."

"Do you promise to protect, guide, and provide for the people of your kingdom, in times of prosperity and in times of adversity, to the best of your ability for as long as you are able?"

"I do."

"Will you uphold the values of the Church of the Creator and, to your power, ensure justice and mercy is executed in all your judgments?"

"I will."

"Then by my power as the most holy servant and hand of the Great Creator, I crown this woman Queen Mercy Myrellis. May your reign be prosperous, your life long and joyful, and your country the better because of it."

Another priestess crossed the dais, this time carrying a

pillow bearing the queen's crown. It was smaller than the one Tamriel had worn at his coronation, but no less extravagant—an intricate work of gold, rubies, emeralds, and sapphires. When the High Priestess turned to him, smiling, he picked up the crown and approached Mercy. She glanced up at him, her beautiful eyes sparkling with excitement and love.

How far we've come over the past few months, he thought as he smiled down at her, his heart swelling with love. *How much we've changed.* Before, he had always doubted that Solari years were blessed, but when he considered everything that had happened since he met Mercy, he realized he'd been wrong. They'd endured betrayals, assassination attempts, wars, and a plague. They'd ridden across the country, crossed the Islands, and braved the Feyndaran court. They'd saved each other more times than they could count. They had lost loved ones, faced impossible odds, and endured more pain than Tamriel had ever imagined possible, but he wouldn't change a moment of it. Everything they had faced brought them to this day, to this moment.

At the start of the summer, Mercy was nothing more to him than an Assassin, yet another person in this cutthroat court who had wanted him dead.

Now, she was his love.

Now, she was his wife.

Now, she was his everything.

The guests began to cheer once again as he set the crown on her head. It glittered with the slightest movement, sending flecks of red, blue, and green light dancing around the room. As he straightened, he looked at the ghosts of Mercy's family, little more than outlines at this point. They had tried to stay for as long as possible, but now it was time for them to return to the Beyond. Somehow, Tamriel knew this would be the last time they manifested in the In-Between. He and Mercy still had a lot of work to do, but now it was up to them to protect each other. Liselle and the others couldn't help them any longer.

One by one, they whispered in his mind, the words as clear as if they had been standing right beside him:

Dayna: *Thank you for saving my baby girl.*

Adriel: *We protected her as best we could; it's your turn now.*

Liselle: *I always prayed I would see my people freed. You two are braver and stronger than your father or I ever were.*

Cassia: *Be good to my Bareea, or I swear to the Creator, I'll haunt you until your dying breath.*

On the step before him, Mercy tensed almost imperceptibly. She tilted her head to the side, her crown sparkling, and Tamriel realized her family was whispering to her, as well. Glancing at the guests, he noticed Ino and Matthias wearing identical stunned expressions.

A tear slipped through Mercy's lashes. Tamriel crouched before her and gently wiped it away. When she looked up at him and leaned into his touch, a small smile tugging at her lips, he whispered three simple words:

"Rise, my queen."

ACKNOWLEDGMENTS

Thank you so much to my family: Mom and Faux Pas, for your unending support, feedback, and attention to detail; Dadd-EEEE, for sharing my books with anyone and everyone; and Ethan, for geeking out about how much you love Calum and the Strykers with me.

None of this would have been possible without my awesome ARC team. Your reviews, messages, and emails mean so much to me.

I am incredibly grateful to Judi Soderberg for your comments, feedback, edits, Patreon support, and all our late-night chats. You have been a cheerleader for this series since book 1, and I am so thankful you took a chance on *Merciless*.

And last but certainly not least, thank YOU, dear reader, for joining me on this epic adventure! The series may be over, but this is far from the last time we will see Mercy and her friends.

ABOUT THE AUTHOR

Jacqueline Pawl spent her teen years trapped between the pages of books—exploring Hogwarts, journeying across countless fantasy worlds, and pulling heists with Kaz Brekker and his Crows.

But, because no dashing prince or handsome Fae has come to sweep her off to a strange new world (yet), she writes epic fantasy novels full of cutthroat courtiers, ruthless assassins, unforgettable plot twists, and epic battles. She is a Slytherin, and it shows in her books.

She currently resides in Scotland, where she can be found chasing will-o'-the-wisps, riding unicorns, and hunting haggis in the Highlands.

For news about upcoming books, visit her website at:
www.authorjpawl.com

- instagram.com/authorjpawl
- amazon.com/author/jacquelinepawl
- bookbub.com/profile/jacqueline-pawl
- goodreads.com/Jacqueline_Pawl

ALSO BY JACQUELINE PAWL

Defying Vesuvius

A BORN ASSASSIN SERIES

Helpless (prequel novella)

Nameless (prequel novella)

Merciless

Heartless

Ruthless

Fearless

Limitless

A Born Assassin Series Omnibus

THE LADY OF INNISLEE SERIES

Court of Vipers

Printed in Great Britain
by Amazon